Copyright © 2024 by Anthony L. Crawford, Jr.

All rights reserved. No part of this book may be reproduced or used in any manner without written permission of the copyright owner except for the use of quotations in a book review. For more information, address: alcrawfordjr2@gmail.com

Volume II

linktr.ee/krawfpravurb

Black Pain't, Vol. II

To my daughters,
AKiera Samantha Serene Crawford and Kaia Amora Asé Crawford.
I love you two with all my heart and soul,
I wanna tell you both things that I think young women should know,
Number one, leave these dumb, broke, bummy niggas alone,
Don't focus on no man, focus on your growth
Learn how to tap in with your intuitions,
Don't go into love blinded by a nigga's illusions,
Draw the line so you won't have to draw conclusions,
Keep a pistol on you just in case heart burglars try to intrude in,
Know and believe that your perfect the way God made you,
Use the talents and gifts that God gave you,
Don't be out here depending on anyone to save you,
Take control of your own canvas, don't let anyone paint you,
Indigenous indigo women, grow to be modest, self-sufficient, and disciplined,
Grow to be honest, different, and indifferent,
make a change in people's lives better than what your dad did,
I'm glad God chose me to raise y'all, I'm happy I had kids.

Black Pain't, Vol. II

Introduction

  To the ones who supported, invested, acted, attended, and loved the first volume of *Black Pain't* – I apologize for keeping you all waiting. I have been on a quest to not only learn about my genealogy and the truth about us so called "African Americans." I also been finding unique ways of continuous healing and enlightenment. I've been on daddy duties and learning to be a family man. I'm still teaching, coaching, hosting, and doing poetry. I've dropped a couple albums (*R.A.P.* and *T.R.A.P.*) with another one on the way (*To whom it may concern,*) which can all be found on all music streaming platforms. I've dropped two poetry books (*With My Pen Instead* and *Yoni Scriptures*). I've been doing film but haven't been publicizing them nor make the productions I do have accessible.

  On the flip side, I still have a lot of growing up to do, a lot of discipline that I need to gain, and a lot of revamping of my image. No one is perfect and I don't want to make it seem like everything is just positive in my life, because we need the negatives to see a complete

Black Pain't, Vol. II

picture. I'm older now, so I'm getting more in tuned with reality, with ultimate truth, with supreme consciousness.

  Disclaimer, and I should have done this disclaimer on the last book, but these characters, these stories, these situations, and these places are all fiction, I made up. It's a realistic fiction with a lot of truth attached to it, so YOU MUST DO YOUR RESEARCH. I found a unique way to put my poetry, realistic situations, political views, societal issues, mind sets, and many facets of life into an artistic form and called it a novel. I love creating stories, characters, and situations. Even when I used to play video games as a child, I would create my own characters on wrestling games, basketball games, football games, and many others.

  After the first edition of *Black Pain't*, I realize how ignorant and uninformed I was during the time of writing it. Hence why there is a special edition to the first one that I need you all to purchase and read in order to connect the events and situations in the second edition. I wanted to approach the second with more intention for everyone who purchases this book. I want you to go on a journey with yourself. I want you to learn from these characters and their plots. I want you to be interactive in this book.

  At the end of every chapter there's a portion where I want you to write notes about anything you learned, noticed, suggests, comments, or questions about. Let's develop and start an internal intellectual dialogue with ourselves, that divine part of us; and let's have external dialogues with our families, our friends, our colleagues, our co-workers, our politicians, our community leaders, our pastors, and all people about what's really going on in our society. Those in which this country of America labeled as slaves, African American, Black, Colored, Negro, Niggas, Minority, and the new and upcoming one, People of Color (POC), are in need of some strong help financially, mentally, physically, emotionally, academically, and socially. Being feeble with yourself about who you are, where you are financially, and your mindset can free you. Let's get counsel, let's go to therapy, let's get into support groups, go to church, go to the mosque, go to places of worship. Let's heal for real.

Black Pain't, Vol. II

Chapter 1:
InterstelHER
(*interstellar* adj.)

It's late into the night. As she lies down, looking out into the skylight of her bedroom, she's finally able to transition through the period between insomnia and sleep. Within this period, her body falls into deep relaxation. Suddenly, her neurons begin to bring her sleep spindles, and she feels as if someone is pressing her body down. She tries to find the will to move and fight, but her entire body feels paralyzed like a sleep paralysis. She tries to open her mouth to scream, but nothing comes out.

Somehow, she keeps her mind at ease, drifting into a sparkly realm. A realm with unusual, dazzling shapes, illuminating the area around her. She's seeing colors and stars that she has never seen before color the sky and the skyscrapers. There are creative creatures walking to and from in the hills, houses, and mushroom-like buildings that she floats over. She sees disk-like saucers, flying in lines of rows, crossing across the invisible street-sky. She sees martians that look a lot like copper colored people moving in peace and harmony.

She's conscious of this terrestrial experience. During her hovering, a voice unexpectedly appears, asking, *"Who are you? Where are you? Why are you here? Where are you going?"*

The questions make her stomach drop, straining her core. Abruptly, her floating starts to feel like she's falling. Everything and everyone within the realm all begin moving in hasty motion as the answer ascended her consciousness into a dark vortex where she can see phantasmagorias of her past being projected unto the luminous tunnel. She sees moments with her mother and fun times with her father. She sees her mother's fights with her father; she sees nights with her mother. She sees her past flights to see her father. She sees herself crying, she sees her mother crying, she sees her father struggling. She sees her child-self dressed as an adult, interacting with her mentee, Abbyielle, her friend, Tiffany; she also sees Darryl. She sees her abusive, ex-boyfriend, Dennis.

The image of Dennis disturbs her. Unexpectedly, the presentations begin thinning as her consciousness's hyper speed became more of a slow fall. As she falls into the chasm, she immediately awakes as if she just got off a roller coaster ride with her heart beating out of her chest. After realizing that she's home in bed, she grabs her head and slumps backward onto her pillow.

As she closes her eyes to catch her breath, she takes a few moments to say an internal prayer. "Selah," she says while reaching for her phone from the top of bedside dresser to view the time. She immediately drops the phone right next to her to take a deep breath and to turn away on her side. She takes a moment to think about all the responsibilities, all the due dates, all the bills, all the melodramas, and all of the rest of the challenges that's been consuming her mind these past months.

She turns back around to grab her phone, allowing it to scan her face to unlock it. She taps, scrolls, and taps on the screen of her phone. Instead of going through her emails, text threads, and other apps that she knows she needs to give attention to, she decides to scroll through social media. She scrolls through reel after reel as if her soul is searching for something important. She then comes across a video with a subtitle that reads, "Dr. Peseshet chastises Black men at a round table."

She taps on the video of Aaron James sitting at a round table with Dr. Boyce Watkins, Dr. Michelle Alexander, Dr. Claude Anderson, *Dr. Akira Peseshet*, the Honorable Minister Louis Farrakhan, Dr. Joy DeGruy, and Cornel West. They seem to be in a dark arena with the spotlight specifically on the round table.

A crowd of cheers begins as Dr. Peseshet's strong, melodic voice begins saying, "I dislike using the term, Black, because that's just a nickname that was given to us back in the late sixties, but I'll step down to the lower levels of consciousness to get this point across......." She pauses to get everyone's heart attention. "There is NO WAY that 'Black' men can be who they are and where they are today without 'Black' women!"

As the crowd cheers, Dr. Peseshet awaits the perfect moment to say, "Now, Mr. James, brother, and Honorable Farrakhan, and to all other men around the world...... many of you are absolutely correct on many facets of your 'day-to-day arguments' about society, about 'Black' people, and about the plight of the 'Black' race, but you ALWAYS leave out the essential part of it all....... 'Black' women.

"'Black' women have always been the spine and the soul of humanity. That's why the pyramid of Giza is that of a 'Black' woman; the origin of mankind can all be trace back to one and that one is of a negroid woman. Within women is the *Mesosalpinx*, which used to be parthenogenesis, which allowed women to be pregnant without a man's sperm! This is the dawn of man. Every human is born with an ambilocal cord! Check your sources, because the copper-colored woman is God......... Some of you have been giving God man like qualities and man like attributes when you know God is Love, and what better being can be more loving that the female species, don't worry I'll wait............" Dr. Peseshet says while take a few seconds for someone to come up with a rebuttal. "Exactly, that's why most of you men need to repent. You've done God dirty in so many ways."

Suddenly, the evening alarm on her phone appears, pausing the reel that she's watching, reminding her that it's time to get ready for class. She taps the stop button on the alarm, swipes away all the apps that she has opened, and locks her phone. She yawns and takes one big stretch before getting out of her cozy king-sized bed with the off-white bed set, wearing her nude tanga and bra.

For this evening's course, she already has her clothes prepared and laid out on the arm of her room's chair that sits next to the door of her master bedroom's bathroom. She has her lavender blouse on top of her black slacks, lying on top of her black blazer. She also has some black Christian Louboutin heels standing under the chair.

She walks into her bathroom, turning on the light, and removing the head scarf that covered her crown. She gazes at her dark and lovely afro-puffed ponytail and makes sure her edges are laid. She picks up her toothpaste and her toothbrush. She spreads the toothpaste onto the toothbrush to brush her teeth and her tongue. She then takes a small kit of items that she bought from her esthetician to wash and dry her face with the proper facial products. She concludes by oiling her face and neck that helps illuminate the golden complexion of her mocha-latte skin.

She smiles into the mirror, changing the energy of her restless mood. She turns around to turn the lights off and exits the bathroom. She takes her time to put on her clothes. Afterwards, she checks her phone for the time, realizing that she does not have to rush. She sits on the chair in her room to slide her heels onto her feet. She goes into her hallway closet to get her laptop bag and her warm peacoat. She departs from her bedroom and into the living room of her condo. She snatches a snack from out of the refrigerator, grabs her keys from the countertop in the kitchen, and departs.

Once she locks the door, she strolls to the elevator doors with the tapping of her heels echoing throughout the halls. She pushes the elevator button that summons a lift. Seconds later, the lift arrives, opening its doors for from the middle to the sides. She hums onto the lift and the elevator door closes behind her as she presses the letter G which takes her to the garage of the condo.

She gets off of the elevator and strides to her car. She presses the AutoStart on her car keys to make the car start and the doors unlock. Once she enters, she turns to place her lap top bag in the backseat. While in the driver's seat, she finds music on her phone as her phone instantly connects to the car's Bluetooth. She plays a playlist by *Summer Walker*, puts her seatbelt on, and drives off.

While driving, she notices the sun painting the sky orange with shades of purple over the horizon. A strong wind abruptly dashes in various directions, shaking street signs and lamp posts. As the trees wave, and the electric waves sing, she pulls into the main parking lot of Turner University's City Campus, listening and car-dancing to Megan Thee Stallion's music. After parking, she turns the car off and takes a few deep breaths to align herself by being in the present moment. She retrieves her laptop bag from the backseat, exits the vehicle all awhile locking it and walks towards the main building.

With the wind blowing through her slacks, she slowly walks near a human sized statue of Nat Turner and stops to admire the all-bronze figure. He's holding a sword in his right hand that's supposed to symbolize freedom at all costs, and a book in the left hand which supposed to symbolize knowledge and liberation. She notices the statue wearing torn away clothes as she mentally debunks Turner's so-called "rebellion," and his almighty bravery that sounds too much like allegory. She scoffs, knowing that Nat Turner was a fictional character that the Virginia Department of Historic Resources created. She continues her saunter to the building.

Walking through the main doors, a sense of elegance and excellence exuberates her inner being. She can feel the depth of awareness at its zenith. The energy in the main building is compelling, and one can tell that she willing and ready to embrace what's to come. She feels at home. Whenever she is in a sanctuary of knowledge, history, intellect, and enlightenment, she's met with a divine sensation. She's feels excitement, and it influences her to want to comprise the challenges ahead, the long hours of researching and writing, and the anxiety of presenting her dissertation. She pulls out a paper from her lap top bag, scan the paper for a room number on her schedule, and confusedly gazes around the edifice as if adventure awaits.

She searches for help and sees a graceful woman with sister-locs, wearing a brown Turner University staff t-shirt over a white collared dress shirt at the information desk, typing away on a desk-top computer. She's wearing many bracelets on both wrists, spectacles that compliment her lovely wide nose, slight make-up on her face so she wouldn't hide her beautiful features, and a gold necklace with the Ankh symbol dangling as the charm.

"Gone 'head sistah," she thinks to herself, walking closer to the desk. "Excuse me, ma'am, where is room 111?" she asks aloud.

With refinement and a vibrant smile, the woman points towards the left side of the building, charmingly saying in an eastern accent, "Oh, you just go right around there, turn right, and it'll be a hallway; your room will be right in that hallway."

"Okay, thank you so much!"

"No problem at all. I'm here if you need anything."

She walks in the direction that the lady instructed her to go. Thrill grips her as she makes her way down the hallway in search of the classroom. *Room 109...110... and...* she cogitates to herself. She sees room 111 on top of a door and anxiously walks in to see a handful of individuals sitting around, conversing, and awaiting the instructor to start class.

There were three women and two men, all dressed in business-casual clothes, all with energy of enthusiasm and preparedness, and all with an aura of intellect that she enjoys to sense. As soon as the door shuts behind her, everyone in the room instantly stops conversing to keenly look her way to make sure it isn't the professor. Then they went back to their discussions until one of them yells, "Look at what the Universe don' flew in from the heavens of the earth!"

How can this be? She internally questions herself while walking toward the small group. She begins mixing the embarrassment she instantly feels and the will to ignore the man's obnoxiousness together within her moods. She shushes him and tightly but quietly says, "STOOOP!"

He catches her drift and as she makes her way towards the tables. He whispers, "God must truly love me to see you here! I didn't think I'd ever see you again."

She does not know what to make of the situation. She smiles as her mind thinks, *Oh, God, why have thou forsaken me?*

He regenerates, whispering, "Miss Patricia Skinner…….. It is with pleasure, honor, and privilege to see you walking through them doors lookin' all fine and divine! Umph.... you look like God threw in some extra loveliness when he was creating you girl......"

Irritably but kindly, Patricia replies, "Darn Darryl," while shaking her head. "Not only that you're humiliating me in front of strangers, but you're also telling them my slave name, too?"

"Darn Darryl sounds like a good sitcom, don't you think?" Darryl asks in an enthusiastic tone.

"Darryl don't........." she stops to think for a second. "Darryl Don't! I think I like that name better for you," her snappish countenance exhilarates Darryl to stop with his antics.

Darryl drawbacks due to Patricia's warning and sojourns his behavior. He eagerly gets up to sit next to Patricia and asks, "How you been? How have you been treating life?"

Untethered, Patricia answers, "Good, and how are you, Darryl?"

In his weak and fake British voice, Darryl answers, "Aww, I'm bloody good as well, thanks fo' asking. So you've finally decided to get you' docto'ates I see! So exiting, innit?"

"Riveting," Patricia uninterestingly retorts. "Isn't this an Introduction to African American Women Studies?"

"Yes, I hope so, or I'll be in the wrong class…."

"What are you getting your doctorates in, Mr. Jones?"

"African American Studies…. I supposed you are, too, right?"

"No, mine is in African American Women Studies. So I'm confused as to why you have this course."

"Can't have African Americans without African American Women…." Darryl responds with an enormous smile. "Why did you choose African American Women Studies? Have you thought about your dissertation, yet?"

Patricia glares at Darryl and states, "I chose this to learn about the countless tales and false narratives that this education system continues to paint about 'Black' people. My dissertation will have something along the lines about African Americans being the true Natives of America." Patricia concludes as a deep voice captures her and the students' attention.

"Good evening, candidates," the professor says, walking to a desk with his lap top bag, wearing a tan suit, white dress shirt, and confidence to compliment the attire.

"Good evening…" some of the students say in unison while "Good evening, professor…" came from other students.

Whilst remaining untethered and silent, Patricia is stunned to see the one and only, Dr. Phillip Carson, walking into the classroom. While he comes across the computer desk to remove his laptop out of his computer bag, Patricia thinks to herself, *"This nigga,"* as she observes him connecting his computer to the promethean board. *"If it ain't good ol' Dr. Phillip Carson, 'Mister I like sleeping with married women,' Mister Carson, 'Mister too old to be acting like an uncivilized boy' Mister Carson. Mister ……..*

Patricia's inner dialogue is interposed when she hears Dr. Carson say, "Ladies and gentlemen, welcome to the beginning of a long, restless, and promising journey. My name is Dr. Phillip Carson, I am one of the Thesis and Dissertation Department Heads along with being a professor for a few of the master courses and doctoral courses for Turner University's Doctoral Programs.

"I received my bachelor's in education, my master's in urban education, and my Doctorate's in Higher Level Education......ahem...... excuse me........ but I got them all at Turner University. My dissertation was about why Predominately White Institutions are more effective financially for Black Athletes to attend, but they lack the culturally responsive effects needed at Black institutions and Black communities. Can you imagine what it was like bringing forth a dissertation as such? Thank God my committee was majority Black doctors who understood my argument," Dr. Carson stops to acknowledge the student with their hand raised. "Yes ma'am?"

"Is it prohibited to assume that the main reason why your dissertation was approved was because of the biasedness from your committee?"

Dr. Carson breathes in his question as the candidate spoke, and instantly answers, "No, because I did the research, one of the books that I included was by William C. Rhoden, *Forty-Million Dollar Slave*, in which he interviews and highlights NCAA athletes who never got paid for bringing these white universities billions of dollars over the past forty years since they integrated schools. The studies prove it.

"Statistically speaking, if you are not an athlete at a Prehistorically White Institution or at a Predominately White Institution, nine times out of ten, in today's society, you will have the money, especially with these Name, Image, and Likeness deals, but, if you're a regular Black student, on a predominately white college, you'll experience a higher class of discrimination. This discrimination comes in all shapes and sizes; this discrimination affects the mind, body, and spirit of a human being. There is massive research by Dr. Shaun Harper behind the plight of Black people attending colleges and universities where they were once not allowed to attend.

"I've been trying to figure out why any Black parent would send their child, along with their money, talent expressions, and academic skills to intuitions as such," Dr. Carson notices that Darryl's hand is raised and points to him as a gesture for him to speak.

The gorgeous, Shampagne Roberts passionately says, "Dr. Carson, now I did go to Christopher Columbus University for my undergrad, so I know what you mean, but I transferred to Christopher Columbus University from FDU. So I feel as though, like, there's a dilemma……right…… because most HBCUs, like Frederick Douglass University, and I have years of research from top scholars and athletes who left HBCUs to attend those predominately white institutions, they all said that they were terrible with communications, financial aid offices weren't proactive, housing was unlivable, and they received their refunds late. But when they got to those white campuses, they were treated better, operations were smoothly, they communicated with you; you got your refund money on time."

Darryl chimes in, "But then why do those same individuals go through the trials and tribulations of dealing with academic and social racism just to get their degrees, get decent jobs, and move in predominately white neighborhoods!? Why don't they come and make their communities and universities better?"

Another student shouts, "Don't nobody want to live in a neighborhood where they don't feel safe, with dudes gang banging and shooting up neighborhoods, people trying to find places to be peaceful!"

Patricia remains silent and still throughout the class discussion. She detects inauthenticity coming from the room. She watches how everyone is getting excited about common problems that melaninated people tend to endure on an academic level. Without an opinion on the matter, she stays neutral to stay centered within the chaotic conversation until Dr. Carson stops the discourse.

"Wait, wait…. Let's not float off the topic at hand. The sister's question was about the 'biasedness' within our institution. Let's respect and acknowledge everyone's question throughout class discussions with evidence, data, documents, and historically relevance. To help you all understand my answer from a point of view of true justice and equality, I have a question."

Dr. Carson pauses for a moment and resumes, "Do you measure society with that same biasedness assumption? When you attend predominantly white institutions, or when you listen to radio stations, when you watch a film on a major streaming network, when you are studying out of 10th edition of your college books.... Are you measuring the biasedness behind them as well?

"Who owns these major radio stations, television networks, music companies; who makes the decisions when it comes to the politics of education? Who writes these books that teachers have to teach out of? Is that not enough biasedness to you?" Dr. Carson pauses to calm his passion to prove his dissertation every chance he gets.

"Was not America built on biasedness? If a committee of majority Black people were helping another Black person advanced in society, then why not? That's what the Jews do for their people, that is what Whites do for their people; Asians, the Latinos; everyone does it for their own, why can't Black folks...............? Yes sir?" Dr. Carson acknowledges another student, allowing them to speak.

"Well, what about integrity? And honesty, and trust? Can those be built from biasedness?" The student asks.

Dr. Carson answers, "Within that certain group of people, yes. Once that honesty......ahem...... that trust and that integrity are built, then, who knows what that community may accomplish...... especially under a set of principles and values that pushes towards economic growth and prosperity; majority of Black folk do not have that. Not in America.

"Also...... in all actuality, I met all the qualifications, all the requirements, made the deadlines... umm...... I had extensive amount of research, field research studies, interviews, and a significant amount of data to back up my claims.......... My dissertation is about two hundred pages long. I could publish a book about it called 'The Financial Psychotic Decision of Black Athletes committing to White Schools.' But that could be divisive."

During Dr. Carson's discourse, Patricia's attention span drifts off, *"I see why Darryl is in here. Birds of a feather, flock together...... this is who Darryl got ALL his ways from....... No good son of bi......"*

Darryl notices Patricia's trance and slightly taps Patricia's shoulder to get her attention. Patricia immediately jumps, staring at Darryl. "Yes sir?" she sarcastically says.

"Are you okay?" Darryl whispers to Patricia.

"Yes, thank you," Patricia firmly responds with her eyes still fixed on Dr. Caron as Darryl gives his attention back to Dr. Carson as well.

"But once again, I am Dr. Phillip Carson; I am your doctoral professor for the Introduction of African American Women Studies," Dr. Carson says as he pauses to quickly type something on his laptop. He clicks on a presentation on the desktop of the laptop, and watches as it quickly opens onto the screen of the promethean board.

Dr. Carson walks away from his lap-top, inserts his hands in his pockets, and says, "Umm, I am here to see that you set sail on your course for doctoral-ship; I am here to help you understand how to collate your research and information for the ears and minds of those that will be on your doctoral committee. Trust me, it will not be easy."

"Negro, you're just as fake," Patricia says within as all the PhD candidates in the room are zealously listening to the professor with hope and aspiration. Patricia has this mien of disapproval and disenchantment throughout Dr. Carson's introduction. Intuitively, she's not too receptive, Dr. Carson's presence mentally blocks herself from being optimistic about the course. *"You're just here for your degree, girl, don't let these heathens stop you!"*

Dr. Carson breaks her internal interrogation by saying, "We will dive deep in the heart and soul of African American History through the perspectives of African American women. Remember, without Black women, the abducted would not have made it through the Atlantic Slave Trade; without Black women, the enslaved would not have made it through slavery; without Black women, we would not have made it through the Jim Crow era......"

"More lies about the 'Atlantic Slave Trade,' more lies about how bad the Jim Crow era was, blah, blah, blah...." Patricia internalizes.

"It has always been Black women who have paved the way for humanity. In this course, we will learn about those women and how we still rest our livelihood as Black people in this society on Black women. We will learn why Black women have a higher success rate than most people in other ethnic groups, why Black women are more dominant now more than ever before; it is all because of what their ancestors endured, it's the epistemology of it all; but we'll get into all that throughout this course," Dr. Carson concludes. "Are there any questions?"

A tense silence circulates the room. Everyone is excited and nervous at the same time; however, Patricia is more subtle and prepared. Breaking the strain in the room, Patricia bravely raises her hand, and intrusively asks, "If this is a course about 'Black' women, then how come there is not a 'Black' woman teaching this course?"

The candidates look towards Dr. Carson in astonishment, allowing her question to provoke their thoughts, wondering what their professor's answer will be. Darryl adoringly smiles at Patricia, sending a cosmic wave of love and admiration her way.

"Good question," Dr. Carson thoughtfully says as he searches inside for an answer that he did not have. He never thought of the reason why he's been teaching this course for the past few years. Patricia's question pierce through his mind and heart.

Patricia interferes with his internal search and mental processing by asking, "So we are to learn and receive information about Black women's mark in pivotal moments in our history from a man's point of view? We're supposed to read and research Black women authors but with Black male judgement and a white man's academic system? How is this just?"

Feeling intellectually attacked, Dr. Carson collects himself and asks, "What's your name, sistah?"

"Patricia Skinner, I received my bachelor's and my master's from the University of George Washington Carver Science and Medical School; I currently serve as a librarian at W.E.B. Dubois Middle School with goals of starting a Copper Color Sisterhood non-profit organization called CCS to provide a network of resources and mentorships to young Melaninated women everywhere. I am a strong advocate for my people, especially the women."

One of the PhD candidates says aloud, "so basically, you're like a feminist?"

Patricia's demeanor perforates through that student's soul as she contemptuously answers, "Call it what you want, sir, but sex trafficking, molestation, domestic abuse, and sex workers are all at an all-time high; oh and guess what?" Patricia pauses for an intense moment, "The numbers grow immensely generation after generation; nine times out of ten, a woman is the main target. So if that makes me the boot of a 'feminist' then I'll be happy to put those sols on. I'll even tie them in a double knot."

Dr. Carson, with an impressive gaze on his face, states, "Nice to meet you, Miss Skinner, my hope is that you, or any of you other ladies may take over this course once you all receive your PhD...... and Miss Skinner, I really do not have an answer for you at this moment."

"I'll keep that in mind, sir," Patricia responds with a stern smile.

"Miss Skinner, have you ever heard of Dr. Akira Peseshet?"

Patricia shillyshallies and responds, "No, I haven't but it is funny that you ask that because I was watching a video of her 'fact-checking' Aaron James in front of a live audience."

"You're speaking of the annual Black Leaders Round Table discussion. I was actually there in the crowd witnessing it. I call myself 'fact-checking' her by doing my own research on her claims. Her research introduced me to historian and major researcher, Dane Calloway, and meta physicist, Dr. Delbert Blair, and many other prominent researchers.... and she is absolutely correct on so many levels. I believe that you would find her work interesting as well. She's been deemed the commencement speaker for TU's graduation ceremony. You all should make it a point to come hear her speak.

"With that, it is also will hopes that you all will trust in me to do the best I can as your professor for the time being, and if you don't agree with anything discussed in my class or anything that hinders your growth as a scholar, please speak up. And that goes for everyone in this room," Dr. Carson says as he walks back to the desk that his laptop is on.

Dr. Carson grips his mouse and clicks through his presentation. "Listen, I won't keep you all long tonight, this is just to get acclimated with the class and myself. When you log into your school account, click on the course, download the syllabus. You're going to want to buy the required readings, especially for research purposes, references, and to add to your home library; there are only two books to get, and fairly cheap if you buy them online; be prepared to dialogue and write research papers on various topics.

"As your professor, I will have an open-door policy for one-on-one conferences. This is a community; this is how we network and grow as a people. I will make myself available for feedback on your assignments, your progress, and your well-being; that includes moral support and communal support. I know this process will be rough on your mental and probably your mental health. So I want to make sure that I do the best I can to help you succeed.

"When it's all said and done, I want to encourage you to use your degrees to make transformations in the communities where you know you are obligatory." Dr. Carson points to the back of his left hand and continues, "Like W.E.B. Dubois said, we are the *Talented Tenth*! It's up to us to make those changes that we want to see for our people......... Are there any comments, questions, or concerns?"

Dr. Carson awaits patiently for anyone to say anything or to ask anything, but no one takes on the opportunity. "Class dismissed," he says while disconnecting his lap-top from the promethean board. While everyone in the room begin to gather their belongings, he senses that they would want to try to be the first to speak and introduce themselves to him, so he takes his time to pack.

Patricia elegantly takes her time to gather her possessions. Once collected, she walks near the door to observe other candidates interact with Dr. Carson before exchanging a few words with him. *"Kiss asses,"* Patricia thinks to herself. She then views Dr. Carson, discerning, *"I can sense his stench. You can dress a skunk up but it's still going to stink."*

Patricia notices Darryl and Dr. Carson's brotherly interaction. She smirks as if something was inauthentic about their greeting.

"Thank you for all your help in getting me in that program, Doc!" Darryl says.

"No problem at all, brother man, from the motherland, just don't let those that believe in you down now. I'll have to call your mother up and snitch on you!"

"My mother does not even know I'm doing this!"

"Really? Why not?"

"None of my family and close friends know, Doc!" Darryl whispers. "I'm just trying to get through this without the stress that come with it. It's a journey that I'll wish to take on my own."

"I understand that my brother," Dr. Carson says with a big smile. "Just make sure you're taking good care of yourself in the process."

"I will for sure!"

"Peace to the journey!"

"Peace to the journey!" Darryl restates as he shakes Dr. Carson's hand and exits.

As the other candidates slowly disperse, Patricia walks up to Dr. Carson with her hand out, ready to shake his hand, saying, "Hey, Dr. Carson." They shake hands and Patricia vocalizes, "I wanted to reintroduce myself and did not want you to overlook my desire and search for clarity as an attack on you, personally."

Dr. Carson stands his ground, claiming, "I understood where you were coming from; I just never received any scrutiny from it. As I said, you were right. We definitely need more feminine representation within our institutions to teach feministic views and to teach men in ways in how they're misogynistic. Will you answer the call?"

Patricia scoffs, shrugs her right shoulder, and confidently replies, "Let me get my doctorates first and then I'll check their voicemails. Gives me time to weigh my options."

"I understand." Dr. Carson says.

"Enjoy the rest of your evening professor. See you next week."

"See you next week, Miss Skinner."

As Patricia exits, she thinks, *"You no good son of a bi…"*

While waiting outside of the classroom door, Darryl intercepts her thought process and startles Patricia, saying, "Hey my mocha choka latte."

Rolling her eyes, Patricia annoyingly says, "Hi Darryl……. Bye Darryl," and continues strutting down the hallway.

Darryl tries to keep up with her strides, keenly asking, "How was your first day of class?"

"It was quite interesting actually……… Not surprised by the taboo, of course, but quite interesting."

"What made it interesting?"

Patricia hesitates to answer because that would mean more conversation, so she thought of something surface level to say. "Ummmm…… that he allows questions and discussions to go on without any structure or destination."

"Aren't we supposed to arrive at our own destination?"

Patricia gives Darryl a haughty look as he opens the door of the front entrances of the building. "Thank you," Patricia says as she walks out with Darryl on her coat tail. "To answer your question, yes, I think that was his whole point was to make sure that we arrive to our own destinations and conclusions. I guess it would be good to being taught by a woman instead but…… whatever."

"Nah, nah, nah, not whatever…. I really am intrigued as to what you feel and think about that……and everything really," Darryl softly but seriously says.

Patricia stops in her tracks to face Darryl and firmly states, "Darn Darryl, you still using that same charm that got me when I first met you at that bookstore," Patricia says as she scoffs. "Do you use those same lines with other women? I bet they flock to you too, huh?" Mocking Darryl, Patricia continues, "'Oh, love, I am really intrigued as to what you are feeling and thinking, please take my hand and follow me into the romances of passion and desire.'"

Using her regular voice, Patricia proceeds to say, "Then you're going to start one on one dialogue about this and that, you know topics and discussions that I find interesting; you're going to use that as bait to lure me into your conniving and controlling ways...."

With confusion, Darryl tries to hold in his fake laugh, and says, "It's not even like that, Patricia."

"Ummm hmmm," Patricia says haughtily and walks away.

"Wait, wait, wait, Patricia......." Darryl slightly grabs Patricia to stop her from walking and Patricia instantaneously pushes his hands off of her. Darryl stares at her for a moment, looks down at the ground for a second, up in the sky then back at Patricia saying, "Look Patricia, I don't know what I ever did to you. I don't know what made you switch. Till this day, I don't know what happened between us. One moment we we're good and the next moment you stop communicating with me because of who I chose to associate myself with.... I don.."

Patricia interjects, "It wasn't just about who you associate yourself with, Darryl!"

"Then what was it?" Darryl irritably and instantly asks, looking for empathy. "Please tell me, I thought we had something good or at least creating something good."

"I was just not ready for what you wanted, Darryl."

"Was it that you were not ready for what I wanted or was it that you just didn't want what I wanted with me," Darryl pauses to await an answer. "It's okay, you can be honest with me, Patricia. You used to talk about truth and communication being an important part of a relationship, now I'm asking you to be honest with me. What was it, Patricia?"

Patricia feels a deep conviction consuming her heart. She never seen Darryl's heart like this before. It inaugurates up and down his sleeve when he's still. He carries it in his arm movements. Patricia takes a deep breath to find the words, but she couldn't find them. "I can't do this right now, Darryl," Patricia states as she walks away from him, leaving him looking dumbfounded. He walks away to his car trying to remain calm.

Once Patricia gets closer to her car, she pushes the AutoStart on her key chain to start the car. She opens the back door to put her laptop bag inside and closes the door on her way to the driver side. She gets in the car in distress, taking in more deep breaths, trying to stay calm.

She reaches for her phone in her purse before placing it in the passenger seat. She allows the phone to scan her face for it to unlock. She taps, scrolls, and taps some more. She gets to her call log to notice all of her missed calls. She dials the first person that called her.

The phone rings and moments later, a woman's voice answers the phone saying, "Namaste...... Docta... Skinner!"

Patricia chuckles a little, saying, "Not yet girl, I could be done with this program in two to three years if I stay the course."

"Ooooh, I heard that girl. Make sure you speak it into existence! You know we powerful! Sooooooooo.... how was your first day?"

"Mighty adventurous, girl, let me tell you........... guess who is one of my classmates and one of my professors?"

"Girl who? Stop playin'..."

"Darryl the Heart Break Kid Jones and Dr. Phillip I'll Bang Your Wife Carson!"

"Bitch you lyyyyyinnnnnn!"

"Tiffany...... girl, I wish I was lying! My whole mood went down when I seen him. He got all loud right as I walked in, girl...... then what made matters worse, Dr. Carson came strolling on in saying that he was the professor for an African American Woman's course. Like what the entire fuck? Y'all couldn't take y'all shenanigans elsewhere?" Patricia scoffs and continues, "It is what it is at this point. I'm just there to get my credentials baby, ya hear me?"

"I hear you! But hey, you got this, girl. Thanks for calling me back! I was excited to hear about your first daaaaayyy! Yaaayy! My friend gone be docta, my friend gon' be a docta!"

"Thanks, girl!"

"What are you about to do now?"

"Nothing, I guess go home, order something from *Sprint*Door, sip some wine, may read or watch a movie and relax."

"Come on, Patricia! Stop being a homebody and get your body out your home, stop isolating yourself!"

Patricia sighs and says, "I'm not isolating myself. Why would you say that? I got to work in the morning!"

"Patricia, as long as I've known you, you've always isolated yourself....... come on Pat, it's still early! You don't go to bed until about eleven anyway!"

"I got a whole routine, girl."

"That you can probably do in less than ten minutes before bed! Stop playin' Pat....... Oooh, girl, let's go to RED'S! It's Wet Wednesday! They got half off on drinks!"

Patricia hesitates for a moment, takes a deep breath, and says, "Okay, sure. How far are you from there?"

"I'm about 15 minutes away from RED'S," Tiffany claims.

"Okay, I'm about seven to ten minutes away from it. I'll meet you there."

"K, bye."

"Bye," Patricia says as the car's Bluetooth disconnects from the call. She takes an immense sigh and continues driving to RED'S.

On the way to RED'S, Patricia ponders about her encounter with Darryl and the small time that they had together. She feels that the main reason why she did not continue with Darryl was because of the drama that he was a part of. She does not find those situations attractive; it's like a recipe for future drama that she does not want to be a part of. She wishes that she can explain that to him, but he's too unrelentless.

Patricia's thoughts transition to how she has not seen her mentee, Abbyielle, since she stopped being the librarian at W.E. Dubois Middle School. Abbyielle is dealing with so much at her young age. Her thoughts made her ask aloud, "Why do women have to take on the brunt of society?"

She then thinks about her "love-life" and battles if she's ready to be intimate with someone or not. *"Maybe I should wait until after I get my doctorates,"* she wonders. She also ponders if she has become too guarded to the extent that not letting anyone in her personal sanctuary is second nature.

Once Patricia arrives to RED'S, she grabs her purse, exits her car, locks by pushing the lock button on her car keys, and struts inside. While inside, she observes the light crowd and hears the sweet jazz music playing. People are lounging in the seating areas, eating and drinking. She notices the waiters are busily moving to and from. She walks to the bar and finds two open bar stools. She sits her purse down on one of the bar stools and sits in the other.

"What are we having tonight?" A bartender asks.

"Let me get the white-Hennessy mixed in with the margarita-mix," Patricia answers.

"Coming right up," the bartender says as they go prepare the drink.

The man next to her confusingly inquiries, "There's a white Hennessy? I did not even know that exists. And Black people drink this?"

Patricia swiftly notices the man's corniness, but it carried with it a safe presence. She can smell his cologne's scent and senses that he must have some type of taste. He's wearing a black V-neck T-shirt that complimented his body frame. The shirt is tucked into his black, fitted slacks with a smooth black leather belt that wrapped around his waist. He's wearing black dress shoes.

She then musters a smile, and articulates, "I didn't know liquor was segregated, too."

Patricia's comeback twists his neurons, because he didn't think that she was going to have a response towards his

The man is so dumbfounded by Patricia's profound statement, that Patricia notices some sophistication about him, something that she has never seen in a man before; it's attractive, it's ineffable.

"I'm Jase," he says as he holds his hand out to shake hers.

Patricia hesitates but slowly reaches to shake his hand, saying, "Patricia." At the point of contact, Patricia feels his energy. He feels confident. As they gently release each other's hand, his energy still lingered, and she can't help but to feel his intensity.

"You don't come here often, right?" Jase asks, trying to read Patricia.

"Nah, according to my friends, 'I barely go out. I'm a homebody.'"

Jase chuckles and asks, "What brings you out tonight?"

"Well, I had an overbearing first day of school," Patricia scoffs. "Now, I'm just trying to get over the hump."

Jase softly states, "It is Wednesday, so I understand. What are you going to school for?"

"I'm getting my doctorates in African American Women Studies."

"Your PHD?" he enthusiastically, but confusingly questions.

Patricia quickly and confidently says, "What? A melaninated woman can't be a doctor?"

Jase embarrassingly says, "No, no, no, I'm not saying that…" and quickly catches himself. "Wait, I mean yes! Of course, women can be… and are doctors… I just think…….. that's amazing. I stopped with my masters; so when I hear about anyone going to get their doctorates, it's all respect. I have been trying to figure out if I want to go back and get mine."

"What did you get your master's in?"

"Business Administration."

"What were you planning to do with that degree?"

"Learn how to effectively operate multiple businesses all at one time. I wanted to learn how to make money in my sleep.... Be the first Black billionaire that didn't have to dribble or throw a ball, sing or rap, or sell my soul to get there."

Ignoring the nickname given to the natives of America, Patricia gives a genuine giggle and intriguingly says, "I never met an indigenous brother say that?"

"Indigenous. Isn't that like Native American or something?"

"Sure," Patricia says condescendingly. "I mean we are the originals of this land, right?"

Bewilderingly, he asks, "Are you saying that Black people are Native Americans?"

"Yes," Patricia securely says.

He sniggers and states, "So what was slavery? What about the Black people who came from Africa?"

"Slavery was the democracy that the Europeans brought from Europe, Slavery was when these same Europeans conquered and disheveled us into their society, however. There was never an Atlantic slave trade harboring people from Africa to America. There was not two point two million Africans stolen in transported to America over no course of three hundred years.... we were lied to."

"You're making some bold claims there.......... besides if you believed that, then why are you getting your doctorates in African American Women Studies? Your ancestors came from Africa my love. You're from the motherland!"

"I'm getting my doctorates in African American Women Studies to learn the lies and combat them with truth and evidence. My dissertation reflects that.......... and to your second opinion............ Everyone's origin...... the origin of man, yes indeed, came from Africa, but my genealogy, my traces, my ancestors are from here...... our people were already here."

"School must have lied to us then."

"And continues to lie, but you must ask yourself...... do you think school is the proper way to learn your history? Who constructed the school systems?" Patricia interestingly asks as the bartender places a napkin and the drink in front of her. "Much obliged," she expresses to the bartender.

As the bartender leaves to serve another customer, Jase utters, "You may have a point there. But I don't know....... there's so much to consider.... and so much to reconsider.... so much to look into. There are actual accounts and documents of slavery, it's hard to just dismiss the entire thing."

"I'm not saying dismiss the entire outlook of slavery, but slavery didn't happen the way we think.......... You seem like an intelligent man, Jase, do your research."

"Yes ma'am......"

Patricia notices how the truth makes him uncomfortable and switches the subject, "So what's holding you back from investing in you?"

Jase answers, "Money, time, having to get a lawyer for expansions...... it's just so much to do to get that exposure."

"Sounds like you're giving yourself excuses," Patricia jokingly, but firmly pronounces.

Patricia's comment puts Jase in exhalation for a moment. Then he speaks, "Well, really, life is not showing up the way I imagined. I thought by this time in my life, that I'd be settled down, have some children running around, success, et cetera, et cetera...... so many hindrances along this path that I feel like I was caught in an illusion. Life didn't show up the way I thought it was supposed to be."

Patricia observes his innocent demeanor and insecurity, and says, "I completely understand, but you can't let what you thought was 'supposed-to-be' hinder your growth. As humans, we have to get out of this notion of how life is 'supposed-to-be.' It keeps us operating at a low vibration, it creates unrealistic expectations, it gives you a fight that is not needed to fight; it's okay to pursue your goals, but it's not going to show up the way you want it to with a feeling you're thinking of; it's going to show up in a way that's perfectly for you, a way that's going to make you happy. Everything in our life is always happening at the perfect moment, the way it 'supposed-to-be.' Therefore, your life is 'supposed-to-be' the way it is right now."

"What if I'm not happy with it? Not saying that I'm not grateful with it but what if I'm just not satisfied with it? Or what if I'm not seeing the bigger picture."

Patricia quickly answers, "If you're not happy with it then it maybe because you haven't accepted it. Anytime we feel a sense of unhappiness, that's because there are things that we are not accepting or things that we are repelling. Which causes internal friction."

"Hmph, okay......" Jase tries to understand.

"If you're not satisfied with it, then you have this concept of 'more.' You're wanting 'more.' You want to experience 'more.' More what? What 'more' do you want? And that's okay, too, but there's always going to be more."

Jase looks away for a moment and looks back at Patricia, saying "I get it."

"Do you? I mean.... Let's count your blessings. What all do you have going on in your life right now?" Patricia asks.

He ponders for a second and says, "Well...... I have my own place, my own car; I did obtain my bachelors and my masters. I do have a fun-fulfilling career, that many can't say for themselves, umm." After another short pause, Jase proceeds, "I guess you're right, my life is better than what I'm making it out to be."

"Do you feel some joy, Jase?"

He smiles and replies, "I kinda do. Especially talking to you."

Patricia smiles and asks, "Do you feel like an award, Jase?"

"I am feeling a lil bit better about myself... yes."

"And don't your shoulders feel lighter now?"

He gets internally excited and replies, "They do!"

"Like some weights have been lifted off of your shoulders?"

"Yes ma'am!"

Patricia concludes, "That's because you've been carrying baggage that you do not need to carry. You are living how your life is 'supposed-to-be,' you must accept it, give it gratitude....... gratitude leads to 'more' of the things that you want to be grateful for. Then that's when everything begins to change the way you envisioned it."

Jase is captured by Patricia's method of uplifting. Her essence makes him want to confide in her; it's like he wants to tell her all his secrets. He occasionally has to look away to keep from staring into her eyes. He is too distracted by her divine beauty. Her intellect elevates him, and he is moved by her demanding presence.

Patricia perceives Jase as a turtle who just ran back into their shell and laughs, "I don't know where that came from......" She sighs and concludes, "Huuugggghhhh, it's been a looooooong day."

"God had to been using you as a vessel.... because I needed to hear that......... Thank you so much."

He checks the time on his watch, remembering that he has to pick up Braiveri from work while her car is in the shop. He gulps the rest of his drink and says, "I didn't mean to be a party pooper and just start talking about my problems. Just saying that out loud actually made me feel better about my life. Thank you for listening."

"No problem at all. Glad that I can be of service."

"You know, you could be a therapist. Here I am in the middle of this bar, telling my personal problems to a total stranger..." Jase says, and they both laugh.

While Jase stands to take a few dollars out of his wallet and tosses them on the counter. Patricia tries to read him, trying to find the flaw of men. The same flaw that millions of men across the millennium have fall quarry to. The same test that the flaw put them through in which they all fail. It's like forbidden fruit for them.

Jase interrupts her analyses and says, "Well, I hope you enjoy the rest of your evening. Thank you for the therapeutic session; oh, and good luck with your doctoral program, Miss Indigenous. I am of the most certainty that you will make the change that you're hoping to see in this world."

Patricia smirks and says, "Why thank you Jase, that truly means a lot to me. I hope to see you on one of these Forbes' magazines one day, doing your thing."

As he gets up to walk away, he walks slowly to think, *"I shouldn't leave, but she's waiting on someone; should I ask her for her number? What should I doooo? Was she just being nice? I'mma ask her."*

At the same time, Patricia is thinking, *"Wait, he's not going to hound me about my number? He's not pursuing me in a perverted way?*

He's not asking for my social media? Is he married? Is he gay?" She then senses a strong pull within her heart to keep in contact with him.

They both have their backs away from one another as they both turn around to yell "Wait!" at the same time. As Jase comes back to the bar, they both start saying, "Look, I don't normally do this but uhhhh..." They both stop awkwardly and try to laugh away their cumbersome.

"You go first," Patricia commands.

"Nah, you know it's ladies first," Jase responds.

"Okay, okay!" Patricia says, pausing and taking a deep breath to internally collect some courage. "I'm no counselor or anything but let's exchange contact information just in case you ever need someone to talk to and remind you of how life is trying to love you."

"I was going to ask the same thing!" Jase responds with a smile. "Well, not the exact words or perspective, but...... you know what I mean," Jake concludes, taking out his phone and unlocking it with face recognition. He hands it to Patricia as she dials her number and calls her phone.

"Okay, story me in," Patricia sympathetically says. "Don't be a stranger, Jase."

"Will do. You don't be a stranger, either Patricia...... and enjoy the rest of your evening," Jase says as he walks towards the exit. While leaving, he questions himself, *"Why does she remind me so much of Braiveri? Just a lil' too black..."*

Turning back around on the bar stool to face the bar, Patricia becomes full of internal questions. *"Why don't men like that ever take the initiative? Did he think I was married, or did he think I was lesbian?"*

She takes a swig of her drink while in deep thought, feeling a poignant sensation arising from her deep sense of creativity. The alcohol makes an impression throughout her body and goads her mind. It then enflames the burning desire that she constantly feels inside but she's been suppressing the feelings for so long that she kind of gotten used to doing it.

Black Pain't, Vol. II

She spiritually rids herself of the harsh feelings and all the second guesses by closing her eyes for a quick moment. She internally affirms that fear is no longer a factor in her life. She feels a sense of triumph and power charging from her core, enabling her to want to do more of the things that she has always been afraid to do.

She feels her tension ease and her mind's creative juices flow. She picks up her phone and allows the facial recognition to unlock her phone and she taps and swipes her way to her notes. She types the date and time as the title of the notes, and she pauses to see where her spirit is leading her to type.

Patricia finds herself in the present moment, feeling a slight buzz. In the middle of a bar, amid jazz instrumentals, alcohol, and lounge chatter, her life stands still. She types…

No man ever made me feel what I felt from you.
Something you gave off; something fell from you.
I usually sense stupidly from the male species but no hell from you.
In the midst of disorder, we made time stop.
You can't tell that you're on your own time?
You had on a time clock.
We watch as our energies connected.
I'm glad that we share God's complexion.
You felt like the safest haven,
someone I wouldn't mind being vulnerable with.
You're blessed and high favored,
someone I wouldn't mind being comfortable with.
I hope you're not just a figment in my imagination,
I hope your figurations turn into figures as you figure your life out.
I hope you have love during the period of you turning your lights out.
I hope you feel God's love when it's gloomy or when it's nice out.
You deserve it, king.
I can tell that you earned it, king.
And if you ever make a mistake, just learn from it, king.

Black Pain't, Vol. II

Make sure that you enjoy your evening, too, king.

Black Pain't, Vol. II

MY NOTES

Chapter 2:
Pages

She walks in, fidgeting to get herself together from fighting against the vile wind. While in search for her fellow comrade, she finally realizes her at the bar, talking to some handsome fellow. She observes their conversation with good-judgment and joy. She watches for an intense moment as he rises and walks away.

"Will we be dining alone?" a server asks, interrupting her mental inspection.

She glances away for a quick second and says, "No ma'am, my friend is at the bar." When she looks back towards the bar, she sees the guy departing whilst smiling in euphoria. "Don't let him leave, don't let him leave, girl," she silently says to herself.

She then sees her friend and the guy talking again. She perceives him give her his phone and sees her friend typing something in it. Her friend gives the guy his phone back. They say their farewells and, she slithers her way to the restroom as the guy exits.

While in the restroom, she touches up her make up and combs her hair that was rudely interrupted by the strong wind from outside. She washes her hands, dries them, and, on the way out, admires herself in the huge mirror attached on the wall. She gives herself positive energy and a ton of inner self-love. She takes out her phone and takes several pictures of herself in the mirror.

Coming out of the restroom, she slowly slinks her way towards her friend at the bar who is still typing away. "BOO!" She shouts, startling her friend.

"TIFFANY!" she yells while embarrassingly peeping around to make sure no one heard her minor scream. Making a sad, puppy dog face in humiliation, she catechizes, "Why did you scare me like that!?"

Chuckling in thrill, Tiffany asks, "Patricia, girl, who is that grown ass man that you were just canoodling with."

"We were not canoodling!"

"Sure look like some canoodling."

"Oh, God!" Patricia expresses, putting her hands over her face and taking a deep breath. "That's Jase," she settles while signaling to get the bartender's attention.

"Where do you know him from?"

"I just met him," Patricia admits as the bartender arrives. "Get this crazy girl something on my tab, please."

The bartender inquires, "What are we having?"

"What did you get?"

Patricia smiles and covers her face again, saying, "White-Hennessy mixed with a little margarita mix...."

With her mouth wide open and in shock, Tiffany whispers, "A White Hennessy Margarita? What do you have up your sleeve missy? And why don't you have any *water*?"

The bartender politely and patiently asks, "Hey, sorry to interrupt. Do I need to come back?"

"Order your drink, Tiff!"

"Two *waters,* and a Shirley Temple, please," Tiffany requests.

"Coming right up," the bartender says, tapping on the bar twice and instantly walking away.

"Okay, now, who is he? And when did you start talking to strangers? I saw him give you his phone, you gave him your number, too? And you don't really know him? Are you okay?" Tiffany worriedly asks while simultaneously touching Patricia's forehead and neck. "Are you ill?"

The bartender places a glass of water on top of a napkin in front of Patricia as she snickers and replies, "No, girl! I am not sick. It was just something about him that caught my interest. That's all."

The bartender places a glass of water on top of a napkin in front of Tiffany as she jokingly asks, "You ready to blow them cobwebs from your coochie?"

Patricia interjects, "No! Stop that right now! It's going to be a long ten weeks seeing those two every week..."

"Who?"

"Darryl and Dr. Carson!"

"Girl, don't worry about them!"

"I'm not, but between Dr. Carson's inauthenticity and Darryl's deceiving ways, I don't know how I am going to deal with that energy for ten whole weeks," Patricia claims. "On top of that, work has been just...... bluhhhh, overwhelming."

Tiffany comforts Patricia by saying, "I can understand the fakeness coming from those two but one, you just have to remember that you're there to get your credentials! Two, what makes work so overwhelming? You have your own nonprofit! You're your own CEO, girl. You're making a difference."

"I know but it's bigger than just being a CEO! Those young Black girls depend on me in many facets than just being there for them to confide in, I sometimes have to play parent.... which......" Patricia

Black Pain't, Vol. II

stops speaking, noticing something different about Tiffany. "Did you get your hair locc'd?"

While smiling, Tiffany answers, "Why yes, yes, I did." As Patricia examines her hair, Tiffany asks, "You like?"

"I think these are beautiful. These are sister-loccs right?"

As the bartender places the Shirley Temple in front of Tiffany, Tiffany smiles and replies, "Yes, since I've started my *journey*, I decided it was time to have a hairstyle that represents that. A new and improve me."

Patricia bewilderingly stares at Tiffany and rhetorically asks, "Your journey?"

Tiffany timidly says, "Yes, my journey…… the journey towards self-discovery, a journey to my highest self. I've been in my truth; reading, journaling, which the journey lies within the journaling, but that's a whole conversation in itself, girl…. WHOOOOAAA!"

Patricia's humility scans the bar after Tiffany's scream. "Why do you say that?"

"Because, when I write, there's no limit to how deep I can go, or where I can go. I even got to the root of my issues…. My issues with friendships, my issues with the opposite sex, my issues with love and acceptance…" Tiffany says as she pauses for a moment to keep from crying.

Patricia notices Tiffany inner-outcry and rubs her back. In consolation, she says, "Let it out."

"I don'……" Tiffany tries to say as her voice screech. She clears her throat and continues, "I don't know, it's just…. The journey exposes your true self, your past self, and glimpses of your future self if you don't become aware of your present self…. I don't know."

"Sounds like you're healing…. And healing is an ongoing process."

"You're right, but do you think that we can ever truly be healed?" Tiffany asks. "Like can we effectively move on from past traumas?"

"Ummm...... I think we can never truly be completely healed, it's something we work on constantly. We can eventually accept what happened and choose to move forward, but the habits and behaviors that result from our traumas will still be active within you. And that's the part that we must heal."

"That's tough to think about. I guess that's why they say that what happened to you isn't your fault, but your healing is all on you," Tiffany replies. "I start humanistic therapy next week. I think it's about time I learned to move on............ not only do I need to move on, but I need to stay out of the way, like stay out of other people's business."

Sarcastically, Patricia comically says, "You're definitely pretty good at that." They both laugh as Patricia continues, "So tell me more about this Hajj that you're on, Miss Freeman X. I know Tiffany is a Caucasian name."

Tiffany rolls her eyes and retorts, "What type of name is Patricia? Your name sounds like the white slave owner's mistress."

"Come on, girl... we ain't talkin' about me right now."

"Like I said, I do yoga, read, journal, I eat better; I make sure I take myself on dates, rather that's out to eat or a bar; I hike, I travel; especially during the summer since us educators have a summer vacation. Overall though, I'm learning more about me, my traumas, things that make me tick, things that make me happy, the people I associate myself with.... I can go on forever," Tiffany concludes.

In a prophetic manner, Patricia says, "I think that's beautiful. I believe that you're valuable, loved, deserving, and worthy of everything life has to offer. I'm proud of you, goddess!"

"Thank you, and I accept that," Tiffany says while smiling and drinking her Shirley Temple. "When will you go on your Hajj?"

Patricia instantly and firmly answers, "After I get this Ph.D. You know society has this way of pushing us away from our true selves to achieve papers and rewards." She irately shakes her head and resumes, "I just need those credentials to make my arguments and research much more trusting and applicable."

"You need a Ph.D. to do that?"

"Naw, especially with the research I have. It's just that our people have become sooooo conditioned that they won't listen to anyone without the European man's approval stamp."

"Is that important to you?"

Patricia's passion takes over as she says, "Not the European man's approval stamp, but what is important to me is the advancement of my people, especially young melaninated women are important to me. This is how I play my part in the reconstruction and redevelopment of our people in society."

"I love that about you, Patricia. So intentional about who you are and what you represent. I just don't want you to forget to take care of you, too."

"And I appreciate that, Tiffany. I guess it's my selfless divine feminine that gives me the strength to do the things I do. I know who I am," Patricia strongly says while sipping more of the Shirley in her Temple. "I'm a woman of service whose ancestors' land were taken and then violently forced out of those same lands."

Patricia's tension surrounds the bar. People quickly begin glancing on and off at them, wondering where all the loud chatter is coming from. Patricia scolds them all, internally analyzing their energies.

Tiffany breaks the awkward moment by asking, "Girl, you remember my mentee, Rayven?"

"That's............. the one........ who was having an affair........ with the married-preacher man, right?"

Tiffany nods in approval, saying "Yup! That's her. She made me into a god-mom. I was going to say no because I didn't want to be involved in her mess but when I looked at my godson, Rayshawn...... I just knew I had to take on a key role in his life. I can be the rich, fine, and the single auntie."

"She would make you the God-mom," Patricia jokingly asserts.

Tiffany snappishly and instantly asks, "Who else would be a good candidate? Them other broke bitches she calls friends?"

"Ti-ffan-neey!" Patricia motherly says.

"Hey, it's true. That's why she be in mess now because Ella and none of them other hoes wanna tell her about herself, they don't even hold themselves accountable, I see how they move........."

"Tiffany!" Patricia says gently hitting Tiffany's arm.

"..........and you weren't going to have any children no time soon so......."

"Touché."

"Anyways, other than trying to avoid Darryl and Dr. Carson, what are you looking forward to this school year?"

"Going to hear Dr. Akira Peseshet speak at NT's graduation!"

"Dr. Akira Peseshet?" Tiffany fervently asks. "I heard about her! I watched a reel of her going off on Aaron James. She's been pushing for reparations, she helped expose the *Black Lives Matter Movement's* embezzlements and how they've been frauds all along...."

"And she be talking that shit, too...... she knows her history! You know...." Patricia proclaims.

Tiffany denies Patricia's accusation by asking, "Do she believe that the women of melanin complexion are God?"

"Not only that she believes in it, but she got proof!"

"Proof?"

"Proof-proof, like the ads on the pictures before you buy them type of proof," Patricia humorously says.

"I need that type of proof."

"I knew you was going to like that...... that's why you need to come to the commencement ceremony to hear her speak! She gon' tell it how it is!"

Tiffany willingly says. "I'll definitely be in attendance. She better be who she says she is while you right here riding her bike......"

"Ain't nobody riding her bike, you know I love truth in its most rawest forms, and Peseshet provides that......"

"I hear you."

"But what was you saying about Rayven?"

"Yes...... so the paternity results came in her mail a month ago, she called me and asked me to come over."

Patricia confusingly asks, "Why did she want you to come over?"

"I'm God-mama; she needed someone around for comfort, someone to confide in her dark moment of truth. She texted both Tony and the preacher to let them know that she will let them both know what the results are............. Ooooohhhh, when I tell you it was like an episode of Maury when I got there, girl.............. and the preacher was blowing up her phone............ Tony was trying to come over to be there for her."

Patricia impatiently verbalizes, "Girl, who's baby, is it? Get to the mail, get to the results."

"Dang, girl, be patient, you know I have to fill you in on everything; it's been a minute," Tiffany condescendingly states while winking her eye. "Anyways, I laid my Godson down on the couch while Rayven opened the envelop, and she started reading.... Moments later she put her hand over her mouth, began crying, and sat the papers on the table."

"Tiffany," Patricia irately says.

Tiffany giggles and says, "Okay, the results said………"

("It's David's," Rayven's cracked voice announced as tears instantly rushed down her face.

Tiffany embraced her by laying her head on her chest and whispered, "Hey, hey, hey, it's okay. Rayven, look at me...... it is okay, it's going to be okay, love. Do not wake up Rayshawn! He's sleeping peacefully."

While sobbing, Rayven cries, "No, no, no, no, no. He's already has a wife and kids; he's already set where he's at.... My child deserves a father who's going to be there with no obligations outside of him!"

Tiffany dashed to the living room to check on Rayshawn. After she realized that he is still sleep, she came back to the kitchen during Rayven's wailing and said, "Hey, look at me... repeat after me, Rayshawn will be okay."

Rayven took a deep sigh, wiped her eyes, and repeated her, "Rayshawn will be okay."

"All of his needs will always be met!"
She whimpers, "All of his needs will always be met!"
Tiffany's voice gets stronger, "Come on Rayven! I will be the best mother I can be."
Cryingly, Rayven repeats, "I will be the best mother I can be."
"We have all the support we need; we are complete."
"We have all the support we need; we are complete."
Tiffany tightly hugged Rayven before releasing her. She stated, "Everything is going to be alright. Let's take a few deep breaths, relaxing our shoulders and hearts to accept all there is."
Rayven adhered to Tiffany's requests, closed her eyes, and shook off the tension."
"Okay, on three now...... one, two, deep breath in," Tiffany said as they both breathed in heavily. "Hold for a moment............ and release."
Rayven released as a representation of her letting go of her faults, ridding of her unscrupulous choices, and bidding farewell to her regrets.
"One more time, breathe in; hold for a moment............ And breathe out...."
"Thank you so much for being here with me, Tiffany," Rayven said in emotional gratitude.
Tiffany confidently and proudly said, "I'm the God mama! I vowed to be here no matter what."
Rayven took another deep breath and sat down at the Tiffany's table, reading over the DNA results, hoping that somehow the percentages next to the names miraculously changed. She tried to hold back tears and looked away from the paper to avoid them from falling.
"You really wanted Tony to be the father?" Tiffany asked.
Rayven helplessly looked at Tiffany and answered, "Yes. I know he would have been around. He was around throughout the entire pregnancy with the uncertainty that the baby might not be his. He was there when I gave birth. I just feel so stupid!"

Tiffany instantly said, "Hey, hey, don't self-sabotage yourself! You were living in the moments....... and in your truth! You're never stupid for that."

"It's only stupid because David and I never had anything! He was an adulterer who grew a strong addiction to the thrill of cheating. I was just too fond of him....... I knew I wasn't the only one he was cheating with. He was cheating on his wife with men, too! I knew the risks; he was just good at what he did! It's stupid!"

In confusion, Tiffany asked, "Who else was he cheating with?"

Rayven made a slight, crying chuckle, wiped her eyes, and irately said, "Oh, my god? Why am I crying like this?"

"It's okay, it's okay, Rayven. Relax."

"Yeah, he was cheating with multiple people. The choir director at the church, some members in the congregation...... He was into a lot of weird shit.... Tag teaming with other men, all types of porn, women and men eating his ass...... butt plugs...."

Tiffany interrupted Rayven's spill and questioned, "Butt plugs? In you or in him?"

"Girl, in him...... he told me that it helps him have sex better........ at one point, he wanted to take me to a sex party............"

"How does someone like that gets to be a lead at a church? He on his TD Jakes shit?"

"TD Jakes?" Rayven questions.

"Yeah, girl, did you hear about him attending all those Diddy parties? Shits wild!"

"I don't know but David is the real Lucifer. Very narcissistic, knows how to get his way, manipulative; he hides it so well."

"That's petrifying............" Tiffany concludes that conversation after storing it in her mental file cabinet. "When are you going to tell David it's his?"

Tiffany's question reminded Rayven to grab her phone that was in her back pocket. Rayven used the face recognition to unlock her phone and tapped to the call log. Rayven then announced, "I have almost 14 missed calls from David."

Black Pain't, Vol. II

"That's creepy as-fuck...." Tiffany said disturbingly.

"I'm just going to text Tony that it's not his and text David letting him know that it is his," Rayven proclaimed.

"You don't think Tony at least deserve a courtesy call?"

"You're right...... I guess I'll do it when I make it home. Thank you for everything, Tiffany, really," Rayven ended while walking into the living room.

Tiffany followed Rayven into the living room, watching her grab Rayshawn's diaper bag and the car seat, saying, "Hey, anytime. There's no problem at all. You just let me know if you need anything or if there's anything I can help you with. Don't hesitate to ask."

After picking up Rayshawn and strapping him into the car seat, Rayven said, "You will be the first person I call." She puts the diaper bag on her back and picked up the car seat with her forearm.

Tiffany hugged Rayven while saying, "I love you. Be safe. And text me when you make it home. Let me know how everything goes."

Rayven exited Tiffany's apartment and walks to her car. Once Rayven gets to her car, she unlocks the doors, opens the side of the door that has Rayshawn's base to his car seat. She locks in the car seat with base and laid the diaper bag on the passenger seat.

As she got in the driver seat to start the car, Rayven felt that someone was watching her, and she scanned the parking lot. Realizing that there wasn't anyone around, Rayven brushed off the feeling of being watched and drove away.

~

Meanwhile, Trina was observing Rayven leaving out of Tiffany's apartment throughout her living room window. She'd already looked this woman up on her social media pages; she kept looking at the baby's pictures on her pages, wondering if its Tony's. She had strong feelings about the entire situation.

Anger filled Trina. She began feeling that betrayal again. She can feel herself getting infuriated and wanted to go to Tony's house to buss him upside his lips. She turned away for a quick moment to block out her intrusive thoughts. When she turned back to look out the window, Rayven drove away.)

"....and before I walk back in my apartment, I see my neighbor, Trina staring at Rayven from her window while Rayven was driving away," Tiffany concludes.
"Niggas will have you looking dumb...." Patricia indignantly says. "That's why I couldn't do Darryl's ass."
"Darryl seemed sincere when it came to you, but I understand that birds of a feather......."
"Flock together...." Patricia says, finishing Tiffany's idiom. "Our melaninated men.... our melaninated men...... they are in deep, deep, trouble."
"Why trouble?"
"What other way to explain it? Look how they treat themselves, look how they treat others; look how they treat the only valuable resource they have on the face of this planet; the only one that will not leave their sides.............. and they treat women like dog shit......"
"That is troubling...."
"Very troubling, especially when they come from mothers who looks like them......"

~

As the night goes by, Tiffany has had a few Shirley Temples and Patricia has drunk a couple of drinks. An even younger crowd is beginning to enter the bar for club hours. They all look to be in the early 20s. The men are sagging in their tight jeans, the women had on tight dresses that present their physique. They all are on their phones, not giving anyone any genuine human interaction. The only times they look up is when the DJ is playing a song they enjoy.

Patricia and Tiffany notice the short dresses and translucent clothing on the women; they see the men sagging. The music came from Jagged Edge's *Let Get Married* to the DJ playing Blueface's *Thotiana*.

Patricia innocently says, "Buss...... down.... Thotiana? Girl, what the hell is he talking about? Who would name their daughter Thotiana?"

"Um umm, girl, are we getting old? Did we used to dress like that?" Tiffany hyperbolically asks.

While observing the crowd, Patricia declares, "I never dressed like that. I never even been the party type."

"Do you think married women or girlfriends should dress like that?" Tiffany asks.

"People should dress according to how they want to be perceived. Not to judge anyone and how they dress, I'm just not about to reveal my divinity for the public to see."

"In other countries, women walk around half naked."

"Other countries do not have a high rate of predators, prostitution, perverts, and pedophiles like America....... all these sex-trafficking, on-line creeps, and kidnappings going on," Patricia pauses to shake her head. "This is why future sex-workers and strippers will control the economy because sex is becoming a trillion-dollar industry. I respect it, but it's a reflection of how degrading and undignified women have to be in such a society as this one. A society where many women are not valued and don't value themselves, a society where twerking, drinking, and smoking are looked on as having fun," Patricia concludes.

Tiffany absorbs Patricia's profound statements and takes a moment to ponder on them. "What do you expose we do? Not only as women but as a community as a whole."

Patricia contemplates on an answer. She comes to an internal decision and replies, "I really don't have that answer. If you would have asked me five years ago, I would have said a program for young melanated women to learn trades, economics, businesses, educational skills, and entrepreneurship, social skills; now my answer is that we're going to need a generation full of strong melanated families who can not only reiterate those same concepts at home to reverse the curse but also a community of people who are all on the same page."

"That's a lot to think about," Tiffany says.

"But we wouldn't even know how to measure the progress, how would we know if conditions have changed, you know what I mean?" Patricia resolves with a question.

As a young couple walks by them, Patricia says, "See look, why would you want your woman wearing that? We can see her cheeks."

Patricia and Tiffany laugh and decide to leave. While walking in the parking lot, Tiffany asks, "Have you ever gone through a hoe phase?"

"That's a random question..." Patricia bafflingly says, "What's a hoe-phase?"

"You know...... the hoe phase is when you're young, wild, and free sexually; you're either sleeping with multiple men or in a sexual situationship where y'all fucking like rabbits on the consistent bases."

"Nuh...." Patricia says with a puzzling tone. "I can count on one hand how many men I've had sexual activities with and I'm 32 years young."

"That's why you're so uptight, mean, and unembellished, you need some penis. Penis brings hapPenis!"

Patricia chuckles and says, "Ain't no amount of penis is going to fix me or bring me no sense of happiness, unless it's my future husband's penis which I know he would keep for me only. In the meantime, I'm on a mission."

"Well, while you're on this mission, don't forget to make a fun, happy life for yourself," Tiffany encouragingly says. She notices how Patricia's energy is receptive towards her proper claims. "Hey, want to run with me tomorrow morning and do some yoga afterwards?"

"Running? Where? You wanna run and then do some Yoga?"

Tiffany responds, "We can go running around the lake, or on this track at this school in my neighborhood; and yes, there's a yoga dance studio that charges $5 a session or $50 a month to come into all sessions, anytime.... I think it'll be good for you."

"How long is this session?"

"Thirty minutes to an hour."

"And you want to do a yoga session after a run? Girl, I'm no gladiator now.... I may be able to do one or the other.... not both!" Patricia says as they both hoot.

Tiffany enthusiastically says, "We'll run a mile; just a mile."

"Just a mile?"

"Just a mile, then do we can do the yoga and a sauna! I'll pay for the yoga and the sauna!"

"Well, since you're paying.... I'll go!" Patricia hastily and funnily says.

"How you wear Christian Dior's but be acting broke?"

"Girl, I found these at Ross for $20, don't play. You know I'm frugal."

"Great! You can meet me at my house, and I'll drive us!"

"Sounds like a plan."

"Okay, awesome," Tiffany says as they begin departing from one another. "See you tomorrow," Tiffany concludes as she pushes the unlock button on her keys to unlock her car doors. She opens the driver's side door and enters in.

Tiffany sticks the key into the ignition to start the car. She lets the car sit for a moment to let her car's Bluetooth connect to her phone. Once she hears the audio book of the *Four Agreements* by Don Miguel Ruiz playing from her phone to the speakers in her car, she drives out of the parking lot and on her way home.

~

Once Tiffany pulls into the parking lot of the complex, she notices Trina leaving. She shuts the car off and sits for a moment to show a sense of grace for getting home safely. "Thank you, Universe, for the traveling grace. Asé"

She exits the car and pushes the lock button on the car keys to lock her doors. When she gets to the apartment, she walks in with joy and gratitude towards her space and flips up the switch by the door as she closes the door.

Black Pain't, Vol. II

"Thank so much you, Universe, for a place to live, be, and recharge. Asé."

She happily strides to her bedroom to turn on the lamp by her bedside. She saunters into the hallway closet to remove her clothes and toss them in the dirty clothes hamper. She puts on a white tank top and some striped pajamas pants. She grabs her phone, her gratitude journal, and her devotional journal on the way back to the living room.

While in the living room, she grabs the lighter from a bookshelf to light the candle that is on top of the coffee table. Tossing the lighter onto the coffee table, she flops down on the couch, checks her phone one last time before she enters her astronomical, creative zone. She sees text messages from Patricia, Rayven, and a few numbers she does not have saved. She clicks on Patricia's text message and reads, "I made it home. Text me when you make it."

Tiffany replies by texting, "I made it home, too. See you tomorrow." After sending the message, she exits out of her message thread with Patricia and goes to Rayven's message. Rayven wants to know if she'd be interested in having brunch with her and Rayshawn tomorrow.

Tiffany thinks about how she squeezes that into her busy schedule. She responds by texting, "Sure! Let's try that new With Love and Soul restaurant in Westtown. I hear it's Black owned." She sits her phone down on the coffee table to grab a pen from out of the office space in a little room by the main entrance.

While she skips back to the living room, her phone lights up because of a notification from Rayven. She reads, "12 noon?"

"Perfect," Tiffany types and sends to Rayven. She then activates her Do Not Disturb option in the settings. She slides the phone away from herself to escape the matrix. The matrix is full of work, scheduling, and planning. The matrix takes you away from one's true self, separating them from their godly nature.

She sits erect on the couch with her hands rested on her knees, smelling the lavender from the burning candle. She inhales and exhales at a calming pace. She then sits on the floor in the child's pose next to the coffee table.

After a mental twenty seconds, she switches into the downward spiral dog. She then transitions into the *Warrior I* pose for another twenty seconds. Lastly, she went into the tree pose and did both legs for about twenty seconds each.

Tiffany's shoulders are loose, her mind is active and alert from the yoga poses, and she's focus on her devotion for tonight. She sits back down on the couch and grabs her gratitude journal. She flips through three pages of statements of what she is thankful, grateful, and appreciative for. She writes, *"I am appreciative for my profession, I am grateful for endless opportunities, I am thankful for the Universe's divine protection."* She repeats them aloud before closing the gratitude journal and tossing it towards the end of the couch.

She grabs her devotional journal from the side of the couch. She flips through a hand full of pages, searching for one in particular. There are pages full of notes, affirmations, poetry, and prayers; pages full of her venting about her faults and various truths that many of her family members or close friends probably will never know, infused with the providences she knows are owed to her.

She writes in this journal as if she's talking to her inner child, her consciousness, the Universe (God), her current self, an audience, or to her therapist. Her journal is filled with her unscrupulous habits, her plight to wait until marriage before giving herself away sexually; her past alcoholic addiction that she gained and overcame almost a decade ago. Her journal is full of the struggle with herself, dancing with the intelligence of her intellectual ego. She treats the journal like it's her holy scripture that God called her to write.

"Maybe, it'll be a book one day," she thinks to herself as she reads of few of the pages aloud to herself with joy and cheer. She's been thinking of reading some of her pieties at Afro-Culture's open mic night. She has been trying to build the courage to get pass her stage freight. She practices speeches and poems around her students during the school year; she's even began a poetry club for students to share during lunch

Black Pain't, Vol. II

on Fridays, she has gotten teachers and staff members to sponsor lunch for the students who share and attend.

Flipping through more pages, she stops to read a few epistles that are addressed to her ex-fiancé. About his lies and mistreatments; his eyes and how deceitfulness. She internally shows gratitude that she's finally healed and moved on from that situation, however. That left a sour taste in her mouth when it comes to men.

She reads, "What's the problem, Black men? Why must you lie? What is it about cheating that would make you gamble with your lives, your health, your relationships, your families? What is this all for, Black men? A quick nut? We're at war, Black men, but you rather throw your energy and life force away for a weak fuck?"

I wish him nothing but true love and abundance," she thinks to herself as she turns to the next blank page. She grabs the pen from the side pocket of the *journal*, lays it in the crevice of the journal. She closes her eyes to take a few deep breaths. She relaxes her shoulders and soothes her breathing, allowing the rudiments of the earth to satiate her with creativity, slake her with more affection, and gratify her with more gratitude.

After opening her eyes, she opens her journal, and she writes the number 111 on the bottom left of the journal. She ponders on a clever title and writes 111 at the top of the page. She writes:

Page one hundred and eleven,
you're the embodiment of elegance;
you're small, sweet, and powerful girl, you're a peppermint;
I love how you heal and be on your own grind girl, you're everything;
and your homie a clown, I can tell you didn't play that by your
temperament. You don't like when guys come off desperate;
the new years passed, you felt like you missed out on a forever kiss;
but, girl, that don't exist, smh, but anyway,
you were on a different page when I opened you;
never met another drug doper than you,
been drinking tequila out my wine glass; getting litty across the city
with my fine ass; can't be sly and shy now; I can't rewind back;
time to go to work if the Universe assigns that;

Black Pain't, Vol. II

let man take my heart but I kept coming to You to get my mind back;
and I'll do anything to get that time back,
but .... what page are we on?
What page are we on? Is this fiction or non-fiction?
What page are we on? This feeling is beyond mystery.
What page are we on? What page are we on?
I learned that we should never judge a book by its cover.
Never start talking with someone else unless their previous
relationship is truly over; and most of these men's lies be lethal
weapons they get to steppin' like Danny Glover;
Reading the same book, but ended up on separate pages,
We were singing the same songs but performing on different stages,
You said that I was acute, and that you saw me from different angles,
Lost in the translation, didn't understand each other's love languages
I learned to never judge a person by the chapter I started reading them
on until I've read the previous chapters and where they came from;
Understand their family dynamics and where they get they name from;
Ask about their influences and where they get their game from;
when you're overthinking situations, you put a different lens on;
different perspective,
what we had was the most beautiful deception;
in the dream of love, you left, but I kept you in my inception;
What page are we on now? What page are we on? What page are we
on now? What page are we on?
What page are we on? Is this fiction or non-fiction?
What page are we on? This feeling is beyond mystery.
What page are we on? Not only did we have chemistry, we got history.
What page are we on?

    She slides the pen in the side pocket of the journal and closes it. She sighs and takes an even deeper breath to release the energy she created from within that ode she just wrote. Ignoring the new souls in the room, she walks into her bedroom, hurdles in the bed, and digs her way under her comforter to get comfortable. She feels at peace, coming into the climax of her night where she has to deal with her subconscious alone.

    She says to herself, "As I lay myself down to sleep, I pray to the Lord, my soul to keep; if I should die before I wake, I pray to the Lord my soul to take. Amen." She turns her lamp off and lies down on the pillow. Tiffany does her eight to ten seconds breathing technique to try to sleep, hoping that insomnia does not visit her tonight. It usually arrives when she has to be up early in the morning, or when she's in desperate need of rest. However, Tiffany is able to fall right to sleep, thinking of all the blessings heading her way.

~

The next day, Tiffany awakens from the sound of her alarm. She turns off the alarm and whispers a short affirmation to herself, *"Today's going to be a happy, fun, and loving day."* She retrieves her phone and immediately calls Patricia.

"I'm uuuuuuuuup! I'll be there in 10-15 minutes," Patricia says as soon as she answers the phone.

"See you shortly," Tiffany pronounces as they both hang up the phone. She checks her messages and her social media apps before hoping out of bed and walking into the bathroom, tapping and scrolling.

While piddling in the bathroom, she continues to tap and scroll through her social media apps. She taps, scrolls, and swipes from nothing but reels, reels, reels. Reels about relationships, reels of women twerking, reels about speeches, reels about sports, reels about podcasts, reels about deaths, reels about fights, reels about celebrities, reels about sermons and preachers preaching about nothing, just reels after reels.

"Just a bunch of nothingness," Tiffany thinks to herself, placing the phone on top of the bathroom sink to wipe and flush the toilet.

She washes her hands then brush her teeth. She ties her hair in a ponytail. Removes her clothes to put on some green yoga pants and a green sports bra to match. After putting on her socks and shoes, she grabs her sports jacket from out of the hallway's closet and walks to the kitchen to grab two bananas from off of the kitchen table, a couple of multigrain bars from out of the pantry, and two water bottles from the refrigerator.

Seconds later, the doorbell rings. Tiffany goes to open the door and Patricia walks in, wearing black and red joggers that brought out

Patricia's gorgeous frame, and a black Sports-Tek shirt. After Tiffany gives her one of the bananas, she says, "Grand rising!"

Patricia replies, "I haven't woken up this early to go workout in a long time," slumping down on the couch to peel her banana.

"Oh, you're going to love the trail that we're running on, you can hear the birds, the bugs, and feel the Friday morning cold as you warm up in it," Tiffany says whimsically.

"If I stop and walk during this run, I'll just meet you at back at our starting spot!" Patricia says as they both snigger.

"You'd be fine! I'll walk with you. I be having to walk, too. I'm not a Sha'Carri Richardson or anybody, I just been.... moving... yeah... moving my body, making sure it gets its health and fitness! Let's just stay in the present moment, give our bodies the love it deserves."

Patricia grunts and teasingly says, "Okay, okay, okay, geeesh, Iyanla Vanzant!"

The name lit a light bulb in Tiffany's mind as she instantly says, "Hey, I think I've actually read some of her books...... look right there. Third shelf."

Patricia rises to go guise at all the paperbacks and hardcovers standing in alphabetical order by the authors' last names. The bookshelf has multiple shelves mounted on the walls of her living room. Patricia mumbles to herself, "*Yesterday, I Cried; Acts of Faith: Meditations for People of Color;* and *Peace from Broken Pieces: How to Get Through What You're Going Through.*"

"I'm reading *Until Today! Daily Devotions for Spiritual Growth and Peace of Mind* by her right now! It actually impelled me to begin my journey."

As Patricia continues to scan at the other books by other authors on the shelves, she comes across a picture of a beautiful woman who appears to be in her mid-50s. "Is this your mom? Did she play any sports in high school or college?" She courteously inquires.

"Girl, that's Althea Gibson, the first Black woman tennis player to be invited to Wimbledon. I got this up because at one point, I wanted to be the First Black .... something.... I didn't care what it was I just wanted to be the first Black person to do it."

"Y'all killin' me with this Black word," Patricia says.

"Oh, my apologies, my Indigenous queen...." Tiffany playfully says. "But that was before I learned that we was always the first to do everything.... to be the first Black anything is the European narrative."

"You got that right," Patricia says while glancing. "You don't have any pictures of you and your mother?"

"I barely know anything about my mom, my dad raised me. I know he played football back in high school, but that's about it."

"What happened with your mom?" Patricia enigmatically asks.

Tiffany sighs and states, "Her and my dad split up when I was a toddler. She already had kids with her ex-husband, and eventually went back to him after her and my dad broke up. My dad told me that my mom was having an affair with her ex-husband while they were together."

"Ouch."

"I know...... he told me he got a DNA test with me to make sure. I don't blame him because when it was all said and done, he did everything in his power to make sure I had a good life."

Empathetically, Patricia asks, "She never kept in contact with you after that?"

"I mean........ she tried. I just felt awkward around her husband who never made me feel welcomed or a part of their family. My mom wouldn't hug and kiss me like she did their other kids. My step siblings treated me like an outcast. I remember telling my dad about how they were treating me, and my dad flipped out on my mom and her husband."

"Why did you tell your daddy?"

"I didn't tell him, tell him...... he was just curious as to why I didn't want to go visit my mom or go to outings with her and her lil' family," Tiffany says, bouncing her shoulders. "So I told him why."

"I can only imagine what Mr. Freeman did!"

"Girl, you know he let freedom ring! He let freedom ring!" Tiffany shouts as they both laugh. "Ready to knock out this mile?"

"I'm as ready as I'd ever be," Patricia claims, rising from the couch to throw her banana peelings away in the kitchen and walking towards the door.

Tiffany grabs her purse, keys, banana, water, and multigrain bar while walking towards the door. Patricia opens it and exits; Tiffany follows suit and locks the door on the way out.

They walk down the block of Tiffany's neighborhood, heading toward Kennedy High School. As Patricia and Tiffany walk through the gates into the school's track and field stadium, there are other people from the neighborhood walking on the track as well.

Patricia properly and sarcastically says, "Oh, good ol' *John F. Kennedy*, the one who is acknowledge as someone who was trying to help colored people; was he assassinated for his role in equality or because he was trying to expose the elite? The world will never know...."

"What's the female version of a Hotep?" Tiffany jokingly asks as they make their way on the track.

They begin jogging, still conversing, and laughing at one another. After four laps around the track, they walk back to Tiffany's car. She drives them to the yoga studio.

Once Tiffany parks the car, they get out and walk inside to see about 20 people in there, mostly White women, sitting or standing on their yoga mats in shorts or yoga pants. The yoga instructor is by her office, speaking with clients and collecting money. Tiffany and Patricia get in line to pay the instructor.

Tiffany pays and takes Patricia to where the extra yoga mats are located. They both get a yoga mat and some Lysol wipes. They wipe and clean their yoga mats, finding space on the floor to set up. They begin stretching before the session begins.

Moments later, they hear soft, meditation music playing louder than before. The yoga instructor announces, "Okay, everyone, let's begin in the lotus position to align our chakras and then we'll move into the downward facing dog." Tiffany notices Patricia's calm spirit a few times during the yoga session as everyone in the studio mimic the yoga instructor. She feels a sense a relief knowing that Patricia came, hoping that she will want to attend more.

Once the session is over, Tiffany and Patricia roll up their yoga mats, place them back in the yoga mat box, and exit, feeling accomplished. Tiffany does not have time to sit in the sauna, because she has to meet with Rayven at noon. She only has time to get home to shower and drive to the brunch spot. The drive on the way back to Tiffany's is a soothing, quiet drive, giving Patricia time to reflect on how she's been neglecting her body and should start exercising more.

After Tiffany parks in the complex, Patricia says, "Thank you for everything! I didn't know I needed that. I want to do this again."

"Anytime! Just let me know!" Tiffany says as they exit the car. "I could use a gym partner!"

"Aight, girl... byyyeee!"

"Be safe, Pat!"

"I will," Patricia says, walking to her car a while Tiffany walks in her apartment.

While in the apartment, Tiffany opens her music app on her phone to play more meditation music in the duration of her showering and preparing to leave to meet with Rayven.

Black Pain't, Vol. II

MY NOTES

Chapter 3:
Rayshawn Little

    As she walks in, she notices a beautiful server, looking to be in her early 20s, at the front desks. She keenly announces, "Hello! Welcome to With Love and Soul! How many will be joining you?"

While smiling, she responds, "One more."

The server grabs two menus, humbly says, "Right this way," and leads her to a table booth. She lays the menus on each side of the table as she sits down and says, "Your waiter would be here shortly," and walks back to the front desk.

    While sitting down, she scans the room of all of the beautiful, copper, bronzy people, and all other sanctified shades of melaninated ladies and gentlemen of all ages, enjoying their Saturday brunch. The restaurant is full of friend groups, families, and couples. *"It smells like somebody grandma, mama, grandpa, and auntie is in the kitchen,"* she thinks to herself. The music is full of songs by Monica, Babyface, Lauryn Hill, Blackstreet, Boys-to-Men, and more soulful artists.

She takes a second to look down to read the menu of the various meal options. A waiter comes and impedes on her thought process with his good looks and attraction, saying, "Welcome to With Love and Soul, I'll be your waiter this afternoon, my name is Tray; what can I get you started with to drink?"

"Hey, Tray," she says while flipping over the menu to see the drinks. "Ooh, I'll take a glass of water, and a pineapple mimosa."

"Coming right up! And are we waiting on anyone?"

"Yes sir!"

"Okay, so I'll bring you your drinks and wait till they get here to order y'all's food."

"Perfect, thank you, Tray."

"With love."

As the waiter walks away, she examines the room again. She notices a handsome gentleman sitting at a table by himself, wearing a nice, grey, fitted suit with a white button up. He's scanning the room and examining everything and everyone as if he is monitoring or evaluating something.

Amid to her staring, his eyes find hers in the midst of all the chatter, music, chewing, tapping, laughing, and boundless food smell. It's as if she can feel and sense his energy across the room. They lock eyes for a few seconds too long and they both look away, smiling. He looks back at her to make sure she can see him staring.

"That's a few seconds over the thirsty limit," she thinks to herself.

Tray comes back to place a glass of water and a mimosa in front of her and walks away. As Tray walks away, he passes by the individual that she was just staring at. She watches him call out for Tray to say something to him, and watches as Tray gives a dry response. Then they both quickly look towards her and then back to one another for more dialogue.

She notices their glare and turns her head in slight confusion. When she looks back, Tray is walking away, and the individual had his back towards her. She awkwardly smiles and continues to drink her mimosa. Once she looks away, she sees her guest walk in, and she says, "My Ray of Sunshine, Rayshawn!!" She says softly grabbing the baby from off Rayven's hip.

"Hey, Tiffany!" she says while putting the diaper bag on the seat and sitting down.

"Hi, Rayven!" Tiffany says while sitting down with little Rayshawn in her arms.

"Oh, my God, Rayshawn, you just get more cuter and bigger every time I see you! Yes, yes, you do, yes, you dooooo," Tiffany says while kissing and tickling the baby. She then asks, "How are you, lil' Ray Ray?"

Rayven skims the menu and says, "I haven't been here since it first opened...... They don' updated everything......"

"Yeah, they did...... but how are you? How are things at night? He's allowing you to sleep in?"

"For the most part now, but you know in the beginning, he had me up every hour on the dot, always feeding and changing him."

"That's normal, that comes with it....... How's David's interactions? How's his participation?"

"He's actually not that bad. He has him three times out of the week, and he has him involved in church......"

"I'm happy that he's taking full responsibility. Is him and his wife still together?"

"Nope, she reached out to me on SnapChat, too..."

"Saying what?" Tiffany interposes.

"Saying she want to meet up and talk about it our affair.......... she said that she would love to have this talk 'woman to woman.'"

"Like wanting to fight...or...."

"Nah, nothing like that...... she just wanted answers. She was trying to put all the puzzle pieces together in her mind. You know he was a piece of shit......"

Instantly, Tiffany says, "Don't be cussing in front of my Ray!"

"Sorry," Rayven whispers. Then she proceeds, saying, "Yeah, but I met with her while I was pregnant, I told her everything......" Rayven says. She smiles, watching Tiffany hug and love on her Babyboy. Then she precipitously asks, "You think I'm a homewrecker?"

"Girl, he was wrecking his home looooong before you; your pregnancy is what gave his wife the strength to leave and move on with her life, you really did her a favor....... as if the men she found out about wasn't enough........ but don't take the blame for that. He was already battling demons."

Tray appears and politely announces, "Excuse me, ladies" to get their attention. Then he directs his energy towards Rayven and asks, "My name is Tray and I'll be taking care of you this afternoon. What can I get you to drink?"

Rayven quickly grabs the menu and searches for the drink menu. "What you drinkin'?" she asked Tiffany.

"Water and a pineapple mimosa!"

"I'll think I'll have a raspberry mimosa and a water with lemon please."

"I got ya...... are we ready to order? Do I need to come back?"

Tiffany looks at Rayven for confirmation. "Just a few seconds, you can take her order," Rayven says as she continues to gaze over the menu.

Tiffany says, "Yes, ummm, I'll take theeeee Chad's Chicken and Chunky Waffle, please...... oh, and can you warm up the syrup, please?"

While writing the order, Tray says, "No problemo, and you madam?"

Rayven asks, "What does the BBW stand for on the BBW and a BLT?"

Amusingly, Tray replies, "Big Belgium Waffle."

"That's creative," Rayven impressively states. "I'll take the BBW and a BLT on avocado toast, please."

"How would you like your eggs?" Tray asks.

"Sunnyside up, please."

As Tray writes, he politely expresses, "Sunnyside up, all coming right up! Can I get you all anything before your food arrives? How about another mimosa?"

Tiffany says, "I'll definitely take another mimosa."

"Yes, ma'am......... and by the way, your food and drinks are on the house. That gentleman over there is treating," Tray declares while walking away.

Tiffany and Rayven are stunned by the generous deed. Tiffany looks over to see that the man is gone. She fervently searches around the restaurant for him.

"Who are you looking for?" Rayven confusingly asks.

"For the guy who paid for our food, I at least want to thank him."

Rayven notices the glare in Tiffany's eyes as she searches for him with the feeling of gratitude spilling from her pores and a sense of admiration from her energy. She tauntingly says, "Aww shoot, Miss Tiffany has a secret add-mire-yi-yeeerrrrr......"

"Oh, stop it....... I never seen this man until today, girl.... but he was sitting right over there, not even eating, just staring......"

"Sounds like he found him something to eat......" Rayven slyly says, making Tiffany blush.

Tiffany rolls her eyes and says, "Anyways...... have you heard from Tony?"

"Not since we found out the baby wasn't his......."

"Understandable.... he really loved you."

"Yeah........ it was the history of us that he was in loved with.... I think he just missed who we were to each other. Or who he was when he was with me."

"You think he wished Rayshawn was his?"

"I don't know.... I doubt it......"

"I think he wished it was his....."

"Why you say that?"

"He was around throughout the whole pregnancy. He was there when Rayshawn was born! That says a lot...."

"True...... I'm just happy that David's church has a daycare that Rayshawn can attend too girl........ for the freeski......"

"Free daycare?" Tiffany questions but then quickly recollects something and says, "Oh, because David's the deacon?"

"Yes, ma'am.... remember my homegirl, Jazmine?"

"Sure do........ your sorority sister, Jazmine, right? Y'all used to sing in the choir together........"

"Yes, her...."

"The one who walked in on you and the Deacon......"

"Yeah, her........ you could have left that part out......" Rayven embarrassingly acknowledges.

"My bad...."

"Nah, you good...... but David used to allow her daughter to attend for free. After everything came out, the church began charging her."

"That's because the deacon didn't have anything to hide once news got out about him getting you pregnant," Tiffany says while pondering. "I heard of the truth setting you free, but I never heard of it taking away your freedom......."

"Girl, stop."

"Isn't it funny how the church still allowed him to hold such high position after being in such a wicked quandary. If it was embezzlement of the church's money, then they would have kicked him out in an instant.... but noooooo......." Tiffany sarcastically states. She finishes her first mimosa as Tray brings two more to the table.

"Thank you," Rayven says to Tray as he walks away.

"No problem, that food should be right out."

Tiffany then resumes her rant, "You can mess around with a few members and you're good, just don't touch that money."

"Yeah, you're right........" Rayven says with a desolate sigh. "I hate how things turned out."

"Fact of the matter is, you were young when he deceived you and treated you like a craving. You were a drug to him. He only went to you when he wanted his fix. You have to remind yourself that you are no one's property, no one's good-temporarily time, nor are you someone's Tylenol. You are worthy and valuable," Tiffany explains.

"Thank you so much, Tiffany. I needed to hear that."

"Anytime, and when you're ready to start your spiritual journey. Let me know.... I believe we're all put on earth for a purpose. I'll help you find yours."

"I would love that."

Several minutes later, Tray brings Tiffany and Rayven their food, along with more mimosas. The individual that paid for their food is right back at that table that he was sitting at before, but Tiffany and Rayven do not notice him just yet.

Tiffany grabs a knife and begins cutting the chicken and the waffle with one hand while firmly still holding Rayshawn in the other. Rayven pours syrup on her BBW. Tiffany gets a fork and commences to eat as Rayven follows suit on her plate.

"Chicken's delicious, seasoned well......"

"This waffle is perfect, sweet but not too sweet, somebody put they foot in this!"

Tiffany notices the guy sitting back at the same spot as last time and tells Rayven, "There he goes right there. At the booth!"

Rayven glances over there for a moment to see him and looks away to not be caught staring. She says, "Oooh girl... he's cuuuuttee."

"Oh, stop it, Rayven."

They continue eating with more conversations about life, Rayshawn, and their futures. It's always like a therapy session when one gets around Tiffany. She just brings that out of everyone.

Tiffany senses and knows that confidently. However, she does not take that for granted. Her nosey nature is innocent and meaningful when she is able to help people find a solution or a mature way of solving their own problems.

When they are almost done eating, the individual from across the room comes to their table, taking them by surprise, and saying, "Excuse me, may I ask you two some questions?"

Rayven looks at Tiffany whilst Tiffany is admiring him. Rayven speaks for speechless Tiffany, saying, "Sure..."

He asks, "How's the food? How's your server, Tray? How's your overall experience?"

Tiffany says, "The food is definitely A-1; I can tell you got somebody grandma back there doing all the work..."

Rayven says, "Yes, the food's good, I need that music playlist too..."

Tiffany chuckles, making the man grin. "Oh, and I love the bottomless mimooosaaaaaaas!"

"Perfect. Very good.... well, I'm Chad Love.... I'm the owner of With Love and Soul."

"Hey, Chaaadd...... I have a question for you," Tiffany bravely initiates. "How many women do you allow to eat on the house? Is this something you do daily ooorrrrr........ do they give you their number before they leave?"

Chad chuckles embarrassingly while warming up a fib. He quickly and internally decides not to lie and states, "You caught me....... you got me there...... I mean, it is a tactic used to make sure they come back; they tell their friends, their family, their co-workers, neighbors...."

Rayven sips her mimosa, minding her own business, as Tiffany proceeds with her friendly interrogation. "Well, it's working, Chaaaad, because my sister and I will be back...... where you from, Chaaaad?"

He chuckles and answers, "I'm from here.... grew up in the neighborhood across the way, learned to cook at a vocational school...... I went to another culinary school after graduating from that one...... I wrote a couple cookbooks that funded many open opportunities, and I was blessed to eventually open my own restaurant," he concludes humbly.

"That's fantastic...... Congratulations on all your success, and it's a pleasure meeting you, Chaaad...... But look, we're HIGHLY grateful for your generosity, we just don't want you to lose your business or your dignity trying to pay for the meals of everyone beautiful woman that walks in here," Tiffany kindly says. Then she whispers to him, "It's way too many of us...... Chaaadd!"

"I love the way you say my name," Chad apologetically affirms. He continues, "Uhhh, but ummm... yes, yes, yes, ma'am..... I'll definitely keep that in mind."

Tiffany then asks, "What are your favorite dishes to make, Chaaadd?" as Rayven surveys their interaction.

"Depends on my mood," Chad states. "Like if it's grown and sexy, or I'm cooking for an occasion then maybe some Salmon, Baked Chicken, or some sort of Steak with rice, mashed potatoes, or vegetables on the side...... but it depends on the occasion."

"That's fascinating...." Tiffany articulates.

Chad takes a card from out of his wallet, sits it down by Tiffany, and says, "Well, here's my card... if you ever need anything, please don't hesitate to ask."

Before Chad gets the chance to walk away, Rayven says, "Come on Chad! This is the 21st Century! We don't keep up with cards anymore...... you gonna have to give her your personal cell, IG, Snap, or something......"

Tiffany gives Rayven a denying countenance as Chad takes out his phone. Tiffany straightens her face and smiles once Chad hands Tiffany his phone for her to put her number in. Tiffany types her name and number as a new contact in his phone.

After handing Chad his phone back, Chad taps on the number, saying, "Let me call it to make sure it's the right number...... you know how the beautiful ones do you......"

Tiffany pulls out her phone from her purse the moment the phone vibrates with Chad's number appearing on her screen. "I'll store you in now...... Chaaaadd..." Tiffany firmly says.

"Perfect... enjoy the rest of your meal," Chad verbalizes as he walks away.

Rayven has a look of approval on her face as Tiffany is finished tapping on her phone. Tiffany catches Rayven's facial expression and stringently says, "What?"

Rayven guiltily says, "I didn't say nothing...." while sipping her mimosa.

"You didn't say it.... but it's all over your face..." Tiffany severely says.

"Girl he's too fine girl to be paying women's meals for pussy...... you gon' reach out to him?"

"I'm going to see where his mind is. I'm focused on my journey right now; I'm focused on me; focused on being a great God-mom!"

"I get it... I definitely get it..."

"Anyway.... what do you have up for the rest of the day?"

Rayven takes a deep breath and widens her eyes for a bit, saying, "I'm gonna drop Rayshawn off at the daycare so he can spend the evening with David while I go to work."

"You work evenings now?"

"Yes, 2p-10p, Tuesday through Saturday...."

"Is it stressful?"

"I think all jobs are stressful, unless you doing something you love. This is only temporarily until I find out what I really need to be doing with my life. I just want to be a good example for Rayshawn. Show him what real women are like."

"I understand......... and you will be a great example for Rayshawn, because your mind is already set on it and...."

"....and I don't really even have a choice..." Rayven interrupts. "Like I have to do this, I have to nurture and love my baby; I can't expect anyone else to."

"Actually, you do have a choice... and because of who you are and your will to do what's right, you made the pro-choice to bear and raise Rayshawn. It's in a woman's nature to. Regardless of the circumstances."

"I hear you......" Rayven says as she proceeds to eat. "But why do mothers always have to bear the weight of society? Why is it our full responsibility to having to raise the kids in and out of the father's absences? Why is that fair?"

"It's not fair, and we don't have to bear the weight of society, we just take it on because it's in our nature to. It's in our nature to fix problems. It's in our nature to nurture and be there for others; to take on the pain."

"Ohhhh."

"Plus, there are laws protecting women and providing them resources to be able to get some help from an absent father......... child support, WIC program, and thousands more for single mothers."

"Why is this even a conversation that we must have?"

"You know they destroyed our families long ago. You destroy a family by first emasculating the men, ruin them with drugs, put them in jail; or just flat out killed them...... now rap music, pornography, LGBTQ, and sexual diseases are being added to the mix of destroying our men.... their masculinity......"

"Yeah, but even before that, Tiffany........" Rayven proclaims. "Men have been the cause of major wars; men will fight whoever to see whose balls are bigger; niggas will fight about who's struggle was or is worse! These same men degrade and devalue women. Most of these men are sick in the head."

Tiffany is lost for words. She's never heard Rayven speak so eloquently about the state of men. "You've had a lot to think about, huh?"

"Yes, girl, be dying to talk to someone about all these intrusive thoughts in my head. All I do is think! It just be me and Rayshawn, all day and night, unless I take him to his grandparent's, or he's with David...... He good company though, he listens very well."

Tiffany giggles at Rayven's comment, thinking of ways to cultivate Rayven in her time of inner development. She says, "I've always said you were a strong woman, Rayven."

"That's because I have no choice but to be...... like motherhood is a whole different type of world."

"I know that's right...."

"Like I be exhausted! Don't get me wrong."
"Right."
"But when I hear Rayshawn's laugh, when I see his huge smile; the way his personality is already being shown...... it makes me wanna go harder...... like I can't give up because I have someone depending on me. No matter how lonely, boring, or hard it gets...... I have to do what I have to do......"

~

After brunch, Tiffany and Rayven part ways. Tiffany goes about her day while Rayven drives Rayshawn down to 18th St. Missionary Baptist Church's Child Daycare Center to drop him off to David. When she arrives, she notices how David hasn't been responsive. She does not want to go inside, but she must.

She grabs Rayshawn's diaper bag and his car seat with him sleeping in it. She embarrassingly walks into the daycare witnessing all the children running around with the staff. She hears babies crying and the sounds of children playing. She witnesses David, Sr. talking to the choir director, Kenneth, and a few other members of the choir by the receptionist's counter.

Once David observes Rayven walking in, his demeanor changes. He feels self-conscious as he walks to her. He gets the diaper bag and throws it over his shoulder. He reaches for the car seat and Rayven gets startled. They have an obdurate moment. Even though it is only a few people witnessing their interaction, but to them two, it feels as if everyone in the world is surreptitiously watching the two giant elephants in the room.

As guilt forms a cloud in the middle of the daycare center, shame brightens their storm like lightening, and the precipitation of embarrassment showers on them. It feels like their natural rhythms of life is off beat. Most of the adults in the room who attends 18th St. Missionary Baptist Church know bits and pieces of their story, Deacon David's infidelities and his affairs. As they work and move around the center doing their daily tasks with the children, they secretively and shyly gaze at their encounter.

"I tried texting you," Rayven says while quickly and distressingly viewing the people in the room, noticing Kenneth's off and on grimy stare. She closes her eyes for another hasty second, groaning, and whispering, "Jesus...." to herself.

"I'm sorry," David says. "My phone has been in my office."

"Damn right, you're sorry," Rayven thinks to herself as she catches her breath. "It's okay," she says aloud.

"There are four bottles of breast milk in there. Put two in the freezer for later, the other two should be fed to him every time he awakens from his naps. Make sure you change him periodically. He pees and poops a lot," she says with a firm, motherly tone. "There's food in there for him and some applesauce that he loves."

"Okay, I got it. Thanks for bringing him," David professionally says as if he's trying to hurry her out of the center.

Rayven silently snarls at his rapid vitality and inquires, "No problem, you want to meet me here later or pick him up from your house?"

"It'll be from my house."

"Okay," Rayven concludes. She kisses Rayshawn and exits the daycare.

While leaving, Rayven sees Jazmine walking towards the center. *"Oh, shit! Can this day get any worse?"* Rayven thinks to herself as the vim of stroppy tension fills their opposite pathways.

Meanwhile, Jazmine is internally startled to see Rayven. She hasn't seen her around since she found out about her pregnancy. *"Speak, Jazmine, speak!"*

As they get closer, something unusual happens within Rayven that provokes her to softly say, "Hey, Soror.... how are you? Long time no see."

Jazmine is caught off guard and cumbersomely embraces Rayven. They do their sorority's secret greeting. While feeling her heavy burden, Jazmine says, "Hey, Ray.... I'm good. How have you been?"

Rayven takes a deep exhale, saying "I've been okay, learning how crazy motherhood can be."

Jazmine lights up and says, "Right... congratulations on your little one.... how is he? What's his name?"

"Rayshawn!"

"Rayshawn? That's a beautiful name! I'm happy for you!"

"Thank you so much! He's so full of life! Greatest gift I can ever ask for," Rayven explains. "How's lil' Miracle?"

"Lil' Miracle is turning into big Miracle," Jazmine says as they both giggle. "She's good though. This is her last week at this daycare. Unfortunately."

"Oh, no, why?"

"They sent me a bill in the mail after Miracle has been going here for free for the last two years," Jazmine tightly says.

Bewilderedly, Rayven slowly asks, "How was she able to go here for free?" in a questioning tone.

Jazmine has a quick flashback within her mind of seeing Rayven and David on his desk having sex, suddenly that flashback jumped towards seeing Kenneth and Deacon David kissing by David's office. Before another flashback came to Jazmine's neurons, she shakes her head to fight the continuous images. She claims, "Because I used to be a regular attendee, and I used to be a part of the choir. They normally wave off their fees."

"Oh, yeah?" Rayven happily states, hoping that David, Sr. wasn't having sex with her, too. "I didn't know that the church's daycare center offered that."

"Yeah, but since I don't attend regularly anymore and I'm no longer in the choir, I was billed like a regular citizen."

"I'm sorry to hear that...."

"Oh, naw, don't be sorry...... I'm finally making things work with Miracle's dad. He has her when I'm at work since he's working from home now."

"God still makes away."

"Amen," Jazmine concludes. "Well it was great seeing you, Rayven. I have to go in here and get lil' Miracle."

Rayven smiles and says, "Yes, umm, and I have to get to work. Is your number still the same. Maybe we can get a bite to eat, catch up? Have a playdate with us and our kids?"

Jazmine internally hesitates, but puts on an inauthentic smile, saying, "Sure, yes, yes. My number is still the same. We can definitely do that.... matter of fact, I'm having a kid-friendly graduation party after I receive my masters. You and Rayshawn can come if you'd like."

"That will be nice, and we can definitely attend!"

"Sounds good!"

"Alright, bye."

"Bye," Jazmine says as she continues walking into the daycare center and Rayven walks to her car.

Jazmine wonders if Rayven will reach out. What would their friendship be like today, especially knowing their past? What would be their intentions with one another?

While in the center, Jazmine walks to the receptionist desk to check out Miracle. She sees David, Sr. and gives him a scowling look as one of the assistant teachers walks Miracle to her. Jazmine changes her countenance into a happier one as she embraces Miracle.

David sees Jazmine and Miracle and rushes to his office to avoid confrontation. While in his office, he gathers his belongings and grabs his keys from inside his desk. He looks outside his window and into the parking lot to see Jazmine holding Miracle's hand as they walk to the car.

While helping Miracle into the car seat, Miracle is telling Jazmine all that she had learn at the church's day care. Jazmine then closes the door and gets into the driver's seat with Miracle still going on and on about her experiences.

Jazmine starts the car and checks her phone's notifications. She has messages from "Juley," "Momma," and "Terry-Bear." She taps on one of the messages and reads something that makes her blush. She texts back, turns the screen off, sits her phone in the cup holder, and looks back to reverse out of the parking lot. She calls Jules while she is driving.

"Hello?"

"Hey, Juley..."

"Hey, babe... how are you?"

"I'm good, just picked up Miracle. What are you up to?"

"Just got off work, about to go home and rest for a bit before I start my second job."

"How long do you plan on working tonight?"

"If I can make an extra two hundred tonight, I'll stop and call it a night."

"Will you have time to come over?"

"I can make time for you. It'll be a lil' late though."

"Well alright, just call or text me to see if I'm still up."

"Okay, will do."

"Have a good nightttt...." Jazmine says sardonically but normally.

"You, too. Aight, bye."

~

Back at the church, David exits his office, knowing that the close is clear for him to get Rayshawn, and get to the house. He starts the car while putting Rayshawn's diaper bag and his things in the passenger seat. He goes back inside to get Rayshawn, and hastily exits full of anxiety. He gets Rayshawn's car seat strapped in and he gets in the driver's seat to back out.

Before he left out of the parking lot, Kenneth tries to stop him to get his attention. Kenneth quickly sends a text to David, saying, "You ain't right," with two rolling eyes emojis.

David ignores and deletes Kenneth's text while driving, listening to Marvin Sapp playing through his speakers. Rayshawn is sleeping, but David can't help but to take a few glints in the rearview mirror at his new and profound bundle of joy. Rayshawn's innocence changes his mood and gives him a divine sense of purpose.

Once David gets to the house, he sits the car seat on the couch in the living room to put Rayshawn's bottles in the refrigerator. Rayshawn begins to cry while David pulls out the toys and books that are in the diaper bag. Rayshawn stops crying once David takes him out of the car seat. David checks to see if he needs to change his diaper, but Rayshawn did not pee or poop in his diaper.

David then places him in a walker for him to practice walking and keeping his back straight. Rayshawn immediately begin strutting around the living room with the walker bumping into furniture. David turns on the television to try to find something on television for Rayshawn to watch.

David and Rayshawn eventually end up watching, singing, and dancing to children's songs on YouTube. They listen to songs from Gracie's Corner, JoolzTV, and Sesame Street. The songs always seem to keep Rayshawn's attention. They are also very good at teaching children their numbers, colors, ABCs, and more.

An hour or so later, David takes Rayshawn out of the walker to feed him one of the bottles. After feeding him, David decides to read the bible story about David and Goliath to Rayshawn. David reads the same bible stories that he had read to Talitha and David, Jr. when they were toddlers to Rayshawn. Stories like Jesus and the sick young girl, Moses's story, the prodigal son, and Job's story.

After reading the bible story, David stares at Rayshawn's eyes as they are getting heavy. "Ahhh, you're sleepy?" David says, feeling the appreciation to have Rayshawn despite his circumstances with Rayven.

"You are not a mistake!" David thinks to himself. "You are perfectly made in the image and likeness of God. God does not make mistakes. You are my holy child. I love you," David announces aloud as if he is in the pew pit speaking to the congregation.

Eventually, Rayshawn falls asleep in David's left arm. David uses his right hand to lay out a blanket on the couch and he used another blanket as a barricade to keep little Rayshawn from falling from the couch. He prays over Rayshawn in hopes that Rayshawn doesn't inherit what he has.

While Rayshawn is asleep, David checks his phone to see messages from Rayven asking about how Rayshawn is doing. David takes a picture of Rayshawn being slumped on the couch and sends it to her.

He also sees messages from members of the church, including the pastor, Kenneth again, and other church members. The church members are asking for prayers and guidance, the pastor is just checking on David, and Kenneth sent angrier emojis.

David sent the church members scriptures to help them with their issues. He thanks the pastor for checking in on him and asks that Pastor Washington pray for him. He ignores and deletes Kenneth's text messages. He texts Tabitha to see the time that she is dropping off Talitha and David, Jr.

After Tabitha replies with the time, David sits back on the couch, pondering on his life and his past actions. *"Am I living in according to Your will, Lord?"* He thinks to himself. He then contemplates his involvement with the church, how long he's been with that church, how he brought harm and healing to the church, and what the church has done for him. He wonders what will be of him and his family if he decided to leave the church.

"Everything is so perfect at that church," David internalizes because the church put him and his family in one of the best financial positions. He feels deep conviction knowing that his actions have not always been holy and that he has sins that must be shared and released. He decides to write in his daily devotion to get his convictions from off his chest.

He goes to his office space to grab a notebook and a pen. He notices the rewards, pictures, and events he has hanging all around the office. *"All of this truly means nothing if I'm not living by it,"* he says to himself.

Black Pain't, Vol. II

      While walking back to the living room, he hears Rayshawn whimpering in his sleep for a moment and then he stops making those sounds. He sits next to him on the couch and flips to a blank page in his notebook to write:

> *Oh, Lord, and Heavenly Father,*
> *Please forgive me for I have sinned.*
> *I have sinned against You; I have sinned against my friends;*
> *my family, my ex-wife, and Your congregation, Lord.*
> *Please see my heart and not my faults.*
> *See me as You saw Moses, who murdered.*
> *See me as You saw King David, who sent off his best friend to be killed just so he can claim his best friend's wife.*
> *See me as You saw Noah and Abraham's drunkenness.*
> *Thank you for looking past my sins and making my life voluptuous*
> *Use me as You still used them for great deeds;*
> *Continue to use me in a special way, to help those with special needs;*
> *I am not perfect, Holy Father, neither was my biological father, who abandoned his family for his sexuality.*
> *Oh, Father please don't allow my genes to control my actions.*
> *Father, please forgive me.*

Black Pain't, Vol. II

MY NOTES

Chapter 4:
__Detached__

      She drives to her past self. She drives to a dwelling full of defamations, deceptions, and dissolutions. A place where she used to be a virtuous wife and mother, but now she's just a righteous 'single mom.' A phrase that she resented since her childhood; a societal expression that men use to deprecate women just so they can feel better about themselves. She comes to terms with this idiom that makes her feel like an idiot.

      She feels as though she lost herself in the name of *Christianity* to a man that did not value the type of woman she is. She feels as though the lifestyle that she had once lived was based on what the religion wanted, not her true self. The old, true her wanted effective communication, she just wanted the same love and honesty that he preached to the churchgoers on the weekly basis. She wanted a covenant with him, but he had, and maybe still has, too many open covenants. *" 'n he move' sneakily,"* her consciousness says internally. Now, she wonders what God expects of her as a single mom.

However, she's become disconnected. Disconnected from everything she once thought was a service to her. She is disconnected from the illusion of what marriage is supposed to be like under God. She's disconnected her feelings from a man that did not treat her well.

She takes a deep sigh to avoid the invasive thoughts that's plaguing her mind. She mumbles something to herself and shakes her head. She thinks, *"You are not weak!* I am strong, modest, and worthy of all good that life has to offer! *You are strong, modest, and worthy of all good that life has to offer!"*

The teenage girl in the front seat stops paying attention to her phone to ask, "Mama, are you okay?"

"Yes baby, I'm okay," she answers. "Got a lot on my mind that I'm tryna shak' off, dats all."

"Is it because of daddy?" the teenage girl inquires.

"Oh, no, sweety," she hesitates. "What happened between me and ya daddy was for da best."

"The best for who?" the boy in the backseat asks while playing a game on his phone.

She vacillates to answer because she did not want to give her children a terrible perspective of their father, nor of men. "Best for the 'hole family so e'eryone can live life the way they choose to," she wavers in the most superlative way she can.

She feels a tightness in her chest as she pulls up to the house and parks the car. As her children prepare to exit, she suddenly sees the choir girl exiting the house with a diaper bag around her arm and the Deacon right behind her, carrying a car seat.

"Wait a minute y'all," she commands her children. "Don't lea'e yet."

She sees the choir girl get in the driver seat as the Deacon straps the baby's car seat in the back seat of the choir girl's car. Moments later,

Black Pain't, Vol. II

the car drives away, and the Deacon stands on the curve, noticing the car parked at the edge of his driveway.

"Okay, le'go," she announces as she and her children exit the car. She watches as the choir girl drives pass.

Seconds later, she hears her daughter say, "Hey, Daddy!" She turns to see her hugging the Deacon and walking in the house.

As her son is walking towards the house, the Deacon greets him, saying, "Wassup, Junior!" and pats him on top of his head.

Once their son walks in the house, she says, "Hello, David."

"Hi, Tabitha.... how have you been?"

"I'm 'lright. And ya?"

"I'm blessed and highly favored...." David says with a pause. "Look, I'm sorry how we turned out...... I was in a bad pla........."

Tabitha interjects with her voice overbearing his, saying, "Ya don' have to be sorry everytime I sees ya, it's okay... it's fine. I just hope ya happy doing what ya want and being who ya are."

David tightly says, "What's that supposed to mean?"

Not backing down, Tabitha replies, "It don't mean nothin' now, David................ I just didn't know who you were............. You could have told me what you were into."

David angrily and quietly yells, "What I was into? I suppressed it because I loved you for you!"

Tabitha cuts him off, saying "Ahhh, here ya go...... stop with the lies now! Just stop now!"

"Our sex life was not the same and you know it! You weren't pleasing me! And I know damn well I wasn't pleasing you!" David says, punching his fist into his hand.

"Aight now, firstoff, you betta stop with this fist pumpin' lil' gesture you doin', I'll beat ya ass Davy.... you kno' how we rock where I'm from boy...... second, if you gon' cheat, at least cheat with women...... when did men come in the picture...."

"AHHH, COME ON!" David yells, storming towards the house.

As David storms off, untethered Tabitha says, "Well.... ummm.... enjoy ya evenin'. I'll pick up the kids tomorrow." She walks to her car, wishing she could have just smacked the bloody taste out of his mouth, but the Lord has been working on the new leaf that she turned since filing for divorce. She spiritual but she can get street, too.

While in the car, Tabitha two pieces the steering wheel and heavy breathes to calm her anger. As she starts the car, she checks her phone and notices a missed call from Phillip. Seeing his notification pop up on her phone brings her instant joy. After driving away and taking a few minutes to calm down, she calls him back.

"Tabitha," he smoothly says while answering the phone.

In her countryfied accent, she says, "Philly!"

Phillip is tickled by Tabitha's response and laughs hysterically. Tabitha chuckles and states, "Boooyy, it ain't even dat funny..."

"I just love your voice......"

"What ya won't, Philly?"

"Tabitha, darling! Are we still on for tonight?"

"Of course, I'm on my way home right now to get ready."

"Okay, great.... ummm... guess I'll see ya later, my country pumpkin'!"

Tabitha sarcastically says, "Oh, cut it out! Okay, see ya later" and hangs up the phone to drive home.

~

When Tabitha gets home, she plays her favorite Jill Scott songs as she prepares for her evening with Phillip. She sings while she glides to her closet to find a nice dress to wear. She takes a beige lantern long-sleeved dress from a clothes hanger and walks in her bedroom to lay it out on the bed. She goes back in the closet to get her black high heel boots and takes them into the bedroom.

She goes into the bathroom to turn on the shower. She strips from her work clothes and enters the shower, still singing. After cleaning and washing her physique, she turns off the shower, grabs the towel hanging on the side, and gets out. She dries her body and wraps the towel around her bodice. She brushes her teeth, washes her face, and oils her face. She slowly lotions her body with the thoughts of Phillip touching her.

She goes into the bedroom to grab some panties and a bra from out of her dresser. She then puts on her lantern long sleeve dress to view herself in one of the mirrors in her bedroom. Suddenly, her doorbell rings. She checks the time on her phone and walks to the door. As she opens it, Phillip is standing at the doorway with flowers in his hand, wearing a white polo shirt, tucked into some nice, dark slacks.

"Phillip! Ya early!" Tabitha says while opening the door wide enough for him to slide in.

As Phillip walks in, he got into Tabitha's personal space, hands her the flowers, and says, "I'm a professor, I have to cum... on time."

Tabitha playfully rolls her eyes and says, "Let me put my boots on and put a lil' make up on," while closing the door behind him and walking back into her bedroom.

Phillip patiently awaits in her living room, looking at all the pictures she has all over the room of her, her kids, and her family back in Louisiana. He yells, "Your family looks like they speak Ebonics."

"Don' come in here talkin' mess now, u kno' I got jokes!" Tabitha yells from her bedroom.

Phillip laughs to himself and sits on the couch. Moments later, Tabitha comes from her bedroom looking like a full course meal. "Tabitha, darling, you look simply amazing...." Phillip sincerely says.

Reservedly, Tabitha humbly asks, "Ya think so?"

"Tabitha, I know so. I hope I won't have to fight nobody over you tonight. It'll look bad on the news that a college professor gets into a fight a restaurant."

Tabitha laughs and says, "Philly, quit playin'!"

"Na, I'm serious! Wow...... Look at you.... You're stunning, Tabitha. It's an honor to take you out to eat tonight. Thank you for agreeing to."

"Okay, stop it.... ya know the pleasure is all mine. Let's go before ya face get stuck starin'."

Black Pain't, Vol. II

Tabitha locks up her crib before leaving. Phillip, being the gentleman he is, opens the car door for Tabitha before he gets in and drives off. There drive to the restaurant is full of good vibes, singing, and intellectual stimulation.

When they pull up to the restaurant, Tabitha notices the weird design of the building. It looks like something from the medieval times. She continues to scan the facility until Phillip says, "We're here! The finest Black owned restaurant in the city!"

"What's dis place called again?"

"*Timbuktu*...... named after a city in the Mali Empire that *Mansa Musa* once governed. Musa was considered one of the richest Africans in history."

"Ohh, nice.... they had castles in Africa?"

"Africans, Moors, they invented castles...... pyramids, sphinx.... Earth!" Phillip says then hurriedly exiting the car to open Tabitha's door.

"Thank ya, kind sir," Tabitha says as Phillip closes the passenger door.

While they walk in together, Phillip talks to the hosts by door as Tabitha observes the fine dining and picturesque people eating and conversing. She notices how active the waiters are, moving to and from the kitchens to their appointed tables. Her gratifying energy surges as Phillip gently caresses her elbow as indication to follow the host to their reserved table.

As they are seated, Tabitha says, "Philly, this is niiicccee!"

"Indeed! Don't you just love seeing Black folks in scenic social settings like this?"

Precipitously, a waitress comes to their table saying, "Grand evening, and welcome to Timbuktu. My name is Tori, I'll be your lovely waitress for this evening. Can I start you two off with some appetizers? Wine?"

"Water with lemon, please," Tabitha says.

"I, too, would like water with lemon with a bottle of your Home Sweet Home as well."

"A whole bottle?" Tabitha questions with her eyes widened.

Phillips chuckles and says, "Yes! Tonight is a celebration!"

Tori says, "I'll go get those waters and that bottle while you two look over the menu."

As Tori walks away, Tabitha asks, "What we celebratin'?"

"You completing your first year of your master's program!" Phillip keenly states. One more year to go!"

Tabitha smiles and states, "Ya just lookin' for a reason to celebrate me? We celebrated the end of my first semester."

"You deserve to be celebrated."

"Thank ya, Philly, I really appreciate ya..." she says while blushing. "But ya know I'ma light weight when it come to that alcohol."

"Studies show that wine is good for your heart and your blood flow.... I know you all don't drink wine back in Louisiana especially with all the high blood pressure out there...."

"Boy, hush!" Tabitha jokingly says. "Ya gon' quit comin' fo' my state, ya heard me?"

"Ya gon' quit comin' fo' my state ya heard me?" Phillip mocks Tabitha and they laugh.

"Nuh, uh, you ain't rite!"

Tori comes back with a pallet of two water glasses and a bottle of wine with two empty champagne glasses. After placing everything on the table, Tori asks, "Are we ready to order?"

"Give us a minute, please," Phillip politely requests.

"No problem," Tori says as she walks away to check on her other tables.

As Tabitha and Phillip view the menu, Tabitha says, "Ooh, dey got double coated chicken fried chicken! I think I'ma get that with mashed potatoes and greenbeans."

Phillip says, "That does sound delicious. I'm going to go ahead and get this salmon with rice and asparagus."

"It's pronounced samon, not salmon."

"I know my countrified pumpkin is not correcting my enunciations."

"I can't let ya go 'round sayin' the word wrong, professa."

Sniggering, Phillip says, "I appreciate you for that, lovely."

Phillip grabs the bottle of wine to read the label. "Nineteen percent? I don't think I ever had wine that was 19% alcohol," he says aloud to himself, amusing Tabitha's interest. After opening it, he asks her, "So tell me, how was your first year?"

While pouring the wine into the champagne glass in front of her, Tabitha says, "Oooh chile, it's ben exhaustin'.......... between my personal life, dese classes, my kids, and my jawb, good lawd.......... there were times when I wanted to just throw in da towel, ya hear me? But I had to remind myself on why I wanted to go back so bad."

After decanting wine into the champagne glass in front of him, Phillip inquires, "What was the most challenging?"

"The divorce," Tabitha claims while taking a sip of the wine. "The separation was by fa' the hardest ting I had to deal wid in my adult life......."

"How did your kids take the divorce? Are they okay?" he solicits while supping his wine glass.

She shillyshallies a tad bit before answering, "They seem to be dealin' wid it pretty cool, no spite from either one of them about what all conspired between David and I; and, to them, David actually became a better parent...."

Phillip interjects saying, "So let me get this straight, he became a better parent AFTER losing you?"

Tabitha sneers at Phillip's enquiry as Tori comes back to save Tabitha from answering that question. "Have you two decided what you would like to eat?" she asks.

"Yes, I'll take the chicken fried chicken with mashed potatoes and greenbeans."

"Got ya," she says while mentally remembering Tabitha's order in such an impressive manner. "Annnd for you sir?" she asks Phillip.

"I'll take the 'samon'," Phillip says with emphasis, putting yet another smile on Tabitha's face.

"Your two sides?" Tori asks.

"Yes, I'm sorry, ummm.... I'll take rice and asparagus, please."

Tori inherits his order along with Tabitha and says, "I have the chicken fried chicken with mashed potatoes and greenbeans, and I have the salmon and rise with asparagus. Is there anything else I can get you?"

"No, ma'am, thank you," Phillip replies as Tori grabs their menus and walks away to place their orders in the system.

"To answer ya question, Philly, I think that he realized who he really is........ it could have been that I was holdin' him back somehow, or sometimes it's jus' best to be single than to drag everyone down witcha, ya know?"

"I understand where you're coming from. Why do you think you could have been holding him back?"

"I don't know, I still don't know his full side of the story...... he didn't even have the audacity to gimme reasons as to why.... when we met up with our lawyers, he couldn't even look me in my eyes," she resolutely says. "Just embarrassin'!"

"He obviously had some personal issues going, because I've been around you for almost a couple of years now...... I haven't found a single flaw...."

Tabitha instantly interjects, saying, "Hol' up now Philly, we all flawed now, all of us....... I just wish that David's flaws wasn't on the expense of my feelings, my time, and my pain... on top of that I had two beautiful children wid'im..... God must have split the last ounce of good in 'im and gave it to our kidz...... I learnt a lot though."

"What did you learn about yourself?"

"Now, Philly, is thisa interview? If so, am I hired yet?" Tabitha questions then taking a gulp of the wine. She continues, "Ooh, ummm. I learnt that sometimes I would rather just deal wid lies and deceit to myself than to confront them; I didn't wanna fight 'im.... I was thinkin' that maybe I be protectin' my children from the effects of divorce, but I was actually hurtin' 'em...like they shouldn't see their mama always sad and depressed. What does that teach them, ya know? I also learnt how..."

Interrupting her, Phillip says, ".... how strong and beautiful you actually are? It's a lot of wonderful in the you, too."

Tabitha blushes and changes the subject by asking, "Sooooo, whatcha been teaching yo students lately, professa?"

"It's interesting that you ask that, because of House Bill 1775, we're technically not allowed to even teach certain issues anymore."

"Issues like what?"

"Issues regarding the impact of slavery; all of America's race massacres...... we all know what happened in Tulsa back in 1920 was happening all over the U.S. like in Central Park, Detroit, Philadelphia, East St. Louis, and other Black towns; issues like Jim Crow and many other racial disparities that many Black people endured over the past four hundred plus years...... we aren't allowed to form our own opinions and share them with our students."

"That makes sense. Don't want to persuade them to think a way, but how to think, right? I mean, you can't be biased, right?"

Hesitantly, Phillip says, "Yeesss, but truth is truth....... if there is a class discussion on sundown towns, and I come out and say that the rules and laws were 'diabolical,' or evil...... am I being biased or am I being truthful?"

"You know what.... you right...... dem white folks is crazy...... how you have so much hate in your heart? I remember when DJ was goin' to that majority white middle school, and them rednecks was trying to bully my boy! How you tryin' to bully someone because they skin different? I was ready to fight anybody at the school! That's critical race theory! Why nobody make a law about dat?"

"Because it does not benefit them....... I didn't know that about DJ; is that why you sent him to the great George Washington Carver Middle School for Arts and applied Sciences? To be around Black children and Black teachers?"

"Yesss, I got tired of following David Senior's views of school and of life. He was tryna live like the white folks. That's why I told DJ that the real fight is amongst our own. Once we com' together than we can take ova this whole country from Main to Florida from Florida to California all the way up to Oregan!"

"I know that's right! Darryl told me that he became one of his favorite students!"

"Who? Mista Jones?"

"Yes."

She smacks her lips and says, "All I heard all day was about Mista Jones..... Mista Jones this, Mista Jones that! I said, 'Who in da heaven is this Mista Jones? David Senior would get jealous....'"

Phillip laughs with Tabitha, saying, "Yeah, he's dealing with backlash from the law, too. The school took away some of his readings and monitors his lesson plans."

"Oh, wow! They ain't doin' nothing but takin' away from the kids! Why would they pass such law, Philly?"

Phillip pauses for a moment to ponder on her question. Once he's able to put his thoughts together, he says, "Well, it started out at the University of Oklahoma! You know a lot of racist activities goes on at this prehistorical white institution, but I'll digress on that topic for now...... Yes, there were 'certain students' who were feeling too 'uncomfortable' during a class discussion about what their ancestors has done to another group of people, so they took these same issues to court. And when I tell you that Republicans ran with it, they ran with it like Barry Sanders and Adrian Peterson found out they were distant cousins! They turned it into a whole ordeal to the point that they made it unlawful to speak on these issues as academic professionals."

"Wow, like we didn' grow up in dis education system feeling 'uncomfortable' about all those lies about European history that made us bored with education then get to Black history mont' just for them to remind us that we was slaves. It's bonkers!"

"Exactly! Then again, it could be a giant leap towards totalitarianism, or a one world government; it could also mean that they're trying to wipe away our history by taking it out of the education system and then we can see books being banned like how the Nazi Germany did during the 1930s.... it's just so much to consider as to what's going on behind the curtain."

Tabitha digests Phillips comments and says, "What are the consequences for talkin' 'bout those things in class? How would anyone even know that you talkin' 'bout those things?"

"Well, if a student files complaints about what's being taught or discussed in class then it could lead to an investigation. They'll view my syllabus, my lesson plans; they'll interview students. It could result in the state taking away my teacher's license or termination."

"Oooh, that's tough, Philly. Ya think teaching students the truth is worth you losin' yo job?"

Phillip takes another moment to contemplate on Tabitha's question, and then he answers, "Yes. I think if I was to go out, I'd want it to be for teaching the truth."

"I think that's commendable," Tabitha says while taking a sip of wine. "You's a great man, professa. A lot of men, especially those who look like us wouldn't go out like that!"

With a grin on his face, Phillip says, "Thank you my country bumpkin."

"I ain't that country now, shit..." Tabitha says as they both laugh.

Moments later, the Tori comes with a huge tray with the food that they ordered on top. After placing their meals in front of them, she says, "If there's anything else you need, please don't hesitate to ask!"

"Thank ya kindly, Tori!" Tabitha announces.

As the night gets younger, Tabitha and Phillip continue to enjoy their time with one another. They eat and continue to drink the wine until it is all gone. They both are tipsy which encourages their excessive laughter and their cunning flirtations. The tension concerning the two is voluptuous, and they do not want their evening to end.

After Phillip pays for dinner, the two exit the restaurant with their fingers interlocked. While walking to the car, Phillip says, "That was fun! I'm happy you finally gave me a night out, Ms. Tabitha......"

Tabitha catches his hint of trying to figure out her maiden last name. She smiles and says, "My maidens name is Harris....... Tabitha Harris."

Phillip starts freestyling a poem, saying "Miss Harris, all hail, Miss Harris; hate to pull your coat tail, Miss Harris, but can I tell you this? You got my heart on a roller coaster when I tell you just how fair you is; Miss Harris, can you put your pubic hair where my facial hair is? Baby, I know you hear this... I wanna hear ya' moaning from where my left ear is..."

Interjecting, she flirtatiously asks, "Is that one of ya freaky poems, professa?"

"Nah, I just came up with that..."

"Oooh, I like it, I like it," Tabitha says as she leans against his car. "Lemme hear more...."

"I'll have to write the rest......" Phillip says as they both hilariously snigger. As they come down from their gut laugh, he asks, "Are we calling it a night, or...."

"Are you trying to get me to come to your house, professa?"

"Yes......" Phillip harmlessly says. "We can drink more wine, watch a movie, lets chill like Guy."

Diffidently, Tabitha states, "I don't think I need any more wine."

"Popcorn and a movie then, pleeeaassseee... I ain't too proud to beg like the *Temptations*."

"Well, this is my kid-free weekend......" Tabitha timidly says as she watches Phillip await her answer. *"Is he tryna get in my panties or does he really want to 'chill'?"* She thinks to herself.

Phillip sings, "If I have to sleep on your doorstep, all night and day!"

"Okay, okay, okay! Stop da singin'! Ya kno' ya can't sing!"

Phillip laughs and says, "So will you spend the rest of your evening with me, Miss Harris? Can we awaken, staring at the ceiling, Miss Harris?"

"Okay, sure...."

"YES!" Phillip says in triumph as he rushes to open the passenger door for Tabitha to get in. He shuts the door once Tabitha gets all the way in and runs to the driver's side to get in.

Phillip starts the car and *Share My Life* by Kem comes on the radio. "What ya know about this my country pumpkin bumpkin!?" he yells.

"Boyyy..." Tabitha says as she starts singing the lyrics as Phillip drives off.

During the ride to Phillip's house, Tabitha can't help but to feel like she's not supposed to be doing this with Phillip. She's recently divorced with her two kids. Her insecurities begin to sink in. She is used to being the church wife. She can't even remember the last time she actually had fun or the last date night she's been on.

"Should I use this time to be alone for a while? I can tell he'll want something more......" her consciousness says internally as they pull into Phillip's driveway.

He parks the car and slowly exits the car, realizing that he does not need any more wine, either. He opens the passenger side door, helplessly helping Tabitha out of the car. They both fell against the door after Tabitha shuts it and laugh aloud.

"Shhhh, you're gonna wake my neighbors!" Phillip whispers to Tabitha.

Tabitha socks Phillip on his arm and says, "That's you makin' all that noise!"

Phillips guides Tabitha to his doorstep, searching for his keys that he has in his hand. After realizing that he has his keys in his hand, Tabitha giggles noticing Phillips blonde moment. He unlocks the door and they both stumble in the house cuddled-up, laughing. They lock eyes, but Tabitha pushes him off of her so they can keep from kissing. Phillip turns on the lamp by the front door and throws his keys and wallet on the table that the lamp is on.

As Phillips continues walking in the house to turn on more lights, Tabitha follows him while noticing the paintings and portraits around his home. She observes the paintings of contemporary art and is amazed at the historical portraits of leaders such as Fred Hampton, Dr. Sebi, Angela Davis, Muammar Kaddafi, and many more. She sees Indian artifacts lying around the counters and hanging on the walls.

Black Pain't, Vol. II

"Make yourself at home," Phillip yells from the bedroom. He checks his phone to see a missed call from Shyla. He texts, "Sorry I missed your call, been a long day. I'm going to call it a night. Talk to you tomorrow." And sends it to her.

Meanwhile, in the living room, Tabitha finally found the courage to take off her heel boots. She sets them on the side of one of the couches. Her comfortability levels just risen as she strolls around to view more Native American souvenirs. "Where'd you get all dese Indian stuff from?" she yells.

"My great grandmother gave them to me!" Phillip yells back. Moments later, he comes back in the living room with his polo shirt untucked and his shoes off to see Tabitha viewing more artifacts. "She used to tell me that I had Indian in my family."

"My daddy told me the same thing," Tabitha says while shifting her focus to the portrait of Leroy and Kathleen Cleaver.

"They were very instrumental during the Black Panther Party for Self-Defense era. An era where Black love and Black power was Black people's number one priority throughout the country.... until the FBI infiltrated them....... jailed them, drugged them, killed them...... some ended up fleeing from the country; it was sooo immoral."

Tabitha loudly and jokingly says, "Oooh, that's critical race theory. Ya breakin' the laws professa. Ya can't talk about those things saa... where do I take my complaints?"

Phillip laughs while making his way to the kitchen. "Can I get you anything? Water? Or anything?"

"I'll take a water, please and thank you," she answers while sitting on the couch. She can hear Phillip getting a glass out of the cabinet and filling it with water from the refrigerator. She notices another portrait of a lady that looks to be in their age range. "Who is this?"

"That's the great Dr. Akira Peseshet, also known as Lady Peseshet! She's a Black feminist who's one of many that's leading the cause for reparations – even though she claims that the U.S. discreetly gave us our reparations," Phillip says while coming back into the living room with the glass of water in his hand. He hands it to Tabitha and sits next to her. "She also claims that the Atlantic Slave trade was a hoax, and that Black people were already here during the beginning stages of America."

"Hmmm....... Do you believe that?" Tabitha asks confusedly.

"Yes and no, but she presents compelling arguments because in Christopher Columbus's memoirs, he stated that there were Black people here whenever he arrived in 'America'.... He thought they were 'Indians' because they look like the Black people in India."

"That's intriguing. We were all over the world it sounds like."

"Indeed, this researcher and historian named Dane Calloway has books and information about it. It all just confirms my theories about Black people being the true natives of the universe," Phillip says while grabbing the remote from the arm of the couch and turning on the television.

"I definitely want to know mo'e of that. I wanna know the truth about the beginning of time and all."

"Why? What would that change for you?"

"A lot! I don't want to live in lies! I maybe a Christian woman but I always question everything.... like... who wrote the bible? Because the many prophets in the bible didn't write anything. I wanna know the one true religion. I wanna know if Adam and Eve is forreal, because if life started with them two then was it a lot of incest going on?"

"Wow, I never heard you talk like that..."

"I'm sorry, it's just..."

Phillip chimes in in the midst of her talking, saying, "No, no don't apologize.... it's totally oka.."

Tabitha talks through Phillip's sanction, saying, "It's just that I spend a lot of time by myself now and my thoughts just be rambling; my apologies, Philly..."

"Tabi, I want to know how you think, what you feel, and the way you see life...."

"Thank you Philly."

"If you don't want to share now, we can just relax and discover more truth of each other," Phillip states while searching on the television. "What would you like to watch?"

Tabitha cluelessly says, "Oooh, I don' know.... I usually just watch kid movies, I don' know what even come on now-days...."

"We can watch this new series called *What 'R Friends 4* on the Melaninated-TV network."

"Sure... what's it about?"

"These three roommates who goes through life trying to figure out relationships, friendships, entrepreneurships, and all the other ships out there.... everything but the slave ships..." he responds while shaking his head.

Tabitha laughs as Phillip searches for the show. She says, "Everything don't have to be about slavery, professa...."

"Why not? America was built off slavery."

"Ya' right......"

After finding the show, Phillip says, "Here we go! We are going to start on episode one!"

Tabitha absorbs the experience. She feels a sense of gratitude overflow from her heart. "Ya have a beautiful home, Philly. Thanks for allowing me to come visit witch ya."

"It's an honor and a privilege to have you here, Miss Harris. I appreciate you for coming to keep me company. Even though I did have to beg you," he says while clicking on season one of *What 'R Friends 4*.

Tabitha sneers and says, "Your begging did something to me. I forgot the last time someone actually wanted me around so bad."

"I want you around more often...." Phillip says while making strong eye contact with Tabitha.

Tabitha is taken by Phillip's manliness. She can feel him trying to stare into her soul. Her body gets warmer as her mind begins to play tricks on her. She feels awkward as he starts looking around her chin as if something is on it.

"You have something around your lips," Phillip utters.

Tabitha wipes around her mouth saying, "Where?"

Phillip kisses Tabitha. Tabitha is shocked at first but then kisses him back, gently wrapping her arms around his shoulders, and leaning back.

The kisses get more intimate and aggressive. He takes a quick break from her lips and commences to kissing around her neck, making her body melt. Tabitha's moaning incites Phillip to grab her and pull her on top of him to continue kissing. Before Tabitha becomes completely engulfed in the moment, she stops and rises off him.

"I'm sorry," Phillip claims. "I got a little carried away..."

"No, don' be sorry..." Tabitha derisorily hesitates. "I haven' been touched or had any sexual attention ina long minute...."

"I understand."

"What we doing, Philly? Is this all that ya want? I'm only asking because ya know I just got divorced. I don't want to be led on or...."

Phillip interjects and says, "Tabitha, I want you; not just sexually, but in a committed relationship. I've been wanting you since the first day I met you at that open mic show. I saw you hurting a long time ago and was so happy when you found the strength to leave the man who was causing the hurt."

He pauses and continues, "I know it maybe too early to be thinking about a relationship, knowing where you are in your life but that is my intention. I'm getting too seasoned to be wanting anything other than commitment, Tabitha. I want you. I'm willing to wait for you as long as we can remain close friends."

Tabitha stares in his eyes for the truth but finds it in her heart that he is being genuine. She doesn't know what to make of their situation. *"Why does a man with no kids want to deal with someone with kids?"* Tabitha thinks to herself. "What about my children?" She asks aloud.

"I love children. It takes a lot for a man to step in to be there for another man's children, but I wouldn't mind being your children's stepdad if it means that I get to be around you more."

Tabitha is filled with uncertainty, and Phillip can sense it. She's never been in this position before and she doesn't know how to respond

Black Pain't, Vol. II

or internalize it. "I hear ya, Philly. I don't want any more children; I'll be 38 this year, Philly..."

"Why not? Ashanti is having a baby and she's in her early forties......" Phillip says.

"Oooh, I ain't Ashanti, and you ain't no Nelly, Philly."

"We just gotta eat healthy and exercise weekly," he says, grabbing the remote to start the first episode over on the television.

"Professa Philly......you ain't giving up ribs and steak," she says. She then notices him starting the episode over and asks, "Why ya start it over?"

"Because you not paying attention! You got to watch it from the beginning. Everything connects...... from the characters, the situations. It's some good television."

"Okay, okay, let me pay attention," Tabitha says as she cuddles up with Phillip on the couch. "You gotta stop talkin' to me."

During the duration of the first episode, they both daze off into a short sleep. Phillip awakens during the third episode of the show with Tabitha lying across his torso.

"Tabi?" he softly says, attempting to wake her. "Tabi, baby, wake up."

She gradually opens her eyes and rises slowly to fix her hair. She melodically asks, "What the time is?"

"Almost midnight," he responds. "Would you like me to take you home or ....?"

"No," Tabitha responds while lying down on his lap. "I'm good where I'm at. Is that okay with you?"

A deep sensation electrocutes every vein in Phillip's body. He's too tired and too weak to fight the tides. He manages to say, "Of course, of course..." with much gratitude. "You want to go lie down?"

"In your bedroom?" She asks firmly.

"Yes."

With improbability but comically, she says, "Okay, don't be trying to get in my panties, professa."

He chuckles as Tabitha lifts herself up from his lap. He stands to take Tabitha's hand to help her up. He quickly grabs the remote and turns off the television. After laying the remote on the arm of the couch, he guides her to his bedroom and releases her hand.

He walks inside his closet to take off his clothes and to view how hard his penis is. He tries to put it in the most appropriate position possible, but he knows that she's going to realize its swell. "Oh, well," he says to himself.

Meanwhile, Tabitha is peeking around his spacious bedroom internally knowing that there's going to be an erotic experience. She tries to decipher if it's the wine that's causing her to accept it or an eager feeling to be desired, loved, and touched.

"We ain't even gon' do anything," she whispers to herself, sitting on his soft, king-sized bed.

Coming from out of the closet, he asks, "You need a shirt or anything?"

She turns to see him half naked, wearing black briefs with his dick print poking out. *"Good lawd, half-murcy!"* she instantaneously cogitates to herself. His endowment captures her. The same apprehension grabs her neck and makes her heartbeat faster. Her eyes slightly roll as she tries to maintain eye contact to avoid looking down at his print.

She's able to utter, "Yes, please."

He goes to his dresser drawer to search through his drawers for a T-shirt, she turns around to take off her dress. Once he finds the shirt, he closes the drawer, turns around to see her placing her dress on the chair in the room.

"Good God all mighty," he deliberates to himself, looking at her wide hips, her marshmallow-looking buttocks, and her motherly thickness. He walks up to her to hand her the shirt.

"Thank ya, Philly," she says in a mellow voice.

"Anytime," he says while making his way to get in the bed.

She turns from Phillip to put on the shirt. She can hear him getting in the bed while she unclips her bra underneath the shirt, tossing it on the chair with her dress. She then makes her way to the bed and gets in under the covers with him. She turns her back towards him to lay in the foetus position.

Seconds later, she can feel him sliding behind her, holding her from the back. She grabs his left hand to hold as he cuddles her. She goes back to feel his body against her backside. She can feel his penis against her bottom.

"It's big," she ruminates to herself.

He tightly holds her to use her soft buttocks as a pillow for the head and the shaft of his penis. He sniffs her heavenly scent and takes a deep breath to keep himself from getting more aroused.

"Did ya jus' smell me?" she confusingly but humorously asks.

"Yes, you smell heavenly, and you feel so right, Tabi."

She turns her head to give him a peck on the lips. That one peck on his lips is enough to send him overboard as he moderately clutches her head for them to kiss more. She turns around for them to kiss each other more easily. He uses his tongue; she matches his energy. He pulls her right legs around his waist and grips her haunches.

They moan in each other's mouths as she feels his hands touching her physique. He places his hands on her vertebral to massage it while he smooches around her neck. She softens in the palms of his hands, allowing the erotic tautness to take over her association.

"I want to taste you, Tabi, I want to taste you," he whispers in her ear.

She gets more turned on, feeling his hand drift down to her waist. He pulls her undergarments down as she lifts her legs for him to take them off. He slithers under the sheets to put his head between her legs. He smooches around her waist, then to her pelvis, and down to her inner thighs.

She jiggles after every kiss in anticipation. She feels his lips press against her urethral orifice; she moans. He licks around her urethral orifice; she moans more. He licks her urethral orifice in circles; she moans gaudier. He sucks her urethral orifice, he slurps her urethral orifice, and he flicks his tongue up and down on her urethral orifice.

Her moaning turns him on even more. He can feel himself wanting to nut, but he squeezes his butt cheeks to hold it in. Holding back his nut made him lock his mouth on her vagina, making her quiver from his lock. He relaxes his shoulders and commence to feasting on her pearly gates.

While enjoying the sensations, she mentally hopes that he doesn't ask her to suck his dick because she hasn't done that in years. She wants to be pleasured. She grabs his bald head with both hands and grinds it against her womanhood, feeling the urge to gush.

Without warning, she spurts in his mouth while still holding his head. He allows the diluted piss to fill up his mouth. Before he almost drowns, he swallows what he can manage, allowing the rest to rush out of his mouth like an overflow. He lifts to allow the rest of her waterfalls to splash on his face.

She looks on in thrilling bewilderment, while trying to keep her composure. After her sprinkler system stops, and Phillip rises to wipe his face, she speechlessly claims, "I'm sorry, I didn't know that was going to happen...."

"I love it," he says with the bottom of his beard soaking and dripping. He grins as he takes off his briefs.

She sees his dick bounce out of the briefs. She wants to touch it before he goes displacing her wet cervix. He climbs on top of her and gets in between her legs in the G-Whiz position. He slowly slides in. She pants for air, biting the skin amid her index and thumb to embrace the slight pain.

He thrusts and strokes to find his rhythm. She's moaning and gripping the pillow, watching him go in and out of her. She can feel the curve of his shaft hitting her G spot. He stops for a second to keep from cuming and pulls her up into the face off position.

While in the position, they both get tantric. She grinds on it as he grips her posterior to guide her movements. They kiss and moan in each other's mouths while they possess one another.

"Wait, wait, stop, stop," he demandingly says.

"What?" she curiously asks.

"I'm not trying to cum until you get yours first."

"I already did twice, baby, u betta cum' on......"

He feels like a huge weight just lifted off his shoulders, knowing he is not going to last any longer. "Ooh, shit..." he says continuously as Tabitha continues grinding on it. He feels himself about to bust. "Ooh, shit!" he says again while gripping her neck with his right hand, placing his left hand on her lower back.

Minutes in, something takes over Tabitha as she's able to bounces harder on his dick. She can't handle much more of him being deep inside her, but she grinds on it anyway. He signals and pushes her off him, ejaculating the semen to come out. Tabitha removes his hand and ejaculates his dick for him. The semen is shooting out onto her hand and on his bed.

Afterwards, he pulls her chin up to his to tongue kiss her. He stops kissing her to ask, "Can I get you a warm towel?"

"Yes, professa."

Phillip rises out of the bed, leaving Tabitha next to their puddle of squirt, semen, and spit, the puddle of love, the river of pleasure. She can hear him turn on the water in his master bedroom's bathroom. Moments later, he comes back in with the warm face-towel and a big towel. He hands her the warm towel and lays the big towel for the puddle of love to soak in.

"I'll wash and dry these sheets tomorrow. I hope you don't mind."

"I don't mind," she says as she finishes dabbing herself with the warm towel. As she gets up, she asks, "Were you want me to put dis?"

"In that dirty clothes hamper in the bathroom."

She walks in the bathroom to toss the towel in the dirty clothes hamper. Then she sits on the toilet to urinate. After urinating, she takes some tissue to dab herself, tosses the tissue in the toilet, and flushes. While she washes her hands, Phillip walks in to urinate as well.

"So now we close enough to use the rest room while we're both in here, huh?"

"I'm sorry, is that a problem?"

"Nah, I guess if you can lick my asshole, we can watch each other use the rest room," she says as they both laugh. She dries her hands and exits the bathroom.

She goes to lie in the ecstasy, feeling like a new woman. Phillip joins her as they cuddle. "How was it?" he asks.

"It was sensational...... I haven' had any of dat in a long time, so it was just right," she says as they both cackle.

"It definitely was heavenly. You taste and feel divinely."

"Why thank ya, sir! I love what ya packin' as well...."

He hesitates, but he finds the courage to asks, "So where do we go from here?"

"I don' know, where do you wanna go?"

"As long as I'm with you...... anywhere......"

They both fall asleep into the abyss; the abyss of the unknown, the abyss of an illusion that can be a great situation for them both on a relationship level. An abyss of possibilities.

~

In the morning, Tabitha awakens alone to the smell of bacon, eggs, and potatoes. She breathes deeply, rising to go see what Phillip is up to. She walks in the kitchen to him in those same black briefs, some house shoes, finishing cooking the eggs.

"You're just in time for breakfast...."

A lovely commotion fills her heart. She hasn't had anyone cook her breakfast since before her and David was married. "Oh, Philly... thank you."

Phillip makes her a plate as she sits on one of his bar stools by the huge kitchen island. He hands her a plate while he makes his. He gets two glasses for some orange juice and grabs two forks after putting the glasses down. He grabs her hands and says, "Dear God, thank you for this food, let it nourish our bodies and nourish our souls; God, thank You for life, thank You for Tabitha. I couldn't ask for anything more perfect. Amen."

"Amen," Tabitha softly proclaims, picking up her fork. "I didn' kno' u believed in God enough to pray like dat....."

"I believe in a higher power......"

"What's a higher power? What do people mean when they say'dat?"

"It's like.... I believe in God, right, don't get me wrong; but, to me, a higher power is the source and essence of everything. I believe that 'God' is all things, all people, and everything this gigantic universe is composed of, acting within itself through individuals....... animals...........and, and, and all other things.... everything."

Tabitha tries to find his understanding of the one true God. *"People are so educated that they're imprudent,"* she internalizes during the rest of Phillips spill.

To change the subject, she asks, "So where do you think we go when we die?"

Phillip smiles and asks, "You remember that saying that we said when we were kids? 'We don't die, we multiply?'" in a childish tone. Then he firmly closes, saying, "I believe that we don't quote on quote 'die,' but we transform........... we move on to a whole new life, a whole new experience... 'Death' is like walking through a door of new experiences, a new perspective, and a new life."

"Like resurrection?" Tabitha simplifies.

"Yes, for lack of better terms...."

"I know he did not," Tabitha says internally and socks Phillip on his shoulder.

"Ouch!" Phillip slightly yells in confusion, smacking Tabitha's rumps. He then runs away after Tabitha gives him a shocking look like she is going to strike him.

Tabitha playfully chases after him. She grew up with brothers, so she loves to get rough and physical. She catches him in the bedroom. She tries to grapple with him.

"Ooh, girl, I used to wrestle in high school," he says while overpowering her.

Tabitha strongly and roughly stands her ground keeping him from slamming her onto the bed. "I wrestled all my life!" she confidently claims, jumping up on his head and somehow getting him in the headlock. Phillip maneuvers towards her legs, lifts her, and body slams her onto the bed. While on the bed, Tabitha rushes to get him back in the headlock. Every time Phillip tries to move, she tightens her grip. "Tap out!" she commands.

Phillip tries to say something, pretending to be put to sleep by Tabitha's submission. Tabitha lifts his right arm high, and it drops. She lifts the same arm high again, and it motionlessly drops. She tries for the third time, however, in the imitation of Hulk Hogan's reenergized signature move that he has done millions of times throughout his pro-wrestling career, Phillip kept his arm in the air. He shakes as if he's having a seizure. He rises while Tabitha struggles to keep the grip on his neck.

Tabitha tries to keep him down with her dead weight, but Phillip lifts her again and body slams her again, going down with her. They both are lying across the bed, trying to catch their breath, feeling the soreness from their two-minute wrestling match. They both receive a fleshly rush that raises the hair on their skins. However, they are too fatigued to act on it.

"I won...." Tabitha proclaims in flirtatious manner.

Black Pain't, Vol. II

MY NOTES

Black Pain't, Vol. II

Chapter 5:
Loneliness

It has been a long day of teaching inner-city Middle School children, talkative colleagues, and opinionated co-workers. A long day of dealing with all the politics surrounding the school systems and the changes that the leadership needs to make in order for Black children to be more successful in academia. The research he needs to finish reading before his doctoral course this evening has been pestering his concentrations all day. He's been struggling with the deliberations about all the bills and debt he has to pay.

Before leaving the parking lot, he sees Miss Luna Hall walking by his car with that snarling look as if she can see right through him. While backing out, he thinks about the times she'd walked through the halls of his neurons with the same disgust on her face since his "fuck-boy" act. At the same time, if she would give him the opportunity to hit again, he'd risk it all.

On top of all of that, his feelings of being on and off with Patricia these past couple of years continues to randomly darken the clouds over his head. Before finding out that they are classmates, he remembers her telling him that she was going to get her doctorate's degree. That inspired him to pursue his. He has no clue as to why she would go to Nat Turner University after all that shit she was talking about Nat Turner when he first met her.

He thinks how it is so ironic how the universe brough them back around one another again, because, lately, he has been thinking about settling down. Patricia is one of the only women who ever made him want to settle down. Settling down sounds too much settling. He has been thinking in hopes that if Patricia and him are meant to be then maybe she'd want to settle with him.

He imagined them both walking the stage, receiving their hoods, taking pictures. He sees himself getting on one knee in front of thousands of people. "I'mma marry that girl," he says to himself. His thoughts are so loud, it made him speak. He spiritually says, "Fuck it!" and decides not to deal with all that's swarming his mind. He then opts to texting his mentee to see if he had some tree for them to chop and screw.

While coming to a stop light, he types, "Break bread," and sends to his mentee. He suddenly begins thinking about how he's going to play as if he read the assigned reading. Scheming through options in his psyche, his thoughts tactlessly begin to override every other thought about his life.

His overthinking is interrupted when a notification from his phone dings with a message from his mentee that says, "Come through, big bro!" While on the way to his mentee's crib, listening to *Mr. Morale & The Big Steppers* by Kendrick Lamar, his thoughts begin to allude him again. He contemplates about what it would mean to his family to be a doctor, how many generational curses he'll be breaking being the first doctor in his family. The act of settling down comes back into his psyche like it did a U-turn on a major street. He deliberates on what his life would be like if he was to settle down and start a family.

Once he arrives to his mentee's apartment, he knocks and waits a second before his mentee opens the door. "Tony! Toni! Toné!" he says, doing a gang-like handshake.

"Darryl from *Coming to America*, wassup big bro?" Tony responds in a jokingly manner.

"Not much man, just needed to escape the matrix for a minute," Darryl says while walking in. He immediately notices a blunt already rolled up on the coffee table.

"You need anything, big bro? Some water? Some chips or somethin'?" Tony concerningly asks, detecting Darryl's dark aura.

"I'll take some water, king, thanks."

As Tony walks into the kitchen to get the water from out of the refrigerator, Darryl also notices all the books on the dining room table with a laptop half-way open. He sees an ashtray with a doobie blunt sitting on the edge of it. He takes a seat on one of the couches in the living room, pulls out his phone, allows the phone to scan his face to unlock it. He scrolls and taps through emails.

Seconds later, Tony brings him the water and flops on the couch a couple feet away. "Thank you," Darryl says as he opens the water and takes a few gulps.

"All love," Tony says as he grabs the blunt and the lighter from the coffee table. He sparks the blunt with the flame of the *Quran*, he closes his eyes to pray over it while inhaling it deeply. He sits straight up to allow the smoke to pass through his chakras like the *Kundalini*. He exhales out a cloud of smoke and slowly opens his eyes to see the smoke abstractly create art within the air. He repeats the process as Darryl continues to tap and scroll on his phone. He tries to hand off the blunt to him, but he's too caught up in his phone to realize it.

"Darryl..." Tony says, breaking Darryl's concentration.

"My bad," Darryl says, slightly flinching and grabbing the blunt to puff. "I appreciate you, family..."

"It's all love big bro... you good? You know you can talk and be yourself around here, fammo."

"Yeah, I'm good... just need a recharge before heading to class," Darryl concludes while puffing again and passing the blunt back. "How's your last semester goin'?"

"Sensational! I'm just ready to graduate...... get this master's and I'm done with school!"

"You might as well get your Doctorate's, Tony."

After clearing his throat, Tony asks, "Why?"

"Retirement benefits, you become a societal source, and it builds your credentials. You know it's all a part of the game."

"Yeah, a game I'm tired of playing......"

"As the great poet, Tupac Shakur, once said, 'play the game nigga, never let the game play you," Darryl says.

"Aren't we all still getting played?" Tony confusingly asks while exhaling the smoke. "There's pesticides in the fruits and vegetables, there's cancer and the meats, there's poison and brainwashing programming on every screen from our phones to the television; we are all getting played! You don't think our education system isn't a vital part in that game that indoctrinating us to think and be a certain way?"

As Tony inhales, Darryl claims, "You take over the controller of the game when you received your doctorate degree.... You can make up shit, when you receive your doctoral degree."

While they both laugh, Tony begins coughing. When he finally catches his breath, he says, "As long as you got evidence, text, and documented experiences to back that muthafucka up, huh?"

Darryl states, ".... but that's the beauty of the game. A pawn can become a King or Queen no matter which side they're on or whichever part of the board you come from."

As they continue their rotation, Tony marinates on Darryl's statements about going back to school after a few years of obtaining his masters. He then begins to wonder what it would be like to be Dr. Tony Givens. *"What would I even get my doctorate's in?"* he meditates to himself. "Will you be coming to my graduation?" Tony sporadically asks, trying to block his thoughts of having to go through another three to four years of school.

"Com' on now, fam, you know I wouldn't miss it for the world. Plus, Dr. Akira Peseshet fine, intelligent, and feisty ass will be there!"

"Everyone keeps talking about her and I have no clue on who she is...."

"Brother, brother, brother.... aight check it.... Dr. Peseshet received her B.A. in Native American studies, did a lot of research on the aboriginals, the indigenous, the Mayans and the Aztecs; the Anunnaki's to further add to her research. She then got her master's, traveled state to state, going to different state departments that holds census records and documents on Native Americans, organizing thrilling information that one day may shock the American civilization. She moved on to get her doctorates, arguing that 'Black' people are the true natives of this country."

Tony stares in puzzlement. He then confusingly says, "Wait... what?"

"Bruuhh! That's the same shit Patricia used to be on," Darryl says. "Dr. Peseshet turned her dissertation into a book and claims to have found the tribe that her ancestors came from before the *1830 Indian Removal Act*. She found her family and friends' tribes, Black people from all over the nation was buying her book, discovering their tribes...."

"What?" Tony incomprehensibly asks.

"Get this...... she discovered that there were never any Slave ships. The only ships that were existing at that time were ships called Rowboats. No rowboat is going to transport millions of slaves across the Atlantic Ocean over no course of four hundred years."

"No way...."

"She spoke about this at Spellman College in Atlanta, Georgia, and provided extensive research on the history of slave ships, claiming that they never existed, that they were made up...... then the students and some staff members at Spellman tried to cancel her on social media, booed her at the end of her presentation...."

"Got on her ass, huh?" Tony laughs in abhor, not wanting to commit to Peseshet's claims.

"Yes, but she did research and found out that Spellman was founded by two white women and did not get their first Black woman president until 1987. She wrote a journal about it, published it, and posted it on her social media platforms with the caption, 'Please Sit Down,' with the subtext saying, 'Your institution was founded by white women.'"

"Scaaaaannnn-da-lous!" Tony sings.

"After that she went ballistic! I'm talking about exposing facts about history that has been kept out of our education systems, exposing the government and government officials; she even exposes our so-called 'Black leaders!' She claims that Rev. Al Sharpton and Jesse Jackson are FBI informants. That the Black leaders that accompanied Dr. Martin Luther King that day of him being shot were the ones who set him up. She's been going in for years!" Darryl says as he closes out his autobiography of Dr. Peseshet.

"I can't wait to hear what she has to say......" Tony claims as he puffs. "We know that the society that was presented to us was all a lie, it's so incongruous that she's speakin' on these subjects."

"Bruh! Dr. Peseshet ain't no joke! She even pressed Aaron James for preaching about collective unity amongst all people, no matter the color."

"Wait, what she say about Brother James' theories?"

"She called him a sellout and told him that 'Blacks' should receive reparations before any Black man and any Black woman talk about any collective unity amongst a people that they fought and forced them out of their lands and reclassified them as a people."

Tony is still wondering on the sellout comment. He eventually says, "A sellout though? Aaron James has been active in our communities for years. Why she go so hard on 'em?"

"Well all Aaron James do is go do lectures at different churches and colleges, but he has no programs within Black communities. Yes, he speaks on Black issues, but he does nothing financially to help the Black communities. It's more than just talkin' my boy; you have to live it too! That's why Dr. Peseshet told him to stop kissing ass. She'll be speaking at your graduation! You know she gon' be talkin' her shit..."

"I bet!"

"Say fam, you hungry?"

"Heaven's yes... starvin' like Marvin over here."

"Trying to hit up this new spot? It's Black-owned."

"I'm with it.... You know I'm ridin', rootin', and relyin' on anyone Black........ I got you on the food too, youngsta, thanks for allowing me to come smoke with you..."

"Ahh, naww, big bro, it's okay..."

"It's my treat fam, don't block your blessings."

"Ahh-man, this ain't no eye for an eye or a tooth for a tooth, but I ain't gon say no to some good ol' food...." Tony claims after smoking until his fingers feel the burn from the cherry flame. Tony smashes the small doobie that was left in a nearby ashtray. He rises to go to his room to put his shoes on.

Darryl rises to put his coat back on as Tony comes back to the living room. "You ready?" he asks.

"Yessir..." Tony answers, grabbing his keys from off of the counter, exiting behind Darryl to lock the door.

They both hop in Darryl's car, arguing about rather COVID-19 was actually a 'deadly virus,' or was it a test-run for the future One-World Government that George Bush, Sr. signed into effect during his presidency.

"COVID-19 was a hoax!" Darryl impatiently says while driving. "If you believe that COVID-19 was an actual real thing, then you are an idiot!"

"Com'on now, big bro. You can't just be saying anything; millions of people died from COVID."

"Who? Who are all of these millions of people? The numbers were fabricated......... there were hundreds of doctors from all over this country, saying the data that the CDC was broadcasting were all inaccurate, the news kept reporting false accounts of people 'suffering' from this 'deadly virus.' This was all propaganda at its finest.......... Population control.............. Pushing mandatory laws for people to take more vaccines. How many people you know personally died from COVID compared to the people you know for a fact died from the foods we eat?"

Hesitantly, Tony says, "I personally don't know anyone who died from the 'Chinavirus,' but umm......"

Darryl comically interjects, saying, "Donald Trump was dead wrong for calling it the Chinavirus......"

"It was funny than a muthafucka though..........." he says while laughing. "Nah, but I do know a lot of people who said they caught COVID tho, big bro....... I also know a lot of people who have or had diabetes, cancer, and other mutated diseases....... caused by the meats they consumed on the daily.............."

In the middle of his confusion and ignorance towards the mediocrity spewing across from him, Darryl bewilderingly says, "Tony?" Then he takes a deep sigh and continues, "The mind is a powerful tool, and if you allow another entity to control it, then that what you fear... will appear."

A moment of silence goes by, tension ascents as Tony comically and sarcastically asks, "Didn't you catch COVID?"

Darryl guiltily laughs and says, "Man," he pauses for a moment, then continues, "I thought I had it, but it felt like the flu; I thought, 'this is fasho the flu part two,' then I was looking at the symptoms of COVID and they were ALL the same as the symptoms for the flu, so I don't know what I had." They both laugh as they come upon traffic and a stop light. Darryl asks, "Did you ever take that booster shot?"

"Darryl, you know I ain't takin' no vaccination nothin', I don't know what Bill Gates put in it.... then, how do you make a vaccine in the short amount of span and get millions of people to take it around the world? No research behind it, no experimentations, no trial runs, no nothing!?"

Darryl responds, "Then to see thousands of young athletes from colleges to some of the pro athletes all over the country passing out and collapsing from having heart attacks and seizures because they were forced to take the vaccines?...... Damar Hamlin............ Bronny James............ Tao Tagovailoa....... just to name a few that are well known.......... Why do you think thousands of nurses and doctors left their hospitals when those same hospitals mandated for their dedicated, hardworking employees to get vaccinated? Come on now! We can't be that stupid. I just don't believe people are that stupid........"

"Speaking of Bill Gates, this demon was talking about 'lowering the population' using new vaccines, healthcare, and reproductive health services back in a 2010 Ted Talk."

"Hell nah! Ted put anybody on his platform. Ted gotta be a white man."

"I wouldn't lie to ya.......... he 'scientifically' went in depth, too...... and the people wanted to take this man's 'new vaccine?' What. In the. Entire fuck. Is wrong with us? What is wrong with our people?" Darryl says in agony.

"What about the people who had to take it? Those other nurses and doctors? Who have families to feed and to provide for? What about those other individuals who had to do what they had to do to survive? What about those other mothers and fathers forced in a compromising and/or financial obligations? What about the old who was constantly told through news stations, and newsreels, and newspapers that they were going to be the most effected?"

"Listen.... no judgment towards them................."

"Big bro, you just called everyone stupid, that's judgement."

"I knoooow but nah, not real judgment towards anyone, but my nonjudgmental factors don't conceal their ignorance. When it comes to the old, after the Tuskegee Experiment, you'd think they would not trust the government to get the vaccine, but many of them took it............ For any billionaire to get on countless international platforms, promoting depopulating the earth through the various factors that people go through for 'environmental protection,' like healthcare and vaccines, and get away with it? It's total stupidity on those who would righteously participate in their nefarious acts."

"That sounds like judgment, big bro," Tony asserts as they pull into a parking lot of the With Love and Soul restaurant.

They get out of the car and concurrently close their doors. While walking, Darryl asks, "What's up with you and Trina? How's that working out?"

"I ain't going to lie to you, it's not working out at all. One minute she wants to work things out, next minute, it's 'get the fuck out of my apartment,' or she can't shake what I did," he dolefully says. "I'm just watering dead flowers at this point."

"Damn," Darryl says with a slight chuckle and grin. "King Tony experiencing heartbreak, again; he's back singing like *Tony! Toni! Toné!*......again."

Once they walk in the restaurant, paradoxically, Tony! Toni! Toné's song, *Anniversary*, is playing over the speakers, but their minds do not piously connect the dots. They walk to the takeout line, observing the scene of all the Black people conversing, eating, laughing, singing, and enjoying themselves, a scenery that's serene to them. They love walking into spaces where it reminds them of Wakanda from the movie, *Black Panther*.

Darryl revives the conversation, saying, "Look, family, she's going to keep running back because men like us only come around once every so often. She knows what she's missing. She just can't move on. Women aren't wired that way."

"Women move on big bro! What you mean?"

"They pretend to move on, but deep down inside, they don't move on, young one! Trust me on this!"

"Did Miss Hall come back? Did Ella come back?"

"I won't let Miss Hall back but she be mean muggin' like she wanna come back; Ella came back plenty of times," Darryl says, chuckling and looking away for an instant to observe more of the scene. Suddenly, he doubletakes to see Patricia at the bar talking to someone. A tornado of emotions traveled from his mind to his heart. The whirlwind that's spinning in his heart fights with the tidal wave of pride and delusion, causing an incision on the takotsubo of his nature.

He observes attentiveness energy of Patricia's body. She is giving the gentleman that same smile that she once gave him when you know someone finds you interesting. It makes him choke on the obliviousness he just emitted to Tony.

Darryl notices the handsome fellow wearing a black V-neck t-shirt, tucked inside some black slacks, and nice, black dress shoes. Jealousy tugs at his ego but Darryl finds the strength to fight back and find happiness for Patricia. *"She deserves to be with someone who makes her happy,"* he says within himself.

"Darryl!" Tony shouts, snapping Darryl out of his trance of insensitive and cringed-hearted thoughts. "Are you going to order something?"

Darryl snaps back to reality and orders his food to go. They await in the lounge area of the restaurant where he gratefully can no longer see Patricia philandering with the guy.

Tony perceives Darryl's uneasiness and asks, "Are you okay, big bro? You're acting like you just got some terrible news."

Darryl awkwardly and inauthentically says, "No, I'm okay. Really fine. I was just thinking about the work I have to do for my doctoral program."

"You seem really disturbed by it."

"Yeah, and it's just the beginning, but things got turned up even more now," Darryl says, not revealing that he is truly talking about being in the same classroom with Patricia, especially after seeing her with another man, laughing and playing around. Darryl gets internally frustrated just thinking about her.

Tony is tangled towards Darryl's answer and his energy but does not bother to ask him to explain. Tony can sense a sense of discreteness, so he respects it, and drops that conversation. He then asks, "How's Alvin been? You haven't mentioned bro since......"

Darryl interjects and slyly says, "Since you punched on him?"

After a slight chuckle, Tony says, "He was attacking a woman friend of mine. What do you expect me to do?"

Darryl chuckles and says, "Anyway, I haven't spoken with Alvin in a couple of years. He posted a picture on social media of him joining the Nation of Islam."

"He joined the Nation? That means he's refined. He's anew. That means he's learning to respect Black women. NOI's respect their women," Tony claims.

"They treat their women the same way all these other religions treat their women."

"What you mean?"

"Give them restrictions and limitations on how they're to live, how they're supposed to conduct themselves, and how they're supposed to be with their husbands. We look at it as respect, but how do they see it?"

"Don't those same religions have those same rules and regulations for men, just in a different context?"

"Yeah, but no matter what, men have always had the upper hand on women. In all hierarchy's, except for Ancient Egypt and England, men have ruled and raged war. Not women. Plus, how is forcing women to dress and act a certain way respecting women? Some religions won't allow women to speak from the pulpits."

"They're not forcing women of the Nation of Islam to dress nor act any way. Those are decisions that they make on their own in the name of Allah. Their influenced by them to live righteously and respectfully. There are enough Sexxy Reds, and, and, and, and Ice Spices influencing our young women to pop pussy, to get fucked, and twerk for money."

"Didn't Elijah Muhammad have a baby with a 14-year-old and made her into a house maid while being married to another woman? What are we talking about here?"

"His sins do not change the fact that young girls are twerking before they're learning to read, goddamn! Someone has to teach self-respect, or we'll have more Twitter porn and women with Only*Fans*! And as far as the meaning, you don't see Christians going door to door trying to feed, educate, and serve their communities. You don't see Christians trying give light and truth to the people about Black people's problems!"

One of the waiters intervenes with two bags of food. "Number 22 and number 23," she says as she hands them their bags.

"Thank you, sistah," Darryl says while following Tony out of the door.

As they walk back to the car, Tony continues his rant on his views of the masculine and feminine energies, but Darryl's mind cannot help but to show photographic images in his mind of Patricia and the man he just seen her with. Those images alter his mood, but he tries to play it off.

"...but shiiiiiit, too each its own," Tony concludes as they reach the car and the parking lot. "It's wild hearing you speak up for women when you come across as misogynistic."

"Misogynistic is crazy; besides I love women! Can't get enough of them! I'm a feminist, but I'm also a realist! I tell things how they are," Darryl responds while unlocking the doors. They both enter, strapping themselves with seat belts. As Darryl starts the car, the car's radio instantly connects to his phone and the song *Vanilla Sky* by Big K.R.I.T. begins playing in the speakers.

Tony receives a text from Trina saying, "You should come over tonight."

Darryl looks over to see Tony smiling and automatically knew that it is some pussy over there texting him. He travels through the list of women in his head to see who he can reach out to to help him cover the hurtful feelings that he felt after seeing Patricia with that other man at the restaurant. He could use a decent drink and some sex, but these are the toxic habits that keeps him feeling lonesome.

Black Pain't, Vol. II

As they pull into the apartment complex, Tony can still tell that something is bothering Darryl. While walking into the apartment, Tony gets settle in before sitting down to eat. Once he starts eating, Tony deliberates to turn on the television to watch a girls college basketball game. He says, "Let's see how feministic you really are, big bro! The average male believes that woman's basketball is too boring!"

"I've been watching it! I'm a huge Dawn Staley fan, I love Angel Reese, Flauje, Aaliyah Boston!"

"Okay, okay, my bad, Unc!" Tony says while his childhood big homie, Petey, calls him. "Hey, Darryl, I need to introduce you to one of my big homies."

Tony answers the phone and Petey says, "Tony! Wassup nigga!"

"What's good Pete!?"

"Not much man, just checkin' in on you!"

"I appreciate that fam.... wassgood with you?"

"Man nothin' man, just hiding out from these hoes main!"

"Why you hidin'?"

"These hoes be expecting too much these days, T! And all they have to bring to the table is pussy.... niggas gotta wine, they gotta dine, they gotta pay for this and pay for that, all for that hoe to just give you some pussy.... niggas claiming they don't pay for pussy and women claim they don't sell it but nigga that's far from the truth, T! Nigga, EVERYBODY is selling and buying pussy!"

"Hecks nah!"

"T, if you take a bitch out on a date; you picking her up, you paying for her meal, and may turn up with her in hopes to get what?"

"To build friendship!"

"Nigga, you ain't building no gottdamn friendships, stop lying! Niggas need to stoop lying! We doing all that for some pussy!"

Tony laughs and says, "Nah, we just showing love."

"Showing love? Nigga sound like a trick! Don't be out here trickin' Tony! Be Tony the tiger not Tony the trick! Don't let these hoes get one up on you kinfolk! You'll be paying their bills, their hair, their nails, their wardrobe, their travel and lodging, and all she gon' do is fuck with a nigga who hittin' right!"

"I hear you big bro!"

"But I didn't call you to be talkin' about these hoes main, just checkin' on you! I may pull up to your graduation family!"

"You keep saying that! I better see you!"

"On the hood, I'mma be there. You got everyone talkin' about it and shit, I said, let me gon' head and get my money right."

"You should borrow it from all the hoes you be claiming you got, fammo."

"Come on relly, you know I keep 'em!"

"Let me finishing eatin' fam, I'll holla at you!"

"Aight, T, take it easy, champ!"

Tony hangs up the phone, looks at Darryl and says, "Now that's narcissistic and misogynistic right there."

After they ate, Tony begins to roll up another blunt while Darryl gets back on his phone, texting Ella about how she's been. He then texts Luna about school related issues just to get a conversation out of her.

Darryl looks at what Tony is doing and asks, "You smokin' again, fam? You're an addict."

"Naw, nah, this for later, fam... supposed to be chillin with Trina later on," Tony says while smiling.

"I guess all that you said earlier was just a fluke, huh?"

"Nah, not a fluke, she wants to kick it, and you know I'm not turning that down."

Darryl checks the time on his phone, realizing that he has to get to school for class. "Thanks for the smoke my brother. Let me get to this class and face the music."

"Aight, big bro, be easy."

As Darryl exits, he mentally feels off balance. Once he gets to his car, he checks the notifications on his phone to see that Luna and Ella text him back.

Ella's text message reads, "Boooooyy what u want?"

He deletes Ella's message and goes straight to Luna's. Luna's message reads, "Principal just want everyone to send their lesson plans to the instructional coaches for site visits."

"More tedious work, I see...." Darryl types and sends. He then starts his car and drives to Turner University's graduate building, while internally putting himself in his scholarly mindset. While driving, he tries to read over a few of his notes to have some type of argument for tonight's class discussions.

Upon his arrival, he automatically scans the parking lot for Patricia's car, wondering if she is still out with ole' boy or if she is going to be coming to class. "I don't care," Darryl says aloud and shrugging his shoulders, allowing his thoughts to get the best of him.

He walks toward the building, and before passing the Nat Turner statue, he rubs it for good luck like the acts do at the Apollo Theater. He enters the building and urgently walks to his class. As soon as he walks in, he instantly sees Patricia reading over some text in the assigned book, sitting in the front of the class while other classmates mix and mingle.

Darryl's world tunes out and his focus is directly on Patricia. *"How smart, how brave, how beautiful, how......."*

"Hey, Darryl!" The enthusiastic, Shampagne Roberts, says, snapping him back to reality. Shampagne is fierce, she's country but talks properly, she's brilliant and witty.

"Shampagne, how are you?" Darryl soothingly says, trying not to take his frustrations out on the world.

"I'm sensational, did you get the chance to read the material?"

Darryl hesitates to answer, but manages to respond, "Yes, I did! You?"

"Yesssss! And good lawd!"

"What did you think about it?"

"I did not know that ...." suddenly, Shampagne's voice gets distorted. The indistinct chatter around the room gets clogged along with the distortion. Darryl can't help but to have his entire energy focusing in on Patricia. He has questions, he has assumptions, he has some confessions, but he's full of some perplexity.

"Why am I feeling like this?" Darryl asks within himself during Shampagne's spill about the Physician Crusade, the inquisitions, the experiments that were had on Black women in the medical field; she talks about how Margaret Sanger implemented birth control in America, and how scientist and doctors still uses Henrietta Lacks' cells today.

Moments later, Darryl sees Patricia rise to go throw something in the trash as Shampagne asks, "Ya know what I mean? Like how?"

"Yeah, that's crazy......" Darryl says as if he is totally engulfed in the conversation.

"But who knows, we're just learning history instead of doing something about it right now."

Shampagne's comment intrigues Darryl. She has his spirit's attention. "What you mean, we're not doing something right now?"

"Well, think about it.... we all know the history, we all know the rules, we all know the laws, we all know the game....... but we're not unifying. We're not mobilizing, we're not lobbying, we're not creating organizations and businesses that will put our people in a better position financially, socially.... we're just looking out for ourselves, trying to be stars on the team, while everyone else is playing as a team."

"But it's a condition, Shampagne, no matter what, everyone's actions and mind set stem and result in what they're conditioned to."

"That may be true, but we don't have to accept our conditions, we don't. We can make a better choice. There are Black people who don't like Black people. There are Black people who wouldn't want to live near Black people. There are Black people who would not put their businesses in predominantly Black neighborhoods. There are Black parents who would not put their Black children in predominantly Black schools. There's a problem, Darryl...... because those kinds of Black people are our middle to high class people who have the knowledge, resources, money, and understanding to take our team to the next level of life. But they take those things to predominantly white neighborhoods and institutions. Why?"

Shampagne's perspectives and questions left Darryl with a bunch of interior excuses that he did not want to express aloud. He feels weak and patriarchal because his core beliefs and mind set is being challenge at a stage he's never been challenged before. He realizes that Shampagne is precise on so many levels.

Before Patricia makes it back to her seat, she catches eyes with Darryl. Patricia tries to wave, but Darryl quickly looks away in avoidance. He focuses on Shampagne even more, giving her eye contact and interest. Darryl's gesture leaves Patricia in a puzzle. She scrambles through her brain for more pieces. Once Dr. Carson enters the room, she disregards Darryl's peculiar act and her invasive thoughts about the situation to concentrate on the class.

"Okay, candidates... what stood out to you about the reading? Did you research more on the topics that stood out to you?" Dr. Carson asks with such gravitational pull that it immediately sparks intellectual debate in the class. "Let's get straight to it."

As everyone finds their seats to sit down, Shampagne raises her hand. With Dr. Carson's nod of approval, she says, "The fact that Black women have always played a pivotal role in all civilizations...... and I say this because the only reason why Physician Crusade began was to stop Black women from being midwives and birthing babies. To actually read about the history of why physicians came about in 'America,' about eugenics, abortions, and other crimes against humanity was a hard pill to swallow, because we see it everywhere in all aspects of our daily lives. And ummmm...... I realized that Black women are and have always been the cultivators and epicenter of creation. NO society is able to function without the influence of Black women!"

Patricia displays a sense of impressiveness on her facial expression, nodding her head regarding Shampagne's comments. She notices that Darryl did not sit next to her. "*I guess he found interest in Shampagne,*" Patricia says within. "Interesting," Patricia mumbles to herself, but quickly snaps out of her inner melodrama to concentrate on the class discussion.

~

After almost two whole hours of lecture, in depth discussions and debates about serious topics that seems to have no real solutions, and reading information from their assigned text, Dr. Carson finally dismisses class. The candidates begin to gather their belongings. Darryl and Patricia both feel the anxiety of wanting to speak but not knowing where one another truly stands.

Can they be friends? Can they let bygones be bygones? With their constant dovetailing bonds and Darryl's stalwart attitudes, they always seem to find their way back to one another. It's either that it could be meant to be, or maybe they are reminders on why that just cannot be. Their connection is like that Chingy and Tyrese song.

Two students separate them in a line to briefly talk with Dr. Carson. Patricia senses Darryl's eager glare on the back of her neck, she knows he wants to say something, but that pride won't let him. He looks away when she looks to the side of her right shoulder. He does not want her to see that he's staring, wanting to actually talk to her and not Dr. Carson.

She feels lead to say something to see what's the energy between them, and he feels lead to see if she is going to say anything to him even though he's been distant all night. It feels like that same feeling of separation that they once felt the last time Patricia heard something about Darryl, but she wonders why she feels guilty. What's come over her? Is there unfinished business? What's magnetizing this moment between them?

He sees Patricia step up next to Dr. Carson to ask a question that she probably already know the answer to, or she probably wants to get some old American educational cliché for her write some argumentative response to. He tries to listen in on Dr. Carson's answer to whatever Patricia ask. Patricia appears to have confidently responded to Dr. Carson, because whatever she said has Dr. Carson looking enthralled.

He sees her do a 180 degree turn in the opposite direction, with that same old walk that she does as if she has time in a chokehold. That same time begins to move slower for him. It is like no other moment set up perfectly for him to talk to her and tell her how he feels.

"Should I speak?" He asks within himself as every tap of Patricia's heels taps at his heart like a pacemaker. Annoys like the tap of pen, or when people constantly tap on their phone while the other person is speaking. This is the tap water version of love, giving them both a nauseating taste of depopulation.

As Patricia passes Darryl with no words or acknowledgement, she pulls out her phone to pretend as if she does not see him standing there. Darryl stares straight ahead with an Emmy award winning act of being nonchalant, knowing damn well his heart is beating a hundred miles per hour on the inside.

Outside the classroom, Patricia looks back to see Darryl still awaiting in line to talk to Dr. Carson. "Darn Darryl," she says while shaking her head and walking off.

Back in the classroom, Darryl turns around to see Patricia walking off into the hallway. Once the last candidate that is talking to Dr. Carson moves out of the way, Darryl steps up.

"You seem out of it today, my lad. Is everything alright?" Dr. Carson asks in his British accent.

"Everything is everything," Darryl meekly says, avoiding his true reasons for his despair.

"Well, whenever you really want to talk, I'm here for you, good brother," Dr. Carson says, attempting to walk away.

"Woah, woah, hold up, OG!" Darryl says, blocking Dr. Carson's path to the door. "You trying to go get some grub? I could use your advice on some things."

Dr. Carson hesitates, but manages to say, "Uhh, I have a to meet with someone in the next thirty, brother...... We'll have to see about tomorrow if you're free."

While struggling to be ecstatic for his mentor, Darryl unassumingly says, "Oh, my apologies, OG! I didn't know! My Bad! I know you gon' have a good time, ole fella! Ya' know?"

"It's all good. It's all good."

"Who is it with Ms. Tabitha?"

"Nah, it's actually with Shyla......"

"You're ex-wife, Shyla?"

"Yes, her, she says that she would like to meet with me and that it's urgent. I gotta go check it out."

"Oh, my damn! Hey, Doc!" Darry says while hyperbolically winking an eye. "We.... we both know what that means, Doc! Come on! Live it UPPPPPP! It ain't never too late! Enjoy yourself, OG!"

"It ain't like that, I closed that chapter a long time ago. I am just making sure that she's okay."

Darryl observes Dr. Carson's demeanor and allows him to live within his mirage of self-inflicting fabrications. "Well alright sensei, go handle your business. I'll catch up with you...."

Dr. Carson chunks the deuces and exits the room. Darryl looks around an empty classroom, feeling and looking like Will Smith on the last episode of *Fresh Prince of Bel Air*. He takes a deep breath and exits the room, taking a walk of shame back to his automobile to take a silent long drive to his crib.

When Darryl gets home, he orders some food from Sprint*Door*. After ordering, he subconsciously clicks on his social media apps to scroll and scroll through timelines and feeds full of bullshit, misters and misses know it alls, denigrations, illusions, allusions, misinformation, computer-generated imageries, filters, artificial intelligence wanting to know everything about you, fights, deceptions, false fact checkers, and many different algorithms that are meant to keep users (addicts also known as the people) in their delusions.

He tosses his phone out of frustration, rebelling against the seclusion. He grabs the remote and channels searches to find something intriguing to watch to keep his mind from today's stresses, yesterday's worries, and tomorrow's battles.

Black Pain't, Vol. II

    Not being able to quiet his thoughts, he turns off the television in annoyance. He grabs his phone, thinks for a moment, and unlock it. He swipes and taps on his phone to get to his memo-pad. Of course his mind drifts to thinking about the cycle that he finds himself in with Patricia. As the inspiration possesses him, he types:

How is the universe going to bring us back next go round?
Or will there be another go around?
Ouch, how will our conversations and texts go now?
Knowing that you've moved on with so and so now?
I'm just saying, it ain't fair, I waited for you...
Had self-control and dated for you....
I was elated for you...
That's how I know it's all love, because I should have hated for you
You always say, 'if it's meant to be then it'll be.'
Here we are, walking pass each other, I'm acting like I don't know you,
you acting like you don't know me,
When did we become awkward?
You casted a spell on me like you graduated from Hogwarts
You're always in some heels, I'm always in some oxfords,
How do you mend a heart that someone like you punctured?
We coulda been like Coulda Been Records,
Girl, we coulda had a family and we wouldn't been like the Huxtables,
We coulda had family full of superheroes like the Incredibles
Because girl, you're incredible, and girl, you be looking edible
If love was a school, would I be ineligible?
Or would I flunk out?
Would I step up to the plate would I strike out?
Would I be a man about it, or would I punk out?
Would I come get what I want like a takeout?
We was never together but this feels like a breakup
I guess we'll never know what it means to... make up....

Suddenly, his phone chimes. He sees a notification text from Alvin. He cannot help but to feel some sense of fretfulness because Alvin was one of his best friends and he just went ghost for a couple of years. He easy forgives him because of the motto he lived by growing up: once a friend always a friend. He wonders as to why he's hitting him up out of the blue.

He opens the message and reads, "Peace Seven, hope all is well. Sorry for the distance brother. I had to get me back right with the All Mighty. Let's link up soon. Got a lot to catch up on.... bismillah."

Alvin's message brings Darryl a lot of relief. Alvin did not ask for any money, the energy in the message seems sincere, and Alvin seems to be in a better space. Usually when friends go distant for a minute, they comeback when they need something. It may be a childhood strain still hanging onto Darryl's imaginations and discernments.

"AL!" Darryl types and sends. He then continues to text, "All is well my brother! And man it's all good, no need to be sorry. I understand. I'm free this upcoming weekend, what's your schedule like?"

Unexpectedly, the doorbell rings. Darryl flinches, forgetting that he ordered food. He gets up to answer the door to see a guy that looks familiar to him, holding a cup and a bag. The guy looks at Darryl as if he appears familiar.

"You look familiar, brother! I know I've seen you somewhere before.... just can't put my finger on it."

He takes out his phone to takes a picture of the cup and bag in Darryl's hands. "Can you hold that up for me?"

While holding up the items, Darryl humbly asks, "Where do I know you from?"

The guy is taken back by the thoughts of his mother. He has not been the same since her passing. He still feels a way that one of his sisters did not attend the funeral and has not been on speaking terms with her. "Enjoy the rest of your evening."

"You, too, brother!" Darryl says confusing as he gradually shuts the door and locks it.

The man walks back to his car, feeling like he made enough money for tonight. On the way home, he tries to call his girl, but sometimes his calls are all going straight to voicemail, other times he had to blow up her phone just for her to answer, cussing him out for making sure she was okay. These constant occurrences have been making him feel apprehensive towards their relationship.

He continues to monitor his meddling thoughts to himself in the duration of driving back to his humble of home, wondering what type of excuse she's going to give him this go round about her lack of communication. *"Is she going claim that she was busy?"* he thinks to himself as he turns up the volume on the radio to block out his judgements.

Once he gets home, he unwinds and put away his belongings. Walking into the house that his father left him before his mysterious death, he feels a strong sagacity of aloneness. His insecurities of not having many of the things he owns on his own merit tug his heart. Even the car he drives was giving to him by his mother. All he does is work with anything to show for it.

"Maybe that's why she really don't love me like she claims she does, I don't even have the means to make her happy and satisfied." He feels as if his life is supposed to be somewhere that it is not; that he's supposed to be happy and successful. He then thinks about how he never completed anything in his life, from college to getting his realtor license, to his failed friendships. His nerve cells drift to his sisters. He decides to swallow his pride and reach to the one who didn't show up to their mother's funeral.

"Hello......" she says as she answers with distant chatter and music playing in the background.

"Trina....... you busy?"

"I'm a work, but I can step out and talk for a second, hold on.... it's a little loud," Trina calmly claims, walking outside of Kemet. She pulls out a joint and a lighter. She put the joint in her mout to lit it, saying, "What's up, lil' bro? Everything okay?"

"You know wassup, Trina...... everything is not okay."

"Daayyuuum, well wasssssup? Why you got your panties all in a bunch? I haven't talked to you in months, what's with the beef?"

"Why didn't you come to the funeral, Trina?"

"Didn't think I needed to or if I was supposed to? Why are you calling me with this? Is your girl trippin' or somethin'? You want me to beat her up?"

"Trina...."

"I told you something off about that bitch...... she got you tweakin' on me, and I ain't did nothin!"

"You didn't come to the funeral..."

"I didn't come to the hospital for her first four strokes! I only went to the last one because you, Tony, and Jalisa fuckin' basically dragged me there.... guilt trippin' me and shit......"

"Trina, that ain't the point......."

"Then what is the damn point, Junior!? I'm fucked up because of her...... and yo weak ass daddy...... I wasn't ready to forgive her..."

"Jalisa wasn't ready to forgive her, but she forgave her anyway."

"I'm not Jalisa, lil' nigga!"

"You are her! Y'all look exactly alike!"

Out of nowhere, they both begin to gradually laugh out their frustrations. Trina can't help herself but to be comical in heated situations. This gives Jules some type of relief. All he wants is a better relationship with his sisters since their parents are no longer here.

Jules eventually says, "I know you gotta go to work; I just couldn't let another month go by without talking to you........ you can swallow your pride sometimes, too."

"That's my toxic trait, Junior....... I don't swallow my pride...."

"You should try it, sis...... I love you...."

"I love you, too, junior...."

Black Pain't, Vol. II

    Jules ends the call and sits there, discerning Jazmine's actions and lack of communiqué. *"Wow, still no call or text back?"* he says to himself, nodding his head. "Okay," he says aloud, getting up to look in the refrigerator for some water.
    The silence surrounding his mind and heart invades his solitude with intrusion. He drinks some water and walks back to sit on the couch. Picking up his phone, he decides to create a voice about what he would like to say to Jazmine. He says:

>"Hey, Jazmine,
>you take my breath away like asthma;
>you make me spazz out and you give my heart spasms;
>life been slow, but you got me fasten;
>dying on the inside, I'm tired of acting concerned about your careless actions; why do I continue to let occurrences like these happen? You got me all in my head, but you're the one cappin';
>giving me the signs and symbols, but you're the one clashin';
>calling my emotions reckless, but you're the one crashin';
>I see that you lost interests, but why are you still taxin'?
>Put you first, not knowing we weren't going to be everlastin'?
>Do you still wanna be with me, tell me......
>Would you even wanna be seen with me, tell me......
>You don't wanna really build a team with, huh? Tell me.
>Addicted to you but you won't feign with me, huh? Tell me.
>Just tell me, tell me, love
>Please tell me, tell me, love
>Just tell me......"

Black Pain't, Vol. II

MY NOTES

Black Pain't, Vol. II

Chapter 6:
Chime

The crowd's applause gradually fades into quietness as their eyes are intently fixated on the performer on the stage. Waiters and waitress are moving to and from with the crowd's food and drink orders. The audience is diligently eating, drinking, and enjoying the show. The light in the room is dim and the spotlight lit up the stage.

"For my last song, I wrote this for all the last of the wholesome women left in the world," the performer says as some of the people in the crowd laughs. "In a world full of *Sexxy Red's* and *Sukihana's*, I appreciate you for being true to you, showing a high level of self-respect; for being true to your morals and high standards, and for being true to being the change that you wish to see in the world, especially when it comes to the young women."

Black Pain't, Vol. II

     The instrumental to the song begins to play during the end of the performer's interlude. He watches as the crowd starts vibing to the instrumental as he sings......

"You're pure and perfect, girl.
You know your value,
that's why you're worth it, girl.
Been A-One since your mother had you,
I see where you learned it, girl.
You keep it one hundred, girl.
You ain't about to be nobody's option.
Nobody can put a bid on you,
you're nobody's auction.
You're no one's tight squeeze,
I wanna feel your warm embrace, baby.
Your personality is a slight tease,
You be smellin' good and I wanna know how you taste, baby.
Can I get with you?
Oooohh, yeah, can I get with you?
With you, with yooouuu, with yoooooouuuu
Can I get....
I know you're righteous,
and I'll wait until marriage with you,
I don't do fairytales,
but I'll do the horses and carriage with you,
I don't believe in society's illusion of love,
but I'll cherish it with you,
I'll go to Faris and to Paris with you,
I'll be humorous and hilarious with you,
Like prevention programs, I'll D.A.R.E with you,
I don't be giving a fuck,
but I care with you,
Can I get with you?
Oooohh, yeah, can I get with you?

With you, with yooouuu, with yoooooouuuu
Can I get....
Can I get with you?
Oooohh, yeah, can I get with you?
With you, with yooouuu, with yoooooouuuu
Can I get....
Come on crowd! Sing it with me!"

The crowd sings along with him while he continues to sing. They start adding a clap to the rhythm of the collective.

"Can I get with you?
Oooohh, yeah, can I get with you?
With you, with yooouuu, with yoooooouuuu.
Can I get...."

As the instrumental continues to play, and some people from the crowd are still singing, he says, "Y'all sound so beautiful, we're better together; you see what unity does? You got to love it. Imagine if we came together for other things.... things like...... supporting our friends' businesses, supporting the kids in our communities.......... things like voting, or financially putting our people in a better position...... can we get with that?"

The crowd gives him a round of applause as he chuckles, "I know that ain't got nothing to do with this song, but I felt moved to say that, AMEN?"

"AMEN," the crowd yells.

"God is good?"

The crowd yells in unison, "All the time!"

"And all the time?"

"God is good!"

"Y'all didn't know ya was comin' to chuuuuch this evening. That's how all those pastors who be gettin' paaiiddd paid to preach be saying church....... 'If you sow a seed right now for $100, God will bless you in ways that you couldn't imagine! Are we not having CHUUUUUCHHH?" he asks as the crowd laughs. He concludes, "Nah, but like I said earlier, big shout out to all the pure women, the ones not giving their bodies away to any ol' body, those who lives by morals and high standards. Thank you for not allowing society.... these movies, today's music, and so on and so forth make you think that that's how women are supposed to be......"

He steps away from the microphone stand as the crowd continues to cheer and clap. As the house lights comes on, and the people begin to exit, he interacts with the crowd from the stage. He spots a few women that he knows, looking at him with impious eyes. One of them approaches him and whispers something into his ears that makes his eyebrows rise in surprise. She walks away, biting her lip.

He looks over to the other girl and she gives him the well-known 'call me' hand signal as he nods in agreement. He internally tries to decide who should he entertain, who does he feel like being with during the next couple of hours. He loves the attention that women give him, especially after his shows.

After shaking hands, giving hugs, and expressing gratitude to a few other people that were in the audience, a woman's voice precipitously says to him, "Terry Bear...... it never seems to amaze me how talented you are...." in a taunting way.

He turns to the side to see Jazmine, looking like a full course meal, wearing a short lavender dress. She slips on her coat in a coquettish way. He says, "Thanks Jazzy, I appreciate you for that. You kid free tonight?"

"Yes, I am!" Jazmine replies with enthusiasm. "Are you bitch free tonight?" she asks while staring into his soul, wanting to snatch it, and wanting him to snatch hers.

"Naw, not really, she's supposed to be coming over later...." he answers with perseverance.

"How much time do you have till she come?"

"About two...... two and a half hours."

Staring into Terrance's dark eyes with the attempt of gaining control over his cognitions, she says, "All I need is forty minutes...."

He hesitates for a second, knowing he's supposed to call that other woman to pull up on her and take her to pound town. However, she does not know about his relationship with Jalisa like Jazmine knows about his relationship with Jalisa. She does not care as long as she gets his time, his penis, and his sexual energy. She wants to be driven by his sex drive, she wants something familiar and aesthetic; she wants to be fucked good.

"Well? You wastin' time, sir...." Jazmine demands, breaking his inner dilemma.

"Let me go pack my bag and get paid, you can follow me home."

"Aright then... don't be long..."

He walks off of the stage, strolls backstage through the hallways, and makes it to the dressing room. He drinks some water and packs his bag with his belongings, thinking about the excuse he's going to give that other girl. Jazmine is just too convenient to be sexing another woman who has no clue about his relationship status.

The owner comes in with an envelope, saying, "Great show tonight, Terrance!" After tossing him the envelope, he continues, "See you in a few weeks!"

"Much obliged!" Terrance says as he counts the money in the envelope. He then stuffs it in his bag and exits the dressing room, flicking the light off. While in the parking lot, he can see people still outside in groups, cars still parked, and the streets filled with traffic.

Once he makes it to his car, a car horn goes off twice to get his attention. He looks over to see Jazmine awaiting in her car. He nods at her as he hops in his car. They both maneuver out of the parking lot and into the traffic.

While on the way to his place, he keeps looking into the rearview mirror, making sure that she's keeping up and feeling her erotic vitality. After coming up with the excuse, he calls that one woman who gave him the 'call me' signal.

"Hello," she says as she answers in her harmonious voice.

"Hey Luna love, my Luner love..."

She firmly says, "Boyyyy stooop, you always trying to butter me up. Why do I have to come to your shows to see you? How come I ain't heard from you?"

"That's my fault lovely, been busy with this music and performance thing, you know...... I'm just now able to see the fruit of my labor.... I promise to make time for you soon..."

"Ummm hmmm..."

"How school going?"

She sighs and replies, "School is school.... I'm tired of being Ms. Hall, the science teacher. I want to do more, I want to be more, and I want to see more. So lately, I've been thinking about going back to school, too."

"Everyone wants to go back to school........ why do we think the answer to life's problems are school, a relationship, or working harder?"

"I didn't say it was a life problem...."

"You said that you're tired of being Ms. Hall, the science teacher.... sounds like a problem to me, love......"

"Well...... ummmm...... I guess you're right...... maybe it's the school... maybe it's the coworkers, I don't know......" she cautiously says, thinking about Darryl's presence and how it alters her moods throughout the workday.

"Or maybe.... it's you......." Terrance softly says.

"I knoooowwww! Uhhhhh!" she says, grunting. "I hate that you give me the real and honest truth, but never give me your time and energy."

"I got you Luna! I promise I got you...." he says while looking in the rearview to make sure Jazmine is still behind him. "And I promise to give it to you the way you want it...."

"Ummm hmmm," Luna says as if he's lying.

"Nah, forreal!"

"Okay, Terrance, see you soon."

"Why you trying to get off the phone with me?"

"Because it's the same ol' excuses...... I'm ready to see your actions with those promises."

"I got you, Luna..."

"Okay.... well, enjoy the rest of your night...."

"Okay, love... bye."

"Bye."

When Terrance makes it home, he hurries to straighten his home before Jazmine's arrival. Once she arrives, she immediately tries to play fight with him. Terrance tries to avoid her way of four play, knowing Jazmine grew up rough and rugged. He eventually pins her against the wall, slapping her into her kinkiness, and choking her into submission. They kiss violently, taking off one another's clothes while walking into the bedroom.

They are both ass naked, kissing and breathing heavily in one another's mouths. Jazmine gets on her knees to repeatedly jam his dick down her throat. She clutches his ass cheeks and fucks her throat with his dick.

"Suck that dick good baby," he says while grabbing the back of her head to help her fuck her throat. She takes his dick out to breath, looks up at him just to be slapped again. "Ummm hmmm, look at me while you jerk it," he says while she roughly tries to milk him.

She moans as he lifts her up and tosses her on the bed. She turns around to lift her ass in the air with her face down. She moans and pants while he smacks his dick on her pussy. "Put it in, stop playin' with it," she says before he rams his dick in the way she likes it to be jammed. She grumbles as he fucks her like a plunger plunges a toilet. She yells and groans as it sounds like a standing ovation right in his bedroom.

"Pussy feel good baby."

"Ooooh shitt... fuck me, like that, just like that!" she yells as he rhythmically beat the pussy up from behind.

"Mhhhmm, like that? Like that baby?" he repetitively grunts while thrusting,.

"Ooh, like that! Like that!" she screams while creaming all over his dick. Her body shakes like she's about to have a seizure.

"I like that shit, keep creaming," he commands as he takes his dick out to lick and suck on her cream. He then slaps his dick on her pussy multiple times while she's creaming on him and soaking onto bed.

She wants to taste her cream, so she somewhat lifts to tongue kisses him. Without a moment's notice, he grabs her neck, pushed her back down, and roughly but gently inserts himself back inside her. She holds on to the sheets for dear life as he takes her to pound town.

"You stretchin' me out, daddy! You stretchin' me out! I wanna taste it," she says while barely having any strength to continue.

"You wanna taste it, baby?"

"Yes, I wanna taste it! Cum for me daddy!"

"You want me to cum baby?"

"Yes, daddy, oooh, oooh! Dick big daddy" she says while making more sound effects.

"You want it on your face baby?"

"Yes, daddy!" she replies.

"Oh fuck!" he says while continuing to try to hold back his nut.

"Cum, daddy! Cum for me, daddy! Cum for me, daddy!"

The clapping sounds echoes off the walls, colliding with her high vibrational words. After the collisions, he finally surrenders. Their passions gift wraps the ambiences flowing in and out of them. The magic and the celestial bliss fill the cosmic gaps in the room. Her precious perfume and his cunning cologne infuse with the smell of sex in the room.

"We shouldn't be fuckin' like this," she thinks to herself.

Moments before his climax, he notices her phone ringing with the name, "Juley," on the screen next to a brown heart emoji. He ignores it and so does she. He takes out his dick from inside her and she turns around ready to be baptized. She moans and smiles while she's taking it with her mouth wide open and her tongue out.

She grabs his penis and strokes it while he cums all over her face. While he's grunting and trying to keep himself together, she licks his dick like a lollipop and slurps his balls like she's slurping a Big Gulp from 7/11.

"Women like you deserve to go to heaven," he amusingly says.

"Ummmm," she hymns and spits on his dick, draining him of his life force, and slurping his soul. "Thank you."

He can barely move as his consciousness comes back from the galactic trip. Their eye contact is sensual as they lie into the puddle of spit, semen, sweat, and creaming white stuff on the bed. He looks down to see her smiling and giving him a compelling look. They French kiss for another couple of minutes, enjoying one another's intimacy.

After they intermix their saliva, he rises to walk into the nearby restroom to grab two face towels. He wets them with hot water and rings them out, so they won't be extra soaked with water. He scrubs some soap on his towel before exiting the bathroom.

As he comes back in the bedroom, Jazmine is texting on her phone. She says, "Thank you," as he hands her the hot towel. While grabbing the towel, she immediately wipes her face of all the semen. She folds the towel to dab and vaguely wipe her yoni. She then folds the towel in half again to wipe her ass crack.

"That was some sexy shit!" he says as he cleans his penis with the towel. He bends the towel to clean his testicles.

"Yeah, you nasty...." she says seductively.

"Com' on now Jazzy, you know you like it...." he says combatively. "This that beat it up right dance right here," he jokingly says, trying to do the crip walk.

"Aight 'Jody'!" she responds as they both hoot. "When did you learn how to fuck like that? And why wasn't you fucking me like that in college?"

"I was still learning, you obviously had more experience than me whenever we were together," he answers. Then he thinks to asks, "Is that why you cheated on me?"

A harsh silence and a punitive tension enter the room to go to war with all the blissful, sexual aroma in the room. She ponders on something witty to combat his depressive question. "That's why you be trying to blow my brains and back out every time we do it? You trying to kill me, Terrance?"

He laughs as he puts his briefs back on, stating, "Killing you is crazy! I'll never kill you! Plus the cat got nine lives, you'll be alright."

She laughs and says, "Oh, whatever...."

"I lost my virginity in college, Jazzy, you had me when I was just starting out. I have tons of practice, especially after you dumped me."

"I heard that...." she says while finally finding the energy to get up. "But that's not why I cheated; I was just having too much fun. I wanted to live my college experience. It wasn't to be devious, or spiteful. I was just young, dumb, and full of cum...."

"I understand, but you could have just broke up with me before you went out and did what you did. Then anonymous ass niggas or bitches was talkin' shit about me on Fizz!"

"Terry-Bear, I'm sorry...... I know I was fucked up! We were young! You gotta forgive me!"

"Don't get me wrong, I forgive you...... I really do Jazmine....... but relationship post-traumatic stress disorder is real! I was NOT the same after that, but we can change the subject," he says as he admires her putting on her underwear. "How's little Miracle doing?"

"She's doing good, she's growing like every day," she says while smiling from the thoughts of her baby girl. She continues to get dressed as her phone rings again.

"Need to be somewhere?"

"Yes.... don't you have to be somewhere, too?" She responds with a derisive question of her own.

Chuckling, he replies, "I'm where I need to be."

"Ummm hmmm."

He contemplates for a moment and asks, "When is graduation?"

"It's in two weeks," she sighs while she answers. Then she asks, "Why; you coming?"

"I don't think it would be a good idea."

"But I would love for you to be there. Plus, Dr. Lady Peseshet will be there! You don't want to miss that!"

"Even with our situation? And who is Dr. Lady Peseshet?"

"We don't have to make our situation known! Like... just make it seem like you coming to hear Dr. Peseshet!"

"Who the hell is Dr. Peseshet?"

"She's a world-renowned historian, activist! She's known for going around speaking truth to our people. I heard she has over 100,000 people on standby, ready to go to war against the government."

"What the hell?"

"Yup! She cold wit it! But overall, I just want you to be there, I want to feel your presence. It's a turn on when we're all in the same room or vicinity."

"I hear you......." he says while deliberating his next question. He does not want to ask it but feels led to. "So you're okay with knowing you fucking both me and 'Juley'?"

Jazmine gives Terrance a nonchalant facial gesture and says, "You're fucking his sister....... We both having our cake right now."

"But I'm not fucking Jalisa," he says to himself as the conviction and guilt begin to emerge from within him. "I guess you're right. We both thought it was divine intervention when we saw each other at Aaron James' speech last year."

"We did. What made you reach out?"

(The whole world was supposedly on quarantine. Somehow the powers that be gave the world a taste of their one world government; a world where there are no borders, a world with only one militia, a world of absolutely no freedom and no privacy. A technological world where artificial intelligence has more power control than humans. This world is going to look similar to that in the book, "1984" by George Orwell.

Anyhow, Terrance and Jalisa ended their evening with an at-home dinner date of food and online live music. Terrance had to get creative since no stores, restaurants, or activities was happening in the city and everyone had to be at least six feet apart from one another. Terrance was hoping for a night cap and some late-night cuddling, but all Jalisa gave him was patience and vulnerability mixed with some sexual refutation. Terrance dropped Jalisa at her home and drove back home feeling that patience wearing thin and vulnerability beating at his mind and heart.

While at home, Terrance was feeling lonely. He was feeling horny. He craved to indulge in that feminine energy. He couldn't sleep. He tapped and scrolled through social media to kill the late-night idle time, forgetting that idle time is the devil's workshop. He watched videos of protests, Black Lives Matter rallies, and videos how other countries are managing the Covid-19 pandemic.

He watched videos of how people were profiting from making masks. He saw videos of the people in Florida totally disregarding all the rules and regulations that was put in place by the CDC. He was reading news articles about Bill Gates' new vaccine to combat this "deadly virus."

"They're about to create a new vaccine and have people just take it without any trial runs or a long-term study on the effect of this vaccine?" He ruminates to himself. "Niggas goin' to be dumb enough to take this shit too," he verbally says.

He came across a video of woman shaking her ass. He clicked on the video to see other women commenting with videos of their ass jolting. He clicked on another video of a woman bouncing her ass on a dick. The video engrossed him, inciting his sexual acumens. Porn perverts him, causing him to look through women profiles to see more ass, titties, and sex. Porn damages his sexual desires and sexual protuberances. Porn weakens a man.

Meanwhile, on the other side of town, Jazmine and Jules just parted for the evening. Jules had to get up early in the morning for work. While Miracle slept in the other room, she found some time to use that Tulip that she bought herself for her birthday.

She searched for on some Twitter porn on her phone. She found a user profile with a variety of freaky porn. There are videos of women scissoring one another; videos of threesomes, and, of course, dick sucking videos. Porn detained her psyche. Watching porn made her heart race. Porn is its own spirit that has a psychological effect on her sex-life.

Black Pain't, Vol. II

She stacked two pillows on top of each other and sat her phone up against and amongst them just good enough for the phone to be eye level with her as she laid back on another pillow with her legs spread.

She came across just the right video. Seven minutes of an orgy. The orgy had women sucking dick, men beating pussy up in missionary positions, women getting hammered in doggystyle position by big niggas with big, black cocks. There were women eating each other out while getting fucked from the back. It was a lot of women moaning and screaming in the video.

She turned the volume down. She began touching herself. She had one hand rubbing her nipples, she loved that shit. She had the other hand playing with her clitoris. The video turned her on even more. She wished she had a long and thick dick to suck and sit on.

She grabbed her Tulip. She pushed to turn it on and realized that there were two types of buttons: one that had different vibrations and one that had different suctions. She tried them all. She simultaneously kept pressing both buttons. She liked them all. Every press had her legs shaking, every push did something to her carnal nature. When the Tulip started sucking, it was able to suck harder, slower, faster, gentle. She came multiple times and squirted all over her bed.

She turned the video off and laid there for a moment to enjoy the sensations. She eventually rose to urinate and clean herself up. She got a body towel and laid it across her wet spot. She got some panties from her drawer, slid them on, and hopped back into the bed. She grabbed her phone, swiped off Twitter, and went to Instagram.

In the meantime, Terrance was watching Twitter porn, holding the phone in his left him, while ejaculating his penis with his right hand. He was watching a video of a woman bouncing on and off a dick like she was athletic. He nuts on a nearby handkerchief, wiped himself dry, and tossed the handkerchief into a dirty clothes basket.

He swiped off Twitter and went to Instagram. While on Instagram, he came across a picture of Jazmine, Miracle, and Jules. He liked the picture and clicked on Jazmine's profile to lurk through her page. He even liked more pictures.

He exited her profile just to receive a direct message from her that said, "Dang, are you going to like all my pictures?"

He responded, "Maybe..."

"OMG LMAO," she responded. After three grey dots appear, she sent another message that read, "Hey Terry-Bear! How you been? It was great seeing you at the church the other day! I always was hypnotized by your light brown eyes and your manliness. I hate that we had to have an awkward moment but thank you for playing it off."

"I should be thanking you too! It's wicked how he ran into each other after five whole years! It was like divine intervention! Like God knew we had unfinished business."

"What unfinished business?"

He read their thread while Jazmine was typing up a message, and thought for a moment of where this conversation could lead to. He didn't want to ruin his chance of rekindling their friendship by being inappropriate. He didn't know how she would feel. Even though they have a strong history together, he didn't want to overstep his boundaries and say something that would disrespect her relationship with Jules and his relationship with Jalisa.

At the same time, Jazmine was hoping he would say something that involved sex. She was horny. Her sensual impulses made think about how big his dick was in college and how he pleased her, even though she made it seem like she was always insatiable he always had the right penis size for her to still get hers off. She thought about all the fun and wild moments that they had together.

Between the wine that Terrance and Jalisa had from their dinner early and the temptations that he's been battling, he tries to fight the sexual urges that corrupts his decision making. He typed, "You know what unfinished business I'm talking about chuuuummmp," and sent it to her.

Jazmine immediately responded, "Lol you's the chump... scared to tell me about whatever 'unfinished business' you're talking about."

"I can show you better than I can tell you."

"Well show me then..."

"Text me."

"Is your number still the same?"

"Ain't nothing changed but the year and my maturity, sweetheart."

He waited for her to message him for about ten minutes. He was losing patience and kept going back to their thread to see if she had replied. "Did I say something I wasn't supposed to say?" he thought to himself.

Then he started to regret that he even reached out, thinking that maybe Jules went through her phone and seen their messages. Then he thought that Jules must have reached out to Jalisa after going through Jazmine's phone to snitch on him. He was in and out of his mind.

Suddenly, once he'd finally and internally accepted whatever consequences from this act of adultery, a message from "Jazzy" appeared at the top of his phone's notification bar. Once Terrance tapped it, he read "Terry-Bear?"

He typed and sent, "Jazzy-baby? Is that you?"

"Nah, nah, nah, don't baby me now; you was just talkin' all that shit on social media... don't try to sweet talk me now...."

"What you mean?" Terrance replied, pretending to be oblivious.

"When are you going to 'show' me whatever unfinished business we have?"

"When are you free?"

"I'm pretty flexible. You let me know when you're free and I'll come to wherever you want me to be at."

"Aight cool..."

"So when?"

"Tomorrow?"

"What time? You know tomorrow is the lord's day and I have church at ten."

"What time do you get out?"

"11 a.m. Lol I don't go to one of those black ass churches where the pastor be preaching about nothing for hours. We in, and we out baby, so stop stalling and tell me what time..."

"Lol 11:30am?"

"That's enough time for me to take my baby to my mamma's house. Where am I going?"

"I'll send you my location when you're set to come. How is your mom's doing?"

"Lol... mmmk............. She's good. Still always trying to preach to me about this and that. I appreciate her for always willing to watch Miracle so I can feel free."

"What are you doing up so late?"

"Couldn't sleep.... U?"

"I couldn't sleep either...."

"You want to help put me to sleep?"

"How can I do that?"

"Send me a picture of your dick......"

Terrance read her message and flicked his dick to get it back hard. He swiped to go to Twitter porn to get his dick even harder. He goes to the camera on his phone to take a picture of his dick and sends it to her. He typed and sent, "Your turn."

Jazmine was in awe at the size of Terrance's manhood. It was as if he had gotten bigger. She immediately imagined herself sucking his dick and riding it. Her mouth gets watery, and her pussy instantly got wet. That was enough for her to make a video of her fingering herself.

She sent the video to him, typed, "I want you to do a nut video," and sent it to him.

He watched her video a few times and became more aroused, watching her masturbate. After he read her message, he grabbed a towel from his bathroom, laid it across his stomach, and recorded himself *masturbating, and ejaculating on the towel. Once he wiped himself dry, he sent her the video.*

Jazmine watched the video with intensity, touching herself in the process, pinching her nipples with every one of his grunts, and cumming to his semen shooting from out his dick. When she catches her breath and calms down, she responded, "See you tomorrow ☺."

The next day was like clockwork. Jazmine came to his apartment in her church clothes, and they immediately went at it. Their sexual encounter was aggressive and passionate. Terrance ate her out like she was a "Good Burger", and he was Ed. She sucked and swallowed his dick like it was a freezie. They ferociously fucked and friendly fought. He choked her while he was beating it from the back. She choked him when she was riding him. He pulverized her pussy. She bounced hard on his dick. She came hard and she creamed.

When he was about to cum, she told him that she wanted to swallow his cum. He was fucking her while harnessing her up and down while standing up; she was taking it like a champ. When he was about to cum, he sat her down. She opened her mouth wide, jerk his dick with her mouth on it, and allowed the semen to shoot down her throat and on her chin.

Their sexual encounters were going on for months on in. Jalisa had no clue of what was going on, and Jules had no idea either. During that time, their mother, Mary Ann Ethel, passed away. Jules and Jalisa were grieving from her passing. Though JaTrina helped with the cost for the funeral and the food, she did not attend. JaTrina also did not go to the burial nor the recession. Jules and Jalisa conflicted with their sister about her actions.

During that time, Jalisa needed her space alongside with moral and faithful support from Terrance. Jules needed his space with moral and loyal support from Jazmine. However, because of Jules and Jalisa's absence in Jazmine and Terrance's lives, Jazmine and Terrance's bond grew.

Whenever their grieving subsided, Jalisa was more active in her and Terrance's relationship, so Terrance had to be sneaky. Jazmine

Black Pain't, Vol. II

wasn't trying to be sneaky, because Jules was too much of a simp to stand up for himself to get to the bottom of Jazmine's ways.)

"I wanted to see if the friendship was still there," Terrance sympathetically says, trying to tug at her conviction.

He removes the sheets and comforter from his bed to roll them up into one pile while she goes inside the bathroom to urinate and straighten herself out to look presentable before she leaves. He throws the sheets and comforter in the washer, puts some laundry detergent inside it, and turns on the heavy-duty cycle to remove the stains and smells of lies, deceit, lust, and carnal energy.

She comes from walking out of his bedroom, strutting and still looking as fine as she wants to be. She checks her phone to see a message from Jules. She texts Jules back and puts her shoes back on. "It was good and fun as always, Terry-Bear. I'll see you later."

"Aight, Jazzy-baby," Terrance says as Jazmine grabs her belongings and exits.

Terrance sits there for a moment to relax his mind and body from all the sensations. He grabs his phone to scroll through social media. He ironically comes across a meme that says, "It feels like the best sex comes from the person you're not supposed to be having sex with." He laughs to himself, closes out the apps on his phone, and calls Jalisa with zeal.

Jalisa answers the phone, saying, "Terrance! Hi, honey!"

"Hey baby, what are you up to? I miss you."

"Awww, I'm just waiting on my girls' parents to come pick them up. I'm still at the dance studio."

"Daaannng, dance practice on Sundays? That shows a lot of dedication... y'all forreal forreal!"

"Well, we leave for our dance competition next week. I gotta make sure they're sharp and precise."

"Nah, I get it... I admire that," he says. "How long will y'all be gone next week?"

"From Friday to Sunday. We raised enough funds to not only travel on a charter bus there, but we made enough money for our hotel and food. The girls just gotta bring money for other expenses."

"That's dope, Jalisa! I'm happy for y'all... what are you doing afterwards?"

"I'm going to grab this food and head to your place, I can just shower over there.."

"Sounds good to me......"

"Okay, well, I'll let you know when I'm on my way over!"

"Aight cool! See you soon."

As they hang up, Terrance quickly gets up to deep clean his apartment. He vacuums from the living room to his room. He makes sure that there is no evidence of another woman being present there. He lights some incense to rid the aroma from sex in the air. He washes the few dishes that were left in the sink, cleans off the stove, and arranges the living room.

Before he showers, he sees a notification from Jalisa, saying, "I got all the food and wine bagged up; I'm headed your way."

Terrance replies, "Cool. I'm about to hop in the shower too!"

Jalisa texts back a smiley face emoji. Terrance hearts the emoji, putting his phone on the bathroom counter. He turns on the shower head and steps in to wash away his iniquities. While scrubbing soap over his body in the shower, he hears the wash machine's alarm. After washing the soap from his body, he gets out of the shower to dry and put on some lotion. He then puts on some grey sweats and a wife-beater. He goes to put his sheets and comforter in the dryer and turns it on.

Terrance has his apartment looking fresh and smelling wonderful. He has soft music playing. He dims the lights in his living room to set the mood. Precipitously, the doorbell rings. He rushes to open the door to see the beautiful and humble Jalisa holding bags of food and a wine bottle.

"Hey, beautiful," he says as he grabs the bags, hugs her tight, kissing her neck. He then sits the bags on the counter in the kitchen while Jalisa shuts the door.

Jalisa takes off her shoes to sit them by the door. She takes off oh her coat and walks into his bedroom to hang it up in the closet. She takes a double look at the bed once she sees it with no sheets or a comforter. Her intuition frissons her, sending her internal warning waves. She unconsciously ignores her feelings and walks back to the kitchen, struggling against her deliberations.

In the kitchen, Terrance is taking the food out of the bags. Her perspective of him changes in that moment. Something is completely off about him and she's too aware of it. Wanting to put the pieces together in her puzzled heart, she cannot help herself but to ponderously ask, "Where is your bed set?"

"Oh, they're in the dryer.... haven't washed them in almost a month. When you said you were coming over to spend the night, I had to wash them," he responds.

Something does not sit well with Jalisa in that moment, but she cannot figure out what it is that turned her spirit. Something is pulling at her heart strings, but she cannot hear the song. She tries to block out the chaos that's causing commotion within her, but everything just seems so loud on the inside.

Terrance notices Jalisa's altered mood and asks, "What are we cooking for dinner?"

Jalisa snaps out of her inner turmoil, trying to answer Terrance's question. She answers, "Fried chicken, mashed potatoes, and French cut green beans!"

"Sounds delicious! I'll start pealing the potatoes."

"Can you get the pots and the pans that we need, please?"

Terrance grabs the pots and pans from the cabinet next to the sink, placing them on top of the stove. He then strolls into the living room to play a R&B music playlist from his mounted television. When he goes back into the kitchen, he sees Jalisa washing and seasoning the chicken. Terrance grabs a bowl, the bag of potatoes, and a small knife to begin cutting the skin off the potatoes.

Jalisa sneezes twice, saying, "If ya ain't sneezing, ya ain't seasoning your food well enough!"

"Bless you," Terrance says.

"Thank you, baby," Jalisa says while rubbing the seasonings in the chicken. "So how was the show? What did you do afterwards?"

Terrance has a quick flashback of him and Jazmine fucking next to where Jalisa is standing. He immediately snaps out of it to answers, "The show was good! Before the show, I met with Sir Charles!"

"Sir Charles the singer?" she asks with significance.

"Yup! He was talking about booking me to perform at an upcoming event! That made the show more fun and purposeful! I just came home to clean up. That's about it."

Jalisa notices something is off in his answer. She cannot quite put her finger on what's tainting her spirit. She manages to ask, "So when's this next performance?"

"At the end of this month; it's going to be grown and sexy. You should come."

"I would love to come! I love how creative you are. Gives us something to relate to on an artistic level."

"I agree, you should dance to one of my songs...."

The idea lifts Jalisa's spirit. She asks, "Which song?"

"I'll send you some to see what you can choregraph from it. We can do a music video to it, too."

After placing one of the pots on the stove and twisting the temperature to turn one of the circles on, she does not take long to agree to the project and says, "I would love to. Hey, but not anything sexual, I won't be degrading myself to any of that. I won't be no half naked girl in your video."

Terrance snickers, saying, "Hey, hey, you won't even do that in real life, why would I give it to the world?"

Jalisa adds blackseed oil in the pot while confidently and temptingly asking, "Is that a challenge?"

"At first it wasn't but now it is," Terrance playfully answers after peeping the sexual energy Jalisa is delivering as he cut the potatoes with a little bit more precision and aggression.

"What are you willing to do for it?"

With the knife in his hand, he dramatically hugs Jalisa from behind while she places the chicken in the rectangular crockpot. "I'll kill for you girl; I'll get on one knee for you girl....... dedicated my life and put seeds in you girl......"

She blushes and says, "Stooooopp, Terrance, you're not serious! You would have been did it, if you were... you're probably not really ready for all that and it's okay....... for now."

"What you mean for now?" Terrance asks, turning on the other eye on the stove.

"You know... for now...."

"No, I don't know what you mean by 'for now,'" Terrance replies as he takes the bowl of potatoes he just cut up and pours water in the bowl to clean the potatoes.

As Jalisa slowly places the chicken in the pot, she says, "How long are we going to be on this level, Terrance? Are we even truly working on going to the next level? I have needs too, I want to take it there with you, but I just don't want that to be it. Terrance, I'm ready to be someone's wife... someone's mother. I'm a garden but we're living like concrete......"

Terrance marinates on Jalisa's words as he adds butter to the pot of potatoes. He says, "I understand where you're coming from Jalisa. And those are my intentions...... I just don't have a time limit. All thought we were in this forever?"

"Yeah, but what would we have to show for it? What are we building together?"

"I guess we don't have anything to show for it; I thought we were building upon our relationship?"

"Terrance, we've been together for a few years now, what exactly have we built?"

"Trust?"

"Okay, I'll accept that one."

"Love?"

"Okay.... have we built outside of trust and love?"

Black Pain't, Vol. II

Terrance gets irritated from Jalisa's questions but does not express it to her. He sighs as a relief to combat the anger building up within him. Feeling trounced, he says, "I guess...... I guess we haven't built anything," watching Jalisa flip over the chicken and putting the pot's top back on it. "So.... what would you like to build?"

Instantly, Jalisa answers, "A covenant, marriage, a home, children, more businesses... like what are we really doing? Did you want to stay in the condo for the rest of your life?"

Jalisa's questions tear at Terrance's ego. He feels like he's been pushed into an uncomfortable corner. "I hear what you're saying Jazzzzmmaa....Jalisa!" he stammers almost saying Jazmine's name aloud. He internally prays that she did not hear what he called her. "I guess I have a lot to consider, and I promise to make a stronger effort to build. When's your team's next performance?" he asks.

"We are going out of town next weekend to compete in a dance competition," Jalisa confidently answers.

"I know y'all gon' win!" he says while making a mental note of her being gone.

The dryer's alarm goes off, and Terrance hurriedly wipes his hand on a nearby napkin and walks to take the sheets and comforter out of the dryer. While Jalisa continues cooking, he takes the bed set to his bedroom to put the sheets of a cheater back on the bed. He feels the conviction and ignores the feelings.

Before going back into the kitchen, he picks up his phone. He unlocks it to tap and scroll to his messages. He clicks on Jazmine's thread, types, "Free next weekend?" and sends.

Meanwhile, Jalisa is in the kitchen, trying to shake off her perturbed moods. She notices Terrance's strange demeanor as he comes back to the kitchen. She looks away whenever Terrance puts his phone on the kitchen counter and comes to stir the potatoes.

Terrance's phone chimes. The sound takes Jalisa's temperament away; it made her feel a way. A way she normally does not feel from Terrance. A way that tries to push her intimate feelings towards him away. A way that made her want to interrogate him, so he has no way out but to come clean on who's texting him.

"He normally does not even be on his phone when I'm around him," her intuition said to her.

After he finishes typing, he sends the message. Then he goes to his music application on his phone and plays *Love and Happiness* by Al Green. He proceeds to stir the potatoes, singing and stomping his feet to the music.

Terrance's silliness warms Jalisa's heart. She cannot help but to smile and sing along with him. As the night continues, she sort of forgets about the chime as they spend their night eating, laughing, and watching the movie, *Who Cloned Tyrone?*

While watching the movie, Terrance tenderly rubs Jalisa's juicy buttocks. Jalisa grasps his hand and pulls it away. After a few minutes, he crawls his fingers back to her ass and begins rubbing on it again. "Staawwpp," Jalisa coquettishly says, clutching his hand and pulling it away again. "No, means no!"

He stops, trying to figure out what he can do to seduce her. It does not take him long to ask, "You want a massage?" in hopes that she agrees to it. He sings, "Saaayy yes, or sayyy nooooo."

Jalisa blushes and asks, "Does this massage come with some cuddling?" she replies.

"You can't answer a question with a question."

"Well......" Jalisa says with some sassiness.

Terrance submits and says, "Sure thing. Anything for you."

She sits up from his lap and asks, "Where you trying to do this?"

Terrance sings, "There's a meeting in my bedrooooom!"

Jalisa gives off a fake snigger, all awhile thinking about his bedsheets twists her heart again. Her inner voice gets louder about something that she can't clearly hear. She watches him stand up with his hand out, gesturing for her to give him her hand. She allows him to help her up with a look of resistance. *"He knows what he's doing,"* she contemplates to herself.

He grabs the remote from the couch to turn off the television. He guides Jalisa into his room and sits her at the edge of his bed. He removes his wife-beater and tosses it by the closet. He takes off his grey sweatpants that has been showing his dick print all night long.

Jalisa takes off her tights with her laced panties still on. She removes her shirt with her sports bra still on. She turns to lie on her stomach. As Terrance makes his way to her, she takes off her sports bra. "Where's the oil?" she asks. "You're not going to give me a massage with those dry hands...."

Terrance hastily hops out of the bed to inanely run to the bathroom to get his oil from out of the cabinet. He pours some into his hand as he calmly walks back into the bedroom. With his hands in the air, he slowly climbs on top of the bed and then on top of her lower body with all leg strength. She can feel his manhood on her Georgia peach.

He affectionately commences to tenderly rubbing on her back. He rubs his fingers up and down her spine, doing circles around it with his thumbs, going up and down on the sides of her spine, and gently going across with his knuckles. He makes her back crack in so many places. "You needed this massage," he wittily says. "All that dancing you be doing."

"Gotta keep up with the girls...." she replies while deeply enjoying the massage. "They keep me young."

After a few minutes, she pulls him down to feel his skin on hers. He embraces her from the back as they both lie on their right sides. He interlocks his fingers with hers, he brings her in closer. She can feel his dragon breathing heavily on her butt as he nibbles on her ear.

She slowly and tightly rolls her body against his. He catches her rhythm and revolves his body with hers. He kisses her ear and eventually makes his way down to her neck. She removes her hand from his and reaches back to grab his hair to guide where she wants to be kissed.

She turns around on her back still directing his head movements. He obeys as she makes him suck and kiss her nipples. She pushes his head down to her stomach, arching her back with strong passion. She temporarily let go of his head to take off her panties as they stare into each other's eyes. She lies back down and grips his hair again.

She spreads her legs and directs his head to kiss around her pearly gates. He kisses her inner thighs; he kisses above her thighs. He turns her over to kiss the back of her thighs. He makes his way back to her neck to kiss it while gyrating. She reaches back to try to pull his boxers off, but then he snatches her hand and pulls it away.

He smooches down her back, driving her to arch it again. He kisses her ass and spreads her cheeks. He kisses and licks up and down between her pussy and her butthole. He sucks on her pussy and sips it. He spits on her pussy and licks all the spit off it. He tongue-kisses her pussy while maneuvering his tongue in many directions. She gasps every time. She seizes his head and rubs it while he feasts on her essence.

"I want it," she seductively says while looking back at him.

He removes his boxers. He smacks his dick on her clit, making her moan in awe. He slides it up and down her pussy before inserting it. As he inserts it, she wheezes for air, moaning and grunting with his every stroke. He rolls his body so she can have every inch of him. He slides in and out of her like he's trying to clean the inside of a sink.

He tries to speed up, but Jalisa tells him to slow down. She loves the long, slow, and deep strokes. To keep himself from nutting, they switch positions. Jalisa sits on top of him, slowly grinding on his shaft. Terrance grips her ass and massage her body to take away from his thoughts of cuming.

They switch positions again. Missionary position is Terrance's favorite position when it comes to Jalisa, because she's beautiful and hyperbolic. They both get to watch it go in and out together. They can stare at each other. It's a tantric vibe when it comes to this religious position.

Jalisa already came a couple of times, and she wants Terrance to cum for her. He starts to speed up, ramming his pipe deep within her. She hates to be pounded but allows Terrance to cum how he likes.

He pulls out to ejaculate on her stomach. Jalisa notices how very little sperm came out onto her stomach, and Terrance usually has enough dick for round two. He sits over her for a moment with nothing left to let out. She notices how he hurriedly tries to get her a hot rag, indicating that their sexual encounter has come to an end.

When he comes back in the bedroom to hand her the hot rag, he immediately put back on his boxers. She dabs her rag on her womanhood and wipes away the sperm on her stomach. She hands him the towel to toss in the dirty clothes hamper, she self-consciously grabs her panties from the side of the bed to put them on.

"Are you okay?" she asks.

He answers, "Yes, I'm great! Are you good?" with much conviction.

"Yes, you done?" she asks in disenchantment.

He stammers on his response, knowing that he wasted some of his sexual energy on Jazmine earlier. He is able to say, "I'm just tired my love, real tired. You still want some? I can give you some head."

His answer throws her off. Her feelings incites her facial expression. She says, "No, it's okay. We can just cuddle."

Her response condemns him. His energy concocts his lies and his wrongdoings, but he tries to avoid them. To him, it seems like Jalisa already knew what he has done, but he trusts that because of her ignorance towards his whereabouts, she cannot possibly find out what he's been up to. Him and Jazmine has been very private and discrete with their communications and meet ups.

As he climbs back in the bed to cuddle with her, Jalisa struggles to snuggle with her mind on overload. Minutes later, she can hear his breathing change, implying that he's fallen asleep. She tries to bump him to awaken him because usually they would talk all through the night, but he leaves her hanging again.

"What changed?" she asks herself. *"Did the sex ruin us? He ain't been the same since we started having sex. I mean what could possibly......."* Her thoughts are interrupted when she sees his phone light up on the dresser drawer. She can barely tell whether it was text notification or a call.

"I wonder who that could be," she thinks. The urge to see what or who notified him pulls at her heart strings. She needs to know what's going on, and she will not be able to sleep with these thoughts shooting through her soul.

She struggles to get from under his arm. She pauses, thinking that he is going to wake up. When the close is clear, she stands to go by the dresser where his phone is. She trips over his grey sweats, making a slight thud. While standing, she pauses again, and makes sure that Terrance is still sleep.

Jalisa walks over by the dresser. She taps on his phone to make it light up. Upon tapping, she reads the name, Jazzy, in the notification. She tries to see if she can unlock his phone but does not know his code, and she does not have his face to unlock it with the facial recognition. Not being able to check his phone perturbs her.

Seeing the name taints her spirit. She grabs her phone and goes into the bathroom to investigate whomever this Jazzy is. She researches the name Jazzy on Facebook and Instagram to see who would pop up. Anyone that is a mutual friend of Terrance will inform her on who to investigate. Unfortunately, she is not able to find anyone by the name Jazzy that is mutual friends with Terrance.

She ponders on how she can ask him about Jazzy without giving her true intentions away. She deliberates that she may be able to just mention the name to see how he will respond. If she asks him about Jazzy and he gets uncomfortable or upset, then he's guilty. If he downgrades it, then he's guilty. If he gets angry with Jalisa for asking the question, he's guilty. Either way it goes, she feels that he's guilty of something that she has no idea of, or without proof.

Black Pain't, Vol. II

MY NOTES

Black Pain't, Vol. II

Chapter 7:
Bet

JaTrina comes back into Kemet from having a phone conversation with her brother. She sees how quickly the bar got filled. Knowing the other bar tenders need assistance, she squeezes her way through the crowd and finally makes her way behind the bar. She notices that one of her favorite co-workers are working this evening.

She enthusiastically says, "The Brave Braiveri, I didn't see your car outside...... when did you get in?"

"Hey, Trina! My car is in the shop, had my friend drop me off. I would have spoke before I walked in, but it looked like you was having a serious conversation."

"Yeah...."

"Everything okay?"

Trina grabs the pen and pad from off the counter where all the liquor bottles are stacked and answers, "I'm okay, that was my little brother......"

"I didn't know you had a little brother," Braiveri interjects.

"Yeah, the little snot, almost ruined my night."

"Little? How old is he?"

"Oh, he's like 27..."

"You made it seem like he was four years old," Braiveri proclaims as they both laugh. She takes the two glasses to the individuals standing at the bar. She takes another order from another patient customer and walks off to make the drink.

Someone at the bar buys Trina a shot, and Trina toasts with the random guy as he disappears into the club. Trina takes someone's order and walks next to Braiveri to retrieve the beer.

Braiveri asks, "Girl, how many drinks do men buy you every time you work?"

Trina ponders on her answer for a tad bit. With remorse, Trina says, "At least five."

"And how many times do you work here a week?"

"At least four."

"Wait, Trina...... you mean to tell me, on four nights a week, you are drinking at least five shots of alcohol........ that's twenty shots a week love...... I don't think that's healthy......"

Trina hands a customer their order as the other waiter takes the mixed drink to another customer. They meet back at the counter and Trina says, "I have a high tolerance.......I don't know......... I think I may be an alcoholic or immune to pain."

She takes Trina's comment in with empathy and prayer. She rebuttals, "What if you could be immune to self-love?"

Trina confusingly asks, "What you mean, Braiveri?"

"I mean what would sober you look like? They say sobriety is our biggest weapon; when was the last time you were sober? What if you started limiting your drinking and restricting yourself from alcohol. And you don't have to start big, you can take thirty shots this week, twenty shots next week, 10 shots another week, by the end of the month, you could be down to 3-5 shots; you can be sober you.... you can put that energy elsewhere.... or give your shots to someone else...." Braiveri concludes, having to walk away to take someone's order.

Trina ponders on Braiveri's suggestions. A woman at the bar waves her hand to get Trina's attention. Trina sees her and walks her way to take her order. She makes the lady a drink, grabs a beer out of the small refrigerator on the side of all the bottles that are stacked on a large countertop. She hands the lady her drink and beer and walks back to where Braiveri is standing.

"Yeah, so, like............ Alcohol destroys the liver over time like it can really ruin us.... especially an overuse of it. You can become addicted to it....... you're far too beautiful, real, and strong to allow something like alcohol separate you from your spirit, have you makin' unconscious decisions... that's why when liquor was introduced, they called it spirits because it removes the spirit out of the equation; alcohol destroys our core selves...... I'm only speakin' on this because I grew up around alcoholics. One drink used to turn into five. By the time they got on their seventh one, they was ready to fuss....... they was always ready to fight...... it was like they became someone else! I'm sorry, I hope you don't feel like I'm talking at you."

Trina fondlingly says, "Nah, nah, you good, sis...... go 'head. You tellin' me somethin' I need to hear right now."

"Okay, good................ But Trina, I realized that a life is too valuable for us to be giving it away to substances like alcohol. Give your life to a cause, give your life to a husband, give your life to a child, give your life to God, not something that's going to make you feel more broken......depressed, resentful."

"So you don't drink?"

"Ahh, baby, while I was in college, I had many wasted nights, nights I barely remember...... that's when I saw how that effected and controlled me, too; I became what I resented growing up...... but now, I'll have a glass of wine......... or, if I do drink liquor, my maximum is two drinks but then I won't drink for weeks. I am not going overboard ever again."

"I feel that."

"You deserve peace, Trina...... you deserve more than what you settle for, more than what you accept, and more than what you receive. Stop selling yourself short.... this world we live in will already do that, but you have to want better for yourself."

Trina marinates on Braiveri's encouraging words while she walks off to help some customers. Throughout her shift, she takes a few more shots but passed on shots to other female customers. She feels the alcohol influencing her hormones. She pulls her phone out of her back pocket to see a text from Jules, Jalisa, Tony, and a few other numbers that are not saved.

She taps on the unsaved numbers to see what men are reaching out, trying to either spend on her or get in between her legs. She reads messages like "Wyd" and "Wya" which are turn offs. She reads messages like "Wassup stranger" and other messages like "Wat you ben on?" She hates negroes who can't spell. These types of messages come across so counterfeit that they are all predictable. She knows where each conversation is going to lead to, and no matter how eager she feels to want some love and affection, the forced energy is just not worth it.

She wants something that she can feel. She wants to feel loved, respected, and she wants to feel something big reach the edge of her stomach. Only man to bring her that comfort and penetration last is

Tony. "*I hate this bitch ass nigga,*" she thinks to herself, knowing she's about to tap on his message that she's been ignoring for the last 18 hours.

The purr from her kitty sanctions her finger to tap on the message. He's asking her if he could see her later tonight. Trina scoffs and annoyingly texts back saying, "Why do you want to see me, Tony? So you can eat my coochie, fuck me good, and go back to yo ex and her newborn?"

After sending the message, a customer at the bar says, "Excuse me!" to get her attention.

Trina acknowledges him and takes his order. She makes the drink and hands it to him, saying, "Twelve dollars."

The customer hands her a fifty-dollar bill and says, "Keep the change."

Trina opens the cash register, puts the fifty inside, takes out thirty-eight dollars and tosses it into the tip jar at the bar. She pulls her phone out to see Tony's notification. She taps on it to read, "Yes, to the first two, but you're very wrong with that last one. Plus, I would love to talk and cuddle with you afterwards......"

The 'L' word and the cuddling always does something to the crux of Trina. She loves being caressed and held; she loves being private and intimate with someone she sexually trusts. However, she grows detestation whenever someone destroys that trust, because she nurtures to love them in many ways, a nurturing that she desires to have. Tony once provided that for her.

"Bitch ass nigga," Trina whispers to herself while grappling with the decision to either go against her morals or go to sleep feeling sexually satisfied. And Tony knows that Trina loves physical touch, it's just something about when a man caresses her body that sends a shockwave of fleshly intelligence through her veins. She spiritually can feel his hands on her neck while leaning against the counter by all the liquor, like a succubus.

Her temperature rises as she types, "Off in 43mins. Meet at my apartment in an hour and a half. That gives me time to shower." As she sends the text, her heart becomes weak. She can already feel the shame that is to come after he comes over, give it to her like she likes it, and disperses like he never cheated on her and broke her trust.

Tony's notification comes, and Trina reads, "With pleasure," internally, feeling her juices wanting to feel him now.

"Aight! Bet!" Trina types and sends.

As she unconsciously goes to take orders from customers, her intrusive thoughts take her on a mental flight. She flies over the fact that Tony is the second man she had ever been with in her twenty-eight years of living. The first guy she had ever been intimate with became her classic story of 'right person, wrong time'...........

(It had been three years since JaTrina moved out of her mother's house. She remembered turning 18 and moving into an apartment with a minimum wage job, rage in her spirit, hate in her heart, and determination to be on her own. She figured that struggle was better than the traumatic energy that lingered around her mother's home, provoking, and stabbing at her every move. She couldn't sleep at night being in that house, because even the dark reminded her of everything.

She hated living in that house. She can still see her mother's face as she watched her twin sister getting molested by their own father. During this time, however, she was still confused and perplexed as to why he suspiciously died out of nowhere. She remembered how happy she and her sister were; how his funeral was like a celebration for them.

She labored until she was able to move up as a manager, due to her gift of gab and willingness to work, network, and learn the systems of her job. She worked and explored ventures that she always wanted to do. She took boxing lessons and got into shape. She received her gun license after being taught how to shoot by a gun slinging, hillbilly named Samuel. 'Uncle Sam' is what she used to call him.

Once she turned twenty-one, she quit her job and stopped boxing to get her liquor license. She began working at upper class bars where white men and women tip enough to pay her rent for two years if she worked bars with happy hours and clubs with after hours. From Tuesday to Saturday, she would work strenuous hours to get the financial results she envisioned. She never wanted money to be a reason why she couldn't do anything she wanted or have whatever she wanted. She was a hustler.

Through her sister's nagging and eaves dropping on customers' conversations, she learned to be wise with her finances. Other than the insurances, stocks and bonds, and other residual incomes that she invested in, she moved into an apartment where people could rent to own. Each year, she would have rent paid in advanced, she would have the dividends flowing from her stocks paying for her insurances and other miscellaneous bills, and she would have money put up in savings accounts and an emergency fund.

She didn't like debt or owing anyone. Since she turned 18, she never asked anyone for anything which put a dent on her social life when it came to making friends and networking. She found solitude in her lonesomeness, and she didn't let people get close enough to her.

She did not trust men. The conversations that she would partake in while working at bars with men who were cheating, married men who were always lying, men who were very deceiving. There were men who were creating illusions for their woman to be safe and secure in while they hid their true feelings and emotions. Men being delusional with their spouses. Most of the men were inconsiderate, selfish, narcissistic,

Black Pain't, Vol. II

and undisciplined. There were men who were the type to treat they woman so good but still commit adultery. She grew to believe that the male species was terrible, mentally ill, stupid, dumb, and worthless.

Over the course of three years, she realized that for every 14 to 16 men she would converse with at the bars she'd worked, she would meet two to three women who were out cheating on their spouses. She thought that they could have been trying to get some 'get-back,' or she figured that those women had nigga tendencies that she didn't possess. She would never cheat on anyone. She didn't want a relationship because of it. 'Everybody livin' foul' became her motto.

There were thousands of men, and women, that tried to talk or run game on Trina at these bars. Many men who offered to pay her car note, men who wanted to pay her mortgage, men willing to fly her out of the country just for one weekend. There were married men, men in relationships, and men with irrational baby-mothers who tried to get with Trina. There were women looking for other women to get threesomes for their spouses. Gay, Lesbian, and Queer folks all wanted Trina.

Trina carried a spirit about her that was welcoming, safe, therapeutic, authentic, nurturing, and straightforward. Everyone she had seen in passing while working at these bars absorbed Trina's energy, they all wanted to feel or taste it for themselves. She hated that everything had to be about sex with people, not yet realizing that the common denominator with all these people was their own sexual traumas. Then mix that trauma with some liquor and it begins to alter your psyche, your rational mind; it goes straight towards your hormones.

One night, while working at her first 21+ bar/club, Kemet, a man in a fitted grey sweat suit, sitting on one of the bar stools with a buoyance she never seen before. He looked out of place. The verve of his demeanor was magnetizing. She wanted to know what he knew. She wanted to know what he experienced. She wanted to know where he was from and what was he doing here. He was observing the scene in deep thought.

Curiously, Trina made him a drink and drops it off at the counter on the side of him. "Here you go sugar, looks like you need a drink."

The man humbly said, "I think I've had enough to drink, ma'am, I'm sorry, I highly appreciate you, though," noticing her vigorous vitality. Her beauty provoked his thoughts. It was like he was seeing himself in her. His spirit turned its attention to her whole essence.

"Well, why you takin' up space at the bar?" Trina asked comically, hoping that he would reciprocate her energy.

"I get to see everything from right here."

"What you see?"

The man smiled and said, "I see us," while pointing to his pigment. "In a place where there's no production. A place where people get dressed and come to be seen....... they come to dance.... to drink their pains away, to sing and to rap when their favorite songs come on..........and to waste money and time. This does nothing for them, but yet... they come in every week to do the same things that they did last week and the other weeks before. They buy countless outfits just so they won't be seen in the same outfits twice.... I want to know the science behind this mentality."

Trina looked around to try to see what he sees but she only saw opportunities for her to make money. His judgmental nature made her feel as if he wasn't as true as she felt, but she met him where he was mentally and humorously asks, "What you think they in here celebrating? Failure?"

The man laughed and authentically says, "Hey, that's pretty funny...." while examining her through eye contact. "You should do stand up!"

Trina internally blushed, a sensation that she never truly felt before swam through her core. No one ever suggests anything that she should do artistically, especially a man. She played it cool and didn't react to it, feeling too gangster to show that he made her feel away. She responds, "Naw, not little ole me."

"Why not? I think you'll be good at...."

"Why you say that? I didn't tell no jokes just now. Plus, I got stage freight, I'll get up ther' and start shakin' like scripper..."

The man genuinely laughed and said, "See! Just go up there talkin' about your stage freight...... you could even talk about your bar experiences......... I know you've heard, seen, and experienced some crazy things."

His comments made Trina reflect for a moment at all her experiences at bars. Her favorite memories were the ones when she was counting all her tip money. She replied, "Ehhh, not too crazy and I don't think they would be funny..."

The man enthusiastically asked, "Okay, what was one of the last conversations you had at a bar?"

Trina thought about her last conversation from earlier with a woman who got into it with her boyfriend's wife. The lady told her that his wife is jealous because her and him are in love. Who ever knew that a human being could be in love with someone who is already married?

The thought of it made her chuckle on the inside as she told him about the story. The man laughed as Trina walked off to help other customers. For the rest of the night, Trina's nature and the man's effervescence conversed while Trina was in and out of conversations, serving customers.

He waited all night for her, hoping he didn't come off as a creep or a stalker. They took a few shots of tequila together, cheering to their newfound friendship. "Is she just entertaining me? Should I ask her for her number, her Snap? Should I leave?" he thoughtfully questions himself as he checked his smartwatch to see the time, 3:43AM.

"What are you getting into tonight, cowboy?" Trina asked him while cleaning the bar tops.

"I was going to ask you the same thing...." He yells loud enough for her to hear him while she walks off cleaning. He felt defeated. He doesn't want to come off desperate. "Besides, there's probably hella men, waiting for her, or she probably got a man at home," he thought to himself as she continued to clean. He allowed doubt and fear pull him out of the bar.

When Trina began putting up the bottles, her intrusive thoughts gave her doubt about the connection she just experienced with him. "He could be crazy," she thought to herself. However, she had been in these types of situations before. Between the mace and the Glock 40 in her Coach bag, she knew how to handle these situations if her hands couldn't do the trick.

Once she got done cleaning and putting the bottles away, her and the other bar tenders counted the tips and divided them up by the hours everyone worked. After she received the largest portion, she walked out and noticed that the guy at the bar was gone. She was a little disappointed that he left without saying anything. Maybe it was good that he left, and she did not have to let him down easily.

By the time she walked outside, she was relieved but dejected that he wasn't waiting on her. "Maybe he wasn't that interested," she thought. She couldn't help but to think about him on her drive home. She hoped to see him again.

Black Pain't, Vol. II

When she got home, she felt lonesomeness for the first time since she's been on her own. For the first time she felt a need to have someone around, someone she can trust, and someone worth giving her time and space to. She wanted to call her sister to talk to her about it, but she chose to stick it out and deal with it on her own.

A couple of weekends went by, he did not reappear. After a month, she dismissed the idea of ever meeting someone she was intrigued by, even though she still would search for the guy that she felt interest. After two and a half months, she decided to stop the search and accept the fact that moments come, and moments go.

Then one late night, he just so happened to show up. He sat at the same spot that he sat at the last time he was there. She noticed him right away. He noticed her. He told the other bar tenders that he was waiting on her to take his order.

The bar tenders informed Trina about his request. Trina couldn't help but to blush. Once Trina got the opportunity to take his order, she walked across to him, saying "Well, well, well....... hey, cowboy, back to observe and scout for more meat?"

"I'm vegetarian actually......... I came here for you."

"Oh, boy pleeeaaaaasssssseeeee, what can I get you?"

"I'm serious, but you can get me two shots of Bourbon."

Trina walks off to get the two shot glasses and the bottle of bourbon. On the way back towards him, she simultaneously poured the bourbon in both of the shot glasses until they were full. After she flipped the bourbon on the bar, she slid the glasses to him and then turned around to put the Bourbon back on the rack.

"One of them is yours," *he proclaimed while holding one of the shot glasses midway into the air.*

Tempted, Trina looked around for a quick glance, searching for an excuse not to take the shot. It was just something about him that she could not resist. Then the doubt rushed in like a warning, but she knew that if she takes this shot with him, she will give him the benefit, of the doubt, too.

    Meanwhile, he was internally praying that she will accept his generosity. Then he prayed that she'll give him the same energy that she gave him the last time he was there. After praying that she would want to take this token of gratitude, remembering when she gave him a round on the house. "REMEMBER, you saaiiddd I could repay yooouuu one day! It's been a long time and I think this is the time to repay you...."

    Trina rolled her eyes and said, "You weren't supposed to remember that!" She grabbed the shot he was holding up in the air. He picked up the other and held in in the air.

    "Cheers?" he questioned.

    "Cheers to what?" she curiously asked.

    "To newfound friendship!" he proclaimed.

    She smiled, she shook her head, said, "To newfound friendship," and apathetically took the shot with him. She instantly felt the liquor soar through her veins. "Why thank ya, cowboy."

    "My name is Quincy...... friends call me Q...."

    "This ain't no Love and Basketball, Q! Okay? I am not Monica....I think I like callin' ya' cowboy...."

    He chuckled, "I'll take it."

    "Ya' have no choice..."

    "What's your name?" he wondered.

    "My name is Trina........" she answered. Then she widened her eyes and held her fist out saying, "JUST... Trina...... don't call me anything else."

    "Bet...... never call you JUST Trina...... got it," Quincy comically says as Trina socked him on his shoulder; not too hard, but

Black Pain't, Vol. II

enough to make him feel it. As he takes on the pain, he calmly says, "Ouchhhh...... what you hit me for?"

"I ain't playin'......" she firmly said, letting him know that she is standing on business.

"Sorry," he said, rubbing his shoulder, and realizing the pain in his shoulder hurts more than he gave credit to. He viewed the confidence in her demeanor, but the liquor courage kicked in. He licked the three fingers he used to rub his shoulder one by one to let her know that he ate her little punch to the shoulder.

"Boyyyyy.... you know that hurt," she comically, but softly said, feeling a sensation from within. She walked off to help other customers.

Among customers and having to run to the back for more bottles, Trina and Quincy conversed, flirted, and caught one another's eyes when they were distant. They even took three more shots together.

At the end of the night, he asked her, "Are we going to exchange contact information, or do I have to come here and find you another four months and wait here all night just to talk to you?"

"Boyyy, you wasn't waiting on me...... nor was you lookin' for me... stop it...."

"I was my lady...... I came here during the week a few times when I had the time......You weren't here..."

"That's because I work at other bars during the week.... this is my weekend spot...."

"I didn't know bar tenders could work at different spots. Isn't that a conflict of interest?"

"I don't care who's interests it conflicts but I'm going to get paid regardless of who's in conflict with who, ya feel me? If another country takes over America, I'mma figure out their economic system and get paid... ya dig?" Trina confidently says.

Quincy is impressed and in admiration. He replied, "Aight! Bet!" while taking out money to tip. After placing the money down, he says, "I'll see you next weekend, Just Trina......."

"Byyyee-byyye, Q!" Trina said, clutching her jaws, because Just Trina sounds too much like JaTrina. She watches him exit. The other bar tenders teased her about all the attention she was giving him while she was packing up to leave.

He came back a few more times before Trina even gave him her cell number. They would text frequently, and he would still show up on weekends for more conversations and drinks at the bar. They would drink and talk, weekend after weekend. It was their regular occurrence.

Tired of only seeing her at the bar on weekends, he asked her out on a date one night. She was so confused as to what to do, what to wear, and what to say, because she had never been on a date before. She never let men take her out or do anything for her.

He was a gentleman. He picked her up, kept opening doors for her, bought her flowers, chocolate candy, took her to a Black owned vegan restaurant with live music. They drank and danced.

After their beautiful night out, he pulled up to her apartment to drop her off, and she invited him inside. While inside, she made him take off his shoes and walked into her bedroom to remove her shoes. He was impressed at her fancy apartment as he made his way to the living room.

He saw that she had a blunt, an ashtray, and a lighter sitting on her coffee table. He didn't smoke but he was always willing and ready to do anything with and for her. Coming back into the living room with him, she flopped down on the couch beside him, grabbing the blunt and the lighter. He watched as she inhaled and exhaled like she was a professional.

She tries to hand him the blunt and she sensed that he wasn't about that life from the beginning anyway. She asks, "Why don't you smoke?"

"Never had an interest for it...."

"I respect that... is it a problem that I smoke?"

"Nah, naw, of course not........ Why do you smoke, if you don't mind me asking?"

"You can ask me anything...." she claimed, feeling protected and safe around him.

Quincy looked at her deeply and said, "Bet."

Before he got to ask his next question, Trina hurriedly asks, "Why you always saying, 'Bet'?"

He slightly snickered and said, "Because 'Bet' is like a confirmation! It's like the deal has been made, the exchange of energy is agreed upon; 'Bet' is like saying, 'Amen,' or 'Asé' for my conscious folks."

"Bet," Trina said, vibing to his answer like she just learned something new. She was able to be transparent and open about her childhood. She told him about her hatred for her mother, how her and her sister were molested, and her relationship with her little brother. She told him about why she hustles and works constantly. It was therapeutic for her and helped her keep her mind from her past traumas.

He listened to her. He gave her compassion; he gave her eye contact. Trina did something that was long overdue, she cried. As she apologetically cried, he held her while she cried on his shoulder. He reassured her, he validated her feelings, and told her that her story is like a key to unlocking someone else's prison.

He told her about his life, too. How he came from a single-parent household. He has a big sister who lives in the same city. He went to college, received his bachelor's in business administration and a trade in welding while he was in high school.

After hours upon hours of talking about everything, they fell asleep on Trina's couch. When he awakened, he kissed Trina on her forehead to wake her up. Trina loved it. It sent goosebumps up and down her body. After their lovely night together, feelings emerged, and they were getting more intimate. She wanted more of him, and he wanted more of her.

One night, while playing and fighting over UNO at his duplex, Quincy kissed her. Trina has never been kissed before nor did she ever kiss anyone. They kissed some more. They both got aroused and wild up with passion and spiritual ecstasy. Trina deeply loved the sexual feelings that she was feeling.

Before they took it to the next base, Quincy asked her, "Are you sure you're ready?"

Trina embarrassingly said, "Yes...."

"Bet."

After her consent, Quincy took her to second base, sliding his tongue in her mouth. They touched and tongue kissed each other. She melted in his tough hands, guiding them for him to touch her buttocks and her breast. She loved the way he touched her. She wanted him to kiss other places as well so she kept throwing her head back hoping he would kiss her neck.

He finally caught on as she grabbed his head and forced it on her neck. She began moaning while he kissed and licked her neck. He ended up in the middle of her legs while they were on the couch, kissing and licking down to her breast. She removed her bra for him to kiss and suck on her nipples, and he did so, sliding to third base.

Trina was horny as fuck. She wanted to feel sexually quenched. She wanted to feel him inside her. She wanted his hands all over her.

Black Pain't, Vol. II

She wanted to be kissed and licked everywhere. She wanted some aggression; she wanted some 'move your hand.'
　　"Do you have a condom?" she asked.
　　"Yes," he claimed.
　　"Go get it..."
　　"Bet."
　　Quincy hopped up, ran into to where his coat was, and grabbed some condoms from his coat pocket. He hurried back and Trina stood up to take off his shirt. She was kissing him while she took off his belt. She laid back on the couch to give him time to remove his pants and boxers. She observingly watched as he put the condom on.
　　When he was done, she pulled him down to her on the couch. He gently inserted himself inside her. She gasped, moaned, and grabbed him desperately. As he began slow stroking, he was struggling to keep himself together. He pulled out to keep himself from nutting to quick.
　　Trina looked at him and concerningly asked, "What's wrong?"
　　"Nothing, nothing; it's nice, wet, and tight in there," *he replied, breathing deeply.*
　　"That's a good thing, right?"
　　"Yeah, give me a second," *Quincy answered.*
　　After catching a second wind, he slid himself back in with more confidence. He slow stroked her for a minute or two, watching Trina enjoying every stroke. He was deeply hitting all the right spots.
　　Trina became so emersed in all that she was feeling inside. His rhythm was off, but it was good enough for her first time. She wanted more. She wanted it to hurt a little more, she wanted some pain. She wanted to feel it all!
　　"Take it!" *Trina softly said, moaning.*
　　He began stroking but he was struggling to keep himself together. He would stop occasionally to keep himself from nutting. She

noticed that he was having a hard time keeping himself from nutting too quick. She was getting turned off. She wanted to continue. She was already in the mood. Then he came after two minutes of being inside her. He pulled out, and they both disappointedly watched the tip of the condom fill up with his sperm.

"*Is that it?*" *she asked him.*

"*Nah, nah, that ain't it....*" *he hurriedly took off the condom and tossed it in a nearby trash can. He put on another condom and got back on top of her with every ounce of energy and life he had left. His dick wasn't as hard as before, and she felt it getting soft.*

She sorrowfully pushed him off her. He sat back feeling terrible. Before regretting the entire session, she asked him, "Can you give me some head?"

He got down on his knees while her legs were spread on the couch and gave her some head. She enjoyed it and was able to cum twice, but she didn't give him the satisfaction of knowing that he made her cum. Even though he was the perfect gentleman, his sex drive and sex game was weak.

After their first sexual experience, Trina thought that maybe it was a bad night for him. However, it was the same almost every time they would have sex. She was conflicted because everything was good except the sex. He grew insecure because he could tell how she would still masturbate after their two, maybe three, minute sessions. He grew sexually depressed, thinking she would go to other men for sex. It lingered into their rapport as to which it felt as if it was a dark cloud everywhere they went and within everything they did.

He used to be happy and enthusiastic, but it was like his pride and ego abandoned him, knowing he couldn't satisfy the woman that he loved. It wasn't that serious for Trina, but she grew distant knowing that he was acting weird because of his pathetic sex game. Dates and text

Black Pain't, Vol. II

messages reduced. He stopped coming to the bar, being that he was too embarrassed to show his face around her.

It was absurd to her that something so fun and therapeutic could end because of their sexual performances. Was opening themselves up sexually to one another worth losing their friendship? Maybe they shouldn't have had sex in the first place. If they would have gotten together, she would have found out later about his frail sex game. Would she still be with him? Why does sex have to be the determining factor? Women have their needs, too.

It took Trina some time to get over Quincy. Even though he did not sexually perform well, he was still a down to earth person; a loving individual. He was someone that Trina didn't mind being around. She missed who she was when she was around him.

She seen him out and about a couple of times after their 'trial relationship run.' During both occasions, he was with a different woman. "Guess the first one learned just as quickly as his premature ejaculation," she said to herself the second time she seen him out, feeling some type of way that he brought a different woman to a bar that he knew she worked at.

By the time she got the chance to tell Jalisa about her first time, it turned into a heated argument because Jalisa felt as though Trina should have told her whenever Quincy and her got close outside the bar. This is when Trina began keeping secrets from Jalisa's critical and judgmental views on how Trina lives her life.)

The last forty-two minutes of her shift takes forever. Her mind is battling back in forth with how good Tony lips are going to feel when he whispers to her divinity. She thinks about how good his shaft is going to feel deep inside her. Her body maybe at work, but her mind is in the gutter.

Thirty minutes left of her shift, Trina starts cleaning and putting away the liquor bottles. The anticipation appears at the bar and follows her around like a shadow. It's been months and she has that urge to feel a man's hands all on her; a man that knows what he's doing; a man who can give it to her like she likes.

Fifteen minutes to go, Trina and her co-workers split the tips. Trina folds her bills and exits in a jiffy. She rushes home to get in the shower, allowing the steaming hot water to calm her spirits. Once she gets out, she plays music from her phone, and dances while she oils her body. She throws on her robe over her bodice, slides some panties on, and puts on a bra for the visual.

Suddenly, the doorbell rings. Trina rushes to opens the door, trying to play it cool. Before opening the door, she can feel Tony's carnal energy slides through the tiny cracks of the apartment's door. She opens the door to see Tony smiling and enthusiastic about being there.

As she moves out of his path, The carnal energy fills the emptiness that surrounds the living room of the apartment. Tony observes her apartment, looking at all of the empty boxes along the packed boxes. He notices the blank walls that were once covered with marijuana or sexual art. He sees that she's in the process of moving but has not told him anything about it. He ignores his feelings and notices that she has on her silk robe. Trina's standing on business by her hallway, she does not care to converse right now. She wants it, and he can sense it.

They follow the carnal energy it into the darkness of her bedroom that had no form nor void but a soft light entering from the bedroom window. Tony grabs her from behind, grabbing her neck, and kissing her. The darkness and the carnal energy suffused themselves within them as Tony embraces the depths of her waters, making their own light in the darkness, and creating their own world.

Black Pain't, Vol. II

The room is filled with moaning, tension, sexual sound effects, weed smell, and Jazzmen Sullivan and Ari Lennox in the background singing *Sit On It*. He makes himself down her lane. As she covers her face with her hands, she thinks to herself, "*I should not be doing this…*" Suddenly, the anticipation hovers around her skin, giving her goosebumps.

He gently grips her panties, sliding them from her dark-oily legs. He massages and measures her bodice for a few seconds then stands to removes his shirt, tossing it to the edge of the bed. The eagerness commences to touch her as he eases himself into a sniper position. He pauses for a moment to watch her flower blossom in the silhouette. He worships the wet, shiny lotus by closing his eyes, and whispers a prayer. She widens her legs to peek amid her fingers to see what he is doing, "*Why is he taking so long?*"

"Asé," he says, slithering his head amongst her legs.

She can feel his beard on her inner thigh while the anticipation grips her torso. She throws her head backwards, ready to bless him with her dark, sweet tunes from heaven, and bless him with the essence of femineity. The expectancy for him to remind her of his lick-her-license thrills her as he gently pecks around her outer lips.

She can feel his hands grip her soft firm buttocks as he proceeds to feast. He slowly starts tongue kissing her inner lips for a second or two, just to pull his head up above it, humming, "Ooh shit Trina!"

The sound effect he makes sounded like he is sipping soup. He steadily lies his tongue back on her flower bed to commence. He stops and lifts his head again to make the same sound effect.

"No, no, no, no, no…" she whispers to herself as she clutches his head for him to surmise. It's been a minute, and her resistance encourages her to want more. He repeatedly flips, flicks, and flows his tongue on her clitoris. He rolls his tongue while making more humming sounds. That humming sound turns into a hymn that's familiar to her, but she can't quite put her finger on what he's humming.

Her body floats into the abyss as he makes his way to her urethra. He flicks, sucks, and licks. He puts his right hand's middle finger and ring finger in her mouth, she sucks on them. As she continues to get his two fingers slippery, he continues to flick, suck, and lick her womanhood. He takes his wet two fingers to tenderly insert them inside her while he flicks, sucks, and licks. He penetrates his fingers within her like he is trying to reach for something stuck in a small hole, touching her inner self.

He flicks, sucks, and licks while penetrating her insides with his two fingers. She's conscious during this euphoric trip as her legs vibrate.

"Right there," she professes.

With the same rhythm, he flicks, sucks, and licks while penetrating her insides with his two fingers.

"Don't stop! Right there! Don't stop!" She arches her back becoming still. She tightly holds her breath as she releases an orgasmic blast from her sacred place, gripping her legs around his face to internally walk through the doorway of heaven.

He rhythmically continues to flick, suck, and lick, but stops penetrating his fingers to press on her G-spot. She feels the sensitivity brewing, so she swings his head to the side like a hurricanrana to get him to stop before she squirts. She stares at him as if she just witnessed him commit murder.

He laughs and Trina asks, "What's so funny?" while trying to catch her breath.

"You almost broke my neck..." he jokingly answers, knowing he did an incredible deed. He sits there feeling the enjoyment of watching her shocking face and tensed body. He notices her close her eyes and lay her head back on the pillow.

"You almost made me squirt," she determinedly says as if she is afraid of the experience.

Her comment arouses his sexual desires. He playfully nudges her while stroking his ego. He tries to get her to see his decent size print through his briefs. Thinking that she fell asleep, he windier nudges her. "Trina..." he softly says with a chuckle. "Are you okay?"

Trina holds up her thumb with her eyes still shut. She then holds her other thumb up and says, "You get two thumbs up."

As she brings down her hands, the euphoric feelings she felt from her orgasm suddenly came down with them. Exiting heaven, she inaugurates to mentally question herself, *"How did I let this nigga back over here? Was it the liquor that ......?"*

She opens her eyes and looks at him. He chuckles again, asking, "What?"

She closes her eyes again, discerning, *"I hate this nig.... Ahhh... fuck it. Ahhhh!"* There is a slight pause before Trina completes her inner soap box, *"It was a good munch session though."*

Unexpectedly, the physical attraction, her long-thought interests in him coming over, that beautiful notion she once had of him from when they first met, and all their scenic memories all weather out of the room to be infuse with the pollution from the chemtrails in the open-air. The five and a half minutes of heaven was perfect, and it was what she needed, but now, just the spiritual residue remains.

She can hear him going into his pants to retrieve a condom. "What are you doing?" she softly asks.

"I'm getting a condom..."

"A condom?" she ponders. *"Damn, am I still not the only one he's fucking? What is he protecting himself from? Oh, he can hit that other bitch raw, but don't wanna......"*

"Give me five minutes," she gently but annoyingly says aloud at the same time he tears the golden package. As she pulls the covers over her body, she can feel his energy dive in disappointment. She hears his urges going to war with one another along with him dropping his pants back down on the floor, tossing the condom in her small room trashcan. She can feel him slithering his way under the covers like the snake he is while coddling and cuddling her. She instantly feels the beat of his drum, pounding away on her butt cheeks.

Moments later, the beat gradually stops, the nurturing hold that he has on her inflates, their new norm of disconcertment fills the room. They both can feel the disconcertion fill the room, crashing into the music, altering the mood. Their demons appear from the energy of the discomfiture, dancing to *Church* by BJ the Chicago Kid, featuring Chance the Rapper.

"You good?" he asks to combat the stroppy.

"Yeah, I'm good.... I just needed a break, you tryna snatch my soul?" Trina asks rhetorically. They laugh in unison to fight the discomposure, but the discomfort is too powerful to overcome, especially for Trina.

While swimming in the sea of dismay, and their demons dancing next to Trina's bedroom door, he asks, "You still coming to my graduation, right?"

"Why should I after you embarrassed me muthafucka?" Trina's consciousness contemplates, but aloud, she replies, "Of course, Tony... Why would I miss that? Plus, my lil' brother's girl is graduating with you."

He instantly says, "Just making sure. I know we haven't really been on good terms."

"Because of your STUPID ASS, TONY!" Trina internally says.

Black Pain't, Vol. II

"Guess who the school got to speak at our graduation!?" Tony enthusiastically asks, trying to avoid Trina's rage.

"Who?"

"Dr. AKiera Peseshet!"

"Ain't dat the lady who videos you be watchin'?"

His passion grew, "That's her! She just recently started a book campaign to fight against the Ban on Books!"

"She gon' come talk her shit huh?"

"You already know!" Tony laughs.

"Bet! I guess I'll be there."

Another awkward silence disconnected them. Their demons began dancing against Trina's thoughts and feelings. She grins, but her slight smile is defeated by the confusion that has contaminated her mind and her heart. Tears begin racing down her face to hide from the demons that continue to slow dance in the room.

Trina's skeletons come from out of her empty bedroom closet to give comfort her. Tony's skeletons exit out of Trina's closet to sit stand by the bedroom door. Trina's skeletons walk away to stand next to a rug by her bathroom door. Her skeletons remove some dirt that is under the rug.

A few minutes go by, Trina's tears go through a process of precipitation to form a dark cloud in her brain. She brainstorms ways to get him out of her apartment, hopefully out of her life. Trina's karmas suddenly appear to watch the dirt get muddy from the precipitation. Tony's karmas appear from the mud to mingle with Trina's karmas.

She can feel Tony's body get heavy from falling asleep. She pushes her cheeks against his stomach to wake him. Tony instantly opens his eyes to feel the spiritual uproar going on in the room. He hears Trina's sniffling and sees her rub her eyes in indication that she has been crying.

"Are you okay?" Tony concerningly asks.

"Nah, I'm not okay," Trina says firmly. "You can't sleep hur, Tony. I don't feel comfortable having you around."

Hurtfully, Tony asks, "Why not?"

"I don't think I can keep doin' dis witchu, Tony. We fakin' it. You know I don't do dat pretendin' shit like everything is okay wen it ain't! I can't keep doin' dis witchu...."

"You been fakin' it? Or have I been faking it?"

"You heard what I said...... Stop actin' like you don't feel it. Our vibe ain't the same, Tony. Whatever love I thought was thur, just ain't thur no more," she irately says as her voice cracks.

There is a long, harsh pause. Tony rises to view Trina lying in bed without the courage to look at him. He takes another moment to process Trina's comments, he does not want to believe that she does not love him anymore, but bravely asks, "You don't love me anymore, Trina?"

In fear of her wrath, Trina's skeletons run back into the closet while Tony's skeletons continue to wait for him at the bedroom door. Trina's karmas disappear after walking Tony's karmas to the bedroom door to await with his skeletons. Their demons continued to slow dance to the Adina Howard song that's playing. Trina hesitates to answer his question. The sharp silence pierce through Tony as he awaits her answer.

Trina admits, "I can't love you right now, Tony," she pauses to listen to Tony's internal distress. "I seen how this stage play plays out too many times. I don't wanna be a burden to you, Tony, because I tak' time to heal."

"So, this it for us, Trina?"

Trina interjects and firmly replies, "Hur' you go wid dis ol' bullshit, Tony! What you think was gonna happen? What? ...... I was jus' gon' let that shit go easily. You act like I cheated on you nigga."

Tony interposes, "It's been a year since it happened......... And the baby ain't even mine."

"So! ... you still fucked the bitch behind my back!" Trina turns around to see the nonplus look on his face. He's speechless, as always.

Tony finds the audacity to say, "At least I told you.... Can I at least get that?"

Trina dramatically gathers herself as if she just solved a crime, and asks, "What if the tables were turnt, Tony? What if I would have cheated on you, Tony? Sucked another nigga dick, let him beat it from the back, and didn't tell you for a couple of weeks. Would you would have taken me back?"

Tony reflects on Trina's remarks and questions. He truly wants to say that he would not take her back if she would have cheated on him. However, his ego wants to say that he would take her back just to prove a point that he does not justly have. He cogitates for too long as Trina interrupted his mental processing.

"'Xactly nigga.... Ion even kno' why I deal witchu no-mo Tony. You hurt me knowing I was already hurtin'. I would never do you like that," Trina turns her back towards him.

Tony is speechless. All he can think to do is to apologize. Apologize for pressing on the ideas of love and loyalty, opening Trina's heart to the ideas, and deceiving her. Apologize for not having the discipline and courtesy to just say no, and the decency to leave past connections alone.

Trina interrupts his thought process, "Say something my nigga damn! Acknowledge what I said at least!"

"I'm not ignoring you; I promise, I am not ignoring you, I'm letting what you said marinate," Tony says softly, snatching Trina from behind. He wants to be able to take the *pain* away, to inhale the hurt that she senses behind his actions. He's helpless. He knows Trina is the type of woman that has been through so much in her life. He ruined the assembly that Trina once wanted to assemble with him. This was Tony's final moment to take full responsibility for destroying their foundation by walking away from it.

"But is that what she wants?" Tony thinks to himself.

"Hold me," Trina demands. Even though he's already holding her, she does not feel the grasp that she once felt.

Tony grips her tighter with the last ounce of hope he has for their "relationship," but he knows that he lost her. Lost her trust, lost her love, lost her best interests at heart. He gradually makes his way out of the bed to put on his clothes.

Tony stands by Trina's bedroom door while their demons stop dancing. His karma and skeletons come standing next to him as he proclaims, "I love you, Trina. This is not a goodbye, this is a 'I see you later.' Probably not tomorrow, probably not next month, but I believe that we'll find our way back to each other."

Trina grunts, says, "Okay," and turns around to pull the sheet over her shoulder.

Tony stares at Trina's nonchalant attitude in weakness. *"There is nothing left for me to do,"* he contemplates in his thoughts, but not aloud. His heart resists, telling him to stay while his mind and his body tell him that he needs to leave.

Trina continues to lie there in emotional *pain*, wondering why the same *pain* follows her every move, why that *pain* guides her thoughts, why that *pain* taunts and haunts her, and why that *pain* loves to torment her.

While the *pain* continues to chew at her, Trina hears the door shut, switching her mind to how Tony was before they got together. She thinks of his sweetness, his strong presence, his intellect. She remembers how he always had her back and remained calm in chaotic situations.

Trina's mind switches to his sneakiness, how he never told Trina about his ex-girlfriend, and how he was able to be around her without even mentioning that he had been inside another woman.

Her mind shifts to the time frame of when he could have possibly had sex with her, *"was it around the same time they had sex together, did he bend her over, did he eat her out? I know his nasty ass ate her out; did he let her suck his dick; how he had the audacity to pretend like he wasn't on any fuck shit! How this mutha fuc....."*

"WHY MEN AIN'T SHIIIIIT!?" Trina screams aloud while punching the pillow, trying to break up the thoughts that are parading in her mind.

Her mind proceeds as she closes her eyes to address them from within. *"Why do men live like this? How can a man be pursuing one woman that he claims he loves, but go fuck another woman? Is this cheating? I guess technically we never made anything official, but doesn't this count as disloyalty if we were trying to build something?"*

As Trina's subconscious intervenes, she gets up to take her cotton green robe to cover her nude body. She allows her spirit to lead her into the living room to her weed tray. She flops on the coach to retrieve the tray from under her couch. Not having the energy to roll, Trina feels joy to see half of that blunt that she rolled this morning lying in the corner of the tray.

Trina grabs the lighter from her coffee table, next to the scented candle. She sparks the blunt, deeply inhaling the smoke. She exhales, permitting the smoke to escape through her nose and from her mouth. As the stress eases, she continues to smoke her blunt while accepting the deception.

She gracefully walks back into her bedroom to get her phone from off the dresser and goes back to the living room. She flops back on the couch to scroll through her social media feed to block out the mental war going on through her head.

I should go to his house and tear up some shit but I ain't gon' do it because I'm a changed woman, Trina internally says with a slight grin. She lays the phone down on the arm of the couch, reaches up for a blanket that is lying on the head of the couch, and throws it over her. She violently lies down on her side, facing the back of the couch. She crouches while closing her eyes.

She monitors all of her invasive thoughts and images in her mind until she's able to calm her breathing. Hating that she wants to be held, she falls asleep.

~

The next morning, Trina awakens to silence and the sun beaming through her window. She gets up to search for her robe to cover her naked body, sits down at the edge of the couch, and says a short prayer to herself.

"Asé," Trina says as she reaches for her phone to read her daily bible scripture. After reading, she screenshots the scripture and swipes and taps through her social media pages to post the screenshot in her stories for her followers to see.

She then swipes and taps to her contact list to text the owner of Kemet to see if she can work a shift this upcoming Friday. She feels like she could use some quick and easy cash. She lies back, looks at her phone to see if she has any other notifications, and lays the phone down on her chest.

Moments later, the owner texts back, saying, "Sure. Can you get in at the end of Happy Hour? That's normally when a larger crowd of people begin to show."

After texting back, Trina rises to walk into the kitchen, tosses her phone on the dining room table, and opens the refrigerator to see what she can eat fast for breakfast. She decides to make herself some breakfast cereal with the last pint of almond milk that is left in the refrigerator.

She grabs a spoon from out of a kitchen drawer and sits down at her dining room table near her phone. She scoops and lifts her spoonful of Raisin Bran cereal into her mouth. While eating, she gathers all the thoughts about last night. Feeling inspiration, she grabs her phone, unlocks it, and closes out all of the applications. She then taps and scrolls to get to the memo pad application.

She types........

Dear Lord,
Please grant me the strength to leave fake niggas alone.
Especially those who appear one way but act a different at home.
Lord, teach these niggas what it means to be mature and grown.
Teach women the game so the truth we can know.
provide me with the eyes to see through men's lies and deceits.
grant me the serenity to stop deletin' texts that could be use as receipts. give me the energy needed to not hold the grudges that I keep. Lord, please help me be all that I can be.
keep weirdos and silly scenarios away from me.
Can I have a vacay just for me?
a couple of days where everything's okay just for me?
Can I go to gas stations and lames won't say anything to me?
Lord, tell my mama to rest up, and that I'm sorry for not showing up to her funeral; Lord, the past still hurts till the day, You know?
Gotta get to the commas, I need my money in numerals.

No need for your validations when I already know I'm beautiful.
Imma boss, can't see myself workin' in a cubicle.
When ya real a lot of fake shit happens because the world don't know what to do with you.
Lord, I've been a humble servant, and all I see is You blessin' hoes that will do anything to make bands?
Getting paid from they looks, body types, and they OnlyFans?
Lately, I realized that your loved ones are your only fans.
made a lot of in my life but I should never had made amends.
My ex not only lost a great person, but he lost a friend.
And if h-

    Trina stops writing when she suddenly feels her phone vibrate. Her daily devotion gets cut short when she reads a text from her sister, Jalisa, saying, "JaTrina!!! Wake uppppp!!!! Let's go to church!" next to the prayer hands emoji.

    Trina smacks her lips, texts back saying, "STOP CALLING ME THAT!" and finishes eating her cereal.

    "Be there in thirty, wombmeeee."

    Trina mumbles, "I'm only wombme when she wants something." She then types, "Whatever..." and presses send.

    Three dots appear on Trina and Jalisa's text thread, indicating that Jalisa is typing a response. A half a second later, Jalisa responds, "I love you, too Ja... I mean Trina!" with a kiss emoji.

    Trina reads the text and aggressively drops the phone back on the table to lift the bowl up to drink the milk. She then drops the bowl gently but hostilely on the table with rage building from within her. She gets up screaming, "UUUUGGGGHHHHH! JALISA!"

Black Pain't, Vol. II

Trina quickly walks to her bedroom, flops on the bed, and throws the covers over her head in anticipation of her nagging ass sister. She ludicrously positions herself in comfortable but uncomfortable positions under the cover with frustration. "I should have changed those locks when I had the damn chance," she says as if she's talking to someone in the room.

Trina decides to lie there until Jalisa's annoyances arrives. She internally accepts the day as it will unfold while staring into the covers. She then closes her eyes to get her last 27 minutes of rest.

Trina dozes off, and *she intrusively imagines Jalisa bursting through the door with an innocent, girly facial expression, skipping her way towards Trina's bedroom. Trina's waiting behind the door with a baseball bat, ready to take Jalisa's head off.*

As Jalisa walks in, Trina swings. Jalisa is able to dodge the swing in Neil from the Matrix form. She cartwheels her way out of the door with Trina still swinging the bat, trying to dismantle her legs. Once Jalisa is fully out of the door, Trina hurries and closes the door, tossing the bat on the floor, and doing her B-Boy stance. Trina suddenly and scarcely awakens to Jalisa repeatedly ringing the doorbell.

She hears, "JaTrina! Com' oooon, Sis! You know I got the key!" Seconds later, Trina can hear keys jiggling from her bedroom, the door being unlocked, and Jalisa's squeaky voice getting louder and closer to her.

"JaTrina!" Jalisa yells, walking into Trina's room, looking around at how filthy it is. She makes a face and says, "It smells like Tank and Adina Howard been in here! Get Up, Trina! I told you I was going to be here in thirty."

Still lying under the covers, Trina dully states, "It's been twelve minutes, Jalisa."

Jalisa innocuously considers Trina's statement and says, "Well, this is church, and I want a good seat. You know church is the only thing Black folk can show up on time for." Jalisa opens the curtains in Trina's room, allowing the sunlight to fill the room with its cheer.

"That, and during the times that clubs let people get in for free, before the liquor close, and happy hour. Oooh, we looovvee happy hour," Trina boringly claims, rising with the cover still covering her head. "Jalisa, church is the laaasssttt place where I would like to be today. Can we go get breakfast....... unlimited mimosas? Sunday-Funday?"

Jalisa removes the cover from over Trina's head and rhetorically asks, "And let this church outfit go to waste?" Jalisa scoffs and concludes with "Chile pleeeaassse....." and lies her handkerchief at the corner of Trina's bed before sitting down on it.

Trina notices what Jalisa just did and states, "You bein' extra with that shit..."

"I just know what my lil sister be doing on her spare time...."

"Oh, please, like you and Terrance don't be fuckin!? You be talking all that holy shit but be fuckin' like animals."

Uncomfortably, Jalisa says, "Thaaaatt's not any of your business..."

Instantly, Trina says, "But you can be all in mine?"

"All I said was it smells like Tank and Adina Howard was in here doing the nasty, I didn't say anything else.... not who, what, or how. Now come along, take a quick shower, and get dressed, sister...... please."

Trina grunts and hisses as she gets out of the bed and drags her feet towards the bathroom. "Why are you soooo pressed about church, Jalisa, damn?"

"It's not church that I'm pressed about Trina......" Jalisa falters. "It's just....... well, ever since mama passed, I've been having this strong desire to be around my siblings........ We all we got, JaTrina."

"Don't call me that........"

"Sorry..."

"Where yo' man at? Why you never take his slimy ass to church witchu?"

Trina's question makes Jalisa think about the Jazzy name that popped up on his phone. She says, "He works his second job on Sunday afternoon. I don't want to take away from his rest."

"But you take away from my rest?"

"Yeah, but no, because you're off on Sundays...... matter of fact, you were off last night, too, wasn't you? You could have come over to our dance competition, humph?"

Trina turns on the shower to avoid answering Jalisa's questions. She hears Jalisa talking but her words are distorted through the sounds of the shower and the steam. When Trina gets out of the shower, she notices Jalisa laying out different outfits on Trina's bed.

"Uhh......Jalisa? What are you doing?"

"I'm dressing you...."

"Bitch this ain't Build a Bear.... you ain't dressing me! Da fuck?" Trina says stepping back into the bathroom to brush her teeth.

Feeling like Trina's being rude, Jalisa stops what she's doing to address Trina in the bathroom. She says, "I used to dress you when we were growing up. What's the difference now?"

Trina stops brushing her teeth, spits, furiously says, "I was depressed and suicidal, Jalisa. I didn't care for clothes," and went back to brushing her teeth.

"Oh, I can't tell the difference."

Trina gurgles the mouthwash for a few seconds, all awhile contemplating if Jalisa is being for real or sarcastic. After she spits, she says, "You can't tell the difference between me being depressed and me being my normal self?"

"Nope!" Jalisa answers.

"What you mean 'No?'" Trina yells as she dabs some oil in her hands. She rubs her hands together to rub it on her face in circular motions.

Jalisa comes back arrogantly, saying, "I don't never know when you're genuinely happy, Trina. Hell, you seemed happy with Tony. Matter of fact, what happened between you two? Y'all still together?"

While being naked in her bathroom, Trina hurriedly but softly puts on oils, saying, "We not off this happy question, Jalisa."

"Okay, what about it?"

"I have more fun than you!"

"You having more fun than me is crazy."

"Yes, more fun than you."

"Prove it!"

"Jalisa, you not about that life, sis; come on now."

"You don't know that. You don't know what I'm capable of."

Trina tries to find some fear in Jalisa's eyes and says, "Okay, bet. Let's go on a girl's trip. Just me and you."

"When?"

"Girl, you know I'm as free as a bird, you're the one who be busy, Pearl Primus."

"That's actually a compliment......"

"You're welcome."

Jalisa ponders for a moment and says, "Aight, after my girls win this upcoming competition, we can go to celebrate the victory!"

"Ooohhh-kay, but, what if you.... lose?"

"Then we'll go so I can feel better. I'll hit up my travel agent to see if there are any specials and deals going on."
"Bet."

Black Pain't, Vol. II

MY NOTES

Chapter 8:
deoxyribonucleic acid

He rises from praying on his rug for the fifth time today. He neatly folds the small rug until it is able to fit in his leather backpack. He puts the rug inside the backpack and walks towards his desk to grab his keys and his phone. He notices a few notifications on his phone, taps them to quickly view them, checks the time, and rushes out of the office.

It's Friday. It's been a long week of paperwork, meetings, and long hours, but this is better than the job he had before he was promoted. It's been a quite some time since he sat down and communed with his best friend.

Black Pain't, Vol. II

"*Are we even friends anymore?*" he wonders within, driving to Kemet, reflecting on the many conversations had, and the people who would come and go. It was like Black people's version of the show, *Cheers*. It was truly his favorite spot to wind down and bring the weekend in cheerfully. "*Trina used to have everyone rolling,*" he cogitates as he concludes the reflection.

He can't even recall the last time he's been in a bar, but he knows that Kemet has always been a haven. It is a much-needed conversation that needs to be had between him and his best friend. They've been knowing each other for far too long to have this amount of distance.

He's been pondering on this for some time. However, with his newest promotion, his newfound faith in Islam, along with Jazmine's willingness to let him spend time with his daughter, Miracle, on weekends, he believes this is just the perfect time to reconcile. Especially with everything going right in his life.

While walking into Kemet, he observes the changes that's been made. He notices his best friend sitting down at the bar. He walks over, clears his throat, and says, "Peace, peace; peace, brother."

His best friend stands to his feet to embrace him with a brotherly hug and says, "Alvin Johnson!" He catches himself and humbly corrects himself by asking, "Or is it Alvin X?"

"Darryl!" Alvin cannot help but laugh, which makes Darryl laughs. "It's actually Alvin Muhammad," he answers. "How you been, brother?"

"Better now that you're here, fam. A couple of rough patches but the stitches healed up. I'm getting my doctorates, so I've been busy with that...... Umm......ahh man, the district moved me up to teaching high school Black History. They figured that my class was too advanced for middle schoolers."

"Bismillah, that's awesome, god....... Ahh man, that's great to hear. I know those high schoolers love you, right?"

"Only because I give them knowledge that they won't receive anywhere else. My fault brother, can I buy you a drink?"

"Ahh, brother, I haven't had a drank in about...... two to two and a half years now? I'm losing track. I'm a sober soul."

"Oh, wow; that's dope, my brother. Congratulations on that, I know that takes a lot of discipline," Darryl says as he waves at one of the bar tenders to get their attention.

"Yeah, man, wasn't easy at first but, over time, you just replace it with something else. You remind yourself on why we shouldn't drink and the impact it has on our bodies and our minds. Just another one of the white man's tricks."

"Can I get an Old Fashion please?" Darryl asks the bar tender while handing them his card. "Start a tab!" he yells as the bar tender walks away. Darryl then turns to Alvin and asks, "My bad, what were you saying?"

Alvin does a light chuckle and says, "I was just talking about why I gave up drinking, that's all. I was saying how I replace those urges with other things."

"Other things like what?"

Alvin takes his time to answer, "Prayer...... I pray five times a day; I exercise about four days a week at the Islam Learning Center. I read and study the Quran, taking Arabic classes online.... so much to replace the poisoning that we put in our minds and bodies."

"That's enlightening......" Darryl apathetically replies as the bar tender lays a napkin and the Old Fashion on top of it. Darryl freely takes a sip of his drink and asks, "So what's good and new with you, Al?"

"Ahh, man, staying strong in my faith. Converting to Islam opened up many doors for me. Allah was able to reunite Jazmine and I so I would be able to see Miracle... ummm...... I got a promotion at the job; no more dealing with White Devil John anymore - praise be to Allah for removing me from that colonizer - and..... ahh, man, just finding ways to eternally feed my people. With not only food, but food for thought, food for the soul......know what I mean?"

"I get it, I get it... wow brother.......I'm proud of you man; congratulations on everything. You deserve it, brother! How's fatherhood?"

Alvin hesitates, but fixes himself to say, "Ahh, man, fatherhood is the best hood; I pray that every Black man who's a father can stand erect and do what they have to do to be in their children's life.... but tahh, umm; it's been iffy, too, brother, real iffy... I'm not going to lie........ and don't get me wrong, I'm happy that I get to be around her, but nothing about her screams me.... nothing, from her eyes to the way she is."

"Her eyes? What you mean by her eyes?"

"My eyes are light brown, and Jazmine's eyes are damn near light green. Where did she get these dark eyes from? She doesn't have my nose or Jazmine's nose. She doesn't have my ears nor Jazmine's ears! So what am I supposed to think, especially knowing the type of woman that Jazmine was?" Alvin asks with persuasion. "Then, bro, Miracle is very artistic; very gifted...... I kept thinking this ain't me, nor your mama, so where is she's getting her artistic expressions from?"

Darryl considers Alvin's claims, searching for reasonings and explanations. Giving Jazmine the benefit of the doubt, he says, "Maybe that's just the intelligence of our youth. These babies being born during this age are remembering they're the true Gods of the Earth. They are..."

Alvin interpolates, saying, "Yeah, maybe so.......... but we're all true Gods of the Earth. Even the ignorant ones...... that still doesn't explain the dark eyes, the nose, or her ears. She does not have my complexion nor Jazmine's complexion; she doesn't have Jazmine's hair nor my hair, brother! I can't keep ignoring my intuition."

"Hmm.... I feel that family. Damn.... so what you gon' do?"

"I've been thinking about getting a DNA test."

"A DNA test?"

"Yes, that's the only way I'm gonna know for sure. My intuition kicks in when I'm around her. I can't keep ignoring it. I must know. Miracle deserves to know who her true father is. Jazmine needs to come face to face with her truth as well."

"How are you going to get one? There are no testing centers open on weekends. At-home DNA kits aren't reliable. How are you gonna pull that off?"

"Jazmine needs me to watch Miracle from Thursday to Sunday...... she says she's going to 'be out of town' as a graduation present to herself. I'm going to take off work so I can watch her. I'm scheduling an appointment for Thursday."

"Do you really wanna do this? What do you expect Miracle is going to tell her mother? 'Daddy took me on a field trip to the doctor's office? They took some blood from me, too, mommy!' Any mother would flip out if you don't communicate that......"

"I got to, Darryl.... this ain't about what Jazmine may think! It's for my sanity....... Wouldn't you want to know?"

"Yes, but........" Darryl says, trying to find the right words to say. "I don't know. I see where you're coming from, Al."

"Think about it if you and Patricia had a child.... and the chil..."

Darryl interrupts him and says, "Patricia and I don't speak anymore, Al."

"Ahh, man, what happened?"

"Nothing happened per se because we never really, truly began," he responds while shaking his head. During that time when you got into that car wreck, Patricia found out some stuff about me, Dr. Carson......stuff about Tony....... 'somebody' told her that we were the womanizer crew, and she didn't want any parts of that."

"Ahhh, man..." Alvin adlibs with sympathy. "We all were pretty harsh and unfair to our women."

Darryl gives Alvin a confusing glare and replies, "Are you speaking for yourself? I was never mean or conniving towards our queens, man."

Alvin calmly responds, "What about what you did to Ella?"

Darryl ponders on his situationship with Ella and enthusiastically says, "Nah, nah, bro, she doesn't count! She was doin' her thing with other men, and I was doing my thing with other women............ We were on the same page about that."

"I hear you, seven, but at what point do we hold ourselves accountable for those types of outcomes. You knew that was going turn out bad, you knew that was going to go left, but you still drove that route."

"Like I said, Al; her and I were on the same page about that. We never disrespect each other in the midst, we never lied to one another; we got regular checkups."

"And what page are y'all on now?"

"Oh, that book ended long ago, playa! No beef, no malice!"

"Oh, okay, so the science teacher had nothing to do with your decision for ghosting Ella?" Alvin asks as a quick thought pierce through his skull. "Oh, speaking of the science teacher...."

Darryl objects and says, "Okay, you got me on Ms. Hall. Only because I went back to Ella after I ghosted the science teacher."

"But then you ghosted Ella again when you met Patricia, brother! You have a track and field record of cutting women off while being inconsiderate of their feelings and their spirits.......and then all the confusion, the insecurities, the sexual residue it leaves behind," Alvin says while pausing for a moment. "A cat can always sense another cat's smell. It's like what Malcolm said...... 'the Black woman is the most disrespected and unprotected person in America.' We have not been held to the fire for all of our war crimes against the very persons who should be in our corners......"

Darryl gives Alvin a blank stare and says, "Look who's calling the kettle a pot and a pot a kettle.... what about you and Jazmine? What had you fighting Tony in the parking lot from you wanting to put your hands on her?"

"Brother, no one can tell the difference between salt and sugar. I've always been a one-woman man, and I aspire to be a family man, too. Jazmine just didn't want that. I wanted to be a man to Jazmine at a time when she was just looking for fun. When Miracle came along, I tried to be a father, when she wasn't trying to have anything to do with me. The only thing I'm guilty of here is the fact that I cursed her out. I wasn't fighting Jazmine; I was fighting to see a life that I help create."

"That's not the story I was toooooollllddd......"

"That's because you did not hear the story from the source, brother. The truth can get mistranslated when it falls on deaf ears. The only thing I was guilty of was cursing her out. I was fed up and that was the most effective way of getting her attention at the time. I did not want to get the system involved...... but...... That's how I have custody of my daughter now....... Jazmine and I are fundamentally cordial enough to co-parent."

"Then what's the purpose of the DNA test when you have that opportunity to be a father?"

Alvin searches within for the answer and says, "For my truth, Darryl. I'm not stupid," Alvin smoothly says. "And since I know the type of person that Jazmine.... was.... I want to know the truth about Miracle. Then my soul has the answers for me to be fully present and all in when it comes to raising her."

"What if she's not yours?"

Darryl's question sends Alvin on a mental timeline to when him and Jazmine were "talking." He remembers it like it was yesterday.......

(The Truth's perspective: Alvin left Jazmine's house in a mental frantic. On the ride home, he got angry with himself for feeling like a fool. He couldn't believe what had just conspired at Jazmine's apartment. He thought that he was not the type to be in a domestic dispute, and for it to turn into sex was like a movie playing in his mind over and over. He had never been in a situation like that before. "Terry Bear," he said to himself aloud.

The name would live rent free in Alvin's mind for a year before he finally began to get over the relationship with Jazmine. He would research that name on his apps to see who would pop up. He'd always have questions about that matter; questions that went unanswered and plagued his spirit.

"Were you with Terry Bear during the times when I was blowing your phone up late at night to see you? Have you ever sucked his dick and came home to kiss me? I know you nasty as fuck, so did you bounce

on him like you bounce on me?" were always the questions that flurried Alvin's spirit.

Meanwhile, Jazmine found out that she was pregnant after experiencing morning sickness. Her and her mother was in a frenzy. Jazmine had no clue who the father could be at that time, either. It was between three men that she had in rotation: Alvin, Terrance, and Dennis. Life was swinging at Jazmine all at once. She had just graduated from college, trying to find a steady career in management; she just joined the church and became a part of the choir, all awhile her mother breathing down her neck about who the father of her grandchild.

All in all, Jazmine endured the pregnancy alone, still attended church regularly with the congregation's arbitrations, worked from home as an operator for a computer-programming company, and found a part time job as a certified nursing assistant, a job she used to work when she was in high school.

Jazmine found a steady routine, making good money to support her and Miracle with her mother's financial help. She was able to get Miracle into daycare for free at her church, so that really helped her save a lot of money. She was even considering going back to college. However, life wasn't so precious when it came to her mother.

Jazmine told her mother that it was Alvin's baby, and that they've been in communication in deciding to co-parent. Tension grew between Jazmine and her mother. It was as if her mother was perturbed about Jazmine's entire pregnancy and the stories she told surrounding the pregnancy.

Meanwhile, Alvin isolated himself for a while to get mentally and emotionally passed him and Jazmine's relationship. He would occasionally go out to drink with Darryl on Fridays at Kemet. After a while, he decided to not be in such a funk. He began exercising a few days a week, he changed his diet, and found himself reading more. He received a promotion from his job, making more money, bought a house, and started dating again.

One evening, after Jazmine picked up Miracle from her mother's house, she got in an impactful argument with her mother about who the father was. Jazmine told her mother that Miracle's father was Alvin with so much uncertainty that the mother felt her unsureness. Late that night, Jazmine contacted Alvin by sending him a picture of Miracle sleep, with a caption that read, "This is your child, Miracle Knight."

The next morning, Alvin woke and viewed his notifications. He saw Jazmine's text and clicked on it with extreme anxiety. He stared at the picture while repeatedly rereading the caption for several minutes. With his chest pumping, he zoomed in to see the features of Miracle, but Miracle looks more like Jazmine than anything at that time. It took him time to process the situation, but he then exploded. He blew Jazmine's phone up, calling it almost 30 times before Jazmine even responded, telling him that she will call him back on her lunch break.

When they finally got to talk, Alvin tried his best to remain calm as Jazmine gave him a back story about how he was the last person she had unprotected sex with before the first day of her last period. She told him that she didn't find out until she was three and a half months. Alvin's mind twisted itself within the story; he accepted her timeline as truth, though it was the actual truth when it came to being the last person that she had unprotected sex with.

Confused and mentally disassociated, Alvin wanted to be in Miracle's life. He wanted to get to know her and make something happen with co-parenting. It took them some time to come to a consensus to meet. They met up at a public park and Alvin was so overjoyed; he held her, embraced her, and was very enthusiastic about the whole experience.

Jazmine loved the way Alvin was with Miracle. She trusted him. She allowed him to see her more often than usual, majority of the weekends through the next few months. One night, Jazmine allowed him to come over after he got off work to see spend some time with Miracle and help Jazmine around her apartment. With the erotic pressure high, Jazmine and Alvin were low key flirting with one another in various ways throughout the night.

After putting Miracle to sleep in the bassinet, Alvin put on his shoes and jacket to prepare to leave. He said his goodbyes, but Jazmine *met him at the door. Alvin felt Jazmine's energy and they immediately started kissing violently. All the grabbing, touching, and panting eventually lead to them fucking like rabbits. Alvin spent the night and that was the manifestation of their collective mirage.*

Alvin was around persistently. They were around one another a lot. It was like how they were after Jazmine graduated from college and moved back home, but it seemed like an obligation. Jazmine was growing weary of their partnership. They were sexing constantly; Alvin forgot how great Jazmine's sex game was. They were acting like a happily married couple who just had their first child.

After Miracle turned a year old, the honeymoon phase, and the eccentricity of what they were trying to be for Miracle, and for one another, all gradually expired. Jazmine and Alvin stopped getting along; they could never see eye to eye on anything. They ran into constant conflict about each other's parenting styles, the plans they had for Miracle, the school districts that they wanted to put her in, the need for Miracle to see a happy home, and the constant, back-to-back banter of how terrible they each were as people, let along as parents. It became unhealthy.

Miracle had to see them separate on bad terms. They somewhat agreed to him having Miracle every other week, but Jazmine began keeping Miracle from Alvin, causing conflict. Miracle had to witness constant fights and arguments. She had to witnessed Jazmine at her worst and Alvin at his worst. Miracle did not see Alvin unless Jazmine wanted to go out on a weekend or out of town.)

"Then I think it'll finally be time for me to move on with my truth of naivety, my obsessions with women that give me this sense of love that I crave, and my ignorance towards society's illusion of love. There I may find peace and understanding that will push me forward in life. I've been going to Humanistic Therapy."

"I respect that......" Darryl says while trying to get one of the waiters' attentions.

Black Pain't, Vol. II

Suddenly, Trina casually walks in, immediately sees Darryl and Alvin, and says, "Ahhhh shiiiit, say it ain't sooooo?"

"Trinnnaaa!" Alvin enthusiastically says.

"Wassgood stranger? Long time no see nor talk! You don' forgot about us, huh?"

"Just had to do some soul searching."

After a slight, awkward moment, Trina seriously but comically asks, "Well, did you find it?"

"Most definitely.... ummm....... I joined the Nation...."

Pondering, and with concern, Trina asks, "...Theee.... Nation from WWF...... ooorrrrrrrr...... N.O.I. Nation?"

"The Nation of Islam..." Alvin replies with a slight smile.

"Well alright, now...... congratulations, my brother! It's good to know that you're doing good for yourself," Trina meekly and enthusiastically says. She inquisitively asks, "How has your life changed then?"

"Oooh, a lot has changed........ Now, I'm actually living my beliefs, ya know? Like I'm not as angry and aggressive as I once were. I'm healthy.... I'm..."

Trina interjects and says, "That explains the agua......"

"Oh yes, definitely......I stopped drinking the devil's poison..." Alvin says as Darryl dramatically gurgles.

"That's noble of you Alvin... I'm happy for you...." Trina says. She then turns her attention to Darryl, asking, "You next?"

Darryl brusquely says, "Psst, nah.... I love pork and white women too much...... I'll get kicked out..." Trina laughs. Alvin unaffectedly chuckles, indicating that he still has a sense of humor.

As their night comes to an end, Alvin and Darryl depart from Kemet in hopes to continue their friendship, however. Alvin sorrowfully made up in his mind that he and Darryl may not be the friends that they once were. They are just on different paths, and Darryl just does not want to change.

~

That Sunday, on the religious side of town, it's a quarter to nine at 18th St. Missionary Baptist Church. Deacon David, Sr. paces back and forth in his office, putting his tie on while awaiting on Rayven and Tabitha's texts. After tying his tie, he decides to walk around the church, ensuring that the churches operations are running smoothly, and that everyone is in good spirits for church service.

He passes by the cafeteria to see church members preparing to serve breakfast. "God bless you all, good morning!"

As the members greet back, David swiftly moves pass the cafeteria and into the corridors to see other church members at their post. They were socializing with great love and cheer, anticipating when Pastor Washington will assemble everyone to pray over the work they have to do today. David waves and salutes many of them on his way towards the church's daycare center.

Before making it to the double doors, he receives a message from Rayven, saying, "Outside."

He replies, "On the way," and proceeds through the double doors. Inside the church's daycare center, church members who serve and work as the daycare teachers are getting the rooms, play areas, and tables in order for church service. He passes through the kitchen where some other church members are preparing breakfast for the children.

David ultimately makes it outside to see Rayven parked right in a handicap spot. As he got closer to the side where Rayshawn's car seat is located, Rayven gets out of the car, saying, "He finally was able to sleep through the whole night last night." She hands him the diaper bag.

"That's good," David claims while putting the diaper bag on. He opens the door and covers Rayshawn and the whole car seat with a blanket before pulling it out of the car.

"There's plenty of milk in the bag, some baby snacks that he'll enjoy, and some toys."

"Thank you..." David dryly says while looking around to see which church members are looking at this exchange.

Rayven's energy is depleted by David's awkwardness. She internally wants him to be vocal, nurturing, fun, and open about their situation. "Aight, well, ummmm...... text me or call me whenever church is over? I'll just meet you at your place if that's cool with you?"

"Oh, yes, yes, sure...." David timidly responds.

"Okay," Rayven says while getting back in the car and driving away.

David walks back into the church's daycare center to drop off Rayshawn to one of the toddler teachers. Minutes later he gets a text from Tabitha saying, *"I'm pulling in now."*

He takes a deep sigh and texts back saying, *"Coming."* He hands the teacher the diaper bag and walks right back outside to get Talitha and DJ (David, Jr.). He sees Tabitha pulling in towards the curb and parks.

First, Talitha exits the car with her eyes glued to her phone, barely even paying attention to where she's walking as if a guiding force is controlling her movements. She gives her dad a meaningless side hug as DJ gets out of the car to follow suit while on his phone. He tries to high five his dad without looking, David, Sr. catches his hand motion late, and they both swipe at the air.

After dad and son's not-in-sync air shake, Tabitha drives away without giving David, Sr. any acknowledgement. David then walks them to the church's Teen Bible Study program that allows teens to learn the bible from an adolescent's perspective. DJ hates the program and Talitha just stays on her phone the entire time.

While walking, DJ asks, "Why can't we just come to church service? Why do we have to go bible study for an hour and then church for another two whole hours?"

"Can never get enough of the Lord, son," David, Sr. responds as they enter the room with six other adolescents in there, waiting on the youth pastor to arrive with the same look of boredom and captivity. "Put your phones up whenever youth pastor gets here," David commands as Talitha completely disregards what her dad commands and DJ is looking like he's going to follow his sister's lead.

Black Pain't, Vol. II

David, Sr. walks out of the room and takes a deep sigh. He gaits to his office where he maybe can find some peace before his adult Sunday class. While inside his office, it does not take long for one of the members of the congregation come knocking on the door. "Yes, come in," David calmly yells with a sham smile.

A graciously lady opens the door with her motherly melody, asking, "Hey Deacon, you want sum breakfast from the cafeteria? It'll be served here inna minnit. Just seein' who all won't sum..."

"You're so kind! I would love some. Thank you, sister Sherry."

"No problem, Deacon," Sister Sherry says while exiting. "You want your door closed?"

"Yes, please," he answers as she closes the door behind her. He leans back onto the chair with his eyes, taking it all in. He takes in the position he is in in his life right now. He monitors his emotions and thoughts just to pray for strength to endure his self-made inflictions.

After several minutes of just semi silence, there is another knock at the door. In hopes it is sister Sherry with his breakfast, David sits erect and eagerly yells, "Come in!"

As the door swings wide, the choir director makes his way slowly inside while making sure no one sees him walking in. David surveys the outside from where he's sitting in confusion. As the choir director shuts the door, he put one hand on his hips and says, "Ummm, hmmm."

Knowing he cannot get loud and cause commotion, David makes quiet, angry gestures but professionally says, "Yes, sir.... how may I help you?"

With sassiness, Kenneth says, "Is this how you treat someone who was there for you when your little divorce was happening?" His voice gets louder, "Is this how you treat someone who was there for you during your little affair with that ugly, little girl?"

Heatedly but silently, David says, "Keep it down!" He tries to calm down with Kenneth's apathy irritating his spirit. "Kenny, now is not the good time to......"

"Well when is it a good time...? You obviously don't have time for me anymore," Kenneth interposes. "Which bitch are you fuckin' from the church now?"

"It ain't nobody! Please, just get out of my office!" David quietly yells, pointing toward the door.

"Well which nigga are you fuckin' with from the church?" Kenneth's says with a feisty attitude while folding his arms.

David points to the door again, saying, "Watch your mouth while you're in the house of the Lord."

"Negro, all those times you had sex in the house of the Lord, don't come for my cussin'......"

David stands and comes around the desk into Kenneth's face to intimidate him, knowing Kenneth likes a little aggression. Kenneth melts at his governing frame. "Boy shut the hell up in here," David aggressively but quietly announces as Kenneth grabs him, thinking that David was going to hit him. Kenneth's grab turns into a long-drawn-out intimate hug. They fight their urge not to kiss one another.

Unexpectedly, Sister Sherry walks in with a nice size plate in her hand, saying, "Alllrriiigghhttt, now, I got a hot plate fo......"

David and Kenneth hurriedly and flinchingly push away from one another, causing David to slightly trip over the foot of his desk as Kenneth almost fell into the chair. David tries to play off his clumsiness by reaching and walking toward the plate, saying, "Thank you, sister, thank you." After David takes the plate from Sister Sherry, she still stands there observing David and Kenneth's awkward energies.

Sister Sherry exits with her head shaking, Kenneth says, "That old hag better mind her business," while looking at David walk back to the other side of the desk.

David lays the plate of food down on the desk, saying, "This was the worse time you could have ever decided to come."

"Well when was it a good time? You keep avoiding the conversation that we need to have."

"I don't know, I got kids, I got work, I got church, I got....."

"I got this, I got that... blah, blah, blah....... ba-ba-baba, bye nigga," Kenneth projects while abruptly exiting out of the office.

David flops down on his chair, panting and trying to catch his breath. He gets angry with himself, feeling a surge of resentment and disappointment. He grabs the plastic fork and stabs at the eggs and hashbrowns on the plate. As he eats, he realizes how good the food is. He has not had anything to eat all morning. It helps put him in a better mood but the thought of Sister Sherry spreading what she saw plagued his spirit again.

The more he thought on the situation, the more meaningful it became. It helps him develop his Sunday school message for adults, like him, who's been dancing with demons. *"What happens in the dark, comes to the light,"* he told himself.

He slides the iPad that is sitting on the edge of the desk to him to tap it. He then swipes up, swipes right, and taps on the bible app. He types the phrase in the search bar and the app shows a similar verse to the phrase from the book of Luke, chapter 12. He strategically reads and writes down some notes. He looks at his time, realizing that he's a few minutes late to his class. He fills his mouth up with food, slid his notes within the crest of the bible as a bookmark then exits the office and strolls to the classroom.

When he makes it to the classroom, there are about fifteen members of the congregation in the room awaiting him. "Good morning, good morning, and good morning," he says while walking toward the front of the room. The moment he makes it to the front, he looks up and for a quick second he felt the eyes of the people in the room as if they see all of his deceits, his habits, his demons, and his dark aura.

Even with shame in his energy, he looks around the room and realized something. He hasn't had this many people come to his Sunday school class in years. After laying his book on the table next to the white board, he grabs an Expo Marker and writes Luke 12 on the white board.

"This morning, our topic of discussion is based on the disciple Luke's perspective, starting on chapter 12. Can I have someone read one through three, please?"

Black Pain't, Vol. II

One of the congregation members, Brother Rodney, raises his hand to read and David points at him in confirmation to read: "Meanwhile, when a crowd of many thousands had gathered, so that they were trampling on one another, Jesus began to speak first to his disciples, saying: 'Be on your guard against the yeast of the Pharisees, which is hypocrisy. There is nothing concealed that will not be disclosed, or hidden that will not be made known. What you have said in the dark will be heard in the daylight, and what you have whispered in the ear in the inner rooms will be proclaimed from the roofs.'"

David intervenes saying, "Thank you brother Rodney! Okay, class, what is this verse saying?"

"That what happens in the dark, eventually comes to light," Sister Winnie says aloud. "It's talking about how a man's dirt, their secrets, and true behaviors will ultimately be exposed."

"Exactly!" David says, pointing to another person in the room, who looks eager to speak. "Brother Derrick."

"There's a double edge sword to this scripture. One, yes everything comes to light and things can get nasty, we get that part; and sometimes people love to read into that type of exposure, but two.... listen to me now. Two, John 8:31-32 says that the truth shall set you free. So regardless, if someone gets exposed in a negative light or a positive light, exposure brings closure; gives people a chance to accept who they really are."

"Some people don't accept it," Sister Francis says.

"Why do you think that is, Sister Francis?" David asks.

"That requires work. A lot of inner work.... it's easy to take care of the external, the shell of the soul, but it's hard taking care of that spirit, that internal, that eternal.... we get lazy when it comes to that."

"Why?" David asks. "I'm only asking because a lot of people were never taught how."

"Yes, they have.... yes, they have, because sooner or later in your life, God came to ya........ God communicates with everyone all the time; people just don't listen. I remember...uh, I remember

God trying to tell me, this is when I was married now, He said, 'Francis, you got a good man. Leave yo ex, the one who couldn't cut it. Leave that man alone, he was not the man for you. You bankin' on history and not currently. Next thing you know, I lost that man....''

Another person in the room asks, "How did you lose him?"

"I can't tell ya'll that part now, get out my business, but just know.... what's done in the dark, comes to light! So be whose you are, even when no one's watching...."

David facilitates the conversation by saying, "Now, y'all know me, I like to leave with solutions, so what if.... what if someone was in the dark, but wants to come out to the light so they can stop living in the dark?"

Sister Francis says, "Deacon, this ain't no dog and pony show; everyone is entitled to their privacies and velocities.... we're not talking about going on .... on a... on a.... what's that thing that everyone be on on they phones? They tellin' they business?"

"Facebook?" someone yells aside.

"Yeah, the book of Faces," Sister Francis says as people laugh. "We're not talking about the telephone industry; we're talking about the evils that people do....... those are the things that need to come to light. So when you can see a person for who they truly are then you can move accordingly."

Someone knocks on the classroom door, enters, and announces, "Sunday Service will begin in 15 minutes."

"Okay, thank you," David says, acknowledging the church's messenger. As the messenger exits and closes the door behind him, David concludes, "Ladies and gentlemen, I appreciate your participation in today's class discussion, I think you all asks some really good, insightful questions; lets pray and meditate on those for Wednesday's Worship. Class is dismissed."

Black Pain't, Vol. II

MY NOTES

Chapter 9:
Sprint*Door*

They gradually, tiredly wake up from a much need nap. Yawning, stretching, and snuggling through their soon to be goodbye for a few days. She presses her butt up against his penis in hopes he catches her hint. He embraces her but does not give her the feat she's wanting. After a minute or so, she rises to sit at the edge of the bed with a quick look of disgust.

She wipes off the feeling, knowing what's to come while she's gone. Before she can stand, he gently grabs her from behind and falls back, pulling her down with him. They wrestle for a bit; she's resisting his hands from the places that she loves to be touched. "No, no, no.... don't try to get me going now, I already gave you the chance..."

"So.... give me another one..." he responds while clutching her neck, attempting to meet her sexual standards.

She closes her eyes in enjoyment, hoping he'll slut her out, hoping he does not cum fast this time, and hoping he'll show out. "Come on......" she says in a carnally demanding way. She gets out of the bed, holding his hand, guiding him into the bathroom.

In a sexual manner, she bends over to sit her torso on the bathroom counter. Her sexual appeal sent shockwaves throughout the elements of his body. Her demeanor seemed to have switch so quickly. He is not prepared.

"Let's have a quickie," she erotically says, wanting to be swallowed, devoured, and pounded.

Everything about her just arouses him. Her pretty face, her body motions, her voice, her sexual drive; her touch alone can make him explode right now. He already feels his penis pulsating as if it's already ready to bust. He tightens his booty cheeks to combat the feeling as he squats to lick and suck on her from the back.

After hearing her moans mixing with the rolling of her hips while he grips her pussy with his mouth, he measures how long he can last with his sexual strength at its zenith. He gives himself thirty seconds of his will power, divides it by the velocity of each combustive stroke that could cause a conducive collision, and it all equaled out to be that he really can bust at any moment.

As he feels her hands come from smashing his head in her ass crack while his mouth remains on her vagina, she then stops moving to cum. She does not tell him while he continues eating her pussy. After catching a second wind, she tries to push him off as a signal that she's ready to be penetrated.

"Come on, Juley, fuck me...." she aggressively says. "Fuck me please...fuck me now!"

Jules stands to feel her hand gripping his penis which arouses him in a major way, but it knocks off some strokes that he was going to give her. He tries to push her hand away, but she wants to put it in herself; he's losing strokes with every touch. She smacks his dick up and down her clit. She went side to side with it, moaning. He's losing strokes.

"Oh, shit...." he says aloud.

Ignoring his faintness, she slowly slides his dick inside her. She moans, rolling her butt up and down to feel him deep inside her.

"Jazmine...." he feebly says while she begins bouncing to and from on his shaft. "Jazmine...."

"Fuck me...." Jazmine aggressively says. Jules pulls out to keep himself from cuming. Jazmine grabs it saying, "Put it ba... put it back in.... please......"

Jules is able to hold his nut in, but he awaits a few more seconds before going back inside. Once he goes back inside, he realizes that he has a good ten strokes to give her. He goes deep inside her and holds before he starts thrusting. As he plunges, he takes a long deep stroke, ten; she moans in enjoyment. He gives her the same exact motion again, nine. He picks up some rhythm while repeating the same sequence, eight.

"Faster," Jazmine says demandingly.

Jules speeds up, seven, "Umm," six, "ooh shit," five, "Oh my god," four.

Jazmine sobs, "Harder!"

"Fuck!" Jules says giving her an extra six strokes as he tightens his butthole. "I'm about to nut..."

"Nooo, no, no wait... Juley, no..."

Three, two, Jules tries to pull out, but she does not let him, one. Jules steps back allowing the sperm to shoot out on her back. Jazmine moves her ass in a circle as he came, wanting more. Once he is done, he grabs a towel from the top of the cabinet in the bathroom and wipes her back off, then himself. She rises to turn the shower head on with internal disappoint.

As he stands over the toilet to urinate, she hops in the shower. Once he's done, he puts back on his boxers. He then puts on his clothes to get ready to take her to the airport. Once he gets done, he leans against the bathroom door while watching Jazmine allowing the hot, steamy water to rinse her body from the soap. His mind immediately begins thinking about this sporadic trip she's about to attend to.

He suspiciously asks, "How long will you be gone again?"

"Thursday thru Sunday," she responds while turning the water off and getting out of the shower. After grabbing the towel from off a rack next to the standing shower, she dries herself off and continues to say, "I'll be back Sunday evening. Ooh, matter of fact, I need you to pick me up from the airport Sunday evening. Do you work that night, too?"

"Yeah, but I can still come get you," he depressingly replies with an uneasy sensitivity, watching her wrap the towel around her bodice. He asks, "Who are you going with again?"

While rubbing some oil on her face in the mirror, she innocently says, "I. Told. You... I'm going with some of my sorority sisters from college. It's our line's anniversary." She does some sign language-like gesture with her hands, grabs the lotion, and exits into the bedroom.

"How come I never met any of your sorority sisters?" he asks, watching her remove the towel and tossing it onto her bed.

She thinks for a second and hesitantly says, "I... think... you...... have.... met one, or I told you about one... I don't know, it was something. I don't remember," all awhile putting on lotion.

"Oh, I didn't think so...." he says while gradually whispering into it with his energy feeling indifferently. "Why didn't you all celebrate after graduation?"

Without hesitation, she answers, "This was the most convenient time. Everyone was free......." She then grabs the panties and bra that was sitting on the edge of the bed to put them on.

"Oh," he says, coming to a dead end to his interrogation. He does not know anything about "Greek" life. He doesn't understand lines, line names, being "on-line," "set," probates, or what they stand for. They all sound like organized gangs to him. "Where's Miracle going to be? With your mother?"

After putting on her clothes and sliding into her crocs, she answers, "Nah, she'll actually be with her sperm donor. He picked her up earlier this morning from my mother's." She looks around for her keys, grabs them from off her dresser, and continues, "Alright, I think I'm all ready to go. Can you grab that suitcase for me, Juley? Thank you...." He does as she commands and exits the apartment to put her suitcase in the trunk of his car. She locks up and follows him to the car.

On the ride to the airport, Jules can't help but to get the impression that she does not want to talk to him. She turns up the music and she is too engulfed into what is going on in her phone. The ride was unbearable. Jules has so many questions but don't know how to go about asking.

~

Meanwhile, on the other side of town, Terrance is watching Jalisa rapidly getting props from a closet in her dance studio. He loves watching her doing the things that she loves. "I see you in that mode, 'Lisa...'" he states.

Jalisa asks, "What mode?"

"That mamba mode...... that I'm standin' on business mode!"

"Oh, Terrance, please......" she says.

"I love it."

"Thank you, Terrance; oh, honey, can you grab that box from off the shelf for me?" Terrance rises to get the box from off of the shelf that Jalisa pointed to. "You can put that by the door, too, we're taking that."

A young girl appears at the door, saying, "Coach Lisa, the charter bus has arrived."

"Thanks darling.... go tell the girls to grab their belongings and wait by the bus, here I come...." Jalisa says, watching the young girl run off to deliver the message. Jalisa looks at Terrance and says, "Ready or not, here we come."

Terrance grabs the boxes that Jalisa stacked and exits with Jalisa following behind him to turn off the lights. As they get towards the corridor, they see the girls rolling or carrying their bags towards the bus. As they all got to the bus, the driver got out to lift the storage unit under the bus. Terrance starts grabbing all the suitcases, duffle bags, and props to pack them neatly under the bus.

After all the girls get on the bus and get settled in, Jalisa gives Terrance a tight, sensual hug in appreciation for his volunteer work with her dance teams. She says, "Thank you so much, Terrance. I'mma miss you."

"I'mma miss you too baby," Terrance replies as the give one another a peck on the lips.

"Not too much in front of my girls now, I still gotta be example of a queen...." Jalisa says during their release.

"I know, I know..." Terrance replies. "I love you."

"I love you, too," Jalisa responds as she gets on the bus. After sitting down on the bus, she feels as though she should have asked him about 'Jazzy' when she had the chance.

Terrance walks to his car while viewing the messages in his phone. He taps on one of them that reads, "On my way to the airport now."

"Perfect timing, omw," he texts back as he drives toward the airport.

~

Jules pulls into the various terminals with different airline companies and thousands of people walking to and from. He pops the trunk as he and Jazmine both simultaneously exit the vehicle. He takes out her huge suitcase from the trunk and closes the trunk. He rolls it toward Jazmine as she's looking through her phone. They hug; they slightly kiss with no passion or emotional connection. Even though the hug is strong and drawn out, Jules cannot help but to sense so much distance between them.

"Aight, Juley.... I'll see you Sunday. Call you when I land!" She says while walking through automatic the sliding doors. She watches and waits as Jules gets back into the car and drives away. She calls someone on her phone.

"Hello?" the person says while answering the phone.

"Where you at?" Jazmine cunningly asks while looking out the sliding doors, hoping he was close.

"By Spirit airlines...."

"Alright. Here I come..."

Jazmine exits back outside and walks a few yards down the various outlets. The trunk of a 2017 Red Mustang GT rises, and Jazmine puts her bag inside, closes it, and gets inside the car from the passenger side. After a second or two, the car drives off into traffic.

~

Jules went to work shortly after dropping Jazmine off at the airport. He texts her during his lunch break to see if she got to her destination safely. After lunch, as he spends the rest of his day working, he keeps looking at his phone every twenty to twenty-five minutes, wondering if Jazmine has text him back. A tense feeling evokes his spirit.

Once he got off work, he tries to call Jazmine, but the phone keeps going straight to voicemail. His calls going straight to voicemail has been a common theme during the last year of their relationship. While at home, he cannot help but to think intrusively about where Jazmine is, what she's doing, who's she with, and how is she when they're apart like this. To end the battle with his thoughts, he decides to make deliveries until he is dead beat tired.

Friday morning comes, and Jules awakens to see that Jazmine never responded to any of his text messages or calls. He feels like it is one of the most inappropriate behaviors to do within a relationship. He feels that it is inacceptable because spouses are supposed to check in with one another, right? To shudder away the confusions, he turns on music to get ready for work. From singing in the shower to dancing uncontrollably around the house, the music changes his mood.

He chipperly goes to work. He's greeting and acknowledging his co-workers, joking while fraternizing with the residents, and going

Black Pain't, Vol. II

above and beyond his usual daily duties. Anything to keep himself busy to keep his mind off Jazmine. He gives himself a fifteen-minute break just so he does not spend forty-five minutes of his break thinking about Jazmine and her whereabouts, wherever she's about, and whatever it's about.

Spending eight hours standing and in constant motion took a toll on his mental and physical health. That evening, when Jules makes it home from work, he instantly kicks off his shoes and lies down in his bed for relaxation. He plays some Reggae Music because he heard that the sounds are virtuous for the soul. He closes his eyes to focus on the lyrics, letting the music enter his cerebrum. After a few songs, he gradually dazes off into a dream state in which he appears within a landscape that seems to be at an outdoor concert, crowded with people who are dancing and singing to the sounds of *Stir It Up* by Bob Marley.

In this dream, he walks through the crowd to see couples dancing to the waves of the song. "Stir it up!" the crowd yells as he floats through the crowd as if he's search for something; something that he's been searching for wholeheartedly. He eventually comes to the climax of the dream to see Jazmine slow-dancing and rolling her hips on some guy that he cannot yet see. He angrily approaches them. Everything begins happening in slow motion as he raises his fist to start punching on the guy and Jazmine. Jazmine sees him charging at them, he suddenly wakes up, breathing heavily.

After taking a few deep breaths, he checks his phone to see if Jazmine had replied to at least one of his messages. It's been almost 42 hours since he seen or heard from her. He swallows in his sorrow after realizing she has not responded. *"Maybe she can't respond... maybe she has bad service wherever she's at.... where is she at? She did not even tell me......"* he thinks to himself.

He tosses his phone to avoid looking at it in hopes that a notification from Jazmine would just pop up so he can feel better about their situation. Something inside him knows that she's much of a woman to handle, so it eats at it his manhood, it tears at his ego. He can't keep up with her sexually, and it eats at his flesh. It makes him question his masculinity. He picks up his phone again to check the time and his messages, knowing he must pick up and deliver food orders for extra pay with Sprint*Door*. Still, he desperately hopes that Jazmine finds a way to communicate with him.

"I'm only doing two hours tonight, I'm tired," he says to himself aloud. He turns on his delivery zone so he can start receiving orders. As he waits, he goes to the kitchen to retrieve a snack and some water. On his way back, he sees his phone lights up. He picks it up, unlocks it, and sees that Sprint*Door* sent him an option for his first order.

He reads the assignment and approves of it because of the $10 tip that comes along with it. He gobbles down the snack, puts his shoes on while chewing, and walks back out of the bedroom. Jules decides to take another snack from out of the pantry. Then he grabs his keys from off of the kitchen counter and exits.

While on the way to pick up his first order, he calculates the time he will arrive to his location so he can add the location to his delivery zone. Once he got to the restaurant, he goes to the take-out line to get the bag of food. He drives to the house in which he must drop off the food. After doing so, he awaits a few minutes to retrieve another order within a five-mile radius. He does this throughout the night, knowing that he could eventually end up an hour or an hour and a half away from where he lives by switching delivery zones.

Later that night, after dropping off his sixth order, he realizes that the American people are some lazy bastards. These lazy bastards put too much trust into strangers to pick up and deliver their food. He feels that he has made enough extra cash for the night. Before cutting off his delivery zone, he receives a notification of a food order with the restaurant up the street from where he is, and the house is within four miles of the restaurant.

"This my last one," he states to himself, driving toward the restaurant. He arrives to the restaurant before the food is done and has to wait a bit for the food to be done. Looking around the restaurant, he begins to feel out of place, which ignites his anxiety. Whenever the

Black Pain't, Vol. II

waiter hands him the bag of food, he exits to get the delivery over with so he can get back to his space.

He drives to a house with a Red Mustang GT parked in the driveway. *"That car looks niiiiceee!"* he thinks to himself, subconsciously comparing his Nissan Altima to it. He walks to the door and rings the doorbell. A few seconds later the porch light is lit, and Jules can hear the door being unlocked. Suddenly, Terrance opens the door to see Jules standing at the doorstep with the bag of food. Terrance quickly and nervously blocks his doorway so that Jules can't see Jazmine walking by in the background.

"Jules!" he says while coming outside, shutting the door behind him. "How you doin' man? I didn't know you worked for Sprint*Door*?"

"Wassgood, Terrance! Yeah, man, I've been doing it for almost a year now.... did you move? This is a huge house. This yours?" Jules inquires, trying to get a peak on the inside.

"Nah, nah, nah.... ummm...... this is an Airbnb.... just rented it out for...ummm...... a video.... yes, we are shooting a music video.... yessir...... a music video to my latest song, *Mood Swings*! Yessir......"

Jules notices Terrance's discomfort and commences to wonder if he is shooting a video then why is it only one car present in the driveway. He ponders as to why he's in a white robe. He immediately thinks about the food order for two.

Jules inconspicuously says, "Sure."

To switch the subject, Terrance asks, "How long you makin' deliveries for?"

"This my last one actually. I'm about to get home in relax. Hey, have you talked to my sister recently?"

"She has a competition out of town, she won't be back until Sunday."

Meanwhile, inside the Airbnb, Jazmine and her hunger gets impatient. She rises with her white robe on to go see what's taking Terrance so long to get the food. She can hear conversations but can't make out the voices. She gets by the door and slightly opens it to see what's going on. Terrance quickly turns around to grab the doorknob, but Jules's instincts swiftly see Jazmine's face through the brightly lit porch light.

"What the fuck?" Jules says while dropping the food, trying to get by Terrance. Terrance blocks Jules from the door. Jules violently tries to bowguard his way inside, charging at Jazmine. Terrance blocks Jules from getting inside almost knocking himself off balance. Terrance catches himself, pushes Jules from the porch, but causing Jules to fall unto the grass as he falls forward on the porch.

Terrance instantly tries to get up and rush back in the house, simultaneously as Jules rapidly rises from the grass to meet Terrance at the door. Jules tackles Terrance into the door, bum-rushing their way into the house, wrestling and throwing uncontrollable fists.

"Oh, my God!" Jazmine frightfully says in disbelief, watching Jules and Terrance tussle inside the house and onto the floor.

Jules makes strange sounds, trying to swing on Terrance. As they rise, Terrance dodges Jules's punches, but Jules catches him in face. Counteractively, Terrance hits Jules in his face in between Jules's haymakers. They knock down pictures from off of the wall, antiques fell onto the floor, and glasses shatter.

"STOOOP!" Jazmine yells as she hesitates to stop their fight.

Jules then grapples Terrance, trying to trip him onto the ground. Terrance counters Jules's maneuver and tries to body slam him. Terrance slips and Jules is able to land on top of Terrance, trying to punch him in the face. Terrance covers his face with his arms as Jazmine tries to intervene by clutching Jules's torso, trying to pull him off Terrance.

Jules resists and shoves Jazmine away, saying, "FUCK OFF OF MEEEE!"

Jazmine thuds to the floor while Jules grunts and tries to get back to swinging on Terrance. Terrance spears Jules with his forearm to his head. Their collision pushes Jules towards the wall, banging his shoulder against a nearby console table. Terrance two pieces Jules to keep him down.

Black Pain't, Vol. II

As Jules is laid out onto the floor, Terrance angrily says, "Stay down, nigga!"

"Terrance, what the fuck!?" Jazmine concerningly yells, bending down to check on Jules.

"What the fuck you expect me to do, Jazmine?" Terrance says, rapidly walking towards a room to put on some sweatpants.

Jules groans and stumbles back up. As Terrance comes back around, Jules yells, "IS THIS WHAT IT IS? IS THIS WHAT'S GOING ON? Y'ALL SOME STUPID MUTHA FUCKAS!"

Jules charges at Terrance but Jazmine steps in between, saying, "Quit it! Quit it!" She tries to hug Jules, putting her hand over his mouth saying, "Stop it, right now!"

Jules tries to shove Jazmine out of the way, but slips in the process, still dazed from Terrance's strike. He yells, "DOES JALISA KNOW ABOUT THIS? YOU PLAYIN' MY SISTER? AFTER ALL SHE BEEN THROUGH?" Jules aggressively questions Terrance while getting up and keeping his equilibrium. "This is how you do her?"

"Bruh, just leave!" Terrance implies. "Get the fuck out, nigga!"

"FUCK YOU BITCH ASS NIGGA!" Jules denotes while his voice screeches.

"Jules, please goooooo! We'll talk about it later!" Jazmine intercedes, trying to grab Jules.

"LATER? BITCH, LATER? AIN'T GON' BE NO LATER! IT'S OVER, JAZMINE! I CAN'T BELIEVE YOU WOULD DO THIS!" Jules yells in rage. "AFTER ALL I'VE DONE? AFTER ALL I'VE SACRIFICED?"

"Jules? What are you talking about?" Jazmine confusedly asked.

"YOU KNOW WHAT I'M TALKIN' ABOUT, JAZMINE!" Jules screams while getting in Jazmine's face.

"Nigga, what do you do? I'll wait. What do you?" Jazmine says while clapping her hands. "YOU DO NOTHING FOR ME! YOU DO NOTHING FOR ME!" Jazmine interposes.

"WHA....WHY YOU......" Jules tries to speak but Jazmine continues.

"YOU DON'T DO SHIT FOR ME! YOU DON'T WANT TO LEAVE YOUR MAMA AND DADDY HOUSE, YOU DON'T WANT MORE FOR YOURSELF, YOU DON'T WANT TO FUCK ME PROPERLY! NIGGA, YOU DO NOTHING FOR ME! I PAY MY OWN BILLS; I TAKE CARE OF MY DAUGHTER!"

Jules questions, "WHY BE WITH ME? WHY DIDN'T YOU JUST LEAVE ME? YOU COULD HAVE BEEN BETTER OFF WITH THIS FOOL!"

Terrance closes the door after seeing people outside. "Y'all keep shit down, the neighbors are walking outside, peepin' and shit!"

"FUCK THOSE NEIGHBORS!" Jules passionately states.

"This nigga here...." Terrance infuriatingly comments. "Do you wanna get locked up? Do you want to go to jail, oh stupid ass nigga?"

"Nigga shut the fuck up..." Jules says, walking up to him.

Jazmine notices the police pulling up outside and says, "The police are here........"

Jules feels fearful from the idea of going to jail, so he calms down. Jazmine tries to straighten up the mess, but there is glass on the floor and broken pieces of wood lying around that made it too obvious that something happened in here.

"Nigga wouldn't chill... it's on you fam...." Terrance tells Jules.

Jules replies, "Aight nigga, I don't give a fuck, snitchin' ass......"

Suddenly, there are knocks at the door. Terrance, Jazmine, and Jules all freeze into inertia. Jazmine attempts to open the door, but Terrance grabs her arm and whispers, "Wait, wait...... What are we going to say?"

The policemen knock on the door again, saying, "This is the police department. Open up, or we will be forced to break in!"

Terrance looks at Jazmine and Jules, awaiting a quick response and says, "Well?"

Jules looks nonchalant and ready for whatever as Jazmine's countenance is that of confusion. After the officers knock again, Terrance slightly opens the door and asks the policemen, "How may I help you?"

Both officers put their hands on their guns just in case. One of them says, "We got a call about a disturbance at this house."

"Nah, no sir, no disturbance at all, thank you, bye," Terrance says as he tries to shut the door.

The other officer says, "Excuse me, sir. We're not finished. Are there other people in the house?"

"Yes."

"Who else?" the other officer asks.

Terrance says, "A couple of family members."

"Are there any drugs or firearms in the house?"

"No sir, no drugs and no firearms in here sir...."

"Do you live here?"

"Yes, sir..." Terrance answers. "What? You don't think Black people could own this type of establishment?"

"Funny, one of the neighbors said that the real owner rents this out as an Airbnb...... they're one of the emergency contacts. We can contact the real owner if......."

Terrance says, "Oh okay, what do you need officer?"

"We just need to come in and check out the place that's all."

Terrance steps to the side to let the officers in not realizing he had bruises and blood on his knuckles. As the officers enter, they see debris and assume that a fight might have broken out. They then see Jules and Jazmine standing close to the living room area in grave strain.

"There are other people in the house," one of the officers says and then asks, "What happened here?"

Jazmine sarcastically answers, "Well, you know, playing around......"

Another one of the officers observes Jules's bloody lip asks, "You're okay there, buddy?"

Jules responds, "Yeah, I'm aight......." in an apathetic way.

"Is there anyone else inside this house?"

"No, sir," Terrance answers.

"And everything alright with you Miss?" the officer asks Jazmine.

"Yes," Jazmine nervously replies.

Both officers look at one another in hesitation. Then one of them says, "Okay, well, try to keep the 'playing' down to a minimum," and slowly walks out with the other officer trailing behind him.

As the policemen exit, Terrance shuts the door behind them and leans against the door in relief. Jazmine sighs in respite as Jules still have this visage as if he's ready to fight again. Terrance angrily attempts to clean up the mess in the house, knowing that they're not getting their deposit back.

Jules looks at Jazmine and says, "Guess this is goodbye....... I hope you're happy." He then looks at Terrance and asks, "So are you going to tell my sister, or do I have to? Since you couldn't be a man to tell her you were cheating......"

Terrance intensely thinks for a moment, wanting to knock Jules's head off of his shoulders, but answers, "I would appreciate it if you let me tell her."

"Okay, you have until the end of this night, nigga," Jules exclaims and exits.

After Jules's departure, the Airbnb fills up with a ferocious friction. Terrance senses it and Jazmine sanities it. As they continue to clean up the debris, Terrance yells, "FUCK!"

Jazmine flinches and stares at him in confusion. She watches as he punches a hole in a nearby wall and says, "We definitely not getting our deposit back......"

"Fuck, fuck, fuuuck!"

"All that yelling ain't gon' solve nothin'...." Jazmine states while helping Terrance sterile. "What are you going to do?"

"I'm going to tell her, Jazmine......"

"Good, you didn't like that borin' bitch anyway......"

"I did like her.... I do like her......"

"Terry, if you did, you wouldn't be fuckin' on me......"

"Just because I fuck on you, doesn't mean I didn't love her."

Jazmine disgustedly says, "Ewww, why do men act like that shit mean something. You obviously don't love her if you're cheating my nigga, be real......."

"You cheated on me, does that mean you didn't love me," Terrance instantly asks.

"Terry, I wasn't loving myself... especially in college. Don't act like I didn't hear about them bitches you was sleeping around on me with. I was really returning the favor...... I don't cheat but I would cheat back."

"What bitches, Jazmine?"

"You want me to name drop? Our campus was small, news spreaded like wildfires, Terrance."

"Who was I fuckin' with Jazmine?"

"You don't wanna go there, Terry."

"Naw, come on! Say how you feel? What bitches, Jazmine?"

"Come on now, Terrance...... Neicey?" Jazmine pauses to let the name sink into Terrance. She continues, "Does the name ring a bell? What about Rhi-Rhi? Oooh, what about that Kappa bitch, Francis? What about all them?"

"Some of them was before you."

"You was still fuckin' on them while you were with me, Terrance! I knew! I'm not stupid! That's why I did my own thing.... I knew what you was on. Then you tried to play victim when I was about to graduate."

"Tried to play victim? How?"

"You don't think your weak as frat brothers told me what you was on?" Jazmine instantly replies while Terrance gives a look of betrayal. "Yeah, a few of them niggas came at me foul about our situation, but you didn't give them my side of the story. And a couple of your frat brothers tried to holla at me when they found out about me and you breaking up......"

"Bitch ass niggas," Terrance says under his breath.

Their argument continues for another half an hour before Jazmine decides to pack up her belongings to leave. She orders a

*Down*the*Street* and does not say anything to Terrance while he continues to clean. She leaves without speaking, which was the same way they broke up back after she graduated from college. Everything ends the way it starts.

Terrance is left with thoughts of intrusion. He feels guilty for the hurt he's about to inflict and all the drama that comes with it. He worries, knowing that he will lose Jalisa. Jules's comments replay in the back of his mind, convicting him of his love crimes. Then stress begins to take a hold on him. How is he going to tell Jalisa about his deceit, his lies, his infidelity? How is he going to be able to be one hundred percent honest with her during the questions she will ask?

In synchronicity, Jalisa messages him. Terrance's heart drops as he sees her name appear on his phone. *"Did this lil nigga tell Jalisa already?"* he thinks to himself before clicking on the notification. "Bitch ass," he says aloud as he clicks on the message. A sagacity of relief flows through him after seeing a picture of Jalisa and her dance team holding up a check for $25,000 for first place.

Her caption reads, "Biggest win yet baby!!!!!" Instant guilt and shame cover his aura, he does not know what to type back. He does not want to prolong what he must tell her. He wants to tell her before her brother does. The thought of Jules telling her angers him.

He types, "CONGRATULATIONS BABY!!!!!!!! SO PROUD OF YOU AND YOUR TEAM! Please call me when you get alone," and sends it to her. He sits down on the couch, thinking she is going to call him right away.

Several minutes later, Jalisa texts back saying, "Okay!"

Waiting on her call has his heart racing. He cannot not think about the upcoming conversation with Jalisa. Time passing eats at his soul, so he chooses to leave the Airbnb, even though he has it for another day and night. As he is packing his possessions in the bedroom, Jalisa calls him. He takes the deepest breath as he can before accepting the call.

"Hello?" he says in a sobbing way.

"Hey baby! We won! I'm so tired......" she says while yawning. After her big yawn, she resumes, "Uhhhh.... we just came back from dinner; I treated the girls to some restaurant owned by some famous Black woman named Nyesha Arrington...... it was actually great. The girls loved it."

"That's good to hear," Terrance says sadly.

"What's wrong? You don't sound too good?"

"Well, umm, I..... uhh...," he stumbles over his words. He takes a strong sigh and manages to say, "I have something to tell you...."

"What is it?" Jalisa concerningly asks.

Rubbing his face, Terrance says, "You're not going to like this at all, Jalisa. Are you alone?"

"Why, Terrance? What happened? Yes... I'm alone.... stop stalling and tell me," Jalisa irritably says.

"I cheated on you, Jalisa......"

"You cheated on me?"

"Yeah," Terrance disappointedly answers.

"What?" Jalisa says with the utmost confusion. "With whom?"

"Someone I used to mess around with before you."

Jalisa searches for something to say, and suddenly think about the name that popped up on his phone. The pain and the bewilderment keep her mind and vocal cords from working properly. She asks, "Why now, Terrance? After the biggest night of my career as a choreographer?"

"I know, I know... I'm sorry. I didn't want to ruin your night with it, but I had to tell you before you heard it from someone else...."

"Was it Jazzy? If so, what's her real name?"

"Jazmine."

"Jazmine who?"

"Your brother's Jazmine......"

"Terrance, please don't tell me that you were fucking around on me with my brother's girlfriend?"

Terrance apologetically says, "I'm sorry, Jalisa, I really a...." but Jalisa hangs up on him before he got the chance to say his excuses. Terrance tries to call back but the line keeps ringing. On his sixth try, the call goes straight to voicemail. The next four calls, he realizes that she probably has her phone on do not disturb.

He decides to text her, types, "Jalisa," and presses send. He wonders why his message went green and then he comes to the conclusion that she blocked his number. He sits on the edge of the bed in the excruciating silence. The silence plagues his thoughts and conscience. His heart throbs in fury. It almost feels like he's in a movie because of what transpired today. "You can't make this shit up," he says to himself. He eventually lifts himself up, grabs his duffle bag, and exits the Airbnb with a new reality.

Black Pain't, Vol. II

MY NOTES

Black Pain't, Vol. II

Chapter 10:
Humanistic therapy

She asks him, "So how does that make you feel?"
He takes his time to answer the question and says, "I feel a huge relief but a deep, deep grief.... ya know? Like I lost someone."
"Why relief?" she asks in correspondence, trying to get to the root of his feelings. She notices that he dazes out for a moment and says, "Alvin?"
"Yes ma'am," Alvin says, shaking his head away from what he was just thinking a moment ago.
"Why do you feel relief?"
Alvin ponders for a second and answers, "I don't know."

"Alvin, you're never going to get passed it by holding it in; it's only going to get worst. Let's try another question. How did it all conspire?"

"Well," he says while remembering the details of the story. "Oh, god, where do I begin?"

(It was Sunday afternoon. Alvin was driving to Jazmine's crib to drop off Miracle. As he pulled up, he called Jazmine to let her know that he was outside. While waiting for Jazmine to come downstairs to get Miracle, he opened the trunk to take out a huge tote. Once Jazmine got downstairs, she noticed Alvin walking towards her with Miracle along with Miracle's small suitcase, and the huge tote.

"What's all this?" she asked while picking up Miracle.

Alvin ignored her question to walk back to the car to get document sized envelope. He walked to hand her the envelope and walked back to his car to get in and drove away.

Jazmine stood there with Miracle, looking confused and upset. "Go in the house, baby, and take your suitcase with you," she commanded Miracle, putting her down.

"Yes mommy," Miracle said, running up the stairs with her small suitcase and into their apartment.

Jazmine opened the envelope and read the paternity test results. She put her hand over her mouth in surprise. She finally came face to face with reality. She picked up the tote and walked it upstairs to their apartment. Once she got inside, she texted Terrance, saying, **"We need to talk. ASAP."**

Alvin cried on the way home with sadness and with anger, thinking about how much he's going to miss being Miracle's 'father.' He was thinking that after all these years of oblivion, confusion, and drama. Though it felt like a huge weight was lifted off of his shoulders, total despair filled his heart. He is not a father.)

"Did you tell, Miracle?"
"No, I didn't...."

"Why not?"

"Wasn't my obligation to?"

"So if you found out the results Friday morning, what did you two do till Sunday? Why didn't you take her to her grandmother's?"

"I spoiled her," Alvin says. He resumes, saying, "Yeah, I took her to the movies; we went to the zoo, skyzone, and this kid museum for kids to play with fake ancient artifacts, freaking amazing and fun. We had the time of our lives."

"Did you do all that, knowing this was going to be the last time you seen her?"

"Naw, I took her to the circus before, took her shopping hundreds of times, we went to the park mostly, but we would always go places, I've taken her many places."

"Why not keep that bond?"

Alvin reflects on the therapist's question and says, "It'll be unjust to take time away from the man who should be doing those things, you know? Like who am I to rob the real father of that beautiful experience? Ya know?"

"I understand completely. How has your week been since you saw or talked to Miracle?"

"It's been rough; sooo rough like...... I had to develop new routines and fill-ins to fulfill that void. I have to give my time to a different attention. I don't have to pay child support anymore so where do I place that extra money? Life feels, notice I said, 'feels,' Mrs. Townsend," Alvin says while they both share some laughter. "But life feels...... empty."

"I understand. What does it mean to be empty to you?"

Alvin contemplates the opposed question. It provokes his thoughts. He answers, "To be empty means to be unfulfilled. All my life, I thought like money motivated me, I thought that success shielded from sadness, and I thought that sex satisfied me...... but when I was a father, even for that short period of time, I learned that my daughter really motivated me. I learned that I don't need to be shielded from anything in life, it's okay to be vulnerable; I was vulnerable around Miracle. I wanted her to know that I fought to be in her life, and I feel empty without her in it.

"Life...... Life just feels pointless when you have no one to pour into; especially a child, like...... Miracle was actually a miracle for me; she gave me purpose. I found my religion because of her, I found Allah because of Miracle. Even though everything happened the way it happened, I'm so grateful for the experience. I'm saved now."

"What did that situation teach you about you?"

"That I'm a real man. Like I know I am a real man. A man that will do anything to be in their child's life.... I mean absolutely anything. Now, don't get me wrong, I was inappropriate the way I went about things in the beginning, I was very disrespectful to her, Allah forgive; I was terrible in a lot of occasions between Jazmine and I. She didn't deserve it.

"I think the most messed up thing is...... that, Jazmine probably knew that Miracle was not my daughter, that's probably her reason for keeping her from me. Not to give her any excuses but maybe it allowed her to accept something that I was eagerly willing to give."

"You really put up a fight, I see," she states.

"Something like that...." he replies.

"What did the situation teach you about fatherhood?"

"Oohhh........." he adlibs, rationalizing the answer to Mrs. Townsend's question. He presumes, "That...... one, no matter the relationship, situationship, or whatever you have with the child's mother to try to communicate effectively, show her that you can be trusted with the child because a mother is going to be a mother.... ya know? She's going to be loving, nurturing, mean, overly protective, 'extra,' ......inquisitive.... observing.

"As fathers, we have to be cognizant that some small sperm cell just grew a human body within her. She was giving a God-given contract to watch over this human to the best of her ability. Us, men, have to move according to that and know when to intervene and discuss disagreements or the hard conversations.

"Both parents come from two different worlds so we all may have different ways of teaching......... of disciplining, loving, thinking; traditions maybe different while trying to implement things that you may have picked up on the way...... That's why you can't go around having kids with just anybody..." Alvin concludes.

"Alvin, I love where your head is with all of this. My only question for you is what now? Where is all this going to do for you now? What will you take from all of this?"

Alvin ponders for a moment and says, "I don't know.... I know I want to get deeply involved in the Nation of Islam. I want to build my own insurance firm; I'm tired of working with White people.... I don't care if they were featured in Forbes; fuck Forbes.

The therapist looks at her time piece and says, "Well, looks like our time is up. Is there anything you want to say?"

"No, no ma'am...."

"See you next week?"

"Same time as always..." Alvin says as he stands to exit.

"Hey, Alvin," she says, stopping him in his tracks.

"Yes, ma'am?"

"It's not the end of the world; I know you feel like you're getting older, but you'll have that family that you want one day."

"Thank you, Mrs. Townsend," Alvin says, shutting the door.

Mrs. Townsend takes time to close her eyes and meditate before her next session. Several minutes later, there are knocks on the door. "Come on...." she announces.

Her secretary opens the door, saying, "Hey, Debra, you have a phone call on line seven."

"Thank you, Tracy," Mrs. Townsend gratefully says, picking up the phone. "Hello? This is Mrs. Townsend."

"Hey, ummm... Hello.... this is Terrance, Terrance Robins. I am calling to see if you have any consultations. Just so we don't waste each other's time, and I want to vibe with you before we open some flood gates."

"Mr. Robins, I understand completely. We can set something up this Thursday if you'd like......" Mrs. Townsend says while looking through a planner for an appropriate time. "I am available at 11am and 2pm."

"2pm would be perfect."

"2pm it is then," she says, writing his name down in the calendar. "Hey, how did you hear about me?"

"I can't tell you that right now, but you come highly recommended."

"Okay, Mr. Robins, thank you.......... Alright....... bye," she says, hanging up the phone. After she hangs up, she remembers how one of her old patients used to tell her about a person named Terrance Robins. She thinks long and hard about it but cannot put her finger on it.

~

That evening, Jase invites Patricia to Kemet during their Friday Happy Hour and Appetizers where drinks and appetizers are all half off. Patricia knows that Kemet is Darryl's favorite spot to be at on Fridays, so she was iffy about going. Hoping that she does not run into him, she asks if they can sit far away from the bar to avoid all the traffic that will flow in and out of there.

While in a booth, they proceed to talk about topics that Jase does not find meaningful. After receiving their drinks and appetizers, Patricia continues her rant, saying, "I'm not trying to sound like one of those 'tin foil hat' people, or a 'conspiracy theorists' but think about everything that happened since 2020.... it was a well-known fact that our government was falsifying those Covid case numbers. They lied about the numbers of deaths, they lied about everything........ all to get people to take a vaccines that was supposedly supposed to cure people from this illness when it really made it worst for people's immune systems. I heard it even disrupts people's reproductive systems."

Jase replies, "Yeah, but I can't imagine our government wanting to kill off people......"

"Jase....... are you living under a rock?" she metaphorically asks, testing his common sense. She continues, "The crack epidemic, the war on poverty, Jim Crow south, the burning and destroying of Black towns all across America, the Tuskegee experiment.... and you dare to say that our government does not want to kill us off?"

"Okay...... you do got a point there......" he humbly says.

"Oh, I know..........." she confidently states. "Did you hear about how the Clinton family was exposed for being child traffickers and pedophiles?"

"Parliament, George Clinton? Or the first Black president, George Clinton?"

"Boy, you know I'm talking about Bill and Hillary. Bill is definitely not 'Black' he's as white and pedo as all the other white and pedophilic devils out there in Disney, Nickelodeon."

"Nah, I haven't heard about all of that," he interestingly says, hoping that she would stop this rant about her view society.

"Bill Clinton was on Jeffrey Epstein's Island. That's probably why Hillary Clinton deleted 30,000 emails, most of them were about their child sex trafficking rink. Jeffrey Epstein's case exposed a lot, too. Bill Clinton, Chris Tucker, Prince Andrews, Leonardo DiCaprio, Oprah, and many other celebrities visited Epstein Island.... Jeffrey said that Bill Clinton likes them young.

"I know people don't want to hear this but even the royal Black family...... the Obamas....... were in some of Hillary Clinton's emails..... y'all remember those 'pizza' parties that Barack used to throw at the white house? That was code word for little boys.... and they aren't the only ones! There's R. Kelly, P. Diddy, Jay-Z, Beyonce... everyone is getting exposed for their pedophilic and demonic behaviors...... the public is finally able to see these people that we'd admired our whole lives for who they really are."

He asks, "If all of these people are being exposed then why do people still hold these people to a high pedal stool?"

She answers, "I don't know. People are still listening to R. Kelly and P. Diddy. Families are still watching Nickelodeon and Disney, knowing children were being molested by these people that were over these kid shows......it's so crazy how people still think Barack Obama was a great president. Clueless to the fact that he bombed seven countries during his first few months in being in office. He lied about bringing the troops home. He sold us hope."

Trying to get a complete understanding on the discussion at hand, he asks, "So what does this mean for the people of our society? What are the changes that need to be made?"

"Honestly, Jase, I don't think people have the mental capacity to change......"

"Why do you say that?"

"Well, between social media, propaganda, and all these other brainwashing mechanisms to keep us distracted from reality, distracted from our inner worlds, using the sports and entertainment world to control the masses and build this illusion. We are losing sight of humanity.... People aren't seeking God anymore, they're seeking validation, reassurance, and attention....... This new generation that's coming can't read, write, or count, so imagine what they're future is going to look like... then... ah man... let's not get on AI!"

"AI as in Artificial Intelligence?"

"Yes!"

Jase cluelessly asks, "What's wrong with AI? I thought AI was a good thing."

"People are losing their ability to think, because of AI. What's the point of thinking when you have a robot to think for you? This whole ideology of independent thought is dying out; education as you and I know it....... is done....... finito........."

"Not to mention that men are wanting to be women now; men are either on the down low or choosing to be transgender.... No disrespect or judgment toward them, by all means, follow your preferences and do what you love, but at what costs?"

Jase notices her passion behind debatable issues. Though he can hardly agree, it's fascinating to hear a woman speak about topics that most women don't speak on. *"She takes life so serious,"* he thinks to himself.

"Oh, Jase! Everything disturbing is on the rise. Inflation is on the rise, food and housing is getting more expensive, why? Because property taxes are on the rise; we want our youth to go to college, but they can't go survive in college, why? Because tuition is on the rise. Homelessness is at an all-time high. Sex-workers are on the rise...... society as a whole is getting out of hand."

He marinates on her claims and asks, "Where do you think this is all leading to? Like... what's the end game?"

After a few seconds of silence, she answers, "The fall of humanity......"

"I thought humanity fell after Eve and Adam ate the fruit?"

"Nah, Jase, this ain't a religious thing that's happening; this is reality. Plus, this is a whole different fall. This could be the end of the world as we know it. We mentioned celebrities, politicians; what's going on in different aspects of our government, but we didn't mention how there's soon to be a one world government."

Jase jokingly says, "You got me feeling like we're in an episode of the *Twilight Zone*."

They both laugh as she proceeds, "I wonder what we as a people are going to do with the truth. Will that make us look into the mirror? Will that bring about true change?"

"Thank God, that God has the final say."

"What has God done or is doing?"

He smiles and says, "He's blessing us in many ways, Patricia. Think about it; think about all that stuff you mentioned. Ain't none of that happening around you; ain't none of that happening to you."

Jase's statement sends Patricia on a cerebral drive to her past relationship. Looking in the rearview, she sees herself getting abused by her ex. She takes a left to her jagged childhood, where poverty was her everyday living. She comes across the present moment to hear Jase portraying his ignorance through speech. He has no clue and doesn't know anything about what she has been through, seen, or witnessed. *"Yes, God has blessed her but at what cost?"* She thinks to herself.

"You don't think God has the final say?" Jase asks as Patricia lands back to the current moment.

"I don't know. There are too many things to consider. Like why didn't God intervene during slavery? Why didn't God intervene when young girls and boys get molested? Why didn't God intervene when women get abused and assaulted? Why wait twenty to thirty plus years to intervene on past situations? How come God doesn't remove these cults and individuals who bring harm to our children and the people of society? What about...."

Jase interjects, asking, "What if God gave US the power to make those changes and bring those people to justice?"

"Literally or spiritually...... because the judges and lawyers be in on the corruption as well, this whole system is corrupted and centralized for those who incite the corruption. What power do we have when those in authoritative positions do nothing? Or are we supposed to suffer until we die in order to experience good?" Patricia's questions leave Jase stuck and stagnant. Patricia reads him like a book, realizing there is not anymore pages of himself to read, because he's not expanding pass his limited thought process.

He manages to say, "I hear what you're saying, but God is still God, even if we don't understand or can't fathom what's happening, it's all God's plan."

"Sure," Patricia condescendingly says. It is hard for Patricia to be attracted to someone who thinks in this manner, but she tries to accept him for where he is in his life.

After two drinks and some appetizers, Jase and Patricia's conversations becomes lackluster. Patricia gets uninterested in all his selfish, success stories that have everything to do with him and nothing to do with aiding his people.

When it is time to go, Jase offers to pay for everything as a real gentleman would. Patricia rejects, wanting to at least cover the drinks to make everything even. Jase insists that he pays for food. Patricia tips what she was going to pay for the drinks as they both slide out of the booth to leave.

While walking out, Darryl suddenly appears opening the main door. Patricia gets lethargic; Darryl becomes mentally paralyzed to move. Darryl's spirit takes control, making him hold the door for Patricia and Jase to exit in an obdurate gesture.

Naïve Jase gently clutches Patricia's hand, says, "Thanks," to the stranger opening the door, and leads Patricia out of the restaurant. Darryl looks on with intensity while his heart cringes; Patricia looks back over her shoulder a couple of times to see Darryl staring at the two of them walk away.

When they are outside Patricia cannot help but to think about how talking to Darryl about societal issues is far much easier and more welcoming. She remembers how safe she felt around Darryl, even though he was a fuck boy, he still had class, authentic conversation, and charisma.

Jase breaks Patricia's mental monologue, by comically asking "Is it me or that man that opened the door was socially awkward?"

Humbly, Patricia prophetically says, "I don't know. Glad he opened the door though. Plus, any melaninated brother walking into a restaurant that is owned by someone who looks like us isn't awkward at all."

"Are you always this?"

"Always like what?"

"Ummmm......what you call it.... pro-Black?" Jase satirically asks. "Oh, my bad, you're not Black, you're indigenous."

Patricia forces a chuckle and asks, "Why aren't you pro-your-people enough?" in the nicest way possible.

"What does that mean?" Jase chuckles. "You think just because I'm not out there waving my fist and being all about Black people that, I'm not Black enough?"

Patricia snappishly says, "All I'm trying to figure out is why is it that my strong stance for my people offends you?"

"It doesn't offend me, I'm jus-"

Interposing, Patricia says, "Does it make you feel uncomfortable?"

"No not uncomfortable, it's jus-"

Patricia interrupts him again, saying, "If so then there's a problem...... there's definitely a deep-rooted problem."

"Problem? How am I a problem?"

"I said that there's a problem."

"Well, what's the problem?"

"The problem is that there are people like you who do not want true change. There are people like you who are under hypnosis by society's illusions. You're the type that can't see the truth in any way, shape, or form. There are 'Black' people like you who just refuse to accept the fact that these European mutha fuckas took our land and pushed majority of our people into a lower class system? Then blame the way we are without considering the epigenetics behind it."

Jase listens to Patricia intently and starts playing *Fight the Power* by Public Enemy. Patricia fakes a smirk as Jase says, "Come on...... I knowwww you know this song!" while he bobs his head to the beat. "FIGHT THE POWER!" Jase screams prematurely before the song reaches that part in the song, out of the parking lot to drop Patricia off at home.

~

After getting home from making deliveries, Jules gets home to an unfulfilled house, filled with a sense of emptiness, betrayal, and insecurities. Every time he looks in the mirror to see the bruises from Terrance's fist, the situation between him, Jazmine, and Terrance plagues through his mind.

He develops an internal hatred for Jazmine, but even through all of the bullshit, he misses Jazmine dearly. To stop the suffering going throughout his being, he heats some leftovers in the microwave. He lounges in the living room to eat and watch television, maybe catch up on the new season of *Them*. His sister catapults into his mind, and he decides to call her.

"Hey, Jules!" Jalisa says. "I've been meaning to call you."

"Wassup, sis...." he greets. "You've been meaning to call me about what?"

"Ummm......yeah, Terrance and I are broken up, Jules; did you know about him and Jazmine?"

Jules instantly says, "Jalisa, I ran in on them."

"What, I don't unde-"

Jules interposes, saying, "Jalisa, I was making deliveries, I pulled up to some house; I saw Terrance's mustang in the lot. Terrance opened the door after I knocked; I heard Jazmine's voice in the back and she came to the door, sis! That bitch came to the door...."

"Oh my God!" Jalisa struggles to say. Puzzled and in oblivion, Jalisa asks, "He was fucking on your girl this whole time?"

"My ex-girl! I kicked that bitch to the curb! I told him that he had less than 24 hours to tell you before I told you......"

As Jules is talking, Jalisa texts Trina, "Jules walked in on Terrance cheating on me with Jazmine smh," and says to Jules, "That's all that happened?"

In a corny way, Jules says, "Com' on now sis, you know I had to put these hands on him. Can't let anyone disrespect me or my sister!"

"Y'all fought?" Jalisa asks, noticing Trina calling her. "Hold on bro.... I'm about to add Trina to the call."

"Okay."

Moments later, Trina enters the call, saying, "YOOOOOO WHAT THE FUUUCKKKKK? How?"

"Wassup, sis?" Jules aggressively says.

"Who the fuck is that?" Trina violently asks.

"It's Jules, nigga...." he answers condescendingly.

"Lil' ugly lil boy, I'll knock your head smooth out, coming at me like that...."

"I ain't the one who you should be knocking the head off...."

Trina interrupts him and snappishly says, "Oh, please be sure you can be added to my 'On-Site-List!' You and your weak ass girlfriend.... I knew somethin' was off with that skank!"

"She ain't my girl no more!"

"Good, so it'll be even easier to knock some sense into yo ass!"

Jalisa intervenes, saying, "Can y'all please not do this right now? Trina, where you at?"

"I'm outside of Kemet right now, but where do I need to be at? You know I got hands that's one size fit all. My hands bisexual; a nigga and a bitch can get it!" Trina drastically says. "We meetin' up to beat the bitch nigga up or what?"

Jalisa calmly replies, "Nah, the best revenge is removing all access and forgiveness."

Trina asks, "You can't tell me you don't want to smash the nigga head in?"

"Revenge is mine sayeth the Lord," Jalisa answers. "Plus, we just got our nails done for our trip, you don't need to be going anywhere with bruises or chipped nails."

Jules tries to intervene by asking, "Trip? What trip?"

"I'll put on my brass knuckles...." Trina says.

"No, Trina! We are not about to go to jail for assault and battery!"

"HELLLLLOOOO! I know y'all heard my question!" Jules annoyingly says.

"Why would we go to jail for a fade? That's the problem with the world today, niggas don't wanna fade no more......"

"JaTrina, you gon' act like you can't hear me?"

"Jules, on my soul, I'm gonna slap the dog shit outta you, you mama's boy! DO NOT EVER CALL ME THAT!"

Jules quickly hangs up during Trina's rant. Jalisa notices and says, "Trina, he hung up, baby, calm down...."

"Oh......" Trina says, trying to find peace. "The little nigga think he big and bad or somethin'....... Anyways, we fightin' or what!?"

"NO TRINA! We are not fighting anyone. We are going to go on our trip, do some ayahuasca, meditation......"

Trina interjects, saying, "Some drankin, some smokin', some twerkin'!"

"Oh, girl whatever......" Jalisa says, laughing aloud. "What time do you get off?"

"I'm leaving at 10, I ain't gon' be here all night...... just came to holla at Braiveri and make some extra money for the trip...... Let me get back in here though! Call me if you need somethin' sis!"

"I will, twin, love you!"

"Love you too."

After hanging up the phone, Jalisa cries thinking about how hurt she feels. She thinks about all the moments when she felt her intuition trying to tell her, but she had no proof of Terrance's infidelity. She thinks about how dirty she feels from having sex with someone who was having sex with another woman. She cries to the thoughts of having to start anew if she ever dates again.

Suddenly, she begins thinking about her biological clock. She's only getting older. She thinks that maybe one day, she'll be able to have kids with someone she loves and who loves her back; someone who will take her feelings into consideration before committing love crimes. She's been giving all of herself to her dance team, Terrance, and building her non-profit that she forgot about her wellness in the process.

This is the perfect time to get back to Jalisa, to put together a self-love wellness package that someone will have to mirror if they want to court with her. Vacation time with Trina is just the perfect start. Her mind drifts between the pain that she feels, the experiences she wishes to experience while being out of the country, and dance competitions.

To clear her mind, she goes into her office space to grab an ink pen and a notepad. Looking at all the trophies, awards, and pictures around her office, she sits to show gratitude for the life she lives. She meditates over it to bless the words that she is about spell, understanding that people can curse themselves through spelling. She writes:

Black Pain't, Vol. II

I think I loved you too hard,
They say I shouldn't think that way when the bible tells us that we have a heart to guard,
Cuts and bruises by the misconception of love got everyone emotionally scarred,
I didn't deserve what you did to me,
You were selfish and inconsiderate,
you could have just gotten rid of me,
my misunderstanding got me writing these stanzas,
why do women always gotta tell you men to man up,
Man up to your truth and desires!
Man up to your hateful habits and being habitual liars!
Man up to your schemes, man up to your mass manipulations!
Man up to your indecencies and womanizing humiliations!
Man up to your lies and the times you pretended to care,
If you can't face a woman then man up to your fears!
Man up to the tears that you caused and controlled!
Look me in the eyes and man up to a heart that you stole!
Man up,
All these so-called men to need Man up,
Man up,
Stop being lil boys and Man up!

Black Pain't, Vol. II

MY NOTES

Black Pain't, Vol. II

Chapter 11:
Monsters

After a full day of meditation practices, yoga stretching, and getting a long needed full body massage, Trina and Jalisa finally found themselves on the shores of Cata Bay. Sitting on beach chairs in their two-piece bathing suits, sipping green tea with ayahuasca honey, they are extremely relaxed. They are enjoying nature while hearing the waves crash onto the shore with a strong sensation of love flowing through them. They are getting in tuned with their divinity, evoking inner peace.

"I needed this more than I knew sis!" Trina says. "I' ain't ever felt this much peace in my entire life. Oh, my gawwwDa!"

"What is it?" Jalisa concerningly asks.

"I feel like...... like I'm about to cry, but I'm not about to cry, you know? Like my body is going through some kind of emotional cleanse......"

Jalisa responds, "This is why it's important to get out and away from everything and everyone! It's good for the soul."

"I don't say this often but thank you for always pushing me out of my comfort zone, or just trying to make me try new things...." Trina sobbingly says while trying to allow overdue tears to fall.

"Awwwww, Trina! Are you getting sentimental on me?"

"It maybe the aya-hosta," Trina struggles to say.

"Aya-hua-sca...." Jalisa corrects Trina's pronunciation. "Say it with me, aya-..."

Trina ignores Jalisa's frolics and says, "Or it may be that wellness workshop we attended earlier............ I love knowing that I have a wellness toolbox to pull peace from."

"It's the ayahuasca!"

"Or that...... but I'm just in high spirits and I haven't felt like this in forever...... for once in my life, I do not feel angry or hateful......... thank you......."

"No problem, sis.... thank you for acknowledging that. You know you ain't always easy to get through...."

"I know..." Trina agrees in a joyful, sad way. Seconds later, she softly and calmly says, "This is way better than weed."

"I wouldn't know......" Jalisa euphorically says.

"You sure this isn't illegal? I feel like they drugged me......"

"Nahh, they just used natural herbs to remove your ego...... oooh, heeeey, I have an idea! Let's go take a picture by the Atlantic Ocean!" Jalisa suggests while sitting down her mug and freely running on the beach.

Trina sits down her mug in agreement and follows Jalisa's lead onto the shore to horse play. They take pictures of one another and asks a stranger to take a few pictures of them doing silly and sexy poses. Once they got back to their chairs, they go through the pictures to see which ones they like the most.

Trina suggests, "You should post the picture on IG!"

"Why? You know I don't be on there like that!"

"Yeah, but like Kendrick said, 'sometimes you gotta pop out and show niggas,' sis!"

Jalisa hesitates but goes along to uploading the picture. "Oooh, let me write your caption, sis!" Trina asks as Jalisa hands her the phone. "You got to shit on these niggas!" Trina types a caption that reads, "you lost something fabulous, because you're used to living average; like a Shakespeare play, that's tragic; all because of your Iago tactics; you missed out on all this Black girl magic."

After posting it, Trina gives Jalisa her phone back. Jalisa humbly and blushingly says, "Oh my gaawwwdd.... you're so crazy...." while seeing the post load onto the newsfeed.

Moments later, Jalisa receives notifications of people reposting the picture on their stories. People are commenting compliments and gifs on the post. Many men and some women have sent over 30 direct messages to her inbox. Jalisa ignores it all. She turns off her notifications to get back to enjoying her vacation with her Trina.

"JaTrina?"

Trina sits up with her usual reaction to hearing her real name but the ayahuasca got her feeling too lovey dovey to get angry. She says, "You know for once, I don't feel hatred and resentment from you saying the name on my birth certificate."

"Really, JaTrina?"

"Hey, don't blow my high-oo-stica."

"It's ayahuasca...."

"Or whatever! What you want 'Lisa damn?"

"Do you think there are any good, decent men out there?"

"I do but they ass either be down-low gay, weird, boring, or they can't please a woman sexually."

"Oh, my god, Trina!"

"It's true, Hell! Pornography destroying their sensations and hormones, the access to porn keeps their appetite for real women low, these niggas is fucked up Jalisa! The quicker you accept that, the easier it is to make decisions when it comes to intimate relationships."

Jalisa struggles with the thoughts that Trina presents. She asks, "That doesn't scare you?"

"Don't shit scare me, what you mean?"

"JaTrina, you're afraid of spiders and snakes."

"And rats, and pigeons, yes, but what you talkin' 'bout?"

"Like scared of the future? Like.... think about it...... what happened to me and you is still happening to other girls around the world....... it ain't safe for little girls anymore......"

"That's why we got to teach our young girls to fight, shoot, and protect themselves...... just in case another inquisition happens and these men think they gon' kill and enslave women like Great Brittain did...."

"How do you be knowin' all of this?"

"That fuck nigga Tony....... I hate that I love him..."

"Nobody makes you love them, JaTrina."

"Well, he did.... he knew he was a fuck nigga and he knew I was vulnerable and he took advantage of the situation, that's what fuck niggas do!"

"What's wrong with men?"

"It ain't men, it's society........ you can't blame the seed without looking at the soil...... men and women generally navigate to the energy of their environment. Unless they be on some Christ shit, and see pass societal illusions, spread genuine love, and die as a martyr."

~

Meanwhile, back in the United States, Dr. Carson is getting ready to wrap up the pairing group sessions. Before he announces to the candidates that their time is up, he receives a notification from Shyla. After responding, he lays his phone on top of his laptop bag, and loudly proclaims, "That's time candidates."

As the candidates give Dr. Carson their full attention, Dr. Carson proceeds by saying, "Alright, what is the consensus to the Black people's problems in America? What can we collectively see is a inconceivable problem for Black Americans?"

Shampagne Roberts raises her hand and says, "Mr. Jones and I both came to the conclusion that it is a financial problem. This is while individuals like Dr. Claude Anderson and Dr. Boyce Watkins stress and encourage Black people to learn financial literacy. Society is a money game, so we have to know money to survive in it. Dr. Anderson wrote the book, *Powernomics*, to get Black people on the same page when it comes to the Black dollar."

Another candidate waits until Shampagne is done to chime in and says, "Though financial literacy is a huge problem for the Black community, my partner and I actually believe that the root of Black people's problems was slavery. It gave the white man a four-hundred-year head start on economic growth; they were able to profit off of our inventions and culture; they was able to psychologically indoctrinate us into their systems and beliefs, and Black people were never healed or reparated from those atrocious acts."

Darryl interposes, saying, "That translate back to the financial problem of our argument. Because reparations are due. Until the government pays two point five million dollars to every Black man, woman, and child, we will forever be in the position that we're in!"

A different candidate intervenes, saying, "The government is not about to give us no damn reparations, we need to reparate ourselves. The true problem is Black people's lack to mobilize, to stay unified, and to stay on one accord. We can come together for celebrations, clubs, and holidays, but we can't come together to combat the gang violence in our communities. We can't come together to get the high-class and middle-class Black folks to move back into Black neighborhoods. Our top scholars and athletes take their skills, talents, and abilities to white colleges other than HBCUs."

Dr. Carson carefully and calmly rebuttals everyone's statements by saying, "Sometimes the fight is not a financial one, it's not the fight with a government or with another ethnicity........ sometimes the fight is with ourselves, it's the battle that many Black people have within........We have been our own worst enemy. That's why most Black people.... I'm talking about politicians, professions, preachers, middle to high class Black individuals...... don't do anything for our people. Those are the people that Harriet Tubman would have shot."

All but one person laughs in the class. That one person raises their hand, "Dr. Carson?"

"Yes, Miss Skinner?" Dr. Carson confidently acknowledges.

"May I address a couple of the concepts you just mentioned?"

"Of course......"

"Well, one...... our people were conquered and colonized, so everything you mentioned are results of what happens when civilizations become controlled by the conquerors which is the true root of melaninated people's problem, because if you don't know who you are, you wouldn't know what or who to fight....... two, Harriet Tubman would not have shot anyone! She worked as an employee for an underground railroad system. She never freed a soul from any plantation."

There is a complete, dark silence that circulated in the room. The other doctoral candidates give Patricia looks of despair and in ignorance. They look at everyone else to see if they are not the only ones offended by Patricia's statements.

"How do you know?" Shampagne asks.

"How do I know?" Patricia condescendingly repeats.

Shampagne continues, "Yes...... we've been given enhanced memoirs and witness statements from prominent Black men and women about slavery: Phillis Wheatley, Olaudah Equiano, Frederick A. Douglass, Harriet Tubman, Nat Turner....... Slavery happened, the Atlantic slave trade occurred; our people were stolen and brought over here for forced labor, our people were raped and savaged like animals. This is true."

Patricia respectfully heeds Shampagne's words and prophetically rebuttals, saying, "Once again, you can't accept those false narratives without examining where that came from. Who taught you about those individuals? American education? How come there are no other prominent melaninated people who gave an account of slavery? Why are we force-fed this information year after year? You rather believe an education system that was built by the oppressors and colonizers that enslaved our people before you believe a sister who has sought the truth outside of standardize academia? You all never thought that maybe these crooked individuals who conquered and stole our lands want us to know the truth of who we are? If yes, then you must also think that these white 'Indians' that are pow-wowing around here are indigenous to these lands?

"In the words of Malcolm X, you have been bamboozled, run amuck, and led astray. You will never be liberated and educated until you remove the teachings of your 'slave masters,'" Patricia concludes.

"We can end on that note ladies and gentlemen," Dr. Carson proclaims in a lofty manner. "Class dismissed."

Patricia gathers her belongings feeling unheard and unappreciated in a room full of people that share the same melanin as her. While the other candidates gather around Dr. Carson to sign up for upcoming events and opportunities, she exits. Darryl sees her leaving out of the room and chases her down.

"Patricia!" Darryl slightly yells, stopping Patricia in her tracks.

"Yes, Darryl?"

"Are you okay? You seemed pretty upset when you stormed out of the room."

Patricia sarcastically answers, "Well, you know, can't take other people's ignorance and the insolence from their body gestures personally."

"What do you mean, Pat? You can't take someone else's perspectives?"

"I don't have to."

"You don't think that's a problem?"

"Since when did the truth become a problem, Darryl?"

"I did not sa-"

Patricia interposes, saying, "The only problem is the people with internal mental problems, who can only see what these white devils have put in front of them."

"Okay, Patricia...... so I got the mental illness, too? Does that new nigga that you're with meet your standards?"

Patricia scolds, says, "Nah, the 'new nigga' is just as ignorant, misled, uninformed, and dumb as the rest of you," and tries to walk away.

Darryl's voice stops her in her tracks again when he asks, "So you and the 'new nigga' didn't work out or something? Is this what's causing the conflict between you and the world?"

"Why are you coming for the 'new nigga' when you seemed to have your hands full with that girl that's named after liquor?"

"Oh, so this is what this beef is about? You didn't see me out with her like I saw you and this 'new nigga' out."

"Darryl, that wa-"

He interjects, "You didn't even speak to me when I opened that door. Why would you even bring him to Kemet? Knowing I be in there every Friday!?"

"Come on now, he invited me ther-"

Darryl interrupts her again, "Oh, he invited you, yeah right. You just wanted to show him off in front of me."

"Now, Darryl Jones, to think that I would want to show off someone in front of you is bizarre and berserk, but please carry on."

"So what is it then Patricia Skinner? What's your issue?"

"There's no issue, Darryl! Not with you, not with school, not with society, I just dislike debating with folks who just as programmed and ignorant to the true history of our people; and this doctoral degree is allowing you to be more programmed within the ideocracy of this nation......." Patricia says while walking towards the corridors to escape out of this male, egotistical building full of idiots and women who follow them as Darryl scoffs away back into the room to talk to Dr. Carson.

~

On the other side of town, Tony is in his room preparing his clothes for graduation. He can't help but to be excited to see his family members, mentors, professors, and the spirit of Black excellence all in one spot. He thinks of how far he's come in his education journey, and rather he wants to get his doctorate or not.

Once he's done laying out his attire and accessories, he sits down and takes out his phone to scroll through social media. He stops scrolling once he sees Jalisa's post of her and Trina in bikinis on a beach, looking like two angels who took a trip away from their divine duties of being guardian angels. He stares at the picture for a minute, reminiscing on Trina's savory.

He feels a since of longing for Trina. He internally regrets not having enough discipline to deny temptation, not having enough guts to tell Trina right away, and for not being able to share these moments with her. Tony's moods become interchangeable, viewing the comments from hundreds of people. He sees men commenting sweet compliments and some leaving heart eyes.

After liking the picture, he comes to a deep realization that he severely misses Trina. He's been trying to fill in the void of not having her around with sex, alcohol, and weed, but it does not lead to anything but a sense of desolation, terrible decisions, even more lack of discipline, and resentment. He wonders if Trina was going to be at his graduation, but most likely not. She's living it up in a whole different time zone.

Tony tosses his phone onto the foot of the couch to grab his lighter and blunt from the ashtray on the coffee table. After lighting the blunt and inhaling it. As the smoke fills the room with acceptance, forgiveness, and hope, he flips through channels to find something funny to watch.

Moments later, he gets a call from one of his old, childhood, big homies, Petey. "Wassup, Peter fam?" Tony says while answering the phone. "You good?"

"Toni, Tony, Tony! What's up my guy! Ya ready for tomorrow? Da whole hood talkin' 'bout pullin' up. We tryin' to party with the college hoes!"

"How you talkin' about college hoes and ya girl don' blasted you all over the internet..."

"Aww man, you know how it is........ it's just for play play. But booyyyy, I had to humble that bitch real quick. That's why she did what she did, she didn't know how to regulate her dysfunctional ass emotions with the truth about herself. These bitches get out of line and out of hand, Tony."

"What you talkin' about, Petey?"

"What I'm saying is, if a nigga doin' all he can to protet and provide, and her ass barely workin..."

Tony interjects, "Nigga she takin' care of yo kids..."

"Nah, Tony, that's her and I kids....... bitch, you hold a responsibility other than the kids, too! Then she be sayin' slick shit all day, soon as a nigga come home from work, it's no peace," Petey says, stumbling over his words. "So I told the bitch to shut her bummy ass up! I ain't gon' be takin' shit from a bitch who low class. Bitch, get ya' mind and paper up, not ya' mouth and ya' weight up!"

Tony tries not to laugh to condone Petey's perspective on the situation. During Petey's monologue about bitches, Tony's thoughts wonder into the abyss, thinking about Trina. *I would never ever call Trina a bitch or any real woman a bitch; aren't all women real women? Why do we defame them because of their natural duties of humanization? Shouldn't men want to provide, protect, love, and care for their women?* He internally questions to himself.

He comes back to earth whenever Petey says, "I ain't playin' wit' her ass though...... nigga.... my mama seen the post."

Tony thoughts drift away again. He's becoming annoyed by the stories. *This nigga is too old to be acting like a teenager,* he thinks to himself. "I'm pretty sure there's better ways of handling it big bro... like you have to take her feelings into consideration as well."

Black Pain't, Vol. II

"Man fuck all that! Bitches like that will have you out here looking stupid and simpish as fuck! They can take that attitude to those weak, cuckolded ass niggas! Those the type to cheat on they nigga because he soft and can't fuck, better hear me out, Tony too tone! Bitches will always go back to the niggas who did them dirty but fucked them right. Oh yes, they always find their way back to you!"

Petey's words gave Tony a sense of hope. A sense of hope that maybe, Trina will come back to him. She came back a few times after she told him that she wasn't going to keep communicating with him. *Why is sex always the determining factor?* Tony asks himself within.

"No real bitch want a weak ass nigga who can't fuck my guy!"

"What about the queens? The educated women? The faithful, God-fearing women? The pure souls! I'm pretty sure they wouldn't mind a man who's gentle and lovin'."

"Nigga those the main bitches cheatin'!" Petey comically but seriously says. "Trust me on this, Too Tone! I don't be on that school shit like you do, I just got years of experience, ya see what I'm sayin'? So trust me when I say this, the real niggas will always prevail! Society makes these weak muthafuckas who they are, that's why they assassinate the real niggas. But real niggas win in the end!"

~

That same night, while Tabitha and Phillip are eating dinner, Tabitha receives a text from Talitha about David, Sr. being removed from his duties at the church. An insurmountable of joy rushes through her elements while reading the text as she sends laughing emojis to Talitha. She laughs to herself once Talitha sends laughing emojis back to her.

While Tabitha is on her phone, Phillip stealthily views his call log to see that Shyla called him twice since he's been out. He sees that she texted him and silenced her notifications. He slides his phone right back into his pocket, observes Tabitha's snickering, and optimistically asks her, "What's so funny?"

Trying to hold back her outburst, Tabitha giggling says, "It ain't nuthin," and erupts with laughter, quickly stopping herself in realization of where she is.

Phillip keeps her from feeling embarrassed by saying, "Ahh come on! I wanna laugh too!"

"Oh, nah, it's Talitha......... she jus' remindeded me of on ole' lil' insida..." Tabitha says as she puts her phone back down on the table. "What was we talkin' 'bout?"

"We were talking about the differences between your 'type' and your 'kind.'"

"Oh, yeah.... right...... ummm... like.... how can I explain?" she questions herself aloud. "I think like, your type is like your prefe'ences; things that we prefer in a significant other. But our kind is the essence of who we are, someone that we can't help but be attractive to; someone that's a part of our culture or ethnic spirit; it's spiritual, it's natural."

"So was your ex-husband, your 'type' or your 'kind?'"

"He was defenetly a type, that man was my preference."

"So you were attracted to......"

Interceding, Tabitha says, "Church men who are devoted to God and their family, yes, I am."

"Interesting...."

"Well, whatso interesting about that? Was Shyla yo type oryo kind?" Tabitha snappishly asks.

Though Phillip feels some slight frantic within himself, hearing Shyla's name aloud, knowing he has been communicating with her lately. He engulfs the guilt, and he manages to answer, "She was my type. I was bought on the illusion of us, and what could have been."

"What did you want it to be?"

"Real." Phillip answers confidently. "I wanted it to be authentic."

"I get it," Tabitha empathetically says. Then she asks, "Am I yo type or yo kind?"

"I believe that you're both," Phillip instantly answers. "Like you're a predilection, you're a want, I feel divinely connected and attracted to you."

Tabitha melts at his answer. Then she asks, "You didn' feel this way 'bout Shyla?"

"No, because I knew I was lying to myself. The longer I was lying to myself, the longer I prolonged my rude awakening."

"Awww."

"That's why I don't want to waste your time. I want you in my life Tabitha Harris. I know you just got a divorce, and I'm not trying to force anything on you. I'm willing to wait, but I want to share my life with you. I want you to share your life with me."

~

Chad and Tiffany both enter a theater where hundreds of people are sitting down laughing at the comedian on stage. As they take their seats, the comedian exits the stage as the crowd gives her a round of applause.

The host gets on stage to introduce the next performer, saying, "Ladies and gentlemen give that funny mutha fucka another round of applause!" As the crowds' applauses gradually fade, the host continues, saying, "Did she say that she needs a man that's not afraid of murdering the pussy? Did she say that she need that serial killer dick?" The crowd laughs hysterically.

"Can y'all imagine getting on the news and two news anchors come on - a man and a woman - and the man says, 'The Dick You Down Serial Killer strikes again...... this has been the 14th body this year, and many pussies are dying out here. One survivor says that first he chews on it, might lick on it a lot of a bit, and then he fucks you like he's stabbing you, resulting in stimulation!" the host comically says.

As the crowd continues to go through a wave of gut laughing, the host says, "That woman anchor gon' be right there wondering where she can get her pussy murdered. She gon' hire him as a hitman." After

Black Pain't, Vol. II

laughing with the crowd at his own jokes, the host concludes by saying, "I hope y'all ready for this next performer, you've seen him locally, nationally, and one day you'll see him globally, put y'all hands together for the one and only, Terrance Robins!"

As the crowd claps, Terrance walks on stage with his band members. "Peace and love, y'all!" Terrance announces as he cues in his band. After the crowd return his greeting with theirs, an instrumental begins to play. Terrance feels the song and then he begins singing:

I'm sorry, but it doesn't even matter
It doesn't even matter, I guess it doesn't even matter
You say loving me was like living in a pad room,
You found more peace and privacy in our bathroom,
Loved our sex because it released a lot of endorphins,
You were a power ranger, girl, you're might morphin,
Like Maxwell, to have you was so fortunate,
but when I lost you, it became my misfortune,
saw my heart broken in portions,
I tried to play victim, knowing I caused the breakup,
Wrist still bruised from all the lies I tried to scrape up,
Miss seeing you in the mirror putting on your slight make up,
Might have fake my happiness but I never given fake love,
Make sense to why you gave up.
but I guess now it doesn't even matter
It doesn't matter, it doesn't matter
I guess now it doesn't even matter
Those nights that we spent, they don't even matter
All the love that we lent, they don't even matter
All the messages we sent, I guess they don't even matter
Taking long trips, gotta getta grip,
Flippin' because I'm missin' the taste of your lips,
Style was so crips, I even miss the sound of your lisp,
You was the shit girl excellence came out of your piss,
Why you gotta act out like that, why you gotta leave a nigga like this?

> *but I guess now it doesn't even matter*
> *It doesn't matter, it doesn't matter*
> *I guess now it doesn't even matter*

"Thank y'all so much, my name is Terrance 'Terry Bear' Robins; you can follow me on all social platforms, my music on all musical outlets, love y'all!" Terrance says while exiting the stage.

The host claps Terrance's hand and gave him a brotherly hug before walking up to the microphone. "Give it up for that talented brother man...." the host says while the audience cheers. The host then tries to sing, "It doesn't even MATTA! Doesn't even mattaaaahhhaaaaa! It doesn't even matter!" The crowd laughs and tries to sing along. "Alright y'all we're going to take a 10-minute intermission and get back to our next performer. Go get y'all something to drink, use the restrooms, get you something to nibble on, and we'll see y'all shortly."

As people rise to get drinks, walk to the restroom, or order food, Tiffany asks, "I wonder if men ever feel guilty, shame, or conviction from the things they've done to women...... infidelity, gas lighting, mental and verbal abuse? Like do men ever take the time to think about how that affects a woman?"

"Not until they have daughters! And even then, some men won't feel remorse or conviction. They'll just go and make a victim out of someone else. I only know because I too have done these things."

"Do you still do those things?"

"Not at all......"

She hesitates on her response and then says, "That's what all men say."

"Give me the opportunity to show you different."

"Men be saying, 'I'm different from those other men that you've had.'"

"I don't think I have."

"Mr. Love, you just said it in a 'different' way."

"Who healed you?"

"What?" she startlingly asks.

"Who healed you?" Chad calmly asks.

"What you mean, who healed me?"

"You know how when people show a strong defensive trait before opening up completely? And the main question they ask is who hurt you? I change it up and ask who healed you? Because I believe being guarded is a sign of self-love."

"How so?"

"Because the bible says to guard your heart. If a man is willing to court you, then that man should be willing to wait until you're ready to open up your heart to him."

"Okay, so how long should a man wait?"

"Let's see...... ummm...... nine is a perfect number, the true number of completion; I say...... Nine months to a year. You get to know people in their different seasons."

"After they open up, then what?"

"Communicate goals, desires; ummm.... get on one accord on what one another wants out of the courtship; have a covenant not to have sex until marriage."

"Ahhh, you talk a good game, Mr. Love. Tell me, where did all of this come from."

"Well, ummmm, Tiffany...... experience. I think the older I got, I learned that patience and discipline is what makes a relationship lasts. Sex is and has always been the determining factor of the span of a relationship or a situationship."

Tiffany asks, "So how long before a couple should have sex?"

"When you know the bond, the respect, and the intention is secure."

"What if the sex is whack? You know 60% of marriages end because of cheating...."

"If there are sexual desires that your spouse doesn't meet then they need to communicate that wholeheartedly. That is a difficult but meaningful conversation to have. Especially before marriage!"

"So do you believe in sex before marriage?" she asks.

Black Pain't, Vol. II

"Everybody say O-V-HOE!" the host raps to the song that's currently playing. The crowd follows suit, as the host continues, "Say O-V-HOE! Now step this way, step this way!"

"Hold that thought," Chad says to Tiffany during the host's enactment of the guy that danced around Toronto rapping Kendrick Lamar's lyrics to *Not Like Us*.

As the music fade, the host says, "You know...... that entire Kendrick and Drake beef....... you know what that showed me? It showed me that three things: one, it showed me that people will defend pedophiles; two, people are ignorant as fuck when it comes to authenticity, like how many times does Drake have to show you that he's a fraud? Niggas was defending a fraud...... like...... y'all idiots might as well say, 'So what if he has ghost writers, so what if he a bad father, so what if he's a child predator, so what if he hates Black women.'" The host gives the crowd a chance to laugh, after laughing himself, walking away from the microphone to enjoy his humor.

He comes back to the microphone after walking off and says, "And three, America, we're in trouble. We are in deep shit. Our kids are in deep shit. The future generation is in deep shit. Think about it! These lil' niggas and nigglets can't read, can't write...... they can't add, they can't subtract...... can't multiply, can't divide...... but they can do TikTok dances and get people to like and subscribe...."

Dead silence captures the scenes as the entire theater heeds to the host's statements. The host continues, "Yeah, our Black boys are in danger by the LGBTQ plus community." Some people in the crowd begins booing the host and yelling at the stage. The host gives them a chance to go through their semi-like the Two Minutes Hate speech like that off of 1984, but then states, "I'm sorry my gay, bi, trans, queer brothers and sisters, and they's.... but why put those images and skits in cartoons, what the kids got to do with it? Why propagandize that to the youth?"

The dead silence reappears after the host's question. The host allows the question to sink in, before he says, "To get them used to 'seeing it' but you ignore Black people issues for centuries, I don't get it...... Our Black girls are in danger...... to these child predators, to the porn industry, *OnlyFan* industry........ education and our moral values are at an all-time low...... and we just ignore it without seeking internal and eternal help........... we're like okay with being fucked up.... This all sounds like an episode of *Black Mirror*."

    The host pauses for a moment to find an ending to his soliloquy. "I'm sorry, y'all.... this ain't about none of that right? This is Rhythm, Blues, or Comedy's Open Mic Night; we gon' get back to the fun with our next performer, this brother been all over the globe! Performed with hitmakers and over time became a musical genius, right here in our own city; he loves performing here, this is where he grew up, put your hands together for Siiirrrrrr CHHHARRRLLLEESSS!!!"

    As Sir Charles walks on stage with a lapel microphone attached to his ears, a band of musicians get by their instruments on stage. Tiffany is immediately taken back, feeling the disgust that she once felt all over again. She develops a slight metallic taste in her mouth that went away after about five seconds, think about Charles's evil deeds and devious ways. Her stomach churns as she keeps herself from vomiting.

    Tiffany rises out of her seat to leave. By the time Chad realizes that she had risen to leave, he saw her urgently walking up the aisle. He quickly gets up to leave, following her out of the theater. "Tiffany!" he says in deep concern.

    "I'm fine," Tiffany exclaims while coughing. "Just needed some air."

    "Can I get you some water or anything?"

    "Yes, please," Tiffany says while Charles runs back in the theater and to the concession stand for a cup of water. In the meantime, Tiffany begins to feel better. Once Chad made it back out with the water, she says, "Thank you so much," and gulps some of the water down.

    "You had me worried back there."

    "My bad, I felt claustrophobic for a moment."

    "Are you claustrophobic?"

Black Pain't, Vol. II

"Not at all......" Tiffany says while clearing her throat. Suddenly, something came over her to share aloud. She states, "Honestly, that Mister Sir Charles guy is my ex......."

"Oh," Chad says. "Are y'all still talking or...."

"No, no, it's nothing like that. He really hurt me like.........." Tiffany says but pauses to catch her breath to keep from crying. "He really deceived me, played me like a fool. That's what I was asking earlier, like do men ever feel guilty, shame, or conviction from the things they've done to women...... because he had me in and out of my mind, going crazy.... and he just moved on with his life like everything was fine."

"I hate to hear that."

"I'm sorry. I didn't mean to spew that on you like that."

"Nah, nah, it's okay, trust me........"

"You sure? I know most men hate hearing about women's past with other men."

"Nah, nah, actually, I would like to know more...... I would like to know what you learned from it. I wanna know your triggers and what all you've had to overcome from them."

Tiffany firmly states, "Men are my triggers...... whoooooo boyyyy, you could have a whole family, but you out here, having fun."

"Oh, that's definitely not the case; I think if I had a family, you would have known by now."

"Shiiiiit, not with what I've seen. That man, Sir Charles... ooohhh...... he was hiding a whole pregnancy and child from me for two years!"

"Yikes!"

"Exactly...... and all my girlfriends got similar horror stories from men that are supposed to protect, love, and build with us," Tiffany says instantly. As she shook her head, she concludes by saying, "I'm talking the hideous stories you've ever heard of...... from men who are in church, to doctors, teachers; men in corporate positions; down low men...... men are just monsters."

"Well, I don't have any of those heinous crimes, all my break ups ended maturely."

Tiffany gazes into Chad's eyes and says, "That's what a monster would say."

"How can a being show that he's not a monster?"

"To be or not to be, that is the question that plagues all of humanity, but a monster always reveals its true nature over time."

"So does this mean that I get to spend more time with you to show you that I'm not that monster?"

Tiffany cracks a slight smile, but continues her blunt role, "Nice try, Mr. Love......"

"If not, it's all good, I just thought it was an open-door opportunity to prove to you," Chad meekly says. "Hey, are you hungry?"

"I'm starving! We can get some tacos and we can drive around if you'd like......"

"Hey, gas prices is high as hell; let's go eat at the pier and listen to waves or somethin'...."

Tiffany laughs and says, "I would like that."

Black Pain't, Vol. II

MY NOTES

Black Pain't, Vol. II

Chapter 12:
God is a Melaninated Woman

It's graduation day. The Nat Turner arena's parking lot is filled with cars and people walking to the building with families, balloons, gift bags, and more graduation gifts. The graduates all await inside the corridors of the locker rooms, taking pictures and videos of themselves in excitement. Jazmine and Tony are amongst the graduates as well. Dr. Carson is amongst the faculty and staff, getting ready to lead the graduates in the arena.

Inside the arena, there are hundreds of chairs facing a stage with chair facing the chairs off of the stage. In the back of the stage stands the Nat Turner University's flag, the state's flag, and the USA flag.

There are two huge projector screens on each side of the stage. People are walking in, getting to their seats before everything began.

Jules is there incognito, because he still wanted to see Jazmine at her happiest. While walking inside the arena to find a seat, he sees Miracle with Jazmine's mother and decides to walk to the other side of the arena to avoid them.

Tiffany and Patricia arrive together and found seats that gave the best view of the stage. Tiffany eventually sees Rayven walking around with Rayshawn in his car seat. She yells and waves for Rayven to get her attention so they can sit with her and Patricia.

Tabitha and Talitha are there, scrolling away on their phones. Something grasps Tabitha's spirit, making her put her phone down to feel and sense the positive-like-atmosphere. It fills her with the inspiration to finish her bachelor's degree so she can be here in the next year and a half. She sees Phillip walking down a ramp with the faculty and staff.

The audience cheers as pomp and circumstance begins to play over the arena's loudspeakers and the faculty and staff lead all of the graduates out of the tunnels. The graduates were all in lined up in a single file line waving and smiling on their walk towards the chairs in routine-like fashion. Those who are getting their doctorates are right behind the staff, those receiving their masters followed behind the doctoral candidates, and the undergraduates came last.

While walking, Tony is able to spot his family and friends being loud and obnoxious in their own section in the arena. Darryl is sitting next to Petey, looking like they are having a deep conversation about something. Sensations of success roams throughout his body, causing a chilling feeling. He then sees Rayven in the crowd, holding her baby, Rayshawn. He cannot help but to feel a sense of jealousy, but he allows that feeling to surpass through him to find the happiness for Rayven.

Jazmine is behind Tony as the walk in an aisle to get to their seats. She's been looking around, trying to find Miracle and her mother, but can't seem to locate them. She takes out her phone to take a selfie with Tony, yelling, "We made it!"

Once everyone is in their positions, Nat Turner University's Choir sings the *Black National Anthem* by James Weldon Johnson. The president of the university does her welcome and greeting to all those in attendance, the board of education for the state that are sitting on stage, to the platform guests, and to the graduating class. She then brings up the university's chaplain for a word of prayer.

After the chaplain's prayer, the salutatorian says her speech and introduces the valedictorian. Afterwards, the valedictorian is done with his speech, the president presented both salutatorian and valedictorian with scholarships to go get their master's degrees. Subsequently, the president introduces the Student Government Association's president.

The Student Government Association's president announces, "I have the distinct honor of introducing today's commencement speaker, because one, she's not like any other commencement speaker we've ever had. This speaker is from the Boot! This speaker says what she wants to say at any given moment without a care in world. She received her bachelor's and her master's in Black/African American history at United Melaninated University. She went on to receive her doctorate at Nat Turner University in which her dissertation combatted and refuted the lies told to copper children throughout centuries. And till this day, not a single soul on this planet can debate her on the historical facts of what happened to God's children. Author of the book, *Birthmarks*, please give a NT welcome to Dr. Lady Peseshet!

Dr. Lady Peseshet stands as royal as can be, doing an Egyptian pose. She puts her arms down and walks to the podium with God's confidence, commanding every spirit in attendance; even all of the children were quiet. She hugs the Student Government Association's president for introducing her.

Stepping to the podium, she leans towards the microphone and prophetically says, "Thank you madam president. It's always with much gratitude to see copper-colored women in leadership roles........ that's a sign that our future is in good hands. Also, I would like to address a fact that in the last 32 years of Turner University's commencements, melaninated women have outnumbered our kings by 82%, in which I, myself, was a part of back in the '99 and the two thousands' as Brother Terius Gray once said........but judging by the numbers, I think we may need to change the name of Turner University to something much more feminine and non-fictional.

"We need an *Assata Shakur* University, a *Frances Cress Welsing* University, a *Chaka Khan* University Music of Arts and Theater, a *Queen Nefertiti* University for Fashion, Design, Cosmetics, and Health.............. Let's not take a story that those of Caucasian descent gave us, okay? Or as my Christian brothers and sisters say, 'Amen.'

The crowd repeats the word, Amen in unison.

"Amen.... and thank you so very much for your welcoming and being willing to listen to what I have to say this evening. Even though we need to be saying 'Awomen'...."

As the crowd laughs in appeasement, Dr. Peseshet resumes saying, ".... But you know... today...... today is not about me...... it's not about my religious, historical, or societal views...... even though I'm going to say what Malcolm and Martin tried to tell you; what Jesse, Sharpton, and Farrakhan should have told you, and what the Black Panther Party of Self-Defense tried to warn you about. Today, ladies and gentlemen, today is not about the facts on how the government allowed *Five Dollar Indians* to take something that was rightfully owed to us, or what the European settlers claim to be 'Black' or 'African American.' Today is not about how these same European colonizers reclassified the true Natives of America into the names such as 'Negro,' or 'Slave,' they even nicknamed us 'Black' in which we took in these negative connotations and made them beautiful.

"No, no, no, no, ladies and gentlemen, today... today is about these graduates who sit in front of us...... they all, from pre-K to 12th grade, those receiving B. A's, M. A's, and Ph.D.'s..... they all had to go through rigorous, colonizers influenced, and curriculums full of confusions just to get to this moment...... they spent many countless, sleepless, and weeping nights just to get to this moment....... Today is about how these strong, courageous, intellectuals had to beat all the odds; they had to break some generational curses, they had to suppress traumas to get through, and many had to overcome other barriers just to sit here in front you all today just to receive a piece of paper that America deems worthy of being a part of a certain status or class... in America..... they sit here in front of you willing and ready to take on that next challenge in their life, knowing that the road will not get easier. Today, we celebrate, commemorate, and salute these graduates who did what they had to do to get here......

"While you all go on to this next phase of life, I want to remind you all of something that you need to be aware of, even if you don't answer the call....... then God, The Universe, Allah, Jah, or whatever you call your deity, will be calling again...... *all are called but only a few that's chosen*. It's about you and me, and everyone else here in attendance were led into what the late, great Dr. Martin Luther King, Jr. once called..........'a burning house'.......... King understood where America was headed, he learned information about who the 'Negros' really were. He knew political ways to get what he wanted for his people. Yes, equality and peaceful protesting were tools that King used but that's not what got King killed. It was the truth that he discovered about who we were and who we are that encouraged him to push an agenda for *reparations* and to influence the people to an *Economic Withdrawal* campaign when he spoke in Memphis in 1968.

"However, ladies and gentlemen, I want to inform you of something that will break a barrier within you that you had no clue that you needed to break....... YOU.... ARE....... NOT........... BLACK." Dr. Peseshet repeats and pauses for a second to allow people to digest her words. Then she proceeds, "Let me repeat, YOU...... ARE...... NOT......... BLACK," as her strong words echo with a vibration anyone has ever felt before, while allowing another moment for her words to be internalized throughout the stadium.

"YOU....... are not Colored, you are not African American, you are not a Negro, you are not a Slave, you're not a Minority nor are you an American, and you are definitely not Black! YOU....... are the originals........ the true inhabitants of this country, of this land that your ancestors left for you! You NEED to know this. Your ancestors did NOT come to 'America' on any slave ship! Slave ships were NOT real, ladies and gentlemen.

"All of these other ethnic groups of people can trace their lineage to a nationality...... Colored, Slave, Black, Minority, African American, are NOT nationalities....... you are not a person of color, you are a person, a spiritual being, with the original color. You need to know this, brothers...... and sisters...... it's vital to your intellectualism, it's vital towards your values, it's vital towards your standards, and it's vital towards your views of life and liberty. Your perspective of life dictates your reality, but ignorance is bliss and nothing good comes from being in a bliss...... a bliss is a delusion........a bliss can creates confusion, frustration, and hatred amongst oneself and others........ this bliss was orchestrated and castrated amongst the true citizens of this nation!

"This bliss is taught in all institutions, on all music entertainments, through literature. Our so-called 'Black Leaders' push this bliss.............. this bliss about how 'Black' people were somehow just living it up in Africa, these Europeans came, saw their value, kidnapped many of them, put on harboring ships chained together on a four-month voyage to the 'New World' and enslaved for four hundred years? You mean to tell me that no tribes fought back?

This is why Malcom X claimed that 'we didn't land on Plymouth Rock, Plymouth Rock landed on us,' because we were already here in this so called 'America' before Europeans got here. This bliss makes us not question that fact! This system taught us about so-called prominent scholars and leaders like *W.E.B Dubois, Booker T. Washington, Carter G. Woodson*, who added to the bliss........ and these so-called leaders of today who keeps us in this bliss.......... The Harlem Renaissance sealed this bliss within our craniums through the arts, it was an act of war. I don't have the time to name drop them all........ because it's not about these people who sold us out.... it's about these graduates who must take their degrees and give it back to their communities! You must undo what's been done! Through this knowledge!

"Don't take your degrees...... I.E.... your resources, money, connections, jobs, businesses, trades, and entrepreneurship skills to neighborhoods and to people who don't look like you........ Cities and communities of people that look like you are in desperate need of your presence, energy, and resources. Our people are dying out through social media, education, sports, and entertainment, healthcare, politics, and many other facets of government.... THEY NEED YOU! I didn't come here for you to look at this moment as a moment of success but a call to action! You were already born successful, it's what you do with that success! You're people NEED YOU!"

"SO IF NOT YOU, THEN WHO?............... this is the longest streak of financial, social, emotional, physical, mental, spiritual, and historical genocide in the history of humanity............ but we keep it going. We keep things going by not giving back to our people...... This system is about control...... control...... control.... control...... they want to control you, what you watch, what you hear, what you see, where you go....... just so your true self won't awaken to make this world a better place for you and the generations to come.

"But we're not going to go there....... today is NOT about the elites, the boules, the illuminati's, those who have control over the networks we love to pay for and watch. We loved being the programmed and not the programmers......but today is not about the things that keeps up indebted into this illusion, today is about YOU, graduates....... YOU ARE OUR LAST LINE OF DEFENSE! If you don't make the change, then.... WHO?

"I'm going to tell you what EVERY speaker should have told you since Historically 'Black' Colleges and Universities should have been telling since we lost control and resources from one another after integration...........Go on, graduates! Just go! Get involved in law, politics, education, banking, entrepreneurship, arts, sports, entertainment, health, and fitness, culinary, transportation, sciences, inventions....... technology.... just find your niche.... find your niche and create new methods, curriculums, techniques, skills, networks, and positive and meaningful lifestyles that will financially reparate, proliferate, liberate, and rectorate our people! IF NOT YOU, then..."

The majority of the graduates, in unison, yells, "WHO?" while being totally engulfed into what Dr. Peseshet is saying. She pauses for a moment to allow the energy in the room to emancipate those who never heard of such statements. Her words travel firmly into the hearts of those who are not going to accept them.

She continues, "I love messing with my Christian brothers and sisters because the bible has always been one of the biggest controversaries, right? Like how we allowed these colonizers to come onto our land, enforce their god, and makes us believe we were lesser than, right? But any way, in the bible, I think it's Genesis 1:3.... when God said let there be light and then there was light....... well, I'm going to ask you something that no man has ever think to ask........ what light was She talking about, because the bible says that God made the sun on the fourth day?" Dr. Peseshet asks, letting several seconds to go by to build some anticipation of her answer.

"There are over 200 references of the light that Madam God made, but only several are talking about the light from the sun, so what is this LIGHT that God mentions....... I'll tell you; it is the light that dwells on and through you! That light is melanin! Melanin is the Gift of the Gods. This Gift allows you to be able to change frequencies, change vibrations.........this Gift allows you to survive anywhere, in any climate, and in any condition............ YOU CAN SURVIVE IN ANY CONDITION!

"That's why from the Homestead Act to the 1830 Indian Removal Act........ to every Trail of Tear that our Native ancestors had to walk after being forced out of their lands......colonized, murdered, raped, and diseased, pushed into ghettos all across the country, reclassified, forced to work their jobs, and integrate into their systems....... graduates, YOU CAN SURVE IN ANY CONDITION!

"So go on Graduates! Go on to use your gifts and talents! Go on to zeniths you never thought you'd climb, go to places you'd never thought you'd go, and do the impossible that you'd never thought you'd do! Just remember that your people are depending on you! DO NOT CONTINUE THE CYCLE of taking your time, money, resources, connections, and energy to neighborhoods, businesses, institutions, and jobs that don't look like you! YOU ARE OUR LAST LINE OF DEFENSE! Without your representation, this long-lasting genocide will continue....... How many more financial crises would you like to see our people endure? How many more deaths do you want to hear, see, and read about? How many more broken, dysfunctional, and poor generations of families would you like to see? How many generational curses are we going to curate before we destroy ourselves?"

Dr. Peseshet's voice cracks after her last question. She takes a moment to collect herself as every heart in the crowd feels her emotional stance. "You are our last line of defense graduates. If not you, then......"

"WHO?" the graduates and the people in attendance all say in unison.

"I'll conclude with this.......... Know that your graduation caps are just that, they can be taken off, but your true cap... your true cap, ladies, and gentlemen, lies within the capstones of your mind! So go forth, graduates, get back what's rightfully yours. Thank you!"

The crowd gives her standing ovation. The president of Nat Turner University presents her with an award for her commencement speech. Next, the president begins the robbing ceremony for the doctoral candidates and for those receiving their masters. They announce the undergraduates. The senior class president gave the final remarks, and the graduates exit the arena in orderly fashion.

While walking apart from the other graduates, Jazmine spots Jules leaving, dondering if he came to see her graduate. Jules is big on keeping promises. She then feels some indignity for what she did to him. Jazmine eventually finds Miracle and her mother and takes pictures with them.

Rayven and Rayshawn finally finds Jazmine amid the large crowd of people. Jazmine's mother takes picture of them holding

Black Pain't, Vol. II

up their sorority's symbol. "Thank you so much for coming Rayven! I greatly appreciate you!"

"You know I had to come show out for you, Soror!" Rayven says while hugging Jazmine. "Well, enjoy the rest of your day! Congratulations again!"

As Rayven walks away, she sees Tony taking pictures with his family and friends. She wants to walk to the other way to avoid running into him, but she would have to take the long way around back to her car. She decides to face the music and tries to walk pass Tony and his people unnoticed. She tries to keep her head down to pretend she doesn't see him.

Tony's mother suddenly notices Rayven and says, "Rayven Little, how are you, sweetheart?" while hugging her.

"Hey, Mama Tony, I'm fine; how are you?"

"I'm good, I really been good, how's the bay-be...?" Tony mother says but stutters once Tony walks over there to them.

"Hey, Rayven!" Tony says in pleasant surprise.

"Hey Tony, congratulations," Rayven replies.

"How's lil' Ray Ray?" Tony asks as his mother sneaks away to give them some privacy.

"He's good, just growing fast, he's already trying to find ways to be independent, holding the bottle by himself......" Rayven says with a heartfelt smile.

"That's good, I miss the little fellow. Those first couple of weeks with y'all was breathtaking. Never felt so much love in my life."

Rayven humbly and hurriedly says, "Yeah, we don't have to bring that up, congratulations again, Tony, I don't want to take away from you and your family," while trying to walk away.

"Yeah, hey, I get it......" Tony says. "I'm here if you need me Rayven.... you still have a special place in my heart; no matter what."

"Thank you, Tony!" she says while walking away.

Tony watches as she gets down the hallway, feeling sincerity and gracefulness. He walks back to where Darryl and Petey are standing, still discussing their point of views. All of a sudden. Tony can feel someone grabbing his shoulder, saying, "Congratulations, young Pattawan!"

"Appreciate that, OG!" Tony responds while clasping hands with him. "Your class was the best class, Dr. Carson!"

"Thank you, my young lad! I like to consider myself the Magic Johnson of teaching!"

"If he's Magic, then I'm the Kobe Bryant of teaching," Darryl says, chiming in on the conversation. Darryl subsequently sees Patricia walking along side Tiffany. He walks away from Petey, Dr. Carson, and Tony, "Patricia!"

Patricia suddenly stops to see who's calling her. Once she realizes it's Darryl, she internally melts, but hides the feeling outwardly. They meet halfway between Tiffany and Tony's family. Patricia states, "Darn Darryl, how are you doing on this lovely Saturday afternoon?"

"Better since I go the chance to see you."

"I see you two times out of the week, dammit! Don't start with your flirtatious manner."

Darryl humorously replies, "You right, because you call yourself going off on me the other day, you lucky I didn't handle that!"

"Boy you know I'm too hot to handle!"

They both share a long overdue laugh together and embrace one another with a hug. After the hug went over five seconds, Darryl says, "If we hold anymore longer, I'm going to get on one knee in front of all these people in hopes someone takes a picture and send it to your new boyfriend."

"That's not my boyfriend. He's definitely a friend."

"Oh, now, he's a friend."

"He wasn't anything more, you know you got to run a few marathons to get to me."

"Oh, trust me, I know! You ain't gotta explain!" A slight pause when by and Darryl gathers himself to say, "Patricia, I'm sorry. I hope one day you find it in your heart to forgive me."

"You've been forgiven, Darryl, stop living with that regretfulness."

"Yeah but who wouldn't regret you if they lost you? I know Dennis is probably somewhere sick to his life right now....."

"Probably, but I pray that he's alright. I don't wish bad upon nobody." Patricia smiles and says, "I'll see you around, Darryl."

"Hopefully outside of class, too."

Patricia blushes as she catches back up with Tiffany. Tiffany is shaking her head as Patricia gets nearby. "What?" Patricia cluelessly asks.

"Don't act all innocent with me!"

Patricia laughs and says, "I'm really not," as they continue their stroll to find Dr. Lady Peseshet. Once they find her, they see Dr. Lady Peseshet being congratulated for her excellent speech, taking pictures and signing autographs for some of the graduates and for the people in audience. It is a waiting line, but Patricia is determined to ask her something. Once it is Patricia's turn to so speak, she says, "I needed that speech more than you know, Dr. Pesesht! Thank you!"

"No problem at all, God."

"I read your book, *Birthmarks,* and studied your work for countless numbers of years."

"Thank you so much."

"I just have to ask, what is your overall purpose of exposing the truth when you know that our people won't accept or at least do something about it?"

"I just want our people to heal, for real. Stop crying about it, stop prolonging it, stop wasting time on these devices, it's time for us to heal in the most proper ways possible. Our lives depend on it. But we have to be cognizant that not everyone wants to be healed, some people get paid off the lies that are told, some people don't want the truth, but you shouldn't lose sleep over it. Always speak the truth every chance you get, they can't argue with facts, they'll just defame your character."

"I hear what you're saying, but am I wrong to think that our people are doomed? That are people are too lost and controlled to make that change that we wish to see? What's the answer? Our people are too far gone. We lost them to AI, social media, and pornography."

Dr. Lady Peseshet gently touches Patricia shoulder, saying, "Beloved, let me tell you, because I've had those revelations myself; in this third dimension, on this third rock from the sun, you have to understand that in all civilizations and societies, there had always been conflict, there had always been wars, there had always been caste systems of bondage, and there has always been financial social class. This is the assimilation. We're all here to take with us the experiences, the memories, and the sins to not commit in the next dimension, or the next phase of life. Continue to be that guiding light for others to follow, everything else will be added onto you. Take care of you, and the world shall take care of itself. Nature always wins in the end."

Patricia hugs Dr. Lady Peseshet, saying, "Thank you so much for that. I needed to hear it."

"It's my daily reminder," Dr. Peseshet concludes as some security guards come and guide her towards the presidential suite.

Patricia watches as she walks away in the long hallways feeling like the ending of a final chapter, but the beginning of a new book.

Black Pain't, Vol. II

MY NOTES

Black Pain't, Vol. II

New Characters' List

*Get *Black Pain't, Vol. 1* by Anthony Crawford, Jr. for the list of characters for Patricia, Darryl, Jalisa, JaTrina, Jules, Dennis, Dr. Carson, Tabitha, David, Terrance, Jazmine, Rayven, Tiffany, Alvin, Luna, Charles, Shyla, Brittany, Ella, Dionte, Aaron, Tony,

Sprint*Door* – a company specializing in delivering food like DoorDash, UberEats.

*Down*the*Street* - a company that specializes in picking people up and taking them where they need to be it's like a taxi, Uber, Lyft.

Jase Reed– *what women want* - late 20s, nurturing, provider; he's a one-woman man; he used to be in a relationship with Braiveri (must read/watch *What'R Friends'4* by Kieara Smith to get their background story). He received his bachelor's in education and master's in urban education. Works as a program director for a youth program.

Chad Love – *the chef* – co-owns With Love and Soul, a restaurant with Chef Ivory, a businessman, down to earth,

Braiveri – *the comforter* - late 20s, therapist, strong, brave, independent, bar tends for extra money,

Keyon – *the youth pastor* – early 20s, teaches bible to teens at 18th Street Missionary Baptist Church.

Mrs. Debra Townsend – *the therapist* – late 30s, Alvin's therapist.

Made in the USA
Columbia, SC
18 January 2025